THE REALITY OF EVERYTHING

THE REALITY OF EVERYTHING

REBECCA YARROS

USA TODAY BESTSELLING AUTHOR

Entangled Publishing
644 Shrewsbury Commons Ave
STE 181
Shrewsbury, PA 17361
rights@entangledpublishing.com

Embrace is an imprint of Entangled Publishing, LLC.

Edited by Karen Grove
Cover design by Bree Archer
Cover photography by vvvita/Getty Images

Manufactured in the United States of America

First Edition August 2020

embrace

To Karen Grove,
the Original Flygirl.
For 1.3 million words,
some of which had four letters.
Thank you for taking a chance
on Josh Walker—
for taking a chance on me.

Chapter One

Morgan

Take the money. Use it. Don't just give it to charity or stick it in a bank account, Morgan. Spend it on something that brings you happiness. Use it to leave like you always planned. I just wish I were going with you.

Okay. So maybe I was in over my head.

As if the octagon-shaped house agreed with my thoughts, one of the struggling shutters on the third floor gave up its battle with the ocean breeze and came loose with a loud creak.

All three of us leaned to the right, following the slow slide of the doomed shutter until it snapped free, slammed into another shutter, knocking it loose, and finally fell thirty feet to the sand below.

"Let me get this straight," Sam said, sliding her sunglasses down her nose to peer over the frames at the stilted beach house that—as of thirty-six hours ago—I now owned. "Will left you five hundred thousand dollars, and you bought this."

"Not exactly," I drawled. They both turned their heads slowly toward mine. "Will left me a secondary life insurance policy worth five hundred thousand. His attorney invested it until I was ready to do something, and it ended up a little over six hundred."

"And you bought this," Sam repeated, her hazel-green eyes wide with disbelief.

"Yep." Sure it kind of resembled a giant mushroom, but the price had been right.

"To tear down?" she asked.

"I'm fixing it up," I declared, my voice a hell of a lot stronger than my certainty. That had been one of the conditions of the purchase.

The house groaned, and we tilted our heads to the left as the previously assaulted shutter submitted to gravity and plummeted down the gray-shingled exterior, landing next to its partner like a tombstone in the sand.

"Even the exterior is jumping ship," Mia muttered from my other side, folding her arms across her chest. As our only Outer Banks native, her appraisal gave me pause. If anyone knew beach houses, it was Mia. She was more than Sam's sister-in-law; she'd grown up an hour north of here and was currently studying architecture at UNC.

"It survived the last hurricane," I argued on behalf of the house.

"On life support," Mia muttered, walking forward to examine the stilts.

Hence why it had been so cheap.

"It's not that bad." My voice pitched a little high. Maybe it was weathered, rather ugly, odd-shaped, and appeared to be falling apart, but I'd been assured that the bones were good.

I received two doses of side-eye from my girlfriends.

"It was bad enough for you to call in reinforcements."

Sam raised her eyebrows. "Not that I'm complaining. I'm just glad I happened to be visiting Grayson's parents when you called. Plus, it's been ages since I've seen you."

Guilt pricked me right in the heart.

"It hasn't been *ages*. I saw you at your wedding just two months ago."

"Oh, you mean the half hour you were at the reception before leaving Vegas? You didn't even say good-bye to Paisley." Her tone teased, but I felt the underlying worry.

"Yeah, well..." I took a deep breath, searching for the words that had eluded me for the last twenty-two months. How did you tell your best friends that as much as you loved them, you simply couldn't stand to be around them? Or their happiness? "I wanted to stay, but I...couldn't." It sounded lame even to my ears.

"Still?" she asked softly.

"Still."

Sam was the only one in our group of friends I could talk to without being 95 percent fake about how I was doing. Maybe it was because she'd been my roommate for a while in college. Maybe it was because she didn't point to the calendar and push me to be all healed, pretty, and ready for social niceties. Or maybe it was because she didn't shove her happiness in my face. The others...well, they oozed happiness and then left it lying around like glitter you could never get out of the carpet.

And sure, Sam had fallen in love with Grayson, one of our flyboys, while he was in army flight school, but Grayson hadn't been tangled up in what followed afterward.

It was always Josh and Ember.

Then Paisley and Jagger.

And Sam and Grayson.

I had assumed it would be Will and me...until he was killed in Afghanistan.

The girl I'd been, the one who believed in happily-ever-afters, had died with him.

I didn't even know the woman I was now—just that she had a fixer-upper beach house and a master's degree in childhood education and English. The rest of me was a whole lot of empty, and whatever wasn't empty was pain.

"They miss you," Sam said softly. "Ember. Paisley. The guys."

"I'll get there." The promise felt as hollow as my heart. "Just not yet."

"And until then, we get to have you," Mia offered with a supportive smile.

"And maybe being here will help you heal at your own pace instead of everyone else's." Sam's posture softened, and she squeezed my arm gently. "Why don't you show us the inside of this monstrosity?"

"Yeah, let's do that," I agreed, thankful she let me off the hook like always.

We climbed the stairs that led from the pedestal garage to the first floor of the house. The homes around here were all on stilts to protect them from the rising waters brought in from storm surges, and my house was no exception.

My house. It wasn't really mine, though, was it? It was his. Bought with money I'd never wanted from something I'd spent nights praying would never happen.

"Watch the landing." I skipped over the split board halfway up the staircase.

"You know, you could always wait six months for Grayson to get home from deployment. I bet he'd be happy to lend a hammer," Sam suggested as we crossed the dilapidated deck to the front door.

"In six months, this thing might be a heap on the beach," Mia teased, pulling her black curls into a ponytail. She was unlike her brother in almost every way. Petite where he was broad, ivory-skinned where her brother had a perpetual tan, and bright blue eyes where Grayson's were more the color of gunmetal. But her stubborn streak? Yeah, that was all Grayson. Good thing Sam had an even bigger one to put up with him.

"Oh, come on, you haven't even seen the inside yet!" I argued.

"I'm picturing something very *Addams Family*," Mia drawled. "I mean, I'm delighted you took the job at Cape Hatteras Elementary, but maybe I should have come down and checked this out for you. Or sent Joey. Or someone. Anyone."

I paused with my hand on the sun-warmed door handle. It was in the seventies, which was warm for mid-March in the Outer Banks. It was nothing compared to the intensity summer would bring. Luckily, having been born and raised in southern Alabama, I was no stranger to heat or humidity.

"Okay, so buying it when all I'd seen were the pictures on Zillow and the inspection report was risky, but just wait." The door stuck, and I forced it open with a shove of my shoulder before stepping into the small foyer. Aged wood paneling greeted us along every wall as I led them toward the living room.

"Holy shit," Sam whispered, her jaw dropping at the view.

"Exactly." The wall of windows looking out over the Atlantic was what had convinced me to pull the financial trigger and buy.

We walked across the spongy, avocado-green carpet that matched the kitchen walls, counters, and appliances, and I opened the sliding glass door with a cringe-worthy squeak. "Ignore that boarded-up window." I nodded toward the south-most side.

"And that one, too?" Sam pointed toward another segment of plywood.

"Yep. And watch for the missing boards out here."

The salty ocean breeze lifted the hair off my neck and back as the girls followed me across the wide deck until we rested our hands on the splintered wooden railing. Below, the small, fenced yard ended with a gate leading to a short wooden path that climbed over the dune to a deserted beach about a hundred feet away.

Waves crashed with soothing regularity, coming in a hypnotizing rhythm.

Can you believe people actually live here? Talk about paradise. His voice slid across my heart, and my eyes fluttered shut at the sharp, sweet pain the memory inflicted. It had been almost two years since I stood on a deck like this one, farther up the coast in Nags Head, with Will.

Now I was one of the people who actually lived here. He would have loved it.

"Okay, now I can see why you bought it." Mia's gaze drifted north, then south. "What year was this built? Early fifties?"

"Fifty-one," I replied. "How did you know?"

"There are no other houses beyond the dunes. You and your lone neighbor right there are the only ones for miles. Hatteras has a protected beachfront, and my guess is this was built right before the Seashore was established as a national park. Wow. I wonder how it escaped the imminent domain proceedings back then. The land has to be worth a million bucks, Morgan."

"Maybe if you tear the house down, but there's a clause in my purchase contract that if the structure ceases to exist or is extended beyond a certain point, the land reverts back to the government. Fixing it is my only option."

Mia shook her head. "With the damage from last year's hurricane, this must have blended in with all the other fixer-uppers. You have your work cut out for you, but you seriously lucked out with the real estate. Shape of the house isn't bad, either. Looks awkward as hell, but it actually deflects the wind like a champ. Probably why it's still standing."

"So it will always be just you and your lone neighbor," Sam surmised. "By the way, why didn't you buy that one?" She nodded toward the house next door. It was a bit smaller but in perfect condition.

"Because it wasn't for sale. Besides, I like this house… well, the possibilities, anyway." It was twenty-five hundred square feet, had been in my price range, and felt like I did—weathered, beaten, and broken in ways that needed more than just a coat of paint.

It was a kindred spirit.

"Well, I know what I'm checking out next. The beach!" Sam headed toward the northernmost staircase off the back deck.

We followed her through the sandy yard, past the gate, and up the wood-planked path that led over the dune.

"You'll have to shovel the rest of this out," Mia said, pointing to the sand-covered path as we crested the small hill. "The wind picks up the sand from the beach and leaves it right here. Hence the dune. But it protects the house."

"Got it." I made a mental note, and we hiked down the first five feet, then slid the remaining ten or so of the dune until we reached the beach. I gathered my flip-flops in one hand and surveyed the beach. Other than a few families farther up the coast, it was deserted. "It's so quiet."

"Just the way we like it," Mia noted with a grin as we walked toward the water. "It'll pick up in a couple weeks for spring break, and we're slammed in the summer, but once the tourists leave, it will pretty much look like this."

"It's peaceful," Sam remarked.

Peace? I hadn't felt anything close to that emotion in the last couple of years. I wasn't even sure it existed in my reality.

But the water, the sand, and the crisp breeze were soothing. That was enough.

The sand grew firm and damp the farther we walked, and I paused, watching the ocean rush up to meet my toes and then overtake them. The water was deliciously cool, and it wasn't long before I sank slightly, sand eventually covering my feet.

Color flashed next to my toes. When the next wave retreated, I scooped a small handful of wet sand and held my fingers slightly apart as the water returned, letting the sand strain through the gaps to reveal a slightly rounded, quarter-sized piece of frosted blue glass.

"What is..." Sam shielded her eyes from the midday sun as she gawked at something in the water. "Whoa."

I mimicked her pose and saw a man coming out of the ocean a dozen yards away.

Mercy.

He was... Well, for a lit major, I was completely, ironically speechless. Water sluiced down the cut lines of his muscles like he was some kind of ocean deity as he walked out of the surf, the black swim trunks contrasting his tan skin like the black tattoo that ran down his side.

His abs had abs.

He rubbed his hands over a thick head of light brown hair, rolled his broad shoulders, and then jogged down the beach, straight toward us.

"Oh. My. God." Mia drawled out every word. "Is he real? Am I dreaming, or do insanely hot men just appear from the water around here?"

"I don't even know," Sam answered as he got closer.

The wind whipped my long hair across my face, and I quickly fisted the unruly brown locks and the rebellious hem of my dress as he nearly reached us.

Sweet Lord, he was a scorcher if I'd ever seen one. Strong

nose, carved chin, full, chiseled lips with a Captain America edge that made me want to recite the Pledge of Allegiance. It was like God himself had crammed everything I found attractive into one man and dropped him into the ocean by my house.

"Afternoon, ladies," he said with a slight smile, his breathing as even as his pace.

Ocean-blue eyes. Of course. Just a shade darker than the glass I held in my hand. They locked with mine, widening for a second before he passed and continued his run down the beach.

"No southern accent," I said once I'd found my vocal cords. "Must be a tourist."

"Seriously, I'm going to visit you every weekend if this is how the island treats you." Mia walked toward the water and cupped her hands around her mouth. "Chris Hemsworth, please! Or I'll settle for Liam!"

"Seriously, Mia. The ocean doesn't take requests." Sam rolled her eyes. "Not that we don't have a habit of meeting boys at the beach in our little group. What was it Paisley called Jagger?"

"Mr. California," I answered, remembering the day she'd met him on the coast of Florida almost four years ago. *But their story has a happy ending.*

My eyes followed the retreating form of our jogger.

"Ah, that's right. That one doesn't feel like a California, though," she mused.

"More like Mr. Carolina," I offered.

"Ahh, Carolina." The girls sighed in tandem.

He continued down the shore, and relief replaced the butterflies that had assaulted my stomach. As long as men like that didn't pop out of the ocean every day, I was in the clear.

Not like I was in the market for a relationship, anyway. It

was impossible to offer someone a heart I didn't have. Mine was buried over five hundred miles away at West Point.

Mia and Sam chatted while we climbed back to the house and then took the grand tour of what my heartache had bought me. Bedrooms, bathrooms—it all needed to be overhauled.

"Well?" I asked as the girls took stock of the kitchen.

"Honest opinion?" Mia leaned against one of the Formica counters.

"Of course."

She and Sam shared a glance.

"What?"

"We need to call Joey," Mia said.

"Joey, as in your sister?" I asked.

She nodded. "She manages Masters & Co."

"The family boat-building business," Sam clarified.

"That's right. You guys build racing boats or something, right?" I hated that I wasn't as familiar with Grayson's family as I should have been, seeing as I'd met them a couple years ago.

"Or something," Mia said with a smirk. "But Joey knows all the reputable contractors in the OBX. She'll be able to give you a good list to start with…unless you were thinking you'd head to the hardware store and start ripping stuff out yourself?" Her eyes widened. "Please say that's not what you're thinking."

"Kind of." I shrugged at the horrified looks on both their faces.

"Oh, Morgan. Not only no, but *hell* no. You're not…" Sam motioned to the house. "I know you're a huge HGTV fan, but this is not in your wheelhouse, and I say that with all the love in my heart."

"At least the structural stuff needs to be handled by professionals," Mia urged. "Remodeling on the beach is tricky."

My stubbornness softened at the plea in their eyes. What harm could getting a few bids on the bigger projects be?

"Fine. Call Joey. Whatever I can't do myself, I'll hire contractors for. Sound good?"

"Yep."

"Absolutely."

• • •

A couple hours later, Mia had gone in search of pizza, and Sam, tequila.

I, on the other hand, was on a quest for the lights. The sun would set in a couple of hours, and I wasn't going to unload what little I had brought with me with only half the lights on.

I flipped through the file the real estate agent had left for me in the kitchen. "Secondary breaker in the garage," I read aloud. Why in the hell would someone put another breaker box there? Maybe Sam and Mia were right; I'd at least need a contractor for the electrical work.

There was probably another half hour before the girls got back, which meant if I found that box quickly, we could have the whole house lit.

I rushed out my front door, not bothering to close it, and raced down the steps, jumping to the landing—

SNAP.

The sound registered in my brain about a millisecond before I plummeted through the landing. I shrieked, throwing out my arms to catch my weight on the remaining platform. My boobs took the rest of the impact as they slammed against the edge of the hole I'd made with my lower half.

Blinding pain ripped through me as my body scraped to a halt, but I didn't fall through.

The sound that left my mouth was anything but ladylike.

Holy shit, it hurt. Fire raced up my sides from thighs to ribs, and I was pretty sure my full Ds were going to mutiny back to an A-cup, or just fall right off.

I took a few breaths to steady my heart, praying the pain would subside, and then struggled to get my elbows under me. Maybe I could lift just a little…nope.

You have to be fucking kidding me.

There was no moving. None. Nada. Zip. I was firmly wedged in a hole of my own making without enough leverage to hoist myself out.

A huff of self-deprecating laughter slipped free. Talk about a metaphor for my life. Will would have laughed his smug little ass off.

"Yeah, I bet you think this is hilarious and symbolic or some nonsense," I muttered, slipping into the familiar pattern of talking to him when I was alone.

I swiveled my legs as far as I dared, hoping to find some purchase, but came into contact with nothing. *Of course not.* I was easily seven or eight feet off the ground here.

Not deadly. Just annoying. Humiliating, if I was still here by the time Sam and Mia got back. Way to prove that I'd be totally fine out here on my own. I hadn't even made it through one day.

I jiggled a bit and tried to squeeze my girls down through the opening.

Ouch. That wasn't happening. What skin wasn't already raw from the scrape was protesting the pressure from the remaining boards.

The sound of footsteps caught my attention, and I looked over to my neighbor's deck to see a little red-haired girl skipping down her stairs toward me.

She had that kindergarten look about her—all round cheeks and wide eyes. Around five years old was my best guess, which meant there had to be an adult home, too.

"Oh, thank God. Hi, sugar, how are you?" I asked as she raced across the thirty feet or so between our houses.

She paused shy of my staircase, her riot of curls stopping a second after the rest of her.

"Hi. I'm not supposed to be out here alone, but I heard you yell. You're stuck." Her forehead puckered over big brown eyes as her southern accent dragged out that last word just like mine would have. *Not a tourist.* At least that meant the house next door wasn't a vacation rental.

"I am," I admitted. "I'm Morgan, your neighbor."

Her eyes widened. "Our new neighbor? We had old ones. Really, really old ones. They didn't get stuck."

I might have laughed if the wood against my ribs would have let my chest expand that far.

"That's who I bought the house from. What's your name?"

"I'm Finley. Daddy calls me Fin. Like a fish. Or a shark." She wandered under the landing, and I lost sight of her.

My feet stilled immediately. I wasn't taking any chances I'd kick her on accident.

"Hey, I like Hello Kitty, too!" She squealed in delight. "I have the boring Saturday undies on today, but that's because I don't like the Sunday ones. They're green."

"Hello Kitty..." *Oh. My. God.* I assessed my situation more carefully, seeing fabric pooled beneath my breasts in a way it shouldn't be. And that breeze? Oh no. No, no, *no.*

Earth, just swallow me up right now. Right now.

"You're really heavy, Miss Morgan!" Bless her little soul, she tried to push my feet up, but I didn't budge.

"I'm sure feeling that way, Fin. Can you do me a favor?"

She emerged and looked up at me, folding her arms across her chest. "You're really stuck in there. I'll get Dad's saw."

"Oh, that's not necessary! But really, so kind of you to offer. Do you think you could get your mama for me?" *Please,*

God. There was no way I was going to wait another minute stuck in this damned staircase, flashing everyone on Cape Hatteras. Nope. No way. Hello Kitty needed to say good-bye.

"No." The girl shrugged, walking away.

"No?" I questioned, sure my eyes were about to pop out of my head.

"She lives in California."

"Oh–"

"But I'll get my daddy. Don't worry, he's really good at rescuing people!" She raced up her deck stairs.

"No! No, I'm okay! I'll just wait for my friends!" I called out, but she'd already disappeared into her house.

I blinked, hoping I'd wake up from this new take on the naked-at-school nightmare I was currently living. When that didn't work, I resigned myself to the fact that I was about to meet my new neighbor.

In my underwear.

While literally wedged in my landing.

So much for first impressions.

Wait. *Shit.* I'd shaved my legs, but waxing had pretty much ceased since…well, a while ago. My landscaping habits had gone from meticulous to well…au naturel. I hadn't given it much consideration, or even cared until this very moment.

This very inopportune moment.

But my panties were boy-cut, so there was a prayer of a chance that everything would stay covered, right? Could this possibly get any worse?

There had to be a limit on the amount of humiliation someone could endure.

The screen door shut next door, and I bit my lower lip, the pain reminding me yet again that this was definitely not a dream.

"Come on, Daddy!" Finley yelled.

"I'm coming, honey," a deep voice replied. The footsteps

that followed down the steps were heavy, masculine.

"It's okay, Miss Morgan. I brought my daddy. He was showering, but now he's not."

I opened my eyes to see Finley looking up at me with a smile, nodding her head enthusiastically.

"Thank you, Finley."

A pair of bare feet appeared next to hers, attached to muscular legs that led to a pair of blue swimming trunks and then abs that disappeared as a white T-shirt slid over his stomach and a recognizable tattoo.

I looked up into familiar, ocean-blue eyes and groaned.

Oh God. Just strike me dead. Right now.

It was Mr. Carolina.

Apparently, there was *not* a limit on humiliation.

Chapter Two

Jackson

Huh. Well, this was definitely not the way I'd planned on introducing myself to the new neighbor. It was like I'd stumbled into one of those magic acts where the girl was cut in half with a box…except this one sure didn't seem like the willing-assistant type.

Damn if she didn't have the legs for it, though.

"Okay," I said mostly to myself, completing a quick assessment of the situation. She was wedged in the weak spot of the landing, the one I'd suggested Diane and Carl get fixed before they put the house on the market. Hell, I'd been begging them for years to fix it, thinking one of them would meet the same fate.

I forced my gaze upward and found the profile of my new neighbor's face as red as her Hello Kitty underwear, which was the only scrap of fabric between her exposed ribs and her toes. Underwear I definitely shouldn't have seen…or taken notice of.

But, in my defense, they were right there in my face.

She'd taken out both horizontal planks, leaving the surrounding wood intact instead of splintering into her, but she'd definitely be feeling those abrasions and bruises up her sides for a while. Her ribs were scraped raw and bleeding slightly in places.

"Finley, stay here, honey. I'm not sure it's safe to come up the stairs."

After she nodded, I walked around the staircase and started up the steps, dropping to my knees a few steps beneath the landing, so I could look my very embarrassed neighbor in the eye. Well, I would once she stopped squeezing them shut.

Oh, fuck me. She was the knockout from the beach earlier. The gorgeous one with the hair, and the eyes, and the sundress currently keeping her company above the landing.

"Hey there," I said softly.

She opened one eye, then the other—like she was hoping I'd disappeared—and I was met with a stunning set of browns, dark at the edges, paling to amber at the centers, and framed by long, thick lashes. Every word I'd been about to speak evaporated from my head. Her eyes were as striking as she was, but there was something about them—a deep, lingering sadness that I bet had jack and shit to do with the predicament she was currently in. I'd seen a flash of it on the beach, but it was even more pronounced up close, and damn if it didn't trigger a need to save her from whatever caused it, too.

"Hi," she answered, her southern accent thicker than honey.

"Looks like you could use some help." I concentrated on not swallowing my tongue. The phrase *stunningly beautiful* wasn't new to me, but this was the first time I'd ever been actually…stunned.

"I'm really okay," she protested with the fakest smile

I'd ever seen. It would have almost been comical if I hadn't already seen her skin and how much pain she had to be in. "My girlfriends will be back any minute, so there's really no reason to trouble yourself."

Whoa. Yeah, that accent was deeper than anything the natives spoke with around here, and twice as sexy as that Irish girl last summer who'd rented out the place next to Sawyer's.

"Trouble myself? I'm not sure if you've noticed, but you're kind of stuck in your staircase."

"It has not escaped my attention." She kept that stubborn smile.

"How badly does it hurt? Scale of one to ten?"

Maybe it was because I'd softened my tone or the adrenaline was wearing off, but she sighed and dropped the pretense along with her shoulders.

"Five? A little scraped, I think, but mostly just mortified. I'm sure I can pop right out of this—" She tried to push up on her forearms, and I cringed. "Or not."

"Careful, you skinned your ribs."

"Feels like it. Most of the pain is there, in my hips…and my dignity. But I can't quite get a full breath."

"You *are* wedged pretty tight there, Kitty." The nickname slipped off my tongue before I could stop it.

She groaned, dropping her chin to her chest, and even the tips of her ears blushed pink. "Of all the things to be wearing. This is right up there with that one time my cheerleading skirt got tucked into my spankies," she mumbled.

"Spank…what?" I laugh-whispered to keep Finley from hearing.

Her head popped up, and she rolled her eyes. "Spankies. They're…you know—bloomers. They go under cheerleading skirts. I really wish I was wearing them right now, as a matter of fact."

And now that I had *that* image in my head…

"Well, let's get you out of this mess." I scanned the landing, studying the other boards that looked ready to give way if I put any weight on them. "I don't have the right angle to pull you out from here, and if we break any of those boards, we chance hurting you more. We're going to have to lift you out. You good with that?"

She pressed her full lips together in a tight line and nodded.

"Let's do it." I gave her what I hoped was a reassuring smile, then walked down the steps and under the landing, doing my best to ignore her mostly naked lower half hanging in my face. Chances were she was involved with whomever drove that lifted F250 parked by the old boathouse. It practically screamed alpha male from the size of the tires to the light rack. *Takes one to know one.*

Not that it mattered. Anyone who lived next door or knew Finley was off the one-night-stand table, which was all I was capable of.

Fin tripped over my feet, and I caught her by the waist before she smacked her head on the support pillar.

"Fin, honey. Why don't you give me some space, here? I don't want to squash your toes."

Fin nodded, then scurried out from under my feet and retreated to the patio chairs that lined our section of the fence, eager to watch the show.

I assessed the fingers-width of space I had between her ribs and the surrounding wood, and mentally cursed. She was a curved peg in a square hole.

"Okay, you must have fallen at an angle. We're going to have to maneuver you a little to get you through. Otherwise, you'll get hung up on your..." *ass,* I mentally finished. Not that it wasn't spectacular, but in this situation, it was definitely not helping her out.

"Bottom?" she suggested.

"Exactly."

"I might need you to give it a little push…there. I don't have any leverage up here."

Can I borrow a cup of sugar?

Do you have any extra plywood to board the windows?

We're headed out of town for the weekend, could you water the plants?

In the nearly five years I'd owned my home, those were the kinds of things the Hatchers had asked. There had never once been a "could you push my ass at the right angle so I can get out of the hardwood landing I'm stuck in" discussion. Ever.

Looked like I was about to cross every neighborly boundary in the first five minutes of knowing this woman.

I stepped out from under the landing and met her gaze. "Hey," I repeated my earlier line.

"Hey," she echoed, but with a ghost of a smile.

"I'm Jackson Montgomery. I figured I should probably introduce myself first." Not that I ever introduced myself to any of the people I saved. I wasn't the people person. That was Garrett's job. "Friends call me Jax."

"Morgan Bartley. Pleasure to meet you."

Morgan. Perfect. Like my favorite rum, which had a lot in common with the color of her eyes. *Eyes you're not getting involved with, remember?*

"Excellent. Now I don't have to keep calling you Kitty."

"It's kind of growing on me, embracing the situation and all." She laughed lightly. "Lots of worse things I could have been wearing, that's for sure."

Crap. Not only was she gorgeous, but I *liked* her, too. Not many people I knew could keep their sense of humor in this kind of situation.

"Okay, then, Kitty, here we go." I headed back under the landing. Shit, she was streaked with bruises and scrapes from rib to hip to thighs. Only her waist and lower legs had escaped unscathed. "Ready?"

"Reckon now is as good a time as any," she called back.

Without ceremony, I gripped her waist and lifted her.

"*Oompf.*" The sound escaped as her ribs slid free of the landing barrier.

"Better?" I settled her onto my left shoulder, careful to keep my forearm locked over the top of her thighs to avoid brushing her abused sides.

"A little," she answered. "I can get a full breath now. Thank you."

Seeing the new gap between her waist and the planks, I reached with my right hand and tugged gently on the fabric of her sundress, pulling it down in sections to give her as much modesty as I could offer.

"Thank you," she repeated, softer this time.

"Take a second to catch your breath, and then we'll lift you the rest of the way." My head turned at the sound of tires on the gravel driveway. A small sedan parked between the enormous truck and the moving pod, then two women got out. One pale, holding a large pizza box, and the other one with a tawny complexion and a bottle of what looked to be tequila, both wide-eyed and slack-jawed.

"Oh. My. God."

"Morgan!"

They raced toward the steps.

"Whoa, hold up!" I called out through the slats in the stairs, sending them to a skidding halt. "I don't know how much weight that landing can take."

Two heads popped around the base of the staircase, and I gave them a nod. "Hi there."

"Mr. Carolina?" the petite one asked, her jaw dropping.

Mr. *What*?

"Uh. Not the last time I checked. Then again, I don't

really run in the pageant circuits," I answered. The tequila-toting one came over to see my hands locked firmly on the tops of Morgan's thighs—one over and one under her dress. "I'd shake your hand, but as you can see, mine are a little full at the moment."

"Well, then," she said without a trace of southern accent. "Morgan, are you hurt?"

"A little banged up, but nothing to fret over," Morgan answered, shifting a little on my shoulder. She weighed next to nothing. "So, that's Finley, and Jackson here is my next-door neighbor. How's that for luck?"

"Jax," I offered.

Fin waved, and Morgan's friend returned the gesture before looking back at me.

"Well, Jax, how awkward—I mean awesome—to meet you. I'm Sam, and that's my sister-in-law, Mia. And the girl you have perched on your shoulder is one of my best friends, so what can I do to help?"

"Nice to meet you, too," I told the ladies. "Giving Morgan a hand up would be great. The rest of the stairs look sound, but the landing's unstable. If you could go up the back steps and come down these to that last stair before the landing, that would be awesome. See if you can get your hands under her arms to help guide her onto the stairs as I lift her. Don't let her put weight on the landing, if you can help it."

"Done. Mia!" she called to the other girl, and they were gone in a blur.

"You doing okay up there, Morgan?" I asked. What kind of perfume was she wearing? Sure as hell smelled divine. Vanilla and strawberries?

"I should be asking you that, seeing as I'm currently sitting on you."

I almost laughed. "Don't you worry about me. I'm doing just fine." I sent a wink in Finley's direction, who giggled behind her hand.

"You're not going to be too tired to lift me out?" Morgan asked, worry saturating her voice and increasing the number of syllables in that last word. Holy shit, the woman could read the phone book with that accent, and I'd be hooked.

"Trust me, I could hold you all day. I'm not going to let you fall."

I felt a gentle give in her posture. Good, she'd relaxed a little.

"So, you bought the house, huh?" I asked, trying to fill the silence until the girls could get around to Morgan.

"Yeah. Maybe I should have looked at it first." Her voice dropped, nearly unintelligible with the wood muffling the sound between us.

"You didn't look at it first?" *Seriously?*

"I saw pictures!" she shot back. "And the inspection report, and Google Maps. I just didn't visit it…until today."

Holy shit. She'd walked in blind? The house itself was structurally sound, but damn, did it need some upkeep. It hadn't been touched since the Hatchers bought it back in the seventies.

"And is it what you were expecting?"

She tensed.

"Morgan?"

"It's not that I didn't want something to fix. I did. I do. I want to look at something and say, 'I did that.'" Her sigh was loud enough for me to feel it in my chest. "There just happens to be a lot more fixing to do than I initially thought."

"Is your husband handy?" I'd learned that it was always safer to assume a woman was in a relationship than go with the opposite. Plus, with her soft, bare skin under my fingers, it would be handy to know if I was about to get punched in the face by an overprotective partner.

Her thighs turned to stone.

"I'm not married, not involved, and not looking." She bit

out every word.

Damn, I'd just gotten rejected from a girl I hadn't even hit on. That was a first.

"Sorry, I saw the truck and assumed." And there was the number one problem with assuming anything. "Not that a woman can't have a jacked-up truck like that or anything. It's a nice piece of equipment."

"It was left to me by…a friend. I drive the Mini Cooper over there. So, know any good contractors?"

Subject closed. Got it.

"I can dig you up some names—"

"We're here! Sorry, we had to climb over the bottom gate and, well, we're short. It took a second." Sam leaned over the railing. "Ready?"

"Absolutely. Morgan?"

"Yep."

"Here we go. I'm sorry, this might hurt a little. You're pretty banged up."

"Do it. I'm tougher than I look."

I somehow didn't doubt it as I switched my grip to her hips, careful to place my hands outside her dress. "One. Two. Three." I lifted her slowly and watched her progress through the small opening.

"Okay, angle back toward Sam," I ordered as the curve of her ass reached the board. At six-four, I could reach over the seven feet to the landing, but I needed a better grip to get her the rest of the way through.

"My hands are about to get friendly," I warned her.

"What, like they weren't already?" she joked.

"Ha." I switched my grip quickly, grasping the back of her thigh with one hand and sliding below her knee with the other. I powered her through, letting my higher hand slip from her thigh as she rose.

"Gotcha!" Sam exclaimed.

Then Morgan stepped free, and my hands were empty.

"It worked!" she called out, leaning over the railing from the stairs above the landing.

I stepped into the evening sunlight and smiled up at her. "Sure did."

"You rescued her!" Finley called out, running at me in a tangle of curls and limbs. I caught her easily and lifted her to sit on my shoulders.

"Wasn't *really* a rescue," I told my daughter. "Just a few feet."

"Well, it sure felt like a rescue to me," Morgan countered, flashing a smile that hit me right at the knees.

"You definitely saved the day," the petite one—Mia, I think they'd called her—drawled with the local accent I'd grown accustomed to, batting pretty blue eyes at me.

"That's his job," Finley answered. She squirmed, and I let her down. "I'm hungry!" With that declaration, she was off and running up our stairs. "I'm glad you're not stuck anymore, Miss Morgan!" she called out and disappeared into the house.

"Always hungry, that one," I said with a smile.

"Well, thank you for helping get our friend out." Sam started up the steps. When Mia didn't move, she grasped the strap on her tank top. "We'll see you later."

Mia gave me one more grin and followed Sam.

That left just Morgan.

She tucked her hair behind her ears and stared at the banister. "Thank you," she said quietly.

"My pleasure."

Her eyes shot to mine, no doubt thinking of the eyeful I'd received.

Poor choice of words.

"I'll come over in the morning and lay down some plywood. That will give you time to get the contractors out to estimate...well, everything."

"Don't worry. I'll take care of it." Her spine straightened.

She hadn't been kidding about wanting to fix things herself.

"Stubborn much?"

"I'm not sure why you'd think that." She crossed her arms under her breasts and winced.

"Because I'm offering you help, and you're not accepting it."

"I just did!" She motioned to the landing.

"You had no other choice, unless you wanted to wait for your girlfriends to break out a saw." I tucked my thumbs in the pockets of my shorts. "As I recall, you argued that you were really okay…as your feet dangled. Stubborn."

"Yet I still accepted your help. But I'll fix the landing myself."

Jesus, what if she nailed through rotten boards or cut the size wrong? I'd have to haul her out all over again.

"So you have experience with carpentry and all that." Why wouldn't she let me help? Everyone around here helped each other out. Not that she knew that, or that I'd spent my summers on my dad's construction sites until I left for college.

There was a flicker of something in her eyes that told me her admirable determination might not match her skill set.

"Well. No. Not yet, at least," she admitted.

Not your business.

Not your problem to fix.

Don't get involved.

"When you said you wanted something to fix, you meant in the hire-people-who-know-what-they're-doing kind of way, right? Not the pick-up-a-hammer way." *Way to make it your business, jackass.* "Because this house is going to take more experience than a weekend *Fixer Upper* marathon. Unless you and your roommates have some construction history that those soft hands of yours aren't advertising, you're going to need help."

What happened to not-your-problem?

She visibly bristled. "One, they're not my roommates. They're just visiting. I'm on my own and quite capable. For certain things I'll have to hire a contractor, but I have a few months until my job starts, so I'm sure I can figure out the rest through online tutorials—"

"Wait. Are you seriously considering learning how to remodel via YouTube?"

She tensed, and her eyes…those were on fire.

"Holy crap, you are." Was I worried for her or completely in awe? Probably a little of both, to be honest.

"It was really nice to meet you, Jackson," she all but dismissed me. "I wish it hadn't been under such…memorable circumstances—" And now that blush was back, rising in her cheeks again.

"Let me help. At least with the safety things. I did almost the entire remodel on our house by myself—well, with some buddies from work. Your house hasn't been touched since the seventies, and I doubt the structure has ever been reinforced. The Hatchers loved it just the way it was, avocado paint and everything."

For a second, I thought she might relent.

"I'm reliable, I swear." I put my hand to my heart.

Her chin rose at least two inches.

Wrong thing to say.

"Contrary to what just happened—which I'm incredibly grateful for—I am not in the habit of relying on men, even the pretty ones, so I'll be fixing my own landing, thank you very much." She turned me down with a brisk nod of her head.

There was a hell of a story there, but all I could focus on was *pretty*.

"But really." Her voice gentled. "Thank you so much for"—she motioned toward the landing and dropped her gaze again—"you know..." She gifted me with a closed-lip, embarrassed smile and then retreated up her stairs.

Holy whiplash. The woman was soft-spoken one second, then spitting fire at me the next. Much to my dismay, I more than kind of liked it.

"Pushing you out of the hole you fell into?" Crap, I was grinning. How could I not? She was so indignant that I'd offered to help, but I'd literally just pushed her ass out of the staircase.

"Right. That. Thanks." She paused and waved like a queen to a subject but didn't turn around.

"That offer stands. You need anything, just knock, or I can have Finley run over with our phone number."

"I appreciate the gesture."

Lord save me from polite Southern manners.

She stilled, then turned back toward me, her posture relaxed. "Please tell Finley thank you for me. She really saved my butt." Her head tilted, and she winced slightly, then gave me a self-deprecating chuckle. "Literally."

I laughed, the sound more honest than any I'd made because of a woman in a long time. My phone rang, and I reached into my lower pocket to check the caller ID.

Please don't be a rescue.

It was just Sawyer.

"See ya around, Kitty."

She sputtered, smoothing her dress back down around her thighs as I crossed the yard to our house, swiping to answer Sawyer's call.

"What's up?"

"Is it Finley-Free weekend?" he asked with the noise of a bar in the background.

"Nope. That's only once a month and you know it, so whatever it is you want me to do, the answer is no unless it involves you on my couch with *Moana*."

I heard a door shut and glanced over at Morgan's. She'd made it inside without another incident.

"Damn. I mean, I love Fin. I was just kind of hoping you would wingman me here at McGinty's. There's a set of twins with—"

"Nope. You're flying solo." I started up the steps toward my door.

"Come on! Call her grams. You know she'd love to keep her. And don't try to tell me you don't want to get laid."

I always wanted to get laid. Sex was a physical need I had zero guilt or trouble gratifying. But I steered clear of emotional entanglements, clingers, and anyone who saw Finley and thought they needed to step in as her mom—which basically meant I was perpetually single except for the occasional one-night stand with a tourist. Exactly the way I liked it.

My eyes reverted to Morgan's porch. *Yeah, not going there.*

"Wanting to do something and doing it are two different things. It's called adulthood. Call Garrett. I'm sure he'll back you up."

"Come on! Get a sitter. Call Brianna. You should see the legs on these—"

I wasn't calling Finley's aunt or giving up time with Fin.

"Bye, Sawyer. See you Tuesday." I hung up on my best friend, wishing he'd grow the hell up. The thought made me pause. Maybe he was acting our age, and I was actually way too old in my head to be physically twenty-eight.

Funny, I'd seen that same quiet maturity in Morgan's eyes when I'd run past her on the beach today. It had been more than a little at odds with her Hello Kitty underwear.

Not that I was ever going to see those again.

With every step I climbed, I tried to shove the gorgeous brunette out of my head. There was room for only one woman in my life.

And she was five years old.

Chapter Three

Morgan

To be honest, you scared the shit out of me. You always knew what you wanted—even when we were kids. You have this incredible, fearless approach to life that I lost somewhere along the way. But you need to know that, little by little, I've felt it coming back, and it's because of the way I feel when I'm around you. You're bringing me back to life, Morgan.

"I've read your chart, history, and Dr. Meyers's notes, but can you tell me more about how and when the anxiety attacks occur?" Dr. Circe asked, leaning back in the purple armchair across from mine.

She was nothing like Dr. Meyers, who'd simply given me a prescription and walked away. Then again, Dr. Circe looked to be about thirty and had a way better bedside manner than the seventy-two-year-old psychiatrist I'd seen since the attacks started nearly two years ago.

"Sure," I said, adjusting in my own seat. Of course, I

didn't want to go through it all again, but moving here meant I needed a new doc before my current prescription ran out. "My head starts to race, and my heart jumps, like it's trying to keep up with the thoughts. But then..." I swallowed past the familiar tightening sensation in my throat as it took hold, just like it did every time I tried to describe it. "Then my throat closes, like someone has a fist around the base of it, squeezing." I leaned my head back, stretching my neck as I reminded myself that I could still breathe; it was just uncomfortable. It was like my anxiety attacks had a defense mechanism of their own to keep me from talking about them.

"Are you having one now?"

I shrugged, bringing my eyes back to hers. "Sometimes they happen or intensify when I think about them. But mostly it's when I think or talk about..." Mercy, it hurt. I stretched my neck again, breathing past the vice gripping my throat. "Him." I shoved the images and feelings aside that swamped me whenever he came to mind.

"Can you tell me about"—she checked my chart—"Will?"

Without permission, memories crashed through my defenses—a million different moments from thousands of days over twenty-four years. Childhood. High school. Peyton dying. Him coming home from West Point. Paisley. The breakup. His unwillingness to be with me. The ball. The wings. The kiss. The casket—

"No," I forced out, trying desperately to cram everything back in the box. "It's not that I don't want to, but..." I swallowed and swallowed again, until she leaned forward, nudging a bottle of water across the glass coffee table.

I twisted off the top and chugged half the bottle, trying to dislodge the tension in my throat—to swallow it down—but it didn't help. It never did. A few moments passed while I watched the waves crash on the beach outside the window.

"I have trouble talking about him," I finally admitted.

"I don't really know where to start—how to sum him up in words—and then I can't breathe because I know exactly how it…ends, and I can't go there."

"To when he died?"

I nodded. "It's like opening Pandora's box. I can't pick and choose what comes out of it."

"That's fair." She nodded slowly. "How often do you think about him?"

My eyes jumped back to hers. "More than I should." *All the time. Every minute of every day.* If my life was an ocean, then the water was Will. Always there, sometimes calm, deep, and soothing, and sometimes he was a tsunami ready to pull me under in waves of grief so deep I wondered when I'd eventually drown.

"And who told you that there was an appropriate amount of thinking to be done?" She sipped her tea.

I blinked. "Everyone, I guess. Family. Friends. My old psychiatrist. I'm supposed to get over it, right? It's not supposed to still hurt like this."

She studied me carefully, but it wasn't intrusive or judgmental. "How long has it been?"

"Twenty-two months." The longest months of my damn life. Every day felt like it was a personal test designed to see how much I could take.

Some days, I won. Some days, I didn't.

"Has it gotten any better? The grief?"

"Compared to what?"

"Compared to the first month or so after he passed."

He hadn't passed. He'd been taken. Hell, he'd given his life away.

"No," I finally answered. "But I gave up on that a long time ago. Kind of figured this was simply the way things would be now. This is how I am."

"And how is that?"

"Broken." I stared at the water in my hands. "My previous doctor told me it's anxiety and depression. You have my file."

"I do." She put her tea down and scribbled on a little notepad. "But I'd rather hear it from you than read another clinician's notes. When you think of your future, what do you see for yourself?"

What *did* I see? It had been so long since I thought about goals that I wasn't sure I even had them anymore.

"I don't know. I mean, I bought my house, and I need to fix it up. I took a job that starts in September." I shrugged.

"And past that? What about long term?"

"That is long term." Anything past this week was long term as far as I was concerned.

Her brow puckered for a moment before she gave me an understanding nod. "Okay, and friends?"

"I have friends. There are a couple I'm still really close to, but the others..." I looked back out at the ocean like it had the answers I needed. "They moved on, and I'm stuck. Like someone pressed pause and I'm still waiting for him to come home from that deployment."

She scribbled on her pad again. I wasn't sure I wanted to know whatever it was she wrote on that thing. "And moving here...was that looking to the future?"

Yes was what she wanted to hear. A healthy person would have said that moving here was their new start. That they were ready to wake up and greet the morning with the kind of optimism that simply didn't exist for me.

"Be honest," she urged, her eyes kind. "There's no right or wrong answer. I'm just getting a feel for where you are in the process."

"He was everywhere," I said softly. "In Alabama, I couldn't go anywhere without being accompanied by a memory of him. I couldn't teach at our elementary school or eat at the same restaurants, because...he was everywhere.

And everyone in our little town thought I should either be over him or setting up a shrine."

"So you escaped."

I nodded.

"How did your loved ones feel about the move?"

"My mother is pretty unhappy with me. She thinks a woman has no business living alone. Guess she forgets she was raising me on her own at this age. The friends I'm still close to are supportive. One of them is here, actually."

"So you do have a support structure here?"

"Sam's just visiting, and I can support myself."

"And the others? The ones who have moved on, as you said?"

Guilt smacked me.

"I haven't told them I moved. Haven't talked to them in months, really. I can't…I just need a break from them." I finished the last part on a whisper. It was the first time I'd said it aloud to anyone but Sam: I couldn't stand to be near most of my friends. My avoidance was more than declining a call once in a while. It had become methodical.

"And when is the last time you felt happy? Or at least weren't thinking about your loss?"

Happy? I skipped right over that thought. But then again… "A few days ago, I fell through my landing," I said slowly.

"Are you okay?" Her eyebrows rose.

"I'm bruised up, but fine. Thank you for asking." I swallowed. "But this man—my next-door neighbor—he pulled me out, and there were a few minutes where the only pain I felt was from where I'd gotten scraped. I only thought about…Will when Jackson asked about his truck." Heat flooded my cheeks as I twisted the cap of my water.

"I'm glad he pulled you out, Morgan. How did you feel after that encounter?"

"Besides embarrassed that he found me dangling in my Hello Kitty underwear?" The corners of my mouth tugged upward slightly.

She bit back a smile but nodded.

Mine faded. "Guilty that I enjoyed meeting Jackson," I admitted quietly.

She studied me for a moment.

"Okay." She stood and walked over to her desk, then pulled papers from the bottom drawer before coming back toward me. "I want you to fill these out. Be as blatantly honest as you can. Like I said, there's no right or wrong."

She handed me a three-page assessment and a pencil.

"Right now?" My stomach twisted as I looked over the questions.

"If you can," she answered gently, taking her seat again. "I think there might be a little more going on than your last doctor caught, and this will help me figure it out."

I took another drink, then answered the questions as truthfully as I could. *I long for Will every day. Yes, it's disruptive. I've accepted this as my reality. Hell yes, I'm still bitter.*

Each question pricked at the raw center of my soul, scraping and cutting until it drew blood. I finished and handed the papers back to her.

She thanked me, and I walked to the window so I could see the water while she quietly read my answers.

"Okay. Morgan, I don't think it's just anxiety or depression that's causing your attacks."

"You don't?" My brow puckered as I turned to face her.

"No." She shook her head and leaned forward slightly, putting the papers in my file on the table. "I think you have something called complicated grief."

I scoffed. "Because we had a complicated relationship?"

"Maybe that's part of it. Complicated grief happens when

your rational mind has accepted the loss, but your emotional mind hasn't quite gotten there. It keeps you stuck in that first, sharp, acute stage of grief and doesn't let you move forward."

"Okay? And what am I supposed to do with that?" I walked back to her desk, stopping behind the armchair I'd been sitting in.

"I'd help you move forward." She offered me a soft smile.

I clenched the back of the armchair, the fabric warping slightly under my fingers. "You'd help me move forward?" I repeated, each word a little less kind than the last.

"Yes. We do a very specific form of therapy that's been proven to help people just like you move forward in the grieving process." She sat there calmly while my emotions boiled over.

"Move forward?" I shook my head. "Move forward to *what*? To a life without him? To a world where everyone around me is happy because they didn't lose the only man they've ever loved? That's not moving forward—that's where I'm at *now*. There is no forward when it's the same bullshit I've been living the last two years."

"I can help you see past all this," she promised, and the worst part was she believed that garbage.

"You want to help me? Then bring him back," I snapped. "You rewind time and go to that godforsaken valley in Afghanistan and you tell him that his life is worth the same as Jagger's—not less. You keep him from being the martyr." My stomach twisted with something hot and ugly as my nails dug into the upholstery. "Then you go into a grocery store in Alabama and stop my phone from ringing, and you catch that jar of raspberry jam before I drop it all over the floor and it shatters." I shoved the memory away with the chair, and it screeched across the hardwood floor. "You sew my heart back together, and you give us the chance we didn't get!" A razor-tipped fist of emotion forced its way up my chest, prickling my eyes with pain, and I had to shout to be heard around it. "Everyone else got their shot! Josh and Ember, Paisley and Jagger, Sam and Grayson, hell, even Paisley and Will got their shot, but the minute he decides that it's finally time for us to get our chance to be happy together, he dies saving my best friend's husband." I rubbed viciously at my chest, right where my set of aviation wings should have hung—would have hung if he'd lived. "I don't want to move *forward*. I want Will! I want our shot!" I swiped angrily at my face, batting away the tears that had escaped during my tirade.

God, how long had it been since I'd lost it like that?

"I can't bring him back," Dr. Circe said gently. "I'm so very sorry for the loss you've suffered. But I know I can help you if you'll let me. It's four months of some pretty intense therapy, but I know we can lessen some of the pain you're in."

"You *know*?" I snapped. Nothing lessened the pain. Nothing but sleep took it away, and even then, I eventually had to wake up.

"I honestly think we have a good chance of not only lessening your pain but helping you truly move forward. This program has a seventy percent success rate."

"And what happens when I'm one of the thirty?"

"I don't think you are. This isn't something you have to decide today, Morgan. I'll call in your prescription to the local pharmacy. We definitely want to keep the anxiety attacks under control, but I'd also like to treat the underlying cause, not just the symptoms." She rose to her feet.

"No amount of therapy will make me miss him any less."

She walked me to her door. "Give me four months. Just think about it. You meet with me once a week. You do the homework. You'll feel the results. But you would need someone to help support you through it."

"I'm all alone." I shrugged, shutting the door on the possibility.

A corner of her mouth lifted. "Well, like I said, just give it some thought. And while you're over there telling yourself that therapy isn't going to help you, I want you to think about the fact that you just told me what happened to Will without having an anxiety attack."

She opened her door, and I walked into her small, comfortable lobby, where another patient was already waiting.

Maybe she'd help *him* through whatever he was going through, because there wasn't a *through it* for me.

• • •

"Give it to me straight," I said to the fourth contractor Joey had brought out to look at my property in the last two days. At least this guy was closer to our age and didn't look at me like I'd lost my mind or suggest a complete teardown.

He scratched his well-trimmed beard and looked back at the house from where we stood on the driveway. "Well, how much money do you have?"

"Come on, Steve," Joey snapped, folding her arms across her chest. Grayson's older sister had cut her dark tresses to a bob in the years since I'd seen her, but there was no mistaking her for cute when she arched that eyebrow.

"Don't be like that, Joey. You asked me for my opinion, and I'm giving it. That house is a wreck. You need a new deck on both levels—hell, I'm surprised they're still standing, honestly—new siding, new staircases."

I left out the tidbit where I'd already fallen through the landing.

"Okay, but structurally?" I prodded, hoping the inspector had told the truth on the report I'd seen before closing.

"In that, you lucked out. The foundations around the boathouse and pillars are sound, but they both need better drainage and waterproofing. The bones are good, shape is great for deflecting wind, but it could use a dose of storm-proofing—or you're probably going down in the next cat three. I'm surprised she made it through this last one, and she took some damage for it. Definitely needs a new roof, and that weathervane looks like it's about to break off any minute." He pointed up to the heavy brass arrow that spun circles on my roof when the wind changed.

"It stays," I said. "Reinstall it or whatever, but I like it." Arrows were supposed to be meaningful, right? Getting pulled back to release farther and faster, or something. Besides, if it had survived the storms for this long, who was I to yank it down?

He sighed. "Ms. Bartley, the weathervane is the least of your problems. Your electrical system needs to be completely overhauled. I don't know who thought it was a great idea to put a secondary panel in a room that's literally built to *flood*."

And it just keeps getting better. By grace, the house was just as much of a mess as I was.

A long shadow came up parallel with mine, and I knew from the general shape that Jackson was its owner. I wanted to feel annoyance, or a little of that temper that had flared when he'd insinuated that I couldn't fix my own damn house, but neither came. Just a quick kick to my pulse and a weird sense of relief.

Only because he's already pulled you out of the shit once.

And don't forget he's seen your underwear, too.

I mentally cringed for the four-billionth time.

He came close enough to nearly brush my shoulder, tucking his thumbs into his pockets as Steve paused his list of everything that was wrong with my house.

"Jackson, how's it going?" Steve grinned, and the two reached out to shake hands.

"It's going," Jackson answered. "Don't stop on my

account. I'm dying to know your thoughts. If that's okay?" he asked me. "Steve did the major reno stuff on my house a few years ago."

I glanced at him and nodded. He'd be subjected to the noise of the remodel, so it seemed like a fair enough trade.

"Shit, you did most of that yourself," Steve countered with a shake of his head. "Now, Ms. Bartley, that list doesn't even touch cosmetic stuff like the kitchen or the flooring. We're just talking about what the house needs in order to survive the next decade. I've always loved this house, and I want it to stay standing, so when I ask you how much money you have, it's not because I'm looking to inflate your invoice. It's because there's going to be a hefty base price, and then you're going to have to decide what upgrades you need versus what you want and what you're willing to pay for."

"I definitely want everything you would structurally recommend." The rest, I would scrape and clean and sand it to smooth on my own. If it took years and every penny I had, so be it. There would be one thing in my life that was perfect. That no one could take from me.

"What about hurricane-proofing it?" Jackson asked.

"I definitely want to hear about that." I was used to tornados in Alabama, but hurricanes were a whole different ball game on the coast.

Steve nodded. "Sure, if you want to go all-out, you could definitely use some reinforcement." He studied the house quietly for a moment, his eyes darting over the structure. "We'd probably need lifts, but we could drive a steel support alongside the one you have running through the house, but go deeper, and change the positions of anchors on your roof when we put on the new one so it's structurally like those new-built, hurricane-proof ones, but you'd still stay within your legal limits for the remodel. I mean, it's already got those nice faceted lines on the ocean side, which is probably how it's stood this long. But you're digging into cost again."

"And timeline, I assume," I said with a small sigh.

"That part isn't too bad. We'd probably get the supports and roof on in about two weeks, and we actually have an opening if you want to start—"

"So can you give her a couple different estimates?" Jackson interrupted.

I shot him some side-eye. Listening in was one thing, but this wasn't a situation where I needed—or wanted—to be rescued.

"What?" Jackson shrugged. "Don't you want to know the cost of what *has* to be done by professionals versus what you *can* do yourself, versus what you might *like* to have done by experts?" Those eyes of his cut right through me in a way that was more than a little unsettling and left me feeling exposed, like I was still standing there in my underwear.

"Of course, but I can certainly handle my own contractor," I said with a syrup-sweet smile. "And if I want to hire Barnum and Bailey to construct my new roof in the shape of a circus tent, I certainly can."

"That would actually be awesome. Not only for wind resistance but for pure visual effect." He grinned, undermining my entire intent, because I couldn't help but roll my eyes.

The man had the damnedest effect on me.

"Sweet Lord, Jackson, go away. You're distracting me—Steve. You're distracting Steve." *Clever cover-up. Not.*

"Concentrate harder, Kitty," he whispered with a shrug and a wink. Then he waved up to Finley, who enthusiastically returned the gesture as she played on their porch.

Wait. Shit. Was he flirting with me? He couldn't flirt with me. I wasn't available for flirting, or laughing, or…anything. Had I flirted back?

Guilt gripped me by the throat and squeezed.

I'd only known this man a handful of days.

"Where were we?" Steve asked, glancing at his clipboard.

I sucked in a strangled breath and swallowed past the part of my throat that threatened to close up. The last thing I wanted to do in front of Joey or Steve was take the rescue meds I'd been prescribed for acute attacks. *I'm fine. This is fine.*

"You were agreeing to work up three estimates for me." I stood a little straighter, and Joey smiled, unaware that I'd almost lost it. "I'll need one that includes every safety issue you first addressed, then one that includes new flooring, lighting, siding, and removing that wall between the dining and living room." Everything I couldn't do myself. "And one with the works, whatever you think it needs. Give me details on whatever storm-proofing you like. Oh, and I'd love the entire living room to have the ability to retract the windows like one big sliding glass door." With every word, the vice around my neck loosened.

"It gets windy around here," Steve remarked.

"It's an estimate, not a contract. A girl's gotta keep her options open," I quipped so quickly that I almost felt like *me* for a second.

The edges of Steve's mouth quirked up as he took notes. "Give me a couple days and I'll get the estimates over to you." He shook our hands, and when he got to mine, his gaze darted toward the truck, which I still hadn't managed to get into the boathouse that would serve as its garage. I'd tried twice after the moving company had unloaded her but couldn't bring myself to open the driver's door. "Something that big can be a little impractical out here on the islands unless you're in my line of work. Any chance you're looking to unload it? I'd give you a fair price."

My heart galloped, and every hint of sass that had risen to my surface since the Hello Kitty incident sank like a block of cement in that huge ocean behind me.

"She's not for sale." The words came out in a strained half whisper.

"Okay, well, if you change your mind." He turned to talk to Jackson about some upcoming festival or something I immediately tuned out.

I pivoted to look at my house, barely registering when Jackson left for his own.

Once Joey started up the stairs, I followed, pausing on the piece of plywood I'd cut myself with the new saw she had recommended I purchase this morning from the only hardware store on the island.

Sure, it was a little loose and undeniably imperfect, but it was proof I could do this. I'd be okay when Sam left in a few days. I could repair this house. Repair myself.

Jackson and Finley raced down the stairs of their house with battle cries, and I looked up in time to see Finley hit Jackson square in the chest with a spray from her massive water gun.

"Ha! Got ya!" she shouted.

He fell to his knees in the sand, exaggerating his death for a moment before spraying her legs when she came in for a second shot.

She squealed, taking off through the backyard, and he quickly followed over the dune to the beach.

I smiled at how happy they were. It was as simple as that. Sam was right; here, there were no expectations on how long it took me to recover myself. Here, I could have a moment where I missed Will like hell and still smile a breath later. No one was judging.

Here, I could fix my stair— Wait.

The board didn't shift those centimeters when I moved my feet like it had this morning. I peered closer and saw that there were a few screws next to the nails I'd hammered in.

Screws I knew I hadn't used, because I didn't own a drill. Yet.

Maybe Joey had guaranteed my handiwork while I'd gone to see Dr. Circe. It would make sense, seeing as she knew way more about building stuff than I did.

I climbed to the deck and looked out over the beach, past the shadows creeping toward the ocean from the late-afternoon sun.

As Finley sprinted into the water, Jackson ran behind her, grasping her waist and spinning her low enough for her toes to skim the water. I heard her laughter and felt it echo in my chest, somewhere in the vicinity of where I used to think my heart was. I wanted to be that happy, to find joy in…something.

He turned in my direction, and I knew it was impossible—the distance was too great—but I could have sworn our eyes locked and held for a moment.

And as certain as I was that he'd catch Finley when he tossed her up in the air, I knew he'd secured the board.

But it didn't make me feel infantilized or undermined.

Oh no, it was worse than that.

It made me feel protected, and that scared the crap out of me. But that little spark of yearning I felt as I watched Jackson and Finley play in the ocean? That was terrifying.

• • •

"Maybe it makes me a bitch, but I'm kind of glad everyone left yesterday." Sam handed me a cup of coffee and sat across from me the next day, stretching her legs out in front of her on the sun-warmed deck.

"Thanks," I said and took a sip. "I am, too. I mean, I'm glad they came, and I'm thankful, but I've gotten used to quiet." Once Sam had moved out, I hadn't taken another roommate. I'd grown to crave the silent hours I had at home.

"Do you want me to go? I absolutely can," Sam offered.

"No, please stay. It's different being around you." The wind ruffled the spiral notebook pages next to me.

"I can stay longer, too, you know." She tilted her face at the sun. "If you need someone—I'm here. I don't start grad school until the fall, and it's not like Grayson is waiting for me at home in Colorado."

I flinched. She was two months into his first deployment. Will hadn't survived his first two weeks. "How are you holding it all together so well?"

She squeezed her eyes shut. "I'm not. I miss him like hell, and there's not a second that I'm not scared shitless. I guess I just hide it well. Military brat and all that."

I reached across the distance between us and took her hand. "You're the strongest woman I know, Sam."

"Look in the mirror sometime." She stared at me in that way she had, forcing me to accept her words as truth, but I felt anything but strong. "You're going to be happy again. Maybe not today, or tomorrow, but one day. You know that, right?"

I didn't mention Dr. Circe. Her offer was ludicrous... right? But what if it wasn't? What if there was a real chance that I didn't have to feel like this for the rest of my life?

But seeing how my luck ran, I was probably one of the 30 percent.

"Maybe I'm one of those people who doesn't get to be happy. Maybe my chance for happy died with Will."

"I don't believe that," she whispered.

"Happy people never do."

• • •

The sun had barely turned the sky pink over the ocean when I woke the next morning. That same sense of dread hit me that I had to get up, had to move through my day, had to pretend.

The heaviness of it all was unbearable.

I rolled over on my queen-size mattress and stared at the dark screen of my sleeping laptop. One click, that's all it would take. One click and I'd see him again, and for those seconds, everything would be all right. My heart lurched, longing for that ten-minute eternity where he was still alive. But I wouldn't stay for only ten minutes.

All it would take was that first click—the sound of his voice—and I wouldn't leave this bed all day. Some days I won. Some days I lost. Today was a coin toss, and I needed to call it in the air.

You're going to be happy again. Sam's words from yesterday rang in my ears.

But there wasn't any happiness for me outside the video I'd seen thousands of times. I rubbed my chest, like that would somehow take away the pain, but it never left.

Why wasn't I okay when everyone else was?

How long could I possibly live like this, fighting with myself over Will's memory before I even got out of bed?

I know we can lessen some of the pain you're in.

But Dr. Circe couldn't. Or could she?

But what would happen if I tried her way and failed? *Nothing could possibly feel worse than you do now.* And then there was the unthinkable: What would happen if I tried her way and it...worked?

Was there honestly a chance? Probably not. I tried to squash the tiny flame of hope that had flared to life in my chest, but it kept whispering *maybe.*

I ran my finger along the top of my laptop. Will would have called me all sorts of names for not having the courage to try. He would want me to try. He would have wanted me to watch that video *once*, not use it as a lullaby for twenty-two months. He would have wanted me to get out of bed and *try,* even if I failed.

Maybe I couldn't be as happy as Jackson and Finley, spinning around in the ocean, but maybe…just maybe I could hurt a little less.

I slammed my laptop closed. My feet hit the floor, and five minutes later, I turned the key in the ignition of my Mini Cooper—still dressed in my pajamas. By six twenty-five, I was parked outside Dr. Circe's office.

She arrived at seven fifteen, her eyes flying wide when she found me sitting on the wooden steps that led to her office.

"I don't want to feel like this for the rest of my life," I admitted before she could ask me what the hell I was doing there.

"You don't have to," she said softly, moving her bag to her other shoulder and sitting next to me on the step.

"You really, honestly think you can help me?"

She reached over and took my hand. "I do. Now do you think you can find someone to be your support person? This really works better with one."

I nodded, a slight smile curving my lips. "Yeah. I just need to buy a few cases of peppermint mocha coffee creamer as bribery before I ask her."

Chapter Four

Jackson

"Hey, Jax, Connor is looking for the volleyball," Cassidy told me, flipping her blond hair over her shoulder. "Oh, hi, Brie."

Brie gave her a half wave from where she stood, leaned back against my kitchen counter. *So much like Claire.* And yet the two couldn't have been more different. They'd been Irish twins—Claire older by eleven months—but Brie had always acted like the older sister.

"It's in the garage, second shelf, right-hand side. And tell your husband the NA beer is in this one; I know he's on call tonight," I told Cassidy before pouring the bag of ice into the cooler. The heat wave had weekend temps pushing eighty, which meant it was time for the first Sunday barbecue of the season.

"Man, it's weird to be here when Finley isn't," Brie said, swinging a bag of beach towels over her shoulder.

"Yeah, but it's your mom's weekend, and I know how they both live for it." Finley adored her grandmother. Hell, we both did. Vivian filled the massive shoes left empty not just by Claire but by the three other grandparents Fin was missing.

"How's the new nanny working out?"

"So far, so good. I know your mom wasn't keen on Fin spending so much time with a stranger—"

"Look, Jax, your job is utterly unpredictable. You never know if you'll get a call or if a shift will run late. You have no say in what happens out there." She motioned toward the ocean. "Mom's not taking care of her diabetes the way she should, and she's getting older. She's not up for those late-night drop-offs anymore. You absolutely did the right thing hiring Sarah."

I closed the lid on the cooler. "She still pissed about it?"

Brie cringed. "Well, she did go off on Claire for a good twenty minutes this morning."

My stomach cramped. "Claire's here?"

"Oh no!" Brie's eyebrows shot up. "I meant on the phone. They still talk every Saturday."

My jaw flexed, and I bit back every remark that came to mind, like how fucking ludicrous it was that Claire talked to her mother every week when she hadn't bothered to call Finley in the last two months. "How is she?" I managed to ask.

It wasn't Brie's fault that Claire was…well, Claire.

"She's good. Still in L.A. waiting to see if the last pilot she did gets picked up."

"Pilot. Right." How many was that now?

"She really does miss Finley. You, too, of course." Her lips pressed into a thin line.

"Yeah, misses her so much that she's seen her once in the last eight months." I closed my eyes and took a deep breath to calm the ever-present rage that boiled to my surface whenever I thought about the way Claire treated Fin. "You know what?

Let's not do this."

Brie forced a quick smile. "Good idea. Let's get down to the barbecue," she suggested, moving to hold the door open.

"Yeah, let's get out there." I latched the cooler and lifted its hefty weight, then headed out of the house and down the stairs with Brie following close behind.

My gaze caught on the massive F250 parked outside Morgan's boathouse. Sam—her last houseguest—had left two days ago, and I hadn't seen the truck or her Mini Cooper budge.

None of your business.

Except I'd gone and made it my business the minute I'd rescued her over a week ago. But what the hell else was I supposed to have done, left her stranded with her Hello Kitties blowing in the breeze, half in and half out of her staircase?

Maybe if she hadn't fallen through the wood, if Fin hadn't heard her yell, if I hadn't raced out there to dislodge her, I would have had a prayer's chance of ignoring my new neighbor.

Sure, until you saw her or heard her speak.

Yeah, there was nothing ignorable about Morgan Bartley, which was really damned inconvenient.

Not that I was going to act on that attraction. Hell no, my life was complicated enough without messing around with someone I had to see on a daily basis. Morgan was off-limits, which didn't really matter, because something told me she wasn't emotionally available, anyway, even if she had called me *pretty.*

"Thanks for inviting me," Brie said, jarring me from my thoughts as we reached the ground. "You saved me from tagging along to the shipwreck museum for the hundredth time."

"You're Finley's aunt—you're always invited," I reminded

her for the thousandth time since we brought Fin home from the hospital.

I paused by the wooden gate that separated my backyard from the path to the dune and looked up at Morgan's house, unable to let go of the nagging feeling in my chest that I needed to check on her.

"Need a hand?" Sawyer asked as he came up behind me, the volleyball under his arm.

"Nawh, I'm good," I told him.

"You sure? You look a little scrawny to handle that." He motioned to the cooler.

"Fuck off." I spent a hell of a lot of my downtime at work running and lifting, refusing to give into the *dad bod*, as Sawyer once implied. "You can barely handle that ball."

"Speaking of which, you ready to get your ass kicked?"

"Never going to happen." I smirked at my best friend. Movement in Morgan's window caught my eye, and my attention drifted to her house—to her—again. Had she seen sunlight since her friend left? "You know what? Why don't you take Brie to the party? I'll be there in a second."

"No problem—"

"I can wait for you—"

I put the cooler down by the edge of the deck. "Brie, go ahead. I'm going to invite my new neighbor over. Go have some fun."

Brie rolled her eyes at Sawyer's offered arm and took off up the path.

"Prickly as a cactus, that one," Sawyer remarked as she disappeared over the dune. "I swear she hates everyone but you and Fin."

"Nope. Just you. And she's family, which Fin is in short supply of."

"She coming back tonight?" he asked. "Kinda miss your little urchin."

Sawyer acted all tough until faced with a certain redhead. Then he was pretty much butter, just like every other guy we worked with.

"Tomorrow. It's Vivian's weekend, and it's a three-day weekend for the preschool."

"Seriously? We could hit up McGinty's tonight and catch the end-of-spring-break crowd, or you could break your not-in-my-house rule for one of the ladies currently stripping down to their bikinis. Over the dune. Fifty feet away. While we stand here. Where we can't see said bikinis." He raised his eyebrows.

"One, I never break the house rule. My daughter lives in that house, jackass. Two, I'll be there in a second."

"Yeah, yeah. Okay, you go invite your new neighbor, and I'll see you down there. You sure you don't want me to bring the cooler down? I'd hate for you to injure your back. Old age is a bitch."

"You're exactly two months younger than I am," I reminded him.

"I figure Finley's aged you at least a year for every one of hers, so that makes you five years older. Right? She just turned five? Man, you'll be pushing forty soon if you don't watch it."

"I can't wait until you have kids so I can dish all of this shit right back at you," I called as he headed up the path.

"Never going to happen!" he retorted and disappeared toward the party. A steady beat dropped as Imagine Dragons came on the speakers. *At least Garrett got those working.*

I took a steadying breath for the battle that was no doubt about to ensue with Morgan and crossed the yard to her stairs. Pausing on the landing, I bounced a little, testing it. Good, the screws had held.

No doubt she'd give me shit for sticking my nose in where it didn't belong, and she'd be absolutely correct. I had zero right interfering with her contractor, her staircase, or her life in general.

That hadn't seemed to stop me, though.

It wasn't her looks that had me climbing her stairs. It was that smile that didn't reach her eyes. It was the way the other girls had moved closer, flanking her as if they knew she was one step away from crumbling. The way she'd gone white as a ghost when Steve had asked her about selling the truck. The way she stood on her deck in the mornings and stared out at the ocean with sad eyes and her arms wrapped around her waist while I drank my coffee unnoticed on my own.

That girl had some damage, and it ran deep.

Like calls to like.

But when I riled her up, a spark lit in her eyes, which told me she wasn't completely broken.

I knocked on her door and waited. About two minutes later, I did it again. Another minute went by, and I knocked harder. My overactive imagination pictured her lying injured somewhere.

Before I could knock again, the door swung open, and Morgan openly glared at me. Her hair was piled on her head in a casually sexy knot, her face free of any makeup that would cover her flawless skin, and she was dressed in plaid pajama pants and a loose T-shirt that proclaimed that good grammar was sexy.

"What could you possibly want, Jackson?"

Jackson. I liked the way she said it, refusing to drop the formality and call me Jax—like it was an actual barrier to keep me from her.

Too bad she didn't realize her voice had the opposite effect. That drawl was more addictive than the sugar they laced the tea with around here.

Well. Shit. It had been years since I'd been floored by a woman, and that's exactly what this was, wasn't it?

Fucking inconvenient.

"When's the last time you left the house?"

She folded her arms under her breasts. "Why does it matter?"

"You might only be a beard short of a full-blown recluse."

She arched an eyebrow at me. "Maybe I like being a recluse. Besides, I'm enjoying the last day in my house since I have to move out tomorrow."

"You're moving out tomorrow?" *What the hell?*

"Just for a couple of weeks while they jack up the house and drive in new pilings, place the center support, and pop a new roof on."

Relief I had no business feeling hit me all the same. "So you picked a contractor."

She nodded. "Steve gave me some good estimates, and he had this window open up. Plus, he swears I'll only be out for two weeks."

"Then you definitely need a little fun. I'm having a barbecue. You don't even have to get dressed." I motioned my head toward the beach. "Just a few friends. Come hang out with us."

"Just a few friends?"

"Yep, give or take a guest or two. We like to barbecue on Sundays, and looking at the forecast, this is going to be the best weekend for about a month."

"Sunday barbecues." She softened, her shoulders relaxed, and her lower lip found its way between her teeth.

"You're tempted. Come on, Kitty. Take it one step further. Come down to the beach. You don't have to stay long or even talk to me. There's about a dozen other people you could meet. Humans. Vitamin D. Hamburgers. Maybe a beer. Live dangerously."

A corner of her mouth lifted, and a spark flared in her eyes.

Victory.

"I guess it would be rather un-neighborly to turn you down."

"A downright affront to southern hospitality," I confirmed, internally swearing at the jolt of awareness that punched me in the stomach when she gifted me with a full smile.

Why couldn't a nice, middle-aged guy buy this house? Why didn't I get another older retired couple who I'd wave to at the odd times I saw them? Or, better, why couldn't Morgan be ignorable? Just normal?

But hell no, she was a knockout. Stubborn, funny, nice to Fin, with a gorgeous face, soft brown hair, legs for fucking days, and a smile that might actually control the tides if it would appear twice a day—that's who I got as a neighbor. About as ignorable as a nuclear detonation.

Not that I was doing much to keep clear of the blast radius.

"Okay. Let me throw a suit on and I'll meet you down there."

"Or how about I wait right here, outside, while you put one on, and then I walk you down?" I offered.

She scoffed, narrowing her eyes. "You don't think I'll show."

"Would you actually?" I challenged.

"Probably not," she admitted with a scrunched nose.

"Exactly." I leaned back against the deck railing, feeling it burn against my T-shirt. "I'll wait right here."

"Hopefully the banister holds up." She rolled her eyes and shut the door. The song changed twice before she opened her door again, wearing a tank top and shorts with a halter-top tie showing in her neckline. Her beach bag was slung over her shoulder, and her sunglasses ate up about half of her face.

"This doesn't mean I'm giving up my recluse status," she

told me over her shoulder as she skipped down the steps with me hot on her heels.

"Of course not. This is a heatwave miracle."

She shook her head at me, but I saw those lips lift briefly as we crossed to my backyard.

I lifted the cooler and didn't miss the way her eyes widened as her gaze dropped to my arms, then darted away.

She cleared her throat. "Um. Need help?"

"Nope. Lead the way." I motioned toward the path. She held the gate open for me and then closed it once we were through.

"So who all is here?" she asked, then cringed. "Silly question. Like I even know anyone on this island."

We crested the dune, and I scanned over the party as the unblocked breeze off the ocean hit us full force. "Mostly guys I work with and a few friends."

"This is not a few friends."

"I said give-or-take some guests."

She shot me a look, and I grinned.

The volleyball net was up, with a game in full swing. Sawyer and Garrett held down one side with a couple of the mechanics, and Goodwin was teamed up with Cassidy, Thornson, and a few local girls on the other.

Beach chairs surrounded the area, and the grill was already fired up and manned by Moreno.

"What is it with volleyball and the Outer Banks?" she muttered as we descended the dune steps.

"What?"

"Nothing, it's all very *Top Gun*." She motioned to the game and, no doubt, the shirtless guys.

"Except we're not fighter pilots or covered in baby oil. I could probably hook us up with some 'Highway to the Danger Zone' if you want, though." We reached the bottom of the dune and started toward the grill. The sand burned my feet where it poured into my slides—hot but not scalding.

"Damn, and I was hoping you were going to offer the baby oil."

My eyebrows rose with appreciation at her quick comeback.

"What do you guys do, anyway?" she asked, pausing to slip off her flip-flops.

"We're coa—"

"Heads up!" Garrett shouted.

My head snapped toward the game just in time to see the volleyball on a collision course with Morgan's head.

I dropped the cooler and swung my hand out. The ball hit my palm with a slap before Morgan even removed her second shoe, its momentum reversing and sending it into the sand.

Morgan gasped, her eyes wide when she met mine.

"You okay?" I asked, shaking the sting out of my hand.

"Well, yeah. I'm not the one who hit the ball or dropped a cooler on her foot." She glanced down and then looked at me like I was an idiot. "Are *you* okay?"

That explained why the toes on my right foot were a little pissed off.

"Perfectly fine." I grasped the plastic handles of the cooler and got it off my foot. Sweet relief swept over the little digits when the pressure was removed. Luckily, the sand had taken most of the impact.

"Doesn't look like anything's broken, but I'm not exactly a doctor," Morgan drawled as she dropped down to examine my foot.

"I've been through worse."

"Well, thank you," she said, coming to a stand. "But I'm sorry you got hurt."

"Perfectly fine," I repeated like a puppet with a pulled string.

"Those are some serious reflexes you've got there," she

said as we walked the rest of the way to the grill where the sand firmed up.

"Having a five-year-old daughter will keep you on your toes." I deposited the cooler in the sand and slapped Moreno on the back. "How about I take over, and you can go give Garrett and Sawyer a hand? They're getting their asses kicked."

Moreno laughed but handed over the spatula. "Yeah, I'll go save their precious little egos. You got this?"

"Absolutely." I opened the cooler and fished a beer out of the ice as Moreno joined the volleyball game. "Want one?" I asked Morgan.

She peeked around my shoulder at the selection.

"I'd love a Coke, please."

I plunged my hand into the ice again and pulled out a Coke, brushing off tiny bits of ice from the top before handing it over.

"Thank you," she said quietly, popping the top as I used the bottle opener I'd installed on the edge of the grill. "So, where is Finley?"

A smile tugged at the corners of my mouth. Most women who ended up at our barbecues never thought to ask about my daughter unless she was actually there. "She's with her grandmother." I took a swallow of the cold beer and flipped over the first row of hamburgers.

"Oh." Her forehead wrinkled as she watched the game, rotating the silver tab on her soda from side to side.

I nearly laughed—she looked so conflicted.

"You can ask, you know. I'm pretty open," I offered, flipping the second row of burgers.

"Is she with her grandmother often?" She chanced a look at me.

"Vivian takes her a weekend a month. It gives them some girl time."

"And you a little off time?" she asked, no judgment in her tone.

"Yeah, I guess. Lets me get stuff done, take a weekend shift at work—"

"And have Sunday barbecues," she noted with a smile as she reached for the package of cheese slices on the grill's side table. "Want me to unwrap?"

"That would be great, thanks." I glanced past Morgan to see Sawyer and Garrett headed this way. "Okay, forgive whatever comes out of these idiots' mouths. They know not what they speak, but they are my best friends," I warned before they appeared on either side of her.

"Got it." She nodded, already placing cheese slices on an empty plastic plate.

"You couldn't help us out there?" Sawyer accused me, then promptly assessed Morgan while she wasn't looking.

Asshole.

"Hey, I sent Moreno," I answered, bringing his attention back to me.

"Ignore him. He's whiny today," Garrett said, pointing to Sawyer. "Burgers smell good, though."

Morgan glanced at them both and finished peeling the cheese. A tiny—okay, huge—pang of satisfaction smacked my chest that she hadn't lingered on either of my friends the way she had when I'd run past her that first morning.

"Garrett, Sawyer, this is my new neighbor, Morgan," I introduced them.

"Nice to meet you." Her voice was soft, but her smile was fake. She was missing the little crinkles next to her eyes that had appeared when she'd smiled a few minutes earlier.

"Nice to meet *you*." Sawyer poured on the charm. "Where did you get that delicious accent?"

"So subtle," Garrett mumbled.

"Isn't it the same as around here?" she asked.

"Not even close," I answered and was rewarded with her attention. "Yours is deeper. Don't give me that look–it's not a bad thing. It's pretty great, actually."

She smiled, the crinkles appearing at the edges of her eyes, and I mentally fist-pumped.

"Southern Alabama," she answered. "I guess I never realized it was that much stronger. Y'all don't even have accents."

"That's because I'm from Oregon," Sawyer said, like it made him foreign or something. "West Coast."

For fuck's sake, it was Oregon, not Brazil.

"And you?" she asked me.

"Maine."

"My God, could you get any farther north?"

"Not without becoming Canadian."

"Or Alaskan," Sawyer suggested, stepping closer to Morgan.

"That would still be American, jackass," Garrett interjected.

The two started trading insults, and Morgan stepped backward and picked up her beach bag. "You know, that water looks pretty great. I'm going to sneak away, if that's okay with you boys."

Boys? My eyebrows hit my hairline. Between that and *pretty*, I didn't know if I should be charmed or offended.

Her hands twisted in the strap of her bag, and I nodded in understanding when she caught my eye. "Enjoy your alone time. Just a warning: the water's still freezing."

"Doesn't seem to bother you."

"Well, yeah, but I swim it every day."

"Part penguin. Gotcha. I'll watch my toes for frostbite." She flashed me a quick smile and practically ran toward the water.

"That's your neighbor? I mean, holy shit. I'm going to

move in," Sawyer said, grabbing his chest in dramatics.

"It's a two-bedroom house," I reminded him, slapping cheese on half the burgers.

"I'll take the couch. I won't eat much. I swear."

"Do you ever not think with your dick?" Garrett asked, reaching for a beer.

"Nope," Sawyer answered. "Why would I when it has the best ideas?"

"Man, those smell good," Brie said as she came to stand next to Sawyer.

"They're just about d—" My words died in my mouth.

Twenty feet ahead of us, Morgan peeled off her shirt, revealing two straps of a halter top around her back and neck, and was now sliding her shorts over her hips, exposing a cobalt-blue bikini bottom that cut straight across her hips.

"God bless the south," Sawyer muttered.

Once her shorts hit the sand, she bent over, that incredible ass in the air as she retrieved her clothes.

"Seriously?" Brie asked, her exasperation clear at the open male ogling.

"Okay, that is a gorgeous woman," Garrett admitted.

Apparently, we were all watching the same show.

Morgan's arms arched above her head as she twisted her hair around her hand and somehow got it back into a bun. Fuck me, she was perfect. Lithe yet still ridiculously curved in every place my hands itched to touch.

"Jax," Brie chided.

"I'll be…over there," Sawyer declared his intent, his eyes on Morgan.

He didn't even make it a step in Morgan's direction before my arm snapped out sideways, blocking his path. "No."

"But…" He looked at me like I'd killed his puppy.

"No," I repeated, making sure he understood.

"Whoa." His eyes widened, and his mouth dropped open.

"What?" I snapped.

"You calling dibs?"

"Jesus Christ, are we in junior high?" Garrett asked.

"Jax." Brie's annoyance registered somewhere in the back of my mind.

"She's a woman, Sawyer. Not a pre-K snack you lick and say it's yours." My eyes found their way back to where Morgan walked into the water, the water reaching her knees.

"Well, seems like you wanna lick her," Sawyer teased.

I shot him a quick glare and watched Morgan sink to her hips in the Atlantic.

"I mean in a calling-dibs kind of way. Well, and the other way. Every way, really, from what I can tell by looking at you." Smugness practically oozed out of his voice. "But, I mean, if you're not interested…" He shrugged.

"Jax," Brie called, her voice sharper this time.

I put my finger up, wordlessly asking her to wait a second.

"Don't even talk about licking her," I warned Sawyer.

"Oh shit, Montgomery is going primal." Garrett laughed. "This is getting good."

Sawyer shrugged. "I'm cool with it. I haven't seen you legitimately interested in a woman since—" His eyes hit the sand, and I saw Brie tense in my peripherals.

"It's not like that," I protested, my eyes narrowing when I saw waves breaking on either side of Morgan but not in front of her.

"Jax!" Brie shouted.

"What?" I didn't take my eyes off Morgan, hair rising at the back of my neck.

"You're burning the burgers!"

Shit, Morgan was exactly where she shouldn't be and getting deeper. I shoved the spatula at Garrett's chest, kicked off my flip-flops, and broke into a dead run as a bigger wave receded, pulling the water off the beach. My shirt was off two strides later.

"Morgan!" I called out, my pulse kicking up a notch.

She looked back at me over her shoulder and moved forward, the water already tugging at her. It was waist-deep, but she was easily twenty feet offshore on the sandbar.

"Move over!" I pointed north, my feet hitting the water, which immediately slowed my progress.

She startled but moved as the water swept past her, and was already in the safety zone before I reached her.

My hands gripped her shoulders. "God, woman! It's like you're determined to find every possible way to injure yourself!"

"What's wrong? You scared the bejesus out of me!" she snapped, like I was the one in the wrong.

"Hell yes, I did! You were standing in a riptide zone. Any deeper, and I would have been showing off my *Baywatch* moves!" My fingers tensed on her skin, but I was careful not to squeeze, to shake, to let my emotions manifest physically.

"What?" She looked back to where she'd just been. "There's no sign or anything."

What? I held her steady as a wave swept by, bringing the water up past my waist.

"Right, because we didn't put one out." Adrenaline pumped through my system, and I concentrated on keeping my words even and soft. The ocean was an unforgiving bitch who didn't give a fuck about signs. You broke her rules, she ate you whole, and sometimes she changed the rules just for fun.

"Why would *we* put one out?" Her forehead puckered.

"Because we own the beach, at least up to the tide line." Understanding dawned. "You've never been on a private beach, have you?"

She shook her head. "Always public."

I blew my breath out in a long sigh. This girl was going to be the death of me. "Okay. Do you know how to recognize a riptide?"

"No. Otherwise I wouldn't have been headed for one." Her eyebrow arched, and the tension drained out of my muscles as I fought the urge to laugh.

Of course she would throw sass at me right after I saved her ass. Again.

"Okay. Let me show you." I let go of her shoulders and moved to stand next to her as another wave washed by, rising against our bodies. "It's easier to see from shore, but watch the waves break. See how they break over there, and here, but not in that center area?"

I stepped behind her and pointed, my arm grazing her cheek so she could follow easily. Her head came to the perfect height—she'd be able to rest it in the hollow of my shoulder if she turned around. It would be ridiculously easy to kiss her—

Nope. No. Not happening. Stop it.

"I see," she said, nodding her head.

I immediately dropped my arm. "Right. So that area in the center doesn't have any waves breaking, because that's where the ocean sucks the water back out quickly. Hence the term *riptide.*"

She spun, looking up at me with a perplexed look on her face.

Yep, I'd been right. She'd fit snugly against me, and I wouldn't even have to bend far to get my mouth—

I took a step back and hoped I wasn't obvious as hell.

"But I was out in that exact spot when I found the sea glass."

"The sea glass," I repeated like an idiot. What was this, high school? I was sixteen again, getting caught staring at Stacy Anderson during English instead of paying attention. Except Morgan was ten times more…everything than Stacy had been.

"Right. The day you pulled your Aquaman stunt?" She

folded her arms under her breasts, pushing the curves up.

I didn't look.

I deserved fucking sainthood, because that qualified as a miracle.

"Aquaman?" *Stop repeating what she says, you moron.*

"You know, when you came out of the ocean all Lord of the Fish or whatever and then started jogging? Though I honestly thought you looked more like Captain America at the time. Still kind of do, actually." She tilted her head in clear appraisal of my features.

"The day I first saw you?"

"You remember that? It was only a few seconds." Goose bumps rose on her arms, but I'd barely registered the water's temperature until right now. It was way worse last month, but it was still good and chilled in here.

"Yes. Clear as day." How the hell could I not? It was the only time I'd ever seen her completely unguarded, her emotions on full display. "I mean, it might not have been as colorful an impression as the one you made later that day, but yes, I knew it was you."

A blush stung her cheeks, and she mumbled something about burning that pair of underwear.

"Sea glass, huh?" I asked to get both of our minds off her underwear.

She nodded. "I found the prettiest blue piece. I love that something plain like a broken jam jar can be transformed by the cold saltwater and rough sand over years and years. Kind of like what hurts actually refines it, if that makes any sense."

Another piece of the puzzle that was Morgan clicked into place. This woman knew pain, and not just in a general sense. In the very real, raw, intimate way that changed a person—refined them like the sea glass.

"It makes all the sense in the world." My voice dropped, as if it couldn't physically support the weight of the charged air between us. I swallowed, my throat a little tighter than usual. "That day, we were at low tide. You were standing on the same sandbar you are now, but there was no water. The best time to find sea glass, actually. The next time we're both around at low tide, I'll show you how to spot where the rips will be when the tide comes back."

"Thank you. It would be nice to get through a week where you don't have to come to my rescue." She rubbed the tops of her arms quickly.

"I don't mind," I assured her.

"And I appreciate that, but I do mind." Her words were soft, taking the sting out of what felt a little like rejection. "I need to know I can stand on my own. It's why I moved here. Why I chose a house that looks like Morticia Addams did the exterior design."

Okay, I'd give her that one.

"So, if I can get through a week where I don't nearly get myself killed, stuck, or struck in the head by something that you need to rescue me from, that would be a great start."

"Got it." Funny. My need to rescue was as deep as her need to *not* be rescued.

"I'm going to start right now by getting out of the water. Because once again, you were right, and I think my toes are turning blue. But I *am* going to let you feed me."

That smile was back, giving me that same punch in the gut. *Shit.*

"I think I may have burned the burgers." I didn't tell her why.

She shrugged and tossed a grin over her shoulder as she walked away. "I'll take my chances. Thanks for the rescue, though. Now let's hope you don't have to play the hero again," she teased. "It's almost like you have a complex."

"You have no idea," I muttered to myself, waiting until she was on the beach before trudging my way out of the water, getting some much-needed space to clear my head. I yanked off my shirt, grimacing when it stuck to the wet skin of my stomach and lower back.

"Go ahead and say it." Sawyer handed me a plate with a burger already on it.

"Say what?" I took the plate and dressed my burger, noting that Morgan had found a seat in a camping chair next to Garrett.

"That I was right. You're interested in her." He smirked.

I glared.

"Hey, I'm all for it. I'll even wingman you. What can I do? Talk you up? Brag about your list of achievements and qualities? Come on, let me have your back for once."

"God, please don't. She's obviously going through a tough time, and I'm just trying to be a good neighbor." Right? *Right.*

"Oh shit, she's a wounded bird? That's like your fucking catnip."

"I have no clue what you're talking about."

He snorted. "Seriously? Is there not a three-legged guinea pig, a blind turtle, and a one-finned fish living in your house right now?"

"Those belong to Finley. She likes to rescue helpless pets." I shrugged.

"Right, and who exactly let her bring them home?" He stared at me, his eyebrows nearly hitting his hairline.

I blinked, then cursed.

"This is going to be fun to watch," he said before cramming his face with his own burger and walking off toward Morgan and Garrett.

"There's nothing to watch!" I called after him.

He gave me a thumbs-up and kept walking.

"Really, Jax?"

I paused mid-ketchup and found Brie staring up at me

with crossed arms and concerned eyes.

"What?"

"You really think it's a good idea to start something with your neighbor? To bring a stranger around Finley? Let alone one who lives next door?"

"Start what? First, I'm not starting anything, Brie. And second, if I *was* starting something, it wouldn't be any of your business." I tried like hell to soften my tone, but given the way she tensed, I hadn't been successful.

"It's sure as hell my business who spends time around my niece."

Something foul curdled in my stomach.

"*My* daughter. Don't start with me, Brie."

"Sorry. I just think Claire—"

"Claire lost any rights she had regarding who I spend time with the day she walked out on us."

She sucked in a deep breath and blinked a few times, finally forcing a smile. "Just don't turn your neighbor into a stage-five clinger, especially since I have to work with her."

"You work with her?" My gaze flickered toward Morgan.

"Yep. She came into the school two days ago to pick up some paperwork. She's the new fifth-grade teacher—my counterpart next year. So if you can't keep your dick in your pants for Finley's sake, please consider me." She shot me a look that could have had about a dozen meanings—none of them good—and walked off toward a group of mutual friends. I made a mental note to ask Vivian what had set her off today.

So Morgan was a teacher. I could see that.

I took my food over to where Morgan sat with Garrett and Sawyer. She flashed me a smile and motioned to the empty chair, then took another bite of her burger.

"It's not burned?" I asked.

"Totally is. You should stick to saving people, because barbecue isn't your talent," she teased once she'd swallowed, but that didn't stop her from polishing it off.

"Say it," Sawyer whispered from next to me.

I watched Morgan laugh at something Garrett said. It was small but there and honest. I couldn't wait to see who she'd be once she came fully out of her shell.

Fuck.

I should back the hell away from her.

Brie was right in a way. Morgan was my neighbor. Starting anything with her could bring a shit ton of awkwardness to my door that I didn't need—that Finley definitely didn't need.

I should have moved over to that group of women hanging out with the mechanics and picked up someone who didn't live next door. Someone who didn't need me to explain riptides or push her out of a decaying staircase. Someone who didn't wear red Hello Kitty underwear that I still couldn't get out of my head.

Mental note: throw away all Fin's Hello Kitty stuff.

I should have walked the hell away.

Morgan gathered up her things and slipped into her clothes before walking toward me. "My thirty minutes are up. Time to turn back into a recluse." Her tone was teasing, but her eyes weren't.

"Okay. I'm glad you came down."

"I am, too. Thank you for the invite." She slid her sunglasses on, and I immediately lost the ability to read her.

"Anytime."

She gave me a half smile and a nod, then walked away. My eyes followed her until she disappeared over the dune.

"Say it," Sawyer repeated, this time singing his demand quietly. "Call dibs."

"Fuck off."

But we both knew he was right.

I was interested.

Now I just had to decide if I was going to act on it or not.

Chapter Five

Morgan

I know you. You've always been so good at holding it all together.
I know you'll pick up the pieces.

The construction noise overtook Mama's voice as I pulled into my driveway. There were two huge cranes and several smaller vehicles surrounding my house.

"...and that doesn't even start to address my worrying about hurricane season!" Mama chirped.

"Mama, I'm so sorry, but I gotta cut this short. I can barely hear you with all the clamor going on at my house." I pulled the Mini into the spot on the other side of the boathouse and put her in park.

"Okay, honey. Just think about what I said, okay? It can't be good for you to be all the way out there by yourself. You really need to be home where we can take care of you and help you move on. Being out there is just going to let you dwell on it when you really need to pick up and push on with your life." Her intentions were good, and her demands so… not.

"Okay, Mama, I'll keep that in mind, I promise, and I'm not alone. Sam is spending most of the summer with me." There was zero chance in hell I was moving back to Enterprise, but I wasn't even opening that can of worms with her.

Steve waved to me from the table he'd set up across from Will's truck.

"I'm relieved to hear that, but still. Two young girls—"

"Mama, I really have to go." I killed the ignition and reminded myself not to snap at the woman who had given me life.

"Please do, baby. I'd even come help move you out. Love you! Just think about it!"

"Love you, too. Bye, now!" I hung up before she could launch into another ten-minute tirade about why being here was the completely wrong thing for me. I could devote an entire chapter in the journal Dr. Circe had given me yesterday to Mama's well-meaning control issues.

The weather had chilled since this weekend but was still warm enough that the breeze didn't bite at my legs too hard as I walked over to Steve's makeshift command center.

He gave me the quick rundown. The house was up on jacks, giant holes had been cut next to the existing center support of the house, and they were preparing to drill both the new foundation pilings and the center support into the sand.

"Twenty-seven feet deep?" I remarked.

"Twenty-seven," he confirmed. "A storm can easily swipe away a good six feet of the current ground level. Opting for the composite pilings was incredibly smart of you. They're stronger than concrete or steel."

"And more expensive," I muttered. If the house drained my bank account, so be it. I never wanted the money, anyway.

"Honestly, spend the money on the structure. No one gives a shit if you have granite counters when the next cat four comes in." He shrugged.

"True. Are we still on time for moving back in?" My chest tightened in anticipation. Not that I wasn't enjoying the B&B in Cape Hatteras, but I wanted back into my house.

He ran his finger down his calendar, then nodded. "Ten more days, maybe sooner if the weather holds. We're set to start drilling in about thirty minutes. Once we get her resettled on the new pilings and the new roof secured, you're more than welcome to live in a construction zone."

"So fast," I remarked.

"Not going to lie, I'm pushing my team so we can fit you in between projects. We won't be able to start anything on the interior until we finish a job in Frisco."

"Perfect. You can come in and fix whatever I've messed up by then."

He chuckled and slid a binder across the table. "Have you thought about colors for the exterior?"

What color would Will have wanted had this been our house? Probably the dark blue or even the gray. Classic. Stately.

"She's here!" a high voice shouted with glee. Jackson's door slammed shut, and I heard the fast pitter-pat of what had to be Finley's feet coming down the steps. I looked over and waved as she raced across the small space that separated our houses.

"Hi, Miss Morgan!" Fin grinned up at me, and I couldn't help but return it. She was like living, breathing joy—the contagious kind, and even I wasn't immune.

"Well, hi there, Miss Finley! You got here just in time to help me look at paint colors!" I pulled Steve's vacant stool over and gave the seat a pat.

"I can help?" Fin asked, already climbing onto the stool and setting a bright orange walkie-talkie on the table.

"Well, I get the final say, but I could definitely use your opinion, seeing as you'll have to see it every day, too!"

"Hmm..." She touched her chin thoughtfully as she flipped through the laminated pages of colors. "I like the bright ones!"

I looked over her shoulder to see swatches of bright pastels in yellow, purple, teal, and blue. "You don't think we should go with something like your house?"

A quick glance confirmed my memory—Jackson's house was white with thick, gray trim, and the man himself was walking toward the back gate with a bag slung over his shoulder. My belly fluttered, and I put my hand over the waistband of my shorts.

Not for you, I reminded myself and jerked my eyes away from his retreating frame. Going to his barbecue had been good for me—even Dr. Circe said so—but I wasn't about to let myself start needing the reprieve being around him somehow gave me.

"My bed is yellow. Like happy sunshine! Your house could be sunshine, too!" She nodded enthusiastically.

"A lot of the houses out here are bright colors you don't find in the city," Steve agreed.

I eyed the teal swatch. The color was gorgeous, but what would Will have—

"Calling Fin Montgomery, this is Daddy Montgomery, over," Jackson said through Fin's walkie-talkie. Even his voice was attractive, clear and deep. He wasn't in the yard anymore, so where was he calling her from?

Fin grabbed the device and grinned. "Hi, Daddy!"

"You didn't say over, over," he teased.

She giggled, and the sound slipped inside my heart.

"Don't forget your mission, over," Jackson said.

"Oh! Right...over." She turned to me with expectation in her eyes. "I'm supposed to tell you that it's low tide, so come eat." She nodded with a smile, satisfied that she'd delivered her message.

"Eat at three forty-five in the afternoon?" I questioned.

"I like snacks," she told me matter-of-factly.

"Good point. Where are we supposed to go?"

"To the beach. Daddy's there."

The fluttering in my belly quickened, and I mentally cursed myself. It had only been four days since I'd seen Jackson at the barbecue. He'd been at work when I'd stopped by to check on the house, and I didn't attempt to stalk him or make myself obviously available.

Because I wasn't.

Even joking with myself that I might be available was cruel. But I didn't have the heart to deny those big brown eyes looking at me beseechingly. Guess I was a masochist, because I stuck my hand out to take Finley's.

"Okay, we'll go."

"Yay!" She pressed the button on the side of the walkie-talkie. "Daddy Montgomery, she said yes! Over!"

"Good work, Fin! See you soon, over!"

"When do you need my answer on the colors?" I asked Steve as Fin hopped down from her seat.

"If you want us to throw the siding on before the Frisco job, then I'll need it in the next couple of days so I can get everything here." He smiled at Finley. "Say hi to your dad for me."

"Sure thing!" she answered.

"I'll think it over," I told him, my eyes drawn back to the teal even though I knew that was the most ridiculous, ostentatious choice I could make.

We said our good-byes as Steve headed toward the cranes

hovering over my house. Hand in hand, Fin and I steered clear of the construction, then crossed over the dune to the beach.

Jackson had a blanket spread out on the sand, anchored at the corners with a small cooler and a few rocks.

Stop getting all gooey. It's not a date.

Ugh. Did he have to look so good? He walked over to meet us, barefoot in swim trunks, the wind ruffling his hair and plastering his T-shirt against his carved-by-Michelangelo body.

"You made a picnic?" I asked, hoping my voice didn't sound as breathless to him as it did to me. What the hell was wrong with me? He wasn't the first attractive man I'd been around since…everything happened, but he was the first I was attracted *to*, that was for sure.

"Don't get excited. It's just snacks." He shrugged with a little smile that did inappropriate things to my stomach.

"Pickles, and strawberries, and Skittles!" Finley raced over to the blanket.

"And low tide," I said softly. He'd remembered his promise, and damn if that wasn't more attractive than his looks.

"And low tide." We stood there staring at each other for a moment longer than neighborly friendliness suggested. "So, how has your week been?" he asked, leading me to the blanket.

"Full of Steve, and choices, and diner food," I replied, crossing my legs under me and sitting next to Finley. "You?"

"Work and urchin-chasing," he said, digging containers out of the cooler and tossing a wink at Finley. "Maybe I could introduce you to Christina. She's Hastings's wife. Super level-headed, nice, all that. Owns a shop in town, since you're stuck there for another week or so."

"I have friends," I said defensively.

"Here?" he questioned, handing me a plastic container.

"Well, no. I have Mia and Joey up in Nags Head, and Sam will be back in a couple of weeks to spend the summer with me. She had to fly home to Colorado so she could take care of a couple things and grab more clothes. The rest of my friends are, well, a lot of other places."

"Well, it never hurts to have more friends, and I'm happy to hook you up."

I thanked him, and we devoured our snacks while Finley regaled me with tales of her week. She'd baked cookies with her grandmother, then visited the aquarium and the ship museum, and taken a kiteboarding lesson.

"On the ocean?" I asked, letting my mouth hang open in overexaggeration.

"Yep! I had a vest on. No biggie." She brushed a handful of red curls behind her ear, revealing a smattering of freckles that hadn't been there last week. "Can I go search now?" she asked Jackson, already bouncing on her knees.

"Stay close," he instructed, and she was off, racing toward the water.

I helped Jackson pack up our picnic, secured the bag to a large rock, and then we headed toward where Finley walked along the waterline.

"Okay, see where the sandbar has a little break in the middle?" We paused where a shallow rivulet of water ran through the bar.

"This is the riptide?" My eyes narrowed as I studied the water running from the pool in the sandbar back to the ocean. "It's so small."

"Sure, right now. Bring in the tide, and the amount of water it's sucking back out grows exponentially."

"Seems right." I scanned the sand on the bank, hoping to find another piece of glass to add to my collection. "I mean, it's always the things that look harmless that end up wrecking you, right?"

He studied my face for a handful of seconds before nodding. "Yeah, I guess you could say that, if you're the kind of person always looking for the riptide."

"I'm actually the opposite, if you can't tell, just standing in the middle of it, thinking it's harmless, surprised when it knocks my feet from under me." I looked down the beach, where Finley was doing some searching of her own. "So what's she looking for?"

Jackson's eyes narrowed slightly, watching Finley pick something up. "She wants a perfect conch shell. We come out a lot at low tide so she can search."

We passed a family building a sandcastle, and I offered them a smile.

"What's she going to do once she gets the perfect conch?"

Jackson grinned. "Decide she wants something else and start that search."

I chuckled. "Typical girl. We want what we want until we have it, and then it's on to the next thing."

"That's most guys, too," he countered.

"You?"

He shook his head. "Not really. At least not since Finley was born. Kids have a way of changing the way you look at the world and your role in it." He paused, bending down to grab something. He brushed his thumb over it and then grinned, handing it to me. "Here you go. It's pink. That color's really rare."

He dropped a piece of sea glass in my hand. Its peachy pink color caught the sun as I flipped it over in my palm.

"Thank you!" I crossed behind him and dipped it into the water, letting the next wave wash away the sand. "It's beautiful. I didn't realize there were rare colors."

"Oh yeah, there's classifications and everything. Christina makes jewelry with it. Her shop's down by the bakery. I bet she'd be happy to teach you all about the different colors." He raised his eyebrows in an obvious way.

"What are you? The matchmaker for friends?" I teased. It wasn't a half-bad idea to acquaint myself with the local shops, or to make a friend. "Okay. Give me the address, and I'll go visit the shop."

"Good. That's good," he said with a nod. "Hey, slow down!"

Finley turned and nodded, slowing from her run to examine the ground more carefully.

We walked a fair distance in companionable silence, and I let the waves lull my head into a calm sort of quiet.

"Tell me about the truck."

"What?" I startled.

"The giant F250 in your driveway that you said was left to you. Tell me about it." He looked at me with a mixture of expectation and patience, like he knew I'd eventually tell him and was willing to wait for it.

"That…" I ran my fingers over the sea glass as my throat tightened in warning. "That is a really long story."

"That you don't want to tell?"

"It's more complicated than that. Where I'm from, in Alabama, the truck kind of tells the story for me. Everyone knows. It's nice to be somewhere where it's my choice to tell—or not." I left out the part where my anxiety attacks shut down even the possibility of talking about it most days.

"Does it have anything to do with why you bought the house that time forgot?" His tone was easy, and he kept his eyes on Finley, which helped my throat loosen the smallest degree.

"It has everything to do with it," I admitted. The wind whipped a strand of hair over my face, and I twisted it up around my ponytail to keep it out of the way. Gray clouds moved up the coast quick enough that I could visually track the movement. “That’s not serious, right?” I asked, pointing at the sky.

“No,” Jackson answered. “It’s too early for hurricanes or anything. Might mess with your drilling schedule, though.”

“How would you know that?”

“I ran into Steve when I got home and asked. That’s also how I knew that you usually stop by around now to check on the progress. It’s amazing what happens when you ask him things. He gives you answers. Novel concept.” His voice was flat, but his eyes sparkled with the tease.

“Yeah. Yeah.”

“Daddy, look!” Finley raced over to us, a small conch in her hand. “Not big enough, but good for today!”

Jackson dropped down to examine her treasure. “Whoa! It’s gorgeous, Fin! Worth the walk?”

“Yep! I’m gonna see if I can find another one. Morgan, want this one?” Her eyebrows rose in question, and I found myself smiling bigger than I had in a long while.

“I would be honored to have it,” I told her, bringing myself level with her.

She grabbed it from Jackson and presented it to me with a flourish, like I wouldn’t know she’d actually been the one to give it to me if he had handed it over.

“Thank you,” I told her as I held it up to study its markings. “I will treasure it.”

She grinned, big and wide, her nose scrunching in the best way. “Good! I’ll find more!” She smacked a kiss on Jackson’s cheek and then raced off back toward the house, examining the beach with a new intensity.

“Be prepared to own quite a seashell collection,” Jackson warned as we watched her.

I clasped the shell she’d given me in one hand and the glass from her father in the other as a sweet feeling that I was scared to identify swept through me.

It felt too close to peace. Too comforting to rely on.

"She has your smile," I told him as we followed her, walking the path where the water met the sand and swept over our feet every so often.

"Thanks. Lucky for her, she mostly resembles Claire," he mused.

"Is that your wife?" I asked, then cringed. "If you don't like to talk about it, I completely understand. I have no business prying."

"I'm sure prying into your business," he retorted with a grin that quickly faded. "Claire and I were never married. We were engaged for about four months, though." He tucked his thumbs into his pockets and looked ahead to where Finley was digging in the sand. "That's a long story, too."

I walked silently next to him, deciding if he wanted to share, that was fine, and if he didn't, that was okay, too. I didn't move here to poke at someone else's wounds.

"We met in college," he said with a soft smile.

"In Maine?"

"No. She was on a full ride to Boston University for drama and theater, and I was at MIT as a legacy who started majoring in Frat Parties 101 but graduated with a degree in oceanography."

I blinked a few times.

"What? Didn't peg me for an MIT guy?" His smile nearly tied my tongue in knots.

"I don't know you well enough to make assumptions. Even though I may have considering you look…" I gestured up and down his torso.

"Look like what?" he teased.

"Like you want to finish your story." I flashed a sugar-sweet smile at him.

"Uh-huh." His tone dripped with sarcasm.

Something stirred inside my chest, as if part of me had

been asleep for too long and was blinking awake, shielding her eyes from the sun. Except Jackson *was* the sun. For the first time since…ever, I felt a sense of connection to a man who wasn't Will. I jerked my eyes from his and focused on Finley walking ahead of us.

"We hit it off junior year," he continued, either not seeing or ignoring my mini freak-out. "And then after graduation…" He looked away as his voice softened, and I knew he wasn't with me—he was with her. "I joined the coast guard, and Fin was born the next September. I proposed to Claire while she was in labor, and she laughed and called me an idiot." He smiled, shaking his head.

"But she said yes," I assumed. I hadn't taken him for a coast guard guy, but I guess it made sense. The coast guard probably employed tons of oceanographers. It didn't stop the tiny piece of panic from rising in my throat, though. The coast guard was still the military, but he was a scientist, not one of the front-line guys.

"She said yes," he confirmed. "It was the happiest day of my life."

"I found another one!" Finley shouted, waving a shell above her head.

"Good job, honey!" Jackson answered.

Without coming to show us her treasure, Finley continued her hunt.

"She's a big bottle of joy, isn't she?" I asked, watching her fight with her hair.

"She's Claire. A little bit of my recklessness, sure, but that crazy optimism? All her mother." His voice trailed off, but then he took a deep breath. "She left us when Fin was about four months old. Got an offer for a pilot in L.A. and said she'd come back as soon as they finished filming."

"But she didn't?" I guessed. That look in his eyes…he was still in love with her. It was the same look Will got when he'd talk about Peyton—all wistful but resigned.

He shook his head. "Claire's always been easily distracted by shiny things, and there are a lot of stars to shine out there. But who knows? Maybe one day..." He shrugged.

My heart sank. Even if she hadn't really loved Jackson, how could any mother walk away from her child and never come back? "And you became a single father with a baby."

He nodded, watching Fin with the rapt look of an adoring parent. It was the same way Paisley looked at her son, the way my mama looked at me. "My parents were already gone, and Vivian loves Fin desperately, so I moved here—to the only family we had left."

"You're one of the really good ones, aren't you?" I asked before I could stop myself.

His slight laugh was anything but funny. "No. That's the kicker. I'm not. Anything I am that resembles good is because of her." He nodded toward Finley. "I've always been an asshole. Selfish, careless, impetuous, you name it. But for her, I'll be anything she needs. I'll rip the world apart to keep her safe, and I'll make damn sure I don't give her anything to be embarrassed about when it comes to me."

"And you do it without any help. I can't even imagine." I could barely take care of myself, let alone another person.

"I have Sarah—our nanny—and Vivian. She keeps Fin one weekend a month, and she used to take care of Fin while I was at work. I wouldn't have made it through her baby years without Vivian. Brie helps, too. I've never been alone when it comes to Finley."

"Brie was the redhead at the party, right? The pretty one with the black suit?"

"Yeah. I try to include her in what I can."

His words jogged my memory. "Oh wow, she's the other fifth-grade teacher at the elementary school."

"She is. She recognized you."

I watched Finley brush off another shell and add it to her collection. "Does she get to see Claire?"

Jackson's jaw clenched, and I immediately regretted asking.

"She sees her about once a year if Claire decides to visit for Christmas, and she calls, but Claire has never been good about consistency. She'll call once a day for a week and then go another three months without a peep." He shrugged as we followed Finley, who was already at the top of the dune. "That's Claire."

There wasn't any condemnation in his tone. Had I been in that situation, I wouldn't have been able to say the same. Was he still waiting for Claire to come back?

My cell phone rang as we crested the dune, which kept me from asking that very personal, very not-my-business question.

"Hello?" I answered, plugging my ear to hear over the sound of the drills as we neared the house.

My insurance agent started at a million miles an hour, ending with, "So we'll need the VIN and registration to add it to your policy now that it's out of storage."

Right. The truck.

We reached Jackson's backyard, and I examined the truck from a distance. I could open the door and grab everything from the glove box. Easy. It wasn't like I was driving the damned thing.

"Sure, give me a second, and I'll get it," I said to my agent as Steve waved from his command center.

"I just need to grab something out of the truck," I told Jackson, covering the mouthpiece as we closed in on Steve.

Jackson nodded as Finley took his hand, pulling him toward the book of color swatches.

My heart rate spiked as I drew closer to the truck, but I shook it off. Dr. Circe said that part of the protocol would be addressing the things I avoided because they triggered my thoughts of Will. That particular part was supposed to start in five more weeks, but I could jump ahead a little, right?

"Almost there," I told my agent as I braced the phone on my shoulder and entered the code on the driver's side door. It swung open easily, and I used the running board that lowered automatically to climb up into the cab. God, that *scent.*

The memory hit me hard.

"William Carter, how in the sweet hell do you expect me to get up there in these?" I flashed my heels under my gown.

His grin stopped my heart. "I've got you, Morgan. Don't worry." He reached into the pocket of his dress blues and pulled out his key fob, lowering the running board with the press of a button. "This might be easier, though." In a moment that passed way too quickly, I was in his arms as he climbed up on the board and lifted me into the cab. "I wouldn't want you getting that pretty dress all dirty."

I froze, one hand on the steering wheel and one on the console. My gaze rose to the visor, where his wings—the ones I'd pinned on him at graduation—were fastened. I sucked in a breath, but it only made it worse. Everything still smelled like Will, even after all this time. There was no escaping, no swallowing back the uninvited memory, no stopping the vise around my throat that tightened as my breaths came faster and faster.

I arched my neck, trying to make enough room for air to flow freely, but every ounce of breath I sucked in was thick with the scent of Will. I loved him. God, I loved him, and now this was all I had. He was gone. We'd never get the homecoming kiss he promised me, or the chance to be as happy as our friends. Tears pricked my eyes, not just from the thoughts but from the physical pain of my throat closing.

My head swam as a voice called my name. *Please let it be him.* Why was I still alive when someone as good as Will wasn't?

"I've never seen anyone look as beautiful as you do tonight, Morgan."

But that wasn't real. That was two years and a lifetime ago.

I shoved myself sideways and almost missed the running board as I fled the cab. The sand cushioned my feet after falling those last few inches, and I sidestepped only to collapse against the back door and slide to the ground, uncaring of the scraping sensation as my back raked across the running board before my butt hit the ground.

Breathe. You have to breathe.

My cell phone plummeted as I drew my knees to my chest. I braced my elbows and cradled my head, blocking my ears like that might drown out the sound of his voice.

Another muffled voice—different this time—called my name through the raging cacophony of memories that wouldn't shut up. Wouldn't go back inside the box I kept them in.

"Morgan! Look at me!" Strong hands gripped my wrists.

My eyes flew open wide, taking in the set of ocean-blue ones only inches away. Tears leaked in a steady stream down my face as I struggled to get the air in, my breaths coming in quick, rasping pants.

Jackson. It was Jackson who'd been calling my name. Will wasn't here. He couldn't be because he was dead.

"Morgan, what's going on?" Jackson asked, his brows furrowed in concern.

"I can't—" I managed to force out, then threw my head back, trying to dislodge the vise from my throat.

"Okay," he soothed, his grip softening on my wrists. "It's okay. Just breathe."

If it was that fucking easy, I wouldn't be in this position.

"It's okay. I'm right here."

Our eyes stayed locked as his thumbs stroked a steady rhythm on the inside of my wrists, and slowly—so slowly—my breathing eased to match the pace of those strokes. My throat loosened in increments so small they couldn't be measured.

Minutes. Hours. I wasn't certain how long he stayed there, kneeling in front of me, witnessing my utter meltdown, but soon another voice cut through the fog.

"My phone," I croaked. "Can you—"

"Got it." He grabbed my phone and put it to his ear, still stroking my wrist with his other thumb. "Morgan's not feeling well. Can she call you—"

"Help her." Air filled my lungs in great heaps, but the immovable ache in my throat remained.

"This is Jax Montgomery. I'm Morgan's neighbor. She just asked if I could help you. What exactly do you need?" His brows rose slightly as he listened to the reply. "Got it. Morgan, do you want me to get the registration from the truck?"

I nodded. "Glove box."

His lips pursed as he glanced between my eyes and the open door. "Will you be okay for a second?"

I nodded again. It was safer than trusting my vocal cords.

"Give me just a minute," he said into my phone. Then he stroked the side of my face, brushing that thumb over my cheekbone. "Just keep breathing."

My metronome vanished as he climbed into the cab. I heard shuffling, then the sound of the glove box opening.

His strong, sure voice read her the information she'd need to insure the truck properly, giving her the VIN number and then pausing before saying, "It's registered to William Carter—wait, there's a transfer signed here by Arthur Livingston, Personal Representative to Morgan E. Bartley. Right. I'll tell her. Is that all? Okay, you, too. Bye." The glove box snapped shut, and a few breaths later, I managed to turn my head to see Jackson step down from the cab, tall enough that he actually fit the damned truck. He was easily four inches taller than Will had been, wider in the shoulders, too.

Stop comparing them.

I tried to do the mental exercise I'd watched on YouTube, where I visualized myself shoving all my thoughts about Will into the neat little box in my head and slamming the lid shut.

"All done," Jackson said, dropping to my eye level.

"Thank you." I focused on the sand as my face flushed hot.

"Look at me."

Slowly, I let my eyes travel upward until I met his.

"You have panic attacks. That's nothing to be ashamed of." His gaze bore into mine, driving home the sincerity of his words.

"Anxiety attacks," I corrected him. The ache in my throat flared, and I knew it wouldn't recede until I took my rescue meds, which happened to be back at the B&B.

His brow furrowed. "What triggered you?" When I didn't answer, he guessed. "The truck?"

I nodded. "I have to get back to the bed and breakfast. My meds are there."

He stood, then offered me his hand. I took it, and he pulled me easily to my feet.

"Let me drive you."

"No, I'm fine." My fingers busied themselves brushing the sand from my legs. "I can drive." God, I had to get out of here before I embarrassed myself any further.

"Morgan, really, let me drive you. Please." He reached for my arm, then thought better of it, pulling his hand back.

"I can do it myself," I whispered as I pushed the lock button on the truck.

"I just want to help," he said softly as I walked past him to where the Mini was parked.

"You did." I slid into the driver's seat and arched my neck as another wave of tension washed over me like an aftershock. I ran my hands over my steering wheel and sighed as my emotions lowered to a simmer. That was better.

"Who was he to you?" Jackson asked, looking down at me from the open door.

Every label I could put on what I had with Will felt too small, too pale in comparison to what we'd been, and what we could have evolved into, and yet too big for our lack of definition.

"Everything, and yet nothing." I gave him the truth in the simplest terms I could, giving him the best perspective of me he could have and hiding nothing.

Hi. I'm Morgan. I'm a hot mess.

Jackson didn't cringe, didn't roll his eyes or slam the door. No, that would have made this easier—running away from him. Instead, he nodded. "Okay. I can understand that. Drive safe, okay? Maybe you can text me when you get there?" He stepped free of the door.

"I don't have your number." Before he could offer it to me, I swung the door shut. The engine roared to life as I turned the key, and then I backed out of the long drive once he was clear. He understood. Of course, he understood.

And that was exactly why I couldn't let him drive me to the B&B.

Because back on that beach, I'd felt something. We'd connected.

I didn't have anything to offer, and even if I did, I'd be damned if I was ever going to open up to a man who was in love with another woman. I would never make that mistake again.

Ever.

I was done being someone's consolation prize.

"Damn you, Will. I think you ruined me."

Chapter Six

Jackson

"Night, Daddy!" Fin called out for the sixth time since I'd kissed her good night about two minutes ago.

"Night, Fin." I blew her a kiss but gave her the I'm-not-kidding look.

She giggled accordingly. I turned off her light and shut the door without any protest, so I called it a win.

With Fin tucked in, my mind took off racing as I walked downstairs, giving me every reason not to do this—telling me over and over not to violate Morgan's privacy, reminding me that she hadn't given me details for a reason.

I grabbed a bottle of water from the fridge.

Now, if only it had bubbles. And alcohol. And was beer. But I was on call, so water it was.

The weather had turned, which meant there was a good chance I'd get called in anyway. Hopefully, Morgan had made it to wherever she was staying, but it wasn't like I could text her or anything. That would have required having her phone number.

Having her phone number made it something more than neighborly concern, not that I wouldn't have given her mine if she hadn't shut the door and raced away.

I snagged my iPad on the way to the couch, barely glancing at the sheets of rain pounding my deck, and already had the browser open before my conscience could get the best of me.

I had to know.

The second the sun had flashed on the silver wings pinned to the truck's visor, I'd gotten a sick feeling in my stomach.

Basically, I'd been nauseated for the last five hours.

I tapped on the browser, and my keyboard appeared on the screen. *Don't do it.*

I should have waited for her to tell me. Should have been that patient, good guy she thought I was, capable of sitting quietly while she healed enough to tell me what happened to her—to him.

But I'd already warned her that I was a selfish, careless asshole…and the asshole in me wanted to know. I wasn't willing to wait.

Carter, William D. U.S. Army.

I typed the name I'd read on both the registration and the dog tags that hung from the rearview mirror and cursed as the results populated.

A guy in his midtwenties with wavy brown hair and brown eyes appeared on my screen in a series of pictures above a list of links. I bypassed the picture of him in uniform and clicked on the one where he smiled. It took me to a social media profile.

The cover photo stopped me in my tracks. It was a group photo taken at a military formal, with four lieutenants in dress blues and their dates. Instead of one of those posed, formal pictures, it was a candid, everyone laughing, smiling—or in the blond couple's case, kissing. I immediately recognized

Sam, the girl who'd helped Morgan move in, standing near the center with one of the lieutenants.

Next to her stood the guy whose name tag read "Carter."

And *there* was Morgan.

She was midlaugh in a hell of a dress, her nose scrunched and her head tilted slightly toward Carter. So beautiful, joyous, with none of the shadows that haunted her in her eyes. His arm wrapped around her waist, pulling her close, and his eyes were locked on hers in a look full of so much awe that I almost felt like I was intruding on something.

You are, dumbass.

But…I looked closer. There were no wings on any of the lieutenants. I sent up a little prayer that the wings in the truck were just a coincidence. *Any* kind of coincidence. I noted that the picture was taken two years ago December and minimized it.

"I'll only look at a few more," I mumbled, like it was any kind of excuse for what I was doing.

I clicked on the highlighted photos, and the first popped up full screen. It was the same truck, covered in mud in the middle of a field, and leaning against it was Morgan. Her head was tilted down, the brim of a maroon baseball cap covering her face, but I'd recognize those legs anywhere.

The next was a candid of Will wearing the same hat.

Next—*shit.* There was Morgan, her hair pulled back on one shoulder, pinning a set of shiny silver wings on his chest while he stood in his dress blues, looking stoically ahead.

Fuck. Those had to be the same wings on the truck's visor.

Raking my hands over my hair, I let out a deep sigh. Then I closed out the social media page without looking at any of his posts and went back to the search, clicking on the news story listed second.

LOCAL PILOT KILLED IN AFGHANISTAN

The family of William Carter has confirmed the reports that he was killed this weekend in Afghanistan. Carter, an Enterprise High School alum turned West Point graduate, was serving his first tour overseas as a medevac pilot when he fell to small arms fire that followed a helicopter crash. Carter and his crew had been on a rescue mission for another downed aircraft.

According to a spokesman from his unit at Fort Campbell, Carter saved the lives of three other soldiers before his death, personally pulling four pilots from the cockpits of the dual crash, two of whom were already deceased. Going above and beyond the call of duty, and with blatant disregard for his own safety, Carter stood alone, discharging his weapon to protect the wounded soldiers, although he had been wounded in the crash himself. He was killed shielding the wounded men.

"I cannot put our grief into words at the loss of Lieutenant Carter," Brigadier General Richard Donovan, the previous CG of Fort Rucker, told us by phone. "It doesn't surprise me that he gave his life for others. That's simply who he was."

William Carter is survived by—

I put my iPad on the coffee table, having read more than enough.

There was only one reason a unit spokesman would be that detailed to the press, the same reason they used the deliberate phrasing of *going above and beyond the call of duty, and with blatant disregard for his own safety.*

Will wasn't just a pilot, or the guy Morgan was obviously

still in love with.

He was a fucking hero.

The kind who got awarded medals that took years to receive.

No wonder she was torn up as hell. She didn't have to put the guy on a pedestal; he was already up there. Not only that, but the minute she realized what I did for a living, she'd push me so far away that we might as well live on opposite sides of the island. Not that I'd blame her.

I had my own hang-ups about the death of my parents—I couldn't imagine how Morgan felt about the military, or helicopter pilots in general.

And I was both.

And given what I'd just read, I didn't hold a candle to that guy.

Awesome.

I'd never been one for inferiority complexes. I was damn good at what I did. Hell, I was the best, and proud of it. I'd graduated top of my major at MIT, top of my class in Flight School, and guaranteed my first duty station pick. I'd completed hundreds of successful rescues—some of which were seen as unwinnable—and yet none of that compared to what he'd done.

For the first time in my life, I was forced into second place in a race I hadn't been aware I'd been running, and the guy was miles ahead. I was literally losing to a ghost.

Since when did you want to win?

I thought about it for a second, wishing the answer was when she'd come out to the barbecue, when we'd walked down the beach earlier today, or even when she'd had the telltale signs of an anxiety attack at the truck.

But something had drawn me to her the first moment our eyes had locked on the beach and then hooked me the minute I found her dangling through her landing, cool as a cucumber.

Shit, I didn't just like her—I wanted her, and not just in my bed, but in my *life*.

And I didn't have a shot in hell with her.

• • •

Five days later, the ringer on my phone sounded around ten thirty p.m., and I swiped it open before checking the caller ID.

"Montgomery," I answered.

"It's Goodwin. We have a mayday, and the other bird is already in the field."

"Fuck." I stood, immediately sprinting for my stairs. "Run up the bird. I'll be there ASAP." I hung up, hitting the speed dial for Sarah as I dropped my clothes.

I had it timed to seven minutes flat.

"Mr. Montgomery?" she answered.

"Hey, I hate to do this to you, but I just got a call—"

"I'll be there in a second! I'm still dressed and everything!" My twenty-one-year-old nanny promptly hung up on me.

I threw on my flight suit and booted up, hit the bathroom, tossed a few granola bars and a Monster into my bag, and opened the door just as Sarah reached the threshold.

"It's coming down out there!" she said by way of greeting.

"Yes. Thank you. I'm sorry for calling so late." I hated calling her, forcing her to drop what she was doing.

"It's what you pay me for! Now go save people." She waved me off and headed for the living room.

I tossed my rain gear on and ran down the steps.

Exactly seven minutes after I got the call, we took off from the coast guard station with Goodwin as my copilot, Moreno as my mechanic, and Garrett as our rescue swimmer.

As we headed out over the water, into wind and rain, my mind cleared of Morgan, her dead boyfriend, and even Fin, leaving only the bird, the weather, and the mission.

"Time to save some lives," I said over the com, keeping our tradition.

And we did.

• • •

The skyline blushed with impending sunrise as I parked my Land Cruiser in the driveway.

Long. Fucking. Night.

The rain had stopped around midnight, right around the time we'd returned from the rescue, three extra passengers heavy. We'd barely gotten the small family off their even smaller boat in time. It had gone down just after Garrett had hauled the father on board.

Their bad day had a happy ending: two living parents, one living teenage boy.

I trudged up the steps, weariness pulling at every muscle in my body. If I got to sleep in the next fifteen minutes, I could get a solid three hours before Fin woke up.

I woke Sarah on the couch and sent her home, then headed toward the kitchen in search of water.

The refrigerator was stocked, and I took a cold one from the second shelf and closed the door with my hip, already twisting the top open.

My cell phone rang from my back pocket, and I paused mid-drink to yank it free, swallowing and lowering the bottle when I saw who it was.

"Claire?"

"Hey!" Her voice was barely audible with background party noise. "What are you doing?"

I glanced at the clock. "It's five a.m., so I figured I'd sleep while I can."

"Oh! Late night?" A door shut, and the background

noise dropped exponentially.

"Obviously." I leaned back against the kitchen counter. "Look, I just got home from work, and I know you didn't call to talk to Fin, so what's up?" My voice was as gentle as I could make it, but I was fucking exhausted.

"I can't just call to say hello?" Her little laugh was tinged with sadness.

"Sure you can. Just not at five a.m. when you're clearly still out for the night." I rubbed the bridge of my nose.

"I guess…" She sighed. "I guess I just miss you, Jax."

Five years ago, those words would have meant the world to me. They would have kept me hanging on for her next phone call, hanging on to *her.*

"Claire, it's not me you should be missing. It's Finley. She hasn't talked to you in two months."

"If I knew I was going to get a lecture, I wouldn't have called. It's not my fault that my filming schedule isn't conducive to calling."

The urge to tell her off was rising, but Fin was the one who'd suffer if I pissed Claire off and she chose not to call again. "I'm not lecturing you. I'm just being honest."

"How is she?" Her voice softened.

"Good. Happy. Healthy. Everything you want to hear." I blinked hard, trying to stay awake.

"Does she ask about me?"

"Of course she does. You're her mother."

"Don't you miss me even a little, Jax?"

My stomach sank. "Don't."

"I heard your new neighbor is pretty. Brie told me that she met her at one of your barbecues. Said you seemed pretty…what was the word she used? Entranced? Enamored? Enchanted. That was it. She said you seem enchanted by her." Her tone turned sharp.

Hell no.

"She's not up for discussion."

"Oh, so she *is* pretty. Does Finley like her, too?" She bit the question out.

"She is *none* of your business." I snapped each word, hoping she'd get the point.

"I think I have a right to know who my daughter spends time with, don't you?"

She took the words straight out of Brie's mouth. Exhaustion stripped me of my usual caution.

"Do. Not. Start. I haven't slept in thirty hours, and I don't have the patience to do this with you. Go back to whatever party you're at, Claire. I'm going to sleep because our daughter will be up in a couple of hours. You might want to call her sometime." I chugged the rest of the water bottle.

"Jax, don't be mad at me." Her voice dripped with sugar. "You know how much I love Finley. She's the most important thing in my life. I'm working my ass off to make it out here, and it's all for her. For all of us! It's the hardest thing I've ever done, and I miss you. I miss our life."

I tossed the bottle in the trash can and looked up at a framed picture of Fin and me on the beach. "You want to be a part of Finley's life? Make the effort. She's amazing, and you're missing it."

"What about yours?" Again, that damned teasing little lilt of her voice had me shaking my head.

In the past, I would have said something like, "*We'll see.*" I wouldn't have shut any doors on Claire that would have given Fin a chance at having that picket-fenced family I'd mistakenly thought she was being born into. But that dream was just that—a dream. And the reality of it was that I deserved to be happy. Fin and I both did.

"Jax? Did you hear me? I asked about being a part of *your* life."

"Claire, I think we both know that ship sailed a long time

ago."

She gasped. "But Jax—"

"I gotta go, Claire. If you want to call back in a few hours, Fin will be up. Bye." I hung up the phone before she could beg me to change my mind, to assure her that we'd be waiting here with open arms if she ever decided to come back.

She'd always be Finley's mother, but she wasn't her mom. Not in the ways that mattered.

• • •

"Thank you. I really appreciate this. Sarah needed the day off," I told Christina as I picked up Finley from her shop the next day.

"I really don't mind," she promised as Finley got her fingerprints all over the farthest display case in Christina's jewelry store. "It's honestly wonderful to have her. She sells a surprising amount of pendants. Seriously. Besides, it's good practice for when Peter and I decide to have kids. Not that I'm in any rush for that," she added quickly as she knocked on a piece of driftwood. "I mean, we've only been married a couple years. I'd like to have him all to myself for a bit longer." Her brown eyes widened. "Not that Fin isn't great. Shit. Did I just put my foot in my mouth?" she finished in a whisper.

"Not at all," I said with a laugh. "I absolutely get what you're saying."

"Why don't you two come over for dinner? I'm sure Peter would love to see you off duty, and I make a really awesome pizza order."

My watch read four thirty, enough time to take Fin seashell hunting and play a round of her current video game obsession. "Thanks for the offer, but I think we're going to head home. She's been itching to shell hunt lately."

"Daddy! Look at this one!" She leaned over the glass

case, already on a step stool and her tiptoes.

"Don't lean on that, honey," I told her as I came up behind her. "You might break the glass and get blood all over the pretty jewelry."

She shot me a grown-up dose of side-eye. "Look at the pink one. It's pretty!"

And now her face was smashed against the glass. I cringed in Christina's direction, but she waved me off, already wiping down the other display cases.

"It is pretty," I assured my girl, seeing the pale-pink sea-glass pendant encased in silver hanging from a chain.

"Morgan would like it."

Morgan. A week now, and she still hadn't come back when I'd been home.

"I bet she would. Want to buy it for her?" I offered.

"Nah," she said, shaking her head. Then she wiggled out from where my arms had caged her and rushed over to Christina. "Miss Tina?" She tugged on Christina's shirt, just in case her words weren't enough.

"Yes, sugar?"

"Would you make one for Morgan?" Finley asked.

"One what?"

"A sea-glass necklace? I'll find the sea glass." Her blue eyes were puppy-level cute as they widened in expectation.

Christina cocked an eyebrow at me, and I nodded. I guessed I wasn't the only one missing our neighbor.

"Of course. You can help me set it and everything," Christina promised.

"Yay! Thank you!" She jumped, throwing her arms in the air. Once she landed, she ran back to me. "We can go now."

Her permission was given in all seriousness.

"Well, since you're ready," I answered.

She nodded, grabbing her small backpack on her way to the door.

"Reconsider dinner?" Christina asked as she walked us out. "We always worry about you two, or is it you three now?"

"Morgan's just our neighbor." I hefted Fin into her car seat, and she buckled herself in.

"Well, I'm hearing rumors from a certain barbecue that she might not *just* be your neighbor." She gave me a look that said she expected an explanation.

"She's..." What the hell was Morgan? "She's beautiful, and smart, and funny, and my *neighbor.* Fin and I are just taking her under our wings since she's new. Speaking of which, she could really use a friend here, and you're the most level-headed woman I know."

She blinked at me for a second.

"Christina?"

"Oh, I was just trying to decide if level-headed was the compliment I was going for. Fun? Outgoing? Awesome?" she suggested.

"Okay, you are the most fun, outgoing, awesome woman I know. Plus, I think you two would get along great."

Morgan could deny it all she wanted, but she had to be lonely. I had work and friends and Fin, and even I got lonely sometimes. All Morgan had was a house once Sam left after the summer.

"Have her swing by the shop. I'll make sure not to creep her out."

I rubbed my hand on the back of my neck. "Yeah, I'm not sure I can get her to do that. I've tried once already, but she's on the hermit career path at the moment. I swear she's amazing."

"So, you want me to go by her place and actually creep her out?" She stared me down.

"Pretty much. Next week, maybe? She's right next door to us! Thanks!" I hopped into the Land Cruiser and started her up.

"Uh-huh," she said through the open window. "You've got it bad!" she called out.

"Just my neighbor!" I answered as I pulled out of the small parking lot. After what I'd learned about her past, that was all she'd ever let me be.

We turned onto our street a few minutes later. Best part of living on an island was the almost nonexistent commute. Fin slipped her hand out of the window, letting it ride the wind for the last half mile.

Yeah, we were going to be all right, even if Claire never got her shit together in the parenting department.

I noticed two things simultaneously as I pulled into our driveway. The first was that Morgan was home, or at least her Mini was.

The second? Vivian was here.

This had the potential to get really awkward.

I parked, and Fin had already unsnapped her buckles by the time I opened her door. She jumped into my arms, and I shifted her onto my side, shutting the garage behind us as I carried her around the front of the house.

"Morgan!" Fin called out over the sound of men climbing down from Morgan's almost-finished roof. They'd made a huge amount of progress compared to when I'd left this morning. Half the roof was shingled, and it looked like they were quitting for the day. They even managed to save that old weathervane, which two of the roofers were anchoring back in its original position.

There was no sign of Vivian, which meant she was probably in the house.

"Fin!" Morgan waved from next to Steve and subsequently lost her grip on the paperback she'd been holding. She bent quickly to retrieve it, then set it on the drafting table as we walked over.

I was struck by the strangest urge to get a copy of

whatever she was reading. In my experience, what someone read told you almost everything you needed to know about them. Claire had preferred drama, anything that fired up her imagination. Garrett liked war biographies. Sawyer enjoyed not reading. Ever. Me? I went for Griffin, Clancy, or anything that pulled me out of my life for a minute.

What was Morgan into? Did she read chick lit? Romance? Nonfiction? Was she into horror? Or was comedy more her thing?

I put Finley on the ground once we reached the drafting table, keeping my eyes north of Morgan's turquoise tank top and *way* north of those tiny white shorts. I was going to need to join a support group if I couldn't shake my obsession with her legs.

"I missed you!" Morgan said, dropping to eye level with Fin and pulling her into a big hug.

Well, shit. For the first time, I was jealous of my kid.

"I missed you, too! And you almost have a roof! Are you coming back soon?"

"Four days," Steve promised, even though Morgan shot him a disbelieving look. "You'd be surprised how fast a roof goes on," he finished as he packed up for the day.

"How have you been?" Morgan asked Fin.

Fin jabbered a mile a minute, telling Morgan all about her days, like she'd been gone an eternity.

Okay, maybe it had felt a little long.

Morgan nodded dutifully, adding a word here and there as Finley jumped from subject to subject and was now on something related to Doc McStuffins.

Morgan's smile hit me in the gut like a freight train. Shit, I was in trouble.

She shared that grin with me when she glanced up, and I answered it with one of my own, knowing there was no hope of getting a word in edgewise now that Fin was on a roll.

And now she'd moved on to Christina's cat.

"Jackson?" My stomach lurched at the wariness in Vivian's voice behind me.

"Hey, Grammy!" Fin called, breaking her filibuster to hug Vivian quickly, then turning back to Morgan to continue her tale, which had shifted to the lunch menu at her preschool.

"Can we talk?" Vivian asked softly. "Claire called this morning about…what happened last night."

Morgan's eyes met mine.

Steve's eyebrows shot up.

"Fin, why don't we go…" Morgan looked around for a destination.

"We're done for the day." Steve gestured toward his team as they started climbing down from the roof. "You can show her the progress," he suggested.

"That sounds like a great idea! Then you can finish telling me all about your favorite foods!" Morgan clasped Fin's hand and grabbed her beach bag.

"Oh! There's macaroni and cheese and pizza! And ice cream and…"

I shot Morgan a thankful look, and she nodded, already walking back toward her house and out of ear range.

"And I'm going…somewhere else," Steve said with a nod. "Always good to see you, Mrs. Lewis." Then he basically speed-walked toward the nearest piece of equipment.

"Hey, Vivian." I turned to the side so I could see Fin out of my peripherals and give my would-have-been mother-in-law my attention.

"She's lovely," Vivian remarked with a slight curve of her lips. "Good with Fin, too."

I watched as Morgan put her floppy sun hat on Fin, which completely swamped her little head. "Yeah, she is. We lucked out in the new neighbor department."

"Oh, Jackson." Her shoulders sagged. "Claire was so

upset this morning."

"Was she?" I folded my arms across my chest as I glanced over to Morgan and Fin, seeing them sitting on a blanket Morgan had spread out as she pointed to the changes in the house.

"She was really upset. Going on about how you didn't want her in Fin's life and wouldn't even put her on the phone." She smoothed her silver, chin-length bob, which was her most obvious tell for stress.

"And you think I would say that to Claire?"

She swallowed and looked away. "Well, no. That doesn't sound like you, but Claire was crying and carrying on something fierce."

"Did she tell you that she called from a party at five in the morning our time?"

Vivian's eyebrows shot up. "What? No."

"She didn't ask to talk to Fin, and I wasn't going to wake her up that early, anyway. I even told her to call back in a few hours once Fin was awake," I told her gently. I hated laying Claire's shit bare to Vivian. It wasn't her fault that Claire was…whatever she was.

"Oh." She lifted her hand to her face and smoothed the lines of her forehead. "Now I feel foolish."

"Don't. We both know what a good actress Claire is."

"I know, but it's not like her to get so upset over—" She clamped her mouth shut and looked away.

"Me," I supplied, knowing that was the real source of Claire's tirade.

"I know it's none of my business what happens between you two."

I laughed. "Vivian, nothing has been happening between us for *years*. She will always be Fin's mother but—"

One of the roofers shouted, and my attention snapped to the roofline, where the man slipped and began falling.

My stomach clenched as he flung out his arms but couldn't stop, heading for the huge bronze weathervane that perched midway down the roof, right above—

"Morgan!" I shouted, already running as he slammed into the sculpture. The sound of cracking wood followed instantly as the weathervane tore free. "Above you!"

Her eyes flew from the roof to mine and then back up to where a hundred pounds of bronze plummeted toward where she sat with Finley.

Oh God, I wasn't going to make it.

It was going to hit them.

Chapter Seven

Morgan

Just don't be afraid to take another risk, okay?

Oh God.

There was no time.

I side-tackled Finley, taking her down in a mess of knees and elbows, and used my momentum to roll with my arms around her. As the sky filled my vision, so did the falling hunk of death, and I threw everything I had into the move.

Keep her on the bottom!

I landed on top, curving myself around her as much as possible. The object slammed into the ground with a booming thud in the same millisecond.

Sand and rocks blasted the side of my face.

My heart slammed against my ribs, the beat deafening.

"Finley! Morgan!"

I could hear the panic in Jackson's voice, so I wasn't dead. Right? And Finley was breathing under me, so she wasn't, either.

"Oh, thank God!" Jackson shouted, skidding to a halt next to us and hitting his knees. "Are you okay?"

Words wouldn't form, so I nodded.

"I'm okay," Finley announced, her voice muffled under me.

She's okay. She's okay. She's okay. I fell to the side, taking my weight off Fin, and Jackson immediately grabbed her to his chest.

"Are you okay?" he asked again, pushing her to arm's length, looking her over for injuries.

I sat up slowly as workers and Fin's grandmother came running.

The weathervane I'd been so damned insistent about had fallen from the roof. God, it was *huge.*

"I'm fine!" Finley promised.

It had landed right where we'd been a second ago, the enormous arrow stabbing through the edge of the blanket and pinning the fabric to the ground.

"Are you sure?" Jackson's hands ran down her limbs quickly, no doubt checking for broken bones.

Someone helped me to my feet, and I wavered, my heart galloping. Feeling something wet streak my face, I stumbled away from the group. Of all the times to cry!

I made it as far as the base of my temporary steps before I was engulfed in a pair of arms and pressed against a firm, warm chest. The amazing combination of ocean, lemongrass, and soap filled my lungs as I breathed him in.

Jackson.

"Please tell me you're okay," he begged, his chin resting on the top of my head.

"I'm…f-f-f," I stammered, my knees starting to shake. What the hell was wrong with me?

He pulled back, wincing at something he saw on my face

and then scanning down my body. "Are you injured?"

I shook my head.

"Tell me if anything else hurts."

Anything else?

His hands swept down my arms, then my ribs just under my breasts, over my belly, and then framed my hips, his eyes locking with mine every few seconds to see if I'd flinch.

Then he did the same from midthigh to my ankles. "No pain?"

I shook my head. "I'm f-f-fine," I managed to get out.

He rose, standing so my eyes were level with his chest. "You're not fine. You're bleeding," he said softly, his thumb brushing my cheek and coming away red.

Ah, so *that* was the wetness.

"I'm okay. I can wash up." At least my mouth was working again. I turned to head toward my steps, but my knees went all wobbly.

"Yeah, no." Jackson lifted me, putting one arm behind my back and the other behind my knees. "I've got you."

"What's wrong with me?" I asked as my hand trembled. Was this an anxiety attack? They'd never presented like this before.

"Adrenaline rush. It has nowhere to go," he explained as he carried me across my yard, passing the small gathering of construction crewmembers. "It'll pass in a few minutes, maybe a little longer."

"I can clean my face," I protested as he reached his driveway.

"Morgan, you just saved my daughter's life. Could you please just let me help you?" he snapped.

I studied his face as he climbed his stairs. His jaw flexed, his lips pressed into a line, and in his eyes, there was a wildness—fear. Of course he'd been afraid. He'd nearly lost Finley.

All because I'd taken her to the house when Steve told me they'd finished for the day. I'd nearly gotten Fin killed.

The inside of his home wasn't exactly what I'd expected. Not that I even knew what to expect from Jackson. The decorations were simple, clean, a blend of coastal blues and rich wood tones with white accents. The walls were decorated with framed artwork I assumed was made by Finley.

He carried me through the living room and into the kitchen, setting me carefully on the granite counter near the sink.

I yelped as the icy stone came into contact with my sun-warmed skin.

"What hurts?" he asked immediately, scanning me like he could see through my clothes and skin.

"Nothing. Granite's cold," I muttered, bracing my hands on the edge of the counter.

"Oh. Okay. Sorry about that. Wait here."

He disappeared, and I studied his kitchen. It was U-shaped, the opening facing the living room. A long slab of granite to the left served as a breakfast bar. A small dining set filled the space to the sliding glass door, and off to the side, a play nook was happily cluttered with toys in contrast to the immaculately clean kitchen.

Does he keep his bedroom this clean, too?

I blinked that thought right out of my head. God, was this trembling going to stop anytime soon?

He returned, set a first-aid kit on the counter, then wrapped a soft quilt around my shoulders, his arms encircling me for the barest of moments. "That should help," he said softly.

"Thank you." I tucked the blanket closer.

"That's my line." He took my chin between his thumb and forefinger, then gently tilted my head so he could examine my cheek.

"Finley's really okay, right?"

"She's fine. You're both fine." That last part was nearly a whisper.

My heart galloped as the adrenaline ran its course, and the sight of his lips so close to mine wasn't helping slow its cadence. "Your house is beautiful," I blurted, trying to think about anything other than what had just happened…or the warmth of his fingers. Those were dangerous subjects.

"Thanks. It works for us," he said in that way guys had of dismissing compliments and giving me a half smile. He was good under pressure.

I tried to pull myself together while he dampened a washcloth at the kitchen sink, but he was back faster than I could manage the herculean task.

"You got blasted with sand and a few rocks, if your cuts are anything to gauge by. I want to clean it out." He paused. "Unless you'd rather we go to the clinic?"

"No. Here is good." I shifted my legs so he could get close enough to do it.

He stepped between my thighs, his hips resting against the insides of my bare knees. *Mercy.* The flush of heat that swept over my body had nothing to do with the warmth of the blanket and everything to do with his proximity. It had to be the adrenaline, right? One of those *you-almost-died* coping mechanisms?

It's because he's gorgeous as sin, you moron.

"This one looks the worst, but it's not too deep," he murmured, cradling the uninjured side of my face with warm, gentle fingers while assessing the other.

"Okay." I mentally listed every reason I wasn't allowed to be attracted to this man and prayed my body got with the program.

One, I was pretty sure he was in love with his ex and apparently something had gone down with them last night.

Two, he lived next door, which meant when whatever I wasn't going to allow happen anyway eventually didn't work out, I'd be stuck seeing him every freaking day.

Three…

I hissed as the washcloth brushed over an abrasion along my cheekbone.

"Sorry." He dabbed carefully at the skin.

"Don't worry," I replied, trying to keep my eyes anywhere but on his and failing.

Three, his eyes were too blue. Ocean blue. Flawlessly freaking blue. That was a con because…well, because they were too distracting. Who the hell wanted to be constantly distracted like that? I'd never get anything done.

Four, I was in the middle of some pretty intensive therapy and didn't have anything to offer. My emotional tank was on empty, and that wasn't fair to him.

Five—

"This might hurt."

Exactly. He'd said it perfectly. I'd already swallowed all the pain I could take when it came to relationships.

"I know." But it still didn't stop me from staring at his mouth.

He applied antiseptic, taking extra care with a couple of the cuts, and I welcomed the sting, using it to keep me grounded.

"I don't think you need stitches."

"That's good." I looked down at my hands. At least they'd quit shaking. How the hell had I let that happen? I should have known better than to take Finley so close to the construction.

"I don't know how to thank you," he said.

My eyes jerked to his.

"Thank me? I almost got her killed."

His forehead puckered as he braced his hands on either

side of me and leaned forward.

My breath caught.

"Morgan, that was not your fault. Steve said they were done for the day. You had no way of knowing that guy would fall. It was an accident, plain and simple."

"It was so close," I whispered. "She…it was so *close.*" Just the idea of losing—*don't go there.*

He rested his forehead on mine and overwhelmed my senses. Sight, scent, touch, sound…it was all Jackson. "It was too close. But you saved her. You got her out of the way and shielded her with your own body."

"Anyone would have done it." My heart rate picked up again.

His head lifted as he cradled my face. "No, a lot of people would have dived the other way—to safety. You deliberately put yourself between Finley and a hundred pounds of sharp, pointy bronze. That's extraordinary." His gaze dropped to my lips. "You're extraordinary."

Not for you. NOT FOR YOU. My sense of self-preservation screamed at me to run the other way, but a craving for him raced through my veins, flipping on switches that had lain dormant for almost two years. All that adrenaline had been replaced with something far more dangerous: need.

He lowered his head—

The door burst open, and Jackson retreated.

Before I could process what had almost happened, Sam stood at the edge of the kitchen, her eyes wide.

"I can't even leave you alone for two weeks!" she exclaimed before crossing the floor and hauling me into a hug. "Are you okay? Steve and Finley told me what happened. They're both worried sick down there." She grabbed ahold of my shoulders and pushed back far enough to see for herself. "Ouch."

"It's just a scrape, and you're two days early!" I'd never been so happy to see her in my entire life.

"Is that a complaint?" She arched a brow.

"Never."

"Good, because I'd hate to see what would have happened in another two days," she teased with a shaky smile before yanking me into another hug.

"Me, too," I whispered, locking eyes with Jackson over her shoulder.

Yeah, I saw it all too clearly—how easy it would be to step into something I wasn't ready for, assuming I wasn't misreading his signals. How incredible it would feel to kiss him, to have those sculpted arms around me for more than just a few minutes.

How impossible it would be to survive when my ruined heart was inevitably broken again.

Sam had shown up just in time.

...

"That sounds a little harsh," Sam said slowly to Dr. Circe as she sat back in the armchair next to mine four days later.

"It's not about being harsh," Dr. Circe countered softly. "It's about both Morgan and myself being aware of how Will's death has changed her. She's chosen you as her support person through this process, and I know she has immense trust in you. You won't be harsh."

Sam's gaze skittered my way.

"Go ahead," I encouraged.

Sam swallowed and looked back at Dr. Circe. "Before it happened, Morgan was fearless. She commanded every room she walked into and never hesitated to let anyone know what she was thinking. She had a smile that would light up half the state, and she…got out more, I guess you could say."

She glanced my way, and I nodded my support.

"She was something of a social butterfly, and she was

happy. Not all the time, of course—no one's happy *all* the time. She and Will got into a few legendary fights, and her temper was quick, but whatever emotions Morgan felt were there for the world to see. She was always brave like that." She turned toward me. "I always envied that about you. You were never scared to speak up and fight for what you wanted. You never ran away from the hard things like I did."

It took all the energy I could muster to hold her gaze while trying to remember the girl she described.

"And now?" Dr. Circe prompted.

"You're quiet," Sam said to me, as if it was just the two of us and we weren't in my third session of therapy for complicated grief. "You hide your emotions, and I don't know if it's because you're incredibly strong or scared that the people who love you can't handle what's inside."

I focused on my joined hands that rested in my lap.

"She's avoiding the rest of our friends, which is something she never would have done before Will died, and I wish she didn't feel like she had to. She's drawn so far into herself that she's basically a few cats shy of a cliché, and she won't open herself up to even the slightest possibility that she might be happy again someday."

Because it's not possible. I kept the thought to myself.

"But mostly, she's sad. So damned sad. That light she's always had inside is still there. I see it flicker from time to time, but it's almost like she has it buried, and I just want to help her get it back." She reached over and took my hand.

"She will," Dr. Circe promised before she changed the subject, detailing what the remaining weeks of therapy would bring. I hadn't quite made peace with the fact that I was going to have to talk about Will's death in depth next week, but I knew I had to try. I had to beat against the instinct to withdraw and find whatever spark of light in me still lived on.

We were just about ready to stop for the day when Sam

held up her finger.

"One thing," she said to Dr. Circe and then shifted to face me. "I need you to know that you're still *you*. The things that make you amazing haven't changed, Morgan. You're still incredibly brave, and if you don't feel it, just look at what you're doing now. This takes incredible courage. Look at how you saved Finley the other day. You're still the friend who puts others first—"

"Like making you stay here for the next thirteen weeks while I try to get my shit together?" I teased with a watery voice.

"Stop it. You took me in when I had nowhere else to go. You never judged me for my choices, and you still don't. Your grief for Will is just as deep as your love, and that's not something to be ashamed of. I'm so damned proud to be your friend."

She yanked me against her in an awkward over-the-chair-arm hug, and I felt twin tears escape. She might be proud of me now, but I knew the worst was yet to come. I'd avoided the worst of the pain for the last two years, and that came with a price.

Chapter Eight

Morgan

Lean on our friends, Morgan. God knows you've let them lean on you.

"So where are we at?" I asked Steve, handing him a cup of coffee as he stood at my kitchen counter. Longest two and a half weeks ever, but we were back in my house.

"Thank you." He took a sip and then flipped through his binder. "Okay, the new concrete pilings are in place for the deck, and the support ones for the foundation set perfectly, we released the jacks, and your house is still standing, which is good since you moved back in three days ago."

"Considering you told me there was every chance we'd have a major issue during that process, I consider that a victory." I raised my glass, and he grinned.

"Me, too. Your head looks way better, by the way." He motioned to where my cuts were just little pink lines on my forehead. "I can't tell you how sorry I am."

"Stop. You've told me at least twice a day since it happened. It wasn't your fault."

"Still. I grew up with Claire, and just thinking about what could have happened…" He shook his head.

"You grew up with Fin's mom?"

"Yeah." He smiled. "There wasn't a guy in school that wasn't half in love with her, and I guess that didn't change in college, seeing how Jax is still waiting around for her to come back. Guy hasn't had a serious relationship since she left. Anyway, I'm really sorry it happened."

Apparently, oversharing was a bad habit in every southern town.

"I'm just sad that the weathervane's broken. Seems a shame to lose something that's been with the house so long."

"Even if it tried to murder you?"

"Well, stronger things have tried and failed." I shrugged. "How about this monstrosity?" I pointed to the very large, very visible piling that now ran from the roof through the garage level and into the sand below. Granted, it was a great addition for anyone considering exotic dancing for a living, but I wasn't a huge fan of the eyesore or the hole they'd ripped in every story of my house during installation. The five-thousand-dollar investment had been driven straight through the master bedroom, not that I'd even fathomed starting that chunk of the remodel.

"It set well, and— Oh, you're talking cosmetics, aren't you?"

I raised an eyebrow.

"We'll hide it as well as we can once we start the interior portion of the remodel." He flipped to the page I despised. "You're already at a little over fifty thousand."

Ouch. Not that I hadn't known I was racking up the charges. I'd signed enough checks, but Lord, that was a punch to the belly—or, rather, the wallet.

"Okay, and that's for the new roof, the foundations on both the house and the boathouse"—I gestured to the steel pole—"waterproofing the garage level..."

"As much as possible," Steve repeated. "If that ocean comes up, there's nothing we can do to keep the water out of that garage. The house is built for water to flow right under it. The boathouse is another story."

"Right. I understand." Nausea crept up my throat at the thought of Will's truck being swallowed by flood waters. "And next?"

"All of the windows have been purchased. I have them stored. Also, the storm shutters and lumber for the new decks."

"So where does that leave us?"

He flipped back to his calendar. "Deck construction will start once we're done in Frisco. Should be about another two weeks, and then window installation in three. Feel free to start ripping apart the inside now that your foundation is reinforced."

Now that your foundation is reinforced.

The phrase ran through my head as we finished the scheduling talk and I walked him to the door.

Standing in the living room a few minutes later, I looked out over the ocean through the open door. The breeze was heavy with salt and humidity but better than the stagnant air inside the house.

A few weeks and I'd have my deck back instead of this rough, wooden X nailed into the lower portion of the doorway baby gate-style. Like I was going to forget there wasn't a deck there and step into nothingness.

But the pilings were in, ready to support what came next.

The house's foundation was done. Mine still felt cracked.

"Hey," Sam said as she came down the stairs, twisting her hair into a ponytail. "Are you ready?"

I glanced at the tiny cassette recorder that rested on the counter next to the refrigerator and cringed.

Tuesday had been brutal. Turned out that the base of complicated grief therapy was telling the story of Will's death over and over…then listening to myself tell it every single day on that damned cassette player, only to record it again the following week and so on. It was supposed to lessen the emotional impact, which seemed rather like showering before a tsunami. Or, in my case, like the showering actually brought on the tsunami. I still sucked at the *now visualize yourself putting the memory away, just like you're putting away the tape recorder* part of the instructions.

"I don't want to." Instead, I poured another cup of coffee.

"Right, and you know that I respect your choices, so I'll give you one." Sam hopped up onto the kitchen counter next to the tape recorder. "I can hit play on this one or the one I recorded on my phone before I realized we were using that slice of ancient technology."

That earned her a little side-eye.

"Support person, remember? So we listen, and then you get to pick your reward!"

"Already done." I pointed to the hardback of *Mrs. Dalloway* that rested on the kitchen counter, my bookmark peeking from about midway through the novel.

"Virginia Woolf is not a reward. She's a homework assignment," she challenged.

"I happen to love Virginia Woolf. I'm actually about three quarters through all of her books, I'll have you know, you giant math nerd." I sent her a face that made her laugh.

"Uh-huh." She muttered something about English majors as she reached into the drawer to her left and pulled out pamphlets. "We've already done pedicures and the aquarium—"

Someone knocked at the door. I tossed Sam a fake *sorry*

face and ran for the foyer.

"Dad has off today!" Finley exclaimed before I had the door fully open.

"Does he?" I smiled down at her.

"He does! And you're coming with us!" She bounced on her toes.

"I am?"

"Wait, I'm supposed to ask you that." Her forehead crinkled. "We're going to the surf shop opening. Wanna come?" The light and hope in her eyes made it nearly impossible to deny her.

"Sure, she does!" Sam answered for me, wrapping her arm around my shoulder. "Look, Morgan, your reward has appeared like magic!"

My chest tightened.

"Reward?" Finley asked.

"Yep! Morgan has a quick chore to do, and then she'll be right over!" Sam shot me a look that told me I hadn't gotten out of the therapy assignment.

"Okay! Miss Sam, do you wanna come, too?" Finley bounced again.

"I would, but my husband is calling me in a couple of hours, so I need to stay by the reliable internet so I can see his pretty face."

Finley giggled and took off after I repeated Sam's promise that I'd be over momentarily.

"Jackson cannot be my reward." I shook my head emphatically, crossing my arms.

"Well, I said Finley was your reward, and Jackson can be whatever you want him to be. Or were we sitting in different sessions of therapy when Doc said to explore new relationships?" She tilted her head and raised an eyebrow.

"I don't think she meant Jackson!"

"Oh. Right. She meant every other person on the planet

with the exception of Jackson Montgomery. My bad." She sent me a look that said I was full of shit.

My phone rang as we walked back to the kitchen. *Paisley.* Just seeing her name on the caller ID made my stomach plummet.

"What are you going to do about that?" Sam asked.

"I'll just hurt her if I answer it."

"You might be hurting her more by wearing out the decline button," she observed, then turned toward the refrigerator and pulled out one of the dozens of coffee creamers I'd stockpiled for her. "She'll understand if you're honest with her, and Doc said it was okay to ask her for space until you're further along in your treatment, right?"

Right.

The fourth ring sounded, and my thumb hit the green button instead of the red. *Oh holy hell.* What could I possibly say to her?

"Hey, Paisley." *Good start.*

"Morgan? You actually answered!" Her voice was a mix of relief, wonder, and worry.

Yup, I was a bitch.

"Yeah." It was all I could get out as anxiety dug her scaly claws in me, tightening my throat. How could I be out of words for the one person who had learned them with me in the first place?

"How are you? Where are you? I called your mama, but she said you moved and if you wanted to tell me what was going on, you would. Then she said I'm supposed to convince you to go back home."

A small laugh burst through the lump in my throat.

"Yeah, she's been on my case."

"Hold on a sec." She was quiet for a few moments. "Sorry, had to grab the baby monitor. Peyton decided to take a morning nap, and I didn't want to drop the phone on the hardwood and wake him up. Done that before. Never again."

"Of course." I forced a smile, like she could see me. *Peyton Carter Bateman.* Her son was named after Will and her sister, Peyton. Because in her mind—hell in everyone's—Will had always been Peyton's to love. Paisley's to grieve.

Never mine.

That sick feeling I'd done everything to avoid slapped me in the face, and I felt a rending in my heart, the meticulous stitches I'd been sewing since I got here popping one by one, ripping chunks of my soul out to bleed anew.

"So, where did you move to? What's going on?" She sighed. "This hurts something awful—the rift I can feel between us—and I don't know what I did, or what I can do to fix it."

"I'm fine. We're fine," I lied.

"We're not! You haven't picked up a single one of my calls since Sam's wedding, and that was three months ago, so don't tell me that nothing is wrong, because I can't remember the last time we went three months without speaking."

I could. It was after Will's funeral, but I wasn't about to go there. Lies. Fake smiles. I was so sick of it all. She was my best and oldest friend. I could do this. I could ask her for what I needed, but it was impossible not to hurt her in the process.

"I bought a beach house in Cape Hatteras. It's a wreck, but so am I, so we fit rather nicely. Will—" My throat tightened, and I reached for my coffee, taking a quick swallow before starting again. "He left me a secondary life insurance policy and his truck, among some other things."

Her indrawn breath—just shy of a gasp—made me pause.

"I…I didn't know he did that."

"Yeah, well, you didn't know everything." The little sarcastic laugh flew past my lips before I could stop it. This was going to go to shit if I couldn't rein in my mouth.

"I never thought I did," she said softly. "You know, Cape

Hatteras is only a drive away—"

My anxiety hit the panic button.

"Paisley, I love you, but I need some time and space. I have a therapist, and Sam's staying until I complete this program. Please understand. I'm so glad that you called—"

"Program? Are you in rehab?"

"No." I let a self-deprecating laugh slip. "Nothing like that."

"Wait, you have Sam there?"

Shit. Now I'd gone and hurt her feelings, which was the opposite of my intention.

"The therapy I'm going through is for something called complicated grief, and as much as it hurts you to hear this, you are a giant trigger for me." Just talking to her had the vise tightening around my throat.

"I am?" Her breath left in a rush.

"Yeah, and the treatment requires a support person. That's why Sam is here."

Sam gave me a reassuring smile.

"Are you okay? I didn't even know you were struggling. We've never kept secrets from each other," Paisley murmured.

"I kept one from you," I corrected her. "Remember?"

She paused, and I could almost see the gears turning in her head, the way her green eyes would shift side to side when she was trying to work something out.

"Will," she said softly.

"Will," I confirmed. I'd never told her I loved him when it could have mattered. I didn't tell her until she'd decided she didn't want him anymore, and even then, it had been by accident. I'd never wanted to hurt her.

"Complicated grief…is it over Will?" she asked. "Honey, if this is about him, why can't you talk to me? No one knew him better, or knows you better—"

"Oh, stop it!" I snapped. That facade I'd maintained

around Paisley since he'd died—hell, since I'd fallen for him—shattered like glass. I was done having my feelings marginalized or being talked to like I'd been some fifth grader with a crush.

The line fell quiet, taut with tension and more than a little apprehension.

"I'm a trigger," she said slowly.

My stomach sank at the heartbreak in her voice.

"You're a trigger, and my best friend, which makes this really, painfully hard." I sagged against the counter.

"So..." She sighed. "So you need me to leave you alone. Stop calling. That kind of thing?" Her voice broke.

I felt the telltale burning in my eyes and blinked back tears. "Not forever, but for now, yes."

"Okay. I can give you time."

"I know. That's why I love you." My face crumpled, wishing we were back in our kitchen in Enterprise, snacking on popcorn and M&M's. Wishing our worlds hadn't been torn so completely apart that we couldn't find each other... yet.

"Call when you're ready. Can I talk to Sam for a second?" Her voice broke.

"Sure." I handed the phone to Sam, and she started nodding.

"Yeah, I've got her," she promised, crossing from the kitchen to the living room.

I sucked in a deep breath and hit play on the tape recorder. *May as well go through all the pain at once.*

"Okay, Morgan. Can you take me back to the moment you experienced Will's death?" Dr. Circe's voice came through the speaker.

I braced my hands on the counter, steadying myself for the impact of everything that was going to follow on that damned tape.

"I'm in the grocery store, picking out a jar of jam, and my phone rings. It's Sam."

• • •

We left the windows down as we drove up the coast toward Waves and Rodanthe Beach. The miles between Hatteras and Waves were filled with unpopulated beaches, the strip of island so narrow at times it felt like I could touch the Atlantic with one hand and the sound with the other.

Jackson's Land Cruiser reminded me of his house—pristine in the front seats, where he was in charge, and perfectly cluttered in the backseat, where Finley reigned.

Banners' *Riot* blared though the speakers, and with Fin singing at the top of her lungs from behind us and Jackson grinning when she got the words wrong, my heart lightened. This was the best reward I could have given myself after listening to the tape. Sure, maybe it had been a week since I'd been this close to Jackson, but I refused to bring *that* fact into the reward equation. But every time I looked his way, my pulse jumped at the memory of having his mouth inches from mine.

We reached Waves and fell in with a small line of traffic headed for the beach access.

Finley blew hard, moving some of her curls out of her face. "It's all tangly."

Jackson met her eyes in the rearview mirror. "Then you should have let me pull it up before we left."

"I didn't want you to then," she stated like it was the simplest truth in the world.

"Do you want me to now?"

We pulled into a parking lot that was already three-quarters full and parked.

"Yes, please."

"Then it's a good thing I brought a brush and a hair tie, huh?"

She nodded with a little twist of her puckered lips.

We got out of the car, and I sprayed on sunscreen, then hauled my beach bag over my shoulder. The temp had spiked again, bringing us an eighty-degree day.

"Fin, do you need some sunscreen?" I asked, coming around the back of the car.

"Yes, please," she answered.

My breath caught stupidly at the sight of Jackson working a spray into her hair and then brushing the curls into a high ponytail. It was something so domestic, not in the least bit sexy, but that primal piece of DNA we couldn't seem to wipe out with thousands of years of evolution sat up and took notice.

Okay, I could admit it: being a good father was insanely attractive on a molecular level.

Shut up, ovaries.

"All done," Jackson declared.

Finley spun as he bent down, placing a kiss on his cheek in a motion so perfectly timed that it had to be routine. My belly clenched.

There had to be something wrong with this man somewhere. *Anywhere.* Maybe he squeezed the toothpaste from the center of the tube like a monster or something.

"Okay, what's first for you ladies? Kiteboarding? Surfing?" Jackson curved the brim of his baseball hat.

Never mind, *that* was what was wrong with him. Wasn't there an activity that didn't require I fall on my ass in the middle of the ocean? Or something with a motor? I'd never been more aware of my indoor-girl status.

"Shirts!" Finley decided.

"Well, shirts it is," Jackson said, taking her hand in his.

For a split second, I pictured him offering me his other

hand.

Because clearly, I'd gone crazy.

"Come on, Fin, let's show Morgan how we locals open the surf shop for the season."

"It's Hawkins Day!" Fin held up her free hand, and I took it.

"It is?" I asked.

"Mary Ann Hawkins was one of the first women's surfing champions. It's basically a day where you can learn about the ocean and all the fun stuff you can do in it. There are instructors for just about anything you might want to try," Jackson explained as the three of us walked down the path to the beach, where hundreds of people were already celebrating, and it seemed like it was about 90 percent women.

"It's a girl thing," Finley confirmed.

Jackson met my gaze and shrugged. "I'm here in a purely observational capacity, just like last year."

A woman crossed in front of us in a swimsuit that wasn't hiding much.

"I bet you are," I drawled slowly.

He flashed me a grin.

"Jax!" A tall brunette with chin-length hair waved her hands in the air as she ran our way. Holy crap, I could barely run on a treadmill, and this woman hit the beach like it was pavement.

Wait. Was Jackson seeing someone? We'd never had that conversation. He would have said something, though…right? My stomach sank.

"Miss Tina!" Finley let go of our hands and hugged the woman.

"Hey, Christina." Jackson greeted her with a hug, too.

"You must be Morgan," Christina said with a bright, open smile and sparkling brown eyes.

"I am," I said, then partially froze as she hugged me.

"I'm so happy to meet you!" she said, stepping back and doing a quick but open appraisal of me. "These two talk about you all the time."

"We're going to make shirts!" Finley declared.

"How fun!" Christina turned to Jackson. "You take Finley, and I'll take Morgan. We're going to do beach yoga."

"We are?" Yoga pants were something I was intimately acquainted with. Yoga itself? Not so much.

"We are!" She nodded enthusiastically.

Oh God, she was one of those workout people. The ones who declared that exercise healed everything and posted their fourteen CrossFit workouts on Instagram.

We were so not going to be friends.

"Okay, you guys have a good time. Morgan, why don't you meet us over by the surfing lessons when you're done?" He pointed to an area of the beach and walked off with Finley before I could protest.

Of all the inconsiderate—

"So, I've decided we're going to be friends," Christina said, tilting her head.

"Um. Okay?" What the heck did you say to *that*?

"I mean, Jax decided we should be friends, but now that I've met you, I agree. And Fin likes you. She's super picky with people, so I know you're a good one. I already grabbed you a mat, so we're all set up for yoga. And where are my manners? You must think I'm nuts."

A little.

"So, Jax and my husband, Peter, work together."

"They do?" My nausea vanished at the word "husband," not that I should have cared.

"Yep! Jax said you were new in town and might need someone besides his emotionally unavailable butt to talk to. So he stopped by my jewelry store to grab Finley and mentioned Hawkins Day, and I thought what's more perfect than getting to know someone while you're in crazy positions with your asses in the air?"

I couldn't stop the laugh that tumbled past my lips. This woman was sunshine, radiating her happiness.

It couldn't hurt to let it rub off on me.

That's when it hit me. She'd already grabbed me a yoga mat. Jackson hadn't walked off because he was inconsiderate.

"Oh my God. Jackson set us up on a blind friendship date. That's what's going on here."

"Pretty much," she admitted with a little shrug. "Yoga's this way." She led me to a section of the beach where women stood chatting on mats lined up in rows. The women were all different shapes, sizes, and ethnicities, but all had a variation of the same smile.

Wait. Did happy people do yoga, or did yoga make people happy? Or maybe it was just the open, adventurous spirit of the day.

How long has it been since you laughed and smiled like that?

It felt like forever.

"So Jackson and your husband work together?" I asked as we set up next to the empty mats Christina had reserved. What exactly did oceanographers do, anyway?

"Yep. A few years now. But enough about the boys. What do you do?"

I stripped off my outer layer of clothing, leaving me in my swimsuit like the other women.

"I just graduated from college. I did a five-year master's program in literature and education. So in a couple months, I'll start my first teaching job, but right now I'm pretty much a beach bum. Which, thinking about it, isn't a bad way to live."

"It sure isn't. And where did you pick up that delicious accent?" She limbered up a little, twisting her body.

"Southern Alabama. What about you? Or are you one

of those northerners who thinks you don't have an accent?"

She laughed. "Wyoming. More west than north. So, tell me, what's your damage?"

Her words came with such honesty and genuine curiosity. In truth, it was the best kind of way to get to know someone quickly, if they were willing to open up to a complete stranger.

But maybe that was the best time to lay your shit bare, when you had nothing to lose yet. Or maybe listening to the tape this morning had scraped another layer of dust off my avoidance. What the hell. If I scared her off, then so be it. I scared myself most days.

"The man I loved was killed in action almost two years ago, and now I have horrendous anxiety attacks. I moved a thousand miles and cut off everyone I know but my friend Sam and my psychiatrist. Still want to be my friend?"

I looked over at her slowly.

"Absolutely," she answered without hesitation.

"What's yours?" I challenged.

"I'm insanely worried that Peter's career will always come first and I won't matter in the scheme of life. I also hate coffee and can't understand why people willingly drink it. Still want to be my friend?"

"Absolutely," I stole her answer. "The coffee thing was a close call, though."

Her lips curved, matching mine as the instructor took the little platform set up in front of us.

"Okay, ladies! Welcome to Hawkins Day! Now let's get our energy flowing and center ourselves. Begin with the mountain pose." She modeled the pose, standing with her feet wide apart and her hands reaching for the sky.

I copied her, letting myself take in deep breaths of sea air as my whole body stretched to welcome the sun.

After yoga, Christina and I made plans to meet up the next week, and then I chose to step forward into surfing after purchasing a wet suit. Holy crappola, did I suck at that.

"You weren't that bad," Jackson assured me as we drove home that evening.

"Are you serious? Were you watching? Goats are more graceful on a surfboard than I am." I kept my voice low, noting that Fin had passed out in the backseat before we'd even made it out of Waves.

Jackson grinned, and my traitorous heart skittered a few beats.

"See? You know it was bad."

"I was actually picturing goats on a surfboard."

"They'd have a better chance of staying on that thing than I did, hooves and all." I knew I wasn't athletic, but that had just been embarrassing. There was a definite difference between thin and fit, and I was *not* fit. Grief had eaten away at my appetite and my muscles.

"You can always get better through practice, if you want. I do happen to know of a nearby beach…"

I rolled my eyes.

"Speaking of beaches, it's really narrow here." I changed the subject as we reached a particularly tight strip of 12. "What happens when the storms come?"

"It gets hit. Hard. All of 12 does, really. Hurricanes like Irene and Sandy can cut us off from the mainland for weeks. They have to dig out the roads or rebuild them. We can usually get ferries going, but tides make it difficult."

"So they just keep rebuilding roads that continually get destroyed by hurricanes? I mean, those were both in the last decade." Being cut off for weeks? Did I have supplies for that? I'd need to store some food. Maybe get a generator for when the solar panels we'd just installed with the roof didn't hack it. Oh God, I was going to turn into one of those crazy doomsday preppers.

"Well, yeah, people live here. Love it here. You're one of

us now, so you should appreciate the tenacity of the North Carolina Department of Transportation."

"It just seems so...futile to keep fighting for something you know won't last." Beach erosion was a serious issue—I knew that when I bought the house—and houses here had been known to float away into the Atlantic even without hurricanes. Just living here was a risk.

He glanced my way, and then his hands tightened on the wheel. "Maybe it is futile. Maybe one day we'll be forced to abandon it. But it's okay to fight for something you love, to dig it out and build it back up in hopes that this time the foundation will be strong enough to withstand the hurricane. It's just like what you're doing with the house."

"I guess it is." Fixing a house that could eventually sink into the ocean, fixing a heart that might end up useless anyway. Fixing a friendship that I'd all but ghosted?

"And it's okay to do all you can and still lose, still get washed away. It sucks, but it's a far less tragic ending than never having tried."

The air between us thickened as he glanced my way and then back to the road.

"Yeah, it's those lost chances that end up hurting the worst," I said quietly.

"How did the foundation set on the house, by the way?"

"Went without a hitch." If we didn't count the stupid weathervane.

He smiled. "Good. That's good. You can remodel the hell out of just about any house if the foundation is good."

I looked across the car in the dying sunlight and studied his face. *Inches.* He'd been a breath away from kissing me on his kitchen counter. Was it possible to want someone when you had nothing to offer but a ton of baggage and a damaged heart? Was I even allowed to want him in any other way besides a neighbor, or maybe a friend? Did it matter?

Ripping my eyes away, I looked out at the ocean, recognizing that for the first time in years, I wanted a man who wasn't Will. My heart ripped a little, and I raised my hand to rub the spot beneath my collarbone, partially to ease the ache there and partially to see if I could capture the little bit of light and hope that escaped from that tear. I could push my feelings about Jackson away all I wanted, but it didn't make them any less real or any less dangerous.

He lived right next door, so it was only a matter of time before I had to decide what the heck I was going to do about it. Avoiding him and shutting down whatever this was before it had the chance to start was the safest choice, and that's what I needed right now. Safe. That was the logical choice—the only choice.

I'd just have to say no to every invitation he offered and put a lot of distance between us, starting now. How hard could that be? *No,* I practiced in my head. *No, no, no.* See? I could do it.

Fin stirred in the backseat, blinking awake with a stretch.

"What do you say we get rebellious and stop for ice cream?" Jackson asked me with a mischievous grin that raised my temperature by at least two degrees.

"Sure!" I answered before Fin even got the chance.

I was so screwed.

Chapter Nine

Jackson

"I like the pink one," Finley informed me as we scrolled through backpacks online. "Ooh, and that blue one. And the green one."

"Well, you only need one, so which one is your favorite?"

She scrunched her forehead, looking up at me and then back to the screen, seriously pondering her decision with an intensity that almost made me laugh.

"Take your time. Kindergarten is a big deal. I get that, and I firmly support whatever choice you make. You don't even have to pick one tonight. It's just orientation. We still have months before you start."

She took a deep breath and nodded. "The purple one."

"You're sure?"

"That's the one. I know it."

"Okay, because I'm buying it right now." I clicked add to cart.

She nodded. "I'm ready."

"I know you are." Maybe she was, but I wasn't. I faked it well, though. "Okay, all purchased."

"Thanks, Daddy!" Finley plopped a kiss on my cheek and hopped off the couch, brushing her curls out of her face.

"They won't get in the way if you let me pull it up," I reminded her.

"Ponytails are boring," she declared, skipping every age to thirteen.

A knock at the door saved her from my eye roll.

"We could stop by Grammy's and ask Aunt Brie to braid it for you," I suggested as Fin bolted toward the door.

"Nope. She has really long nails."

"What?" That had exactly what to do with braiding?

"It's Morgan!" Finley called out, jumping up and down to see out the glass side panel of the front door.

My heart rate kicked up, and I had the ridiculous urge to check myself in the mirror as I walked toward the door. *Get a damn grip.* But in my defense, I'd only seen her in passing over the last week, and this was the first time she'd ever knocked on my door.

"Can I?" Fin asked, her hands already on the knob.

"Yep. You can always let Morgan in." Which now made six people on Finley's always-allowed list: Brie, Sarah, Sawyer, Garrett, Vivian, and now Morgan.

"Yay!" She flung open the door. "I can always let you in!"

"Awesome!" Morgan held out her hand for a low-five. Fin gave it to her with a megawatt grin.

"Come in!" Finley backed up and held out her arm like a gracious pint-sized hostess.

"Why, thank you," Morgan said, walking in.

She was in a white, thick-strapped tank top and short khaki shorts that reached midthigh, drawing my eyes to her legs. Not that I needed a reason, because my attention always found its way there with Morgan. She was also wearing the same maroon ball cap from the pictures. His ball cap.

Damn, I wished I hadn't gone snooping.

"Did you come to see my daddy?" Finley asked, shutting the door behind her.

Morgan flashed me a small smile before turning back to Fin. "Nope, I actually came to see you." She dropped down to Fin's eye level.

"You did?" Fin brushed her hair out of her face.

"I did! I was walking the beach with Sam this morning, and I found this!" She opened her hand, revealing a small, perfect conch shell.

"Ooh! It's so pretty!" Fin leaned in close, examining the shell.

"It's yours," Morgan said as she handed it over.

"Really? It's *almost* perfect."

Ah, and so the search continued.

"That's exactly what I thought when I saw it!"

Fin grabbed Morgan's still-outstretched hand and examined her fingernails. "Can you braid?"

Morgan blinked at the subject change, but then nodded. "I can."

"Will you braid my hair?" Fin asked, using those eyes on Morgan to get her way. "I have kindergarten tonight."

Oh shit. That tightness in my chest was back, flaring in a fierce surge of emotion I had no right to feel. Finley liked Morgan. She trusted her, which only made my attraction to her increase exponentially.

Morgan's soft brown eyes found mine in silent question, and I gave her a slight nod.

"If you want me to, I can," Morgan replied.

"Yay! I'll get my stuff." Clutching her new prize, Finley raced off to her room, leaving us standing in the entry hall.

"Thanks. She never lets me braid it. Mostly because every time I try, it comes out lopsided and not very braid-like," I remarked, struggling for something to say that wouldn't come out *hey-I-really-like-you-any-chance-you-might-feel-the-same.*

Because I wasn't fourteen.

And the woman still doesn't know what you do for a living, jackass.

"No problem. I'm happy to do it."

I walked her into the kitchen and offered her a drink.

"No thanks, I'm good." She braced her hands on the granite and boosted her ass into the same spot I'd put her when I'd patched her up weeks ago.

If Sam hadn't walked in, I would have—

"So, kindergarten, huh?"

"It's just orientation for next year, but it crept up on me, that's for sure."

"She'll do great."

Fuck me. She crossed her legs and shifted forward slightly, leaning on her palms. Maybe it was the months of celibacy, but my body took more than enough notice of her. *Shit, when was the last time I got laid?* Not since Morgan arrived, that was for sure. Not for lack of opportunity but because I didn't want anyone else.

Holy shit. I don't want anyone else.

So what the hell did that mean? Did I want a date with this woman? A night in her bed? An actual relationship? *Yes to all.*

She took a deep breath, causing her breasts to rise against her neckline, and I turned back to the refrigerator, popped the top of one of those antioxidant drinks Finley liked because they were pink, and chugged the whole thing.

"Thirsty?" Morgan teased.

You have no fucking idea.

"You could definitely say that." I turned slowly, and from the way her eyes widened, I was doing a piss-poor job of keeping my thoughts off my face.

Only a few feet separated us. A heartbeat—maybe two—and I could be standing between her knees, her face in my hands, my tongue finally tasting the curve of her mouth.

As if she could read my thoughts, her lips parted, and the air crackled for all the potential electricity lingering between us.

"Got it!" Fin called out, skidding to a halt in front of Morgan with a tackle box full of hair-care products.

Morgan blinked rapidly and turned to Fin. "Okay! Let's get you started!"

A few minutes later, Morgan had Fin on the floor in front of her as she sat on the love seat. She listened with rapt attention as Finley told her all about the great kindergarten backpack debate.

I watched from the couch, trying to figure out what the hell I was supposed to do about wanting this woman. Hell, I hadn't been on a second date since Claire. Hadn't really been on a *date* at all.

"What if I get hungry?" Finley asked as Morgan sprayed product into her curls. It was the first time I'd heard her voice concern over going to school.

"There's lunch time and snack time," Morgan told her, brushing through Finley's curls with ease. "And if you're super hungry, just tell your teacher."

"What if no one likes my backpack?" she asked quietly, and it took everything in my power not to answer her, because she hadn't asked me.

"Then that's their problem," Morgan stated simply.

I blinked. My first impulse had been to say that everyone would love her backpack, but Morgan's answer was way better.

Morgan threaded Fin's curls through her fingers and wove a braid around her head.

What the hell kind of sorcery was that?

"What if they don't like me?" Fin's voice dropped even softer.

I leaned forward, and Morgan shot me a look that warned against speaking. My eyebrows lifted, but I stayed silent.

"Then they're not the people you *want* to like you. And you already have one friend there, so you're already starting ahead." She flipped her hands and continued the braid up the other side of Fin's head.

"Who?" Fin asked, sitting stiller than she ever did when I did her hair.

"Me. Just think, your first day of kindergarten will be my first as a teacher, so we'll both be nervous. And I bet every other kid in your class has the same kind of worries you do. So if you smile big, you just might make them a little less nervous, too."

"You're a teacher?" Fin started to turn her head but thought better of it.

"I am. At least that's what my college told me. I've never had a class of my own, though, so I guess we'll see. I'll be right down the hall from you in fifth grade."

She finished the braid, winding an elastic over the end and tucking it into the start of the braid before sticking a few bobby pins through it.

"All done!"

Fin popped up and ran to the mirror, where her jaw dropped. "It's a crown! I have a crown!" She flew back in, wrapping her arms around Morgan and smacking her cheek with a kiss. "Thank you!"

"You're welcome." Morgan's eyes slid shut as she hugged Fin tightly.

Then Fin took off to put her hair stuff away, leaving us alone.

Morgan rose from the love seat.

"That was astonishing," I told her as I stood. "How do you know how to do that?"

"YouTube." Her smile was soft but real.

"She adores you." Fin liked a lot of people, but that blatant look of affection she'd lavished on Morgan was usually reserved for me or Vivian.

"Well, the feeling is mutual. She's phenomenal." We locked eyes briefly before Morgan looked away.

"Thank you. You're amazing. You know that, right?"

Pink tinged her cheeks. "Not really. If you knew the real me, I'm not sure you'd think that."

"And what would change my mind?" I hoped she wasn't alluding to the anxiety attack she'd gone through with the truck.

"Okay, I'm ready!" Fin exclaimed, arms up in victory as she twirled in the newest dress Vivian had bought for her. It was a step beneath a ballroom, but it wasn't exactly classroom, either, and on her feet, she wore her favorite pair of black Vans.

"You look absolutely wonderful. I'm sure they'll all remember you when it's time to go back next year!" Morgan praised before I could question my daughter's thought process.

Finley cocked her head at me, motioning to her dress. Her very sparkly dress.

"I love it." I loved even more that she felt good about herself in it. If that was the confidence boost she needed, I'd fill her closet with fluffy dresses.

Morgan gave her a hug. "You guys have a great night, okay?"

"Walk us out?" I offered as Fin slipped on her jacket without the usual fight.

"Sure," Morgan agreed, her hand finding Fin's as we headed out the door.

By the time I locked up behind us, Morgan and Finley were down the steps, lost in some animated conversation that I wasn't privy to, but I heard Fin mention Vivian.

Right. Next weekend was Vivian's with Fin. Usually, I'd grab a drink with Sawyer and Garrett, but what if I didn't? What if I spent the time with Morgan, instead? Would she even say yes? Shit, was I actually nervous about asking a woman out?

Absolutely.

I got Fin buckled in her car seat, then turned the Land Cruiser on so the air conditioning would circulate for my little redhead.

"Hey, Kitty," I called out when I caught her walking away from me.

She turned, tucking her hands into her back pockets just outside our open garage door. "Jackson?"

There it was, that little uptick at the corner of her mouth, the one I couldn't wait to trace with my tongue. God, if the woman said yes, I was going to have to wait an entire week to take her out.

"I hate that I have to work this weekend." Wait, why the hell did I say that? I was rusty as shit when it came to someone I actually wanted.

"That seems fair." She tilted her head to the side.

"Sorry, that wasn't what I meant to say."

She smiled, and it was real.

My brain emptied. She was beautiful in more than her body or her face—that was a given, and in my experience didn't always carry any deeper. Morgan's beauty skyrocketed with that sparkle I caught right now in her eyes, the hint of playfulness, the glimpse of another stunning facet of her I had yet to discover.

Because I hadn't earned it yet.

But I would.

The timing was wrong. I wasn't sure she was ready. I hadn't been interested in more than a few hours with someone in over five years. She had a broken heart, and I had a kid whose heart I couldn't risk. For God's sake, I was standing outside my garage, which wasn't exactly romantic.

But none of that mattered…or maybe it did, but I was going to give her every reason not to *let* them matter.

I was going to earn the right to see her smile and hear her laugh.

"Are you okay?" Her eyebrows furrowed.

"Yeah, absolutely." *Just busy talking to myself.* "So I have to work this weekend, which we've already covered. But I'm off next weekend."

Her eyes widened slightly.

"You feel up for seeing a little more of the island with me? You haven't gotten out much." *Holy shit, Montgomery, did you just quasi-insult the woman?*

"Oh. I'm not really one for bars anymore." She rocked back on her heels.

"I was thinking more along the lines of nocturnal sightseeing."

"Sightseeing?"

"Yes."

"At night?"

"I believe that's the meaning of nocturnal."

She stared at me for a moment, her pause almost awkwardly long, but I waited. I had a feeling that was the key to Morgan, taking small steps and putting the choice in her corner. I'd never been a wait-for-anything kind of guy, but I'd so fucking learn if it meant having a shot with her.

"Okay," she finally answered. "What time?"

I managed to not fist-pump. Barely. It was close.

"Nine on Saturday. Unless you'd rather grab dinner first? I know some great—"

"Nope, nine is great."

Small steps, Montgomery.

"Okay, see you then."

She nodded and damn-near ran back to her house in obvious retreat.

I blocked off Saturday evening on the calendar using my phone and grinned the whole way to the school. We got there thirteen minutes early.

Fin held her head extra high as we walked in through the front double doors. We turned left at the end of the short hall and passed a pair of classrooms, one that had the door propped open.

"Aunt Brie!" Finley dropped my hand and ran toward her aunt, who was seated behind her desk and a pile of papers.

"Hey, Finley!" Brie got out of her chair and gave Fin a hug.

"What are you doing here so late?" I asked, leaning against one of her students' desks.

"Well, I'm grading papers, and I knew this little lady had orientation tonight, so I thought I'd wish her luck! Let's get a picture!" She took her cell phone from the desk and snapped a picture of Fin.

"Do you like my dress?" Fin asked, spinning with a squeak against the linoleum floor.

"Very glamorous. And look at your hair!" she gushed. "If that's not the prettiest thing I've ever seen!"

"Morgan did it!"

"Did she?" Brie shot me a raised eyebrow. "Well, I love it! That Morgan sure is talented, isn't she?"

"Yes! And she's going out with Daddy next weekend!" Fin clapped.

Oh, shit.

"Fin, it's not like a date-date," I told her. We were going to have to discuss expectations. I didn't need Fin's heart set on something that wasn't even on the table right now. "And how do you even know?"

She looked at me sheepishly. "My iPad told me."

Right. She had access to the family calendar and got notifications—my bad. But— "When exactly did your iPad tell you?"

She pressed her lips in a little line.

"Fin?"

"When we left the house."

"You snuck your iPad into the car? Where? How?" I folded my arms across my chest.

"Under my jacket." She shrugged unapologetically.

"That's why you didn't argue about putting it on," I mused, giving my daughter a point for pure mischievousness. "But I didn't say you could bring it. Tech stays home."

Her eyes darted from Brie's to mine and back again. "You didn't say I *couldn't* bring it..."

"She has you there," Brie acknowledged. "What do you say we walk you down to the kindergarten rooms?"

"Yes, please!" Finley bounced with excitement.

We walked out of Brie's room and almost ran right into one of Fin's friends from preschool, which meant Fin was already starting down the hall with Julie, no longer caring about an escort.

I glanced at the door that would be Morgan's next year.

"She's not just some tourist, you know," Brie said softly, motioning toward the door. "If you start something with her and it ends badly, I'm the one stuck hearing about it at work, and more importantly, it will affect Fin."

"Is that why you told Claire about Morgan?" I questioned as we passed bulletin boards full of artwork.

She gave me an indignant scoff. "I told my sister because she has a right to know that you're putting yourself in a position to move on."

"I moved on *years* ago."

"Not emotionally, you didn't. I know Claire is…Claire, but she's still my sister, and I'm just looking out for her."

"I like Morgan. I'm taking her out. I didn't say that we were hopping a flight to Vegas. Fin, baby, wait up!" I called down the hall.

Fin paused outside the kindergarten doors.

"I just wish—"

I turned, halting us both. "You wish she was Claire. That's your baggage. Not mine. Now I'm going to take my daughter into her orientation. The daughter who once again doesn't have her mother here. I'll see you later, Brie." With a curt nod, I left her standing in the hall and headed for Fin.

I wasn't the only single parent there, but I was the only single dad. The usual onslaught of complicated emotions didn't hit me this time, though. Fin wasn't looking around, sad that her own mother hadn't come—that was my baggage, not hers. She was busy twirling in her dress and showing everyone her crown braid.

But then again, how could she miss someone she'd never really had?

• • •

"Oh, come on!" Sawyer begged as he spotted me the next night.

I pushed the bar through my final rep and set it back on the rack.

"Don't give him shit about it," Garrett muttered from the pull-up station.

We'd already flown a patrol, and we were doing what any man of logic would normally do at one a.m.—working out in the station gym to keep from falling asleep.

"Sorry, man, you're on your own," I told Sawyer as I sat

up.

"I made *arrangements*," he whined. "There are two of them. Two. Cousins. What am I supposed to tell them?" He followed me as I headed for the leg press.

"That you made plans without consulting me?" I adjusted the weight, adding twenty pounds.

"That you made plans without consulting *me*. What the hell is so important that you'd blow me off on a non-Finley weekend?" He stared down at me with a mix of real and mock outrage. "You know we only have a few months before we deploy! You're supposed to be mine!"

"A few months before *you* deploy, remember? I'm on rear D for this one." Command had taken mercy on me since I was Finley's only parent. Yes, I had a care plan, but it had been a relief when they told me I wasn't going to have to use it. I hated sending my guys without me, though.

He grabbed his chest in indignation. "We're supposed to be spending every moment we can together so our bromance survives the separation!"

"All three months of it." I laughed. "Now seriously, I'm taking Morgan out." I slid into the machine.

"I'm sorry. Morgan as in your extremely hot, way unavailable neighbor?" Sawyer asked, his expression changing to a shit-eating grin.

"Yes." I started my reps and hoped the conversation would end there.

"Do you even know how to actually date anymore?" Sawyer dropped down so we were at the same level.

Of course he couldn't let it end there.

"Pretty sure it all works the same as the last time I did it," I snapped, breathing through the reps.

"You mean back in the eighteen hundreds?" Sawyer laughed.

"Seriously, leave him alone," Garrett told Sawyer,

dropping after his last pull-up. "Jax, I like her. She might be gorgeous, but she doesn't act like she knows it, and she ate your burnt-ass cheeseburger."

"Thanks for your approval." I grunted as I reached the end of the set.

"I didn't say I didn't like her!" Sawyer threw his hands up in the air. "I'm here for this, Montgomery. What can I do to help you? Do you need tips? Advice? Date ideas? You know that Myspace isn't a thing anymore, right?"

I finished the last rep, then climbed from the machine and put my hand on Sawyer's shoulder. "Sawyer, you know I love you like a brother, but you are the last person in the world I would ever ask dating advice from."

Garrett burst into laughter as I hauled my ass to the shower. I wasn't letting Sawyer get to me, not when I'd gotten Morgan to say yes—even if it was a friend-zone date. I'd take what I could get when it came to her.

My phone rang as I zipped up my flight suit post-shower.

"Fuck," I muttered, but I still answered. "Do you know what time it is, Claire?"

"Ten thirty," she snapped.

"It's one thirty in the morning here." I sat down on the bench in front of my locker and put on my boots.

"Well, you answered, so you must still be awake."

"But you didn't know that when you called—" I sat up and rubbed the skin between my eyes. "Okay, let's start over. To what do I owe the pleasure of this call?"

"We have a giant fucking issue," she seethed.

"Which would be?"

"Did you seriously send my daughter to her kindergarten orientation wearing a damned Easter dress and Converse?" Her voice was pitched high enough to be called a shriek.

I bit back an instinctual reply, which would have been to tell her to fuck off and hang up. *She's Finley's mother.* I repeated the thought four times before I spoke.

"Not that I know of." I leaned down to lace my boots, holding the phone between my ear and shoulder.

"So this picture Brie sent me isn't Finley's orientation? I just sent it."

My phone vibrated, and I pulled it back long enough to see the picture Brie had taken yesterday appear in our text thread. "That's Finley right before orientation," I confirmed.

"Jax!"

"What?" I finished tying the first boot and started on the second. "She's not wearing an Easter dress because it doesn't have a thousand bunnies on it, or eggs, or a giant cross. It's a party dress. And those aren't Converse; they're her favorite pair of Vans."

"And you let her wear that? Do you know what the teacher must have thought? What the other kids must think about her?"

"That's their problem," I retorted, taking a page out of Morgan's book as I tied the second boot. "Look, Claire, she wore whatever made her feel good about herself. If you have a problem with it, then I guess you should have been here to tell her that what people think is more important than how she feels."

"I cannot believe that you just—"

The alarm went off, and I jolted from the bench, racing for the hallway.

"We've got a mayday!" Sawyer called out, running my way, where all of our flight gear was stored.

It was go time.

"Claire, I'm going to have to call you back. There are people who need me to save them from an *actual* issue." I hung up and pocketed my phone without another thought about Claire as I ran back to the locker room. Sawyer and Garrett both came through the door as I grabbed my flight bag, then pressed a kiss to my fingers and touched the picture of Finley I kept taped on the inside of my locker door.

Then I put her out of my mind, too, and focused only on the mission in front of me.

"Let's go save some lives."

Chapter Ten

Morgan

I'm leaving you the truck. The best memories I have of it are with you in the passenger seat, so it seems fitting.

I stared at the door handle of Will's truck and reached, only to drop my hand yet again. Sam had told me to take it easy while she was visiting Grayson's grandparents for the weekend, but I wasn't going to show up at Dr. Circe's office next week having failed with the simple homework assignment of opening the damned door.

But what if I opened the door and had another anxiety attack? Even worse, what if Jackson saw it? How was I supposed to go out with the man if I wasn't even healthy enough to open this door?

A set of tires crunched the gravel of my driveway, and a blue sedan stopped right in front of the truck. Christina climbed out.

Great, now I had a witness to my failure.

"Well, good morning, sunshine." Christina held a cup of coffee as she glared me down in the odd combination of yoga pants over her wetsuit.

"Hardly," I retorted. "I thought we were meeting at your shop? And what's with the wetsuit?"

"I thought so, too, but then you stood me up." She tilted her head. "I even grabbed you coffee. It's nasty when it's hot, so I bet it's extra special tasty when chilled by an hour of waiting."

I looked from the coffee to her and back again. "Wait, we're supposed to meet at nine, right?" It couldn't possibly be that late.

"Yep, and it's now ten." She shook her phone.

"Oh God, I'm so sorry, Christina. I lost track of time." I'd been standing here for an hour and a half? I wasn't sure if I was more upset by the time loss or my ultimate inability to open the door.

"It's okay. We can make the eleven o'clock class." She walked over to the construction dumpster and tossed the coffee over the metal edge. "Now get your wetsuit and let's go."

"For yoga?"

She grinned. "Do you trust me?"

"No." I shook my head.

"Smart woman. What if I ask you really nicely and promise not to ask you to surf?" She batted her lashes at me.

I sighed. "Give me five?" I was supposed to be exercising my body and making new friends, and if that included putting on my wetsuit, then fine. At least I wouldn't fail that section of my homework.

"Take ten," she answered with a shrug.

I raced up my steps and didn't stop until I reached my bedroom, where I went to war with the neoprene piece of hell known as my wetsuit. Good Lord, this thing exhausted every muscle I had just getting it on, but I did. Thank God I didn't go with the full-body model or I wouldn't have made it.

With already aching arms, I gathered my hair at the top of my head and looped it into a bun, then pulled on my yoga pants, grabbed my sunglasses, and headed back outside, where Christina patiently waited for me.

"Good girl. For your speed, I shall offer you a new cup of non-cold coffee on the way," she said with a smirk.

We took her coupe twenty minutes north to Avon, stopping along the way for the promised caffeine hit.

"You going to pry?" I asked when I caught her glancing my way.

"Nope. I figure if you want to tell me why you were staring at a pickup truck like it was your mortal enemy, you will." Her eyes cut my way. "Doesn't mean I'm not dying of curiosity."

I took a sip of the caramel macchiato as we sped along the narrow parts of the island.

"I'm struggling with a homework assignment my therapist gave me." I glanced at her. "Does it weird you out that I'm in therapy?"

"Nope. You already told me you struggle with anxiety attacks. It weirds me out when people know they need help and still don't seek it. Homework, huh? Dead guy problems?" she asked.

Somehow the blunt way she addressed it made me want to tell her.

"Yeah. I'm supposed to open the door to his truck once a day. Just open it, not get in or drive it or anything, and I can't manage to do it."

"Why not?" She pulled into a small parking lot on the inlet side of the island.

"Probably because the last time I opened it, Jackson had a front-row seat to an epic anxiety attack. I'm not too eager to undo all the progress I've made and risk that happening again." I nearly high-fived myself for analyzing my own motives pretty successfully.

She parked, then turned toward me. "Which part? The attack? Or Jax seeing it? Also, it's adorable that you call him Jackson."

I laughed off the last comment. "Both, I guess. I knew better than to try it again, honestly. Sam only left for the weekend because her husband's family asked her to come up for dinner, and I refused to go with her. She told me to give it a day and we'd try again when she gets back on Sunday, but I just stood there in front of that truck for an hour and a half after she left."

"So basically, you had a free homework pass and tried anyway."

"Stupid, right?" I laughed again, forcing the sound out.

"Brave. It tells me you're serious about getting past whatever is holding you back." She killed the ignition.

"And the fact that I just stood there staring?"

"That just makes you human. Now are you done beating the shit out of yourself? Because this is a really cool class."

"Well, you kind of take the fun out of it." This time when my lips lifted, the small smile was genuine.

We got out of the car and walked through the parking lot.

"I'm just glad you were lost in your own little world. I was kind of scared you'd stood me up because of Jax," Christina said, adjusting her beach bag on her shoulder. "I was afraid you were having second thoughts or something and didn't want to see me because we're friends."

"Jackson?" I nearly tripped over my flip-flops.

"You guys are going out tomorrow night, right?" She did a double take at my face and then sputtered. "Sorry, the guys at the station are pretty much a high school gossip club. Everyone knows everything."

"We're not dating or anything," I assured her, just like I had myself about fourteen billion times since he asked me last weekend. "We're just sightseeing."

"It would be okay if you were. You know that, right?"

"Right. But we're not." I shook my head emphatically.

She raised her eyebrows but didn't argue as we walked down the wooden steps to the beach where our class of about half a dozen women waited…with paddleboards?

"Christina?"

"Consider it the American Ninja Warrior of yoga."

Our feet hit the sand, and I shook my head. "I'm more on the chair aerobics level." I brought up my hands to show her my awesome synchronized finger push-ups.

"Push your comfort zone. Let's go."

No excuses, no option to back down. She firmly expected me to haul my uncoordinated butt up onto that paddleboard and do yoga. On the water.

"And what happens when I fall off? Because that's definitely going to happen." I picked up the unclaimed board next to where Christina claimed hers, grateful that I'd put on the wetsuit.

"You can swim, right?"

"Well, yeah."

"Then you get wet." She shrugged. "You can stay on shore the same way you could have stayed in bed this morning. It's your choice. No one can decide to start living for you, Morgan."

She dropped her yoga pants and kicked off her sandals.

I was living, right? I'd bought a house, was remodeling said house, and had managed to make friends with Jackson, Finley, and now Christina. Sure, maybe my outlook was still a little gray, but now my days had blocks of sunshine peering through the space that had only been dark before. Blocks of sunshine that had a lot to do with the guy I wasn't going on a date with tomorrow night.

It was a sightseeing trip with a friend.

Uh-huh.

Kicking off my flip-flops, I wiggled my toes, feeling every nuance of the damp sand from its slight chill to the grit against my skin that I knew would wear away the rougher edges of my feet if I walked far enough. Not abrasive as much as it was refining, comforting as it molded to my arches.

I couldn't manage to open the truck door.

I had weeks to go in this therapy that felt more like torture than healing.

Will was dead.

But I wasn't.

Maybe it was time I started acting like it more than just the times Jackson dragged me out of the house.

It wasn't just one big choice—it was a thousand tiny ones just like this. Just like saying yes to Jackson.

I dropped my reservations and my pants onshore, then headed into the water with the board tucked under my arm and the ankle leash firmly secured—thanks to Christina.

I managed to climb up onto my board in the hip-deep water with the rest of the class and thanked my lucky stars that we weren't on the ocean side of the island.

Then I fell off.

More than once.

But I'll be damned if I didn't haul myself back up on that board every single time.

• • •

This is not a date.

This is not a date.

This. Is. Not. A. Date.

I mentally repeated the phrase as I headed to answer

my front door. Just because I had on a sundress and little matching sweater didn't make it a date. A date would have meant heels, and my toes were currently cocooned in pair of sensible but cute ballet flats. Maybe I'd shaved my legs, but that didn't make it a date, either. Neither did my makeup or the fact that I'd taken the time to curl my hair.

Those small acts had been my own affirmations of life. They had nothing to do with the man who'd rung my doorbell a few seconds ago.

I exhaled slowly as I reached for the door handle, then took a fresh breath, pasted on a smile, and opened the door.

Oh shit. He had that whole beach-casual vibe going on, and he made it look good. Really damn good. His hair had that messy, ran-my-fingers-through-it style, and he'd rolled up the sleeves of his white button-down shirt over a pair of dark blue cargo shorts.

But it was his smile that seemed to stutter my heart.

"Wow. Morgan, you look incredible."

Maybe it was the deep timbre of his voice or the way his gaze warmed my skin as he glanced over me in the same way I'd just done to him, but suddenly this felt very much like a date.

"Thank you," I managed to reply. "You look great, too." That was absolutely an understatement. The man looked edible.

"Thanks." His smile widened. "You ready?"

"You betcha." *You betcha?* Oh God, did I really just say that? Where the hell was the charm I'd been known for? The quick, flirting smile?

He didn't seem to notice that I'd answered him like an eighty-five-year-old grandfather, and a couple of minutes later, we were strapped into his Land Cruiser, heading south.

"So what exactly are you planning to show me in the dark?" I asked, then mentally cursed myself again. "You know, where we can't see anything?" *Stop, you're making it so much worse.*

He tossed a grin my way, then peered up through the windshield. "It's a clear night and a full moon. It's a good night for climbing, wouldn't you say, Kitty?"

I scoffed. "I'm not exactly dressed for mountaineering, Jackson."

He slowed, pulling into the park. "Good, because we don't exactly have any mountains around here."

A turn later and my jaw dropped.

"But we do have lighthouses," he said as he parked the car.

I stepped out into the parking lot, looking up, and up, and up at the black and white paint twisting its way up the enormous tower. This thing was colossal.

"It's the tallest brick lighthouse in the United States," Jackson noted as he shut his door, then came around to my side and shut mine since I'd been too busy gaping.

"And we're going to climb it?" I swore to God, if that man busted out a climbing harness and rope, I was going to—

"We're going to climb the stairs inside it."

"And they let you do that at nine o'clock on a Saturday night?"

He laughed, sending a wave of flutters through my stomach. "Starting next month, they'll do full-moon tours, but tonight, it's just you and me. Come on." He motioned toward the sidewalk that led to the lighthouse, and we walked down the moonlit path.

"Hey, Jax." A tall, heavy man with a thick black beard and wearing a uniform stepped out of the doorway as we approached.

"John. Thanks for letting us in," Jackson said as he shook the man's hand.

"No problem. I owe you a hell of a lot more than a little

late-night access. You going to introduce me to your girl?" He turned a kind smile on me.

"Oh, I'm not his girl."

"She's not my girl."

We spoke at the same time, then let the awkwardness speak for itself.

"Right." He glanced between us. "Okay, well, the stairwell lights are on, but the deck lights are off, so you two be careful."

We assured him we would be and then walked into the lighthouse. I took in the spiral staircase and shook my head. "What exactly does John owe you for, anyway?"

Jackson's jaw flexed before he answered. "I got his brother out of a tight spot once. Nothing big."

The way he looked away told me otherwise.

"You have a thing for saving people, don't you?" *Like me.*

"You have no idea," he answered quietly, staring up the center of the staircase.

"Okay, tour guide," I said as my foot hit the first metal step. "Time to start guiding."

"I promise it's worth it," he swore as we started to climb. "It's thirty-one steps between each landing for a total of two hundred fifty-seven steps," he recited, beginning my evening history lesson.

I fell into the rhythm of my feet and the cadence of his voice as he told me all about why it had been constructed in the eighteen hundreds.

"The Graveyard of the Atlantic?" I questioned. "Don't you think that's a little extreme?" My breathing grew labored, and I noted with more than a little awe and annoyance that his didn't. No sir, he was still breathing deep and even. How in the blazing hell? Did he spend an hour on the StairMaster every day?

"I'll show you," he promised. "This is the last stretch of

stairs before the top."

"You mean this eventually ends?" I teased with mock wonder.

He shook his head, but there was laughter in those blue eyes. "Yeah, yeah. Keep climbing, Kitty."

"Don't you ever do anything for fun that doesn't burn a thousand calories?"

"What do you mean?"

"Come walk the beach, Morgan." My voice lowered in an awful Jackson impression. "Come surfing, Morgan. Look, there's yoga to learn, Morgan."

His laugh echoed through the brick structure.

"Why not, let's see a movie, Morgan? Or my personal favorite, let's order in and watch Netflix, Morgan?" We finally reached a landing with a door, and I turned toward him as he stepped up beside me, drawing my eyes upward again. "Hmmm?" I asked, lifting an eyebrow.

"I will order in with you whenever you want." His gaze dropped to my lips, and the temperature in the lighthouse rose. Or maybe that was just my own body. "I'll even let you pick what we do next time."

Next time. I swallowed, trying to find the levity we'd had just seconds ago. "I hope you're up for a fun night of reading on the couch," I teased.

"I'll come read with you," he offered in what had to be the sexiest voice imaginable. Hell, that was the sexiest *line* imaginable. "What book are you spending your nights with?"

"I just finished *Mrs. Dalloway*, and I'm on to *Orlando* now. I'm on a bit of a Virginia Woolf kick."

"Go figure, you're a classics kind of girl." He grinned. "You almost had me fooled, thinking you were all about night hikes," he joked.

I scoffed. "I'm not exactly an outdoor kind of girl, you know." At least I hadn't been.

"With all the shell hunting, beach walking, and yoga and surfing? You could have fooled me."

"The old me preferred pedicures to four-wheeling, and the only things I hunted on the beach were boys and a tan. Oh, and the occasional Jet Ski trip." My shoulders lifted in a shrug.

"The old you, huh?" He took a few steps to my right and reached for the door handle.

"Yep. She even came with a quick smile and sharp little tongue when the occasion called for it." That was a whole other life—a whole other girl—but the girl I was tonight didn't feel too bad, either.

"You still have those things. Trust me. And I happen to like whatever version of you this is just fine. In fact, I have yet to see any version of you I don't like. They're all just you."

The sincerity in his eyes stripped away another layer of my defenses, but I didn't feel raw or exposed. I felt...seen, which was oddly comforting in a way I really didn't want to examine at the moment. "Thank you. So are you going to open that door, or was this hike just for fun?"

He stepped to the side and opened the door with a flourish. "After you."

I stepped onto the deck, and my hair went wild, flying varying directions in the strong breeze that whipped at me from the ocean. I fisted the strands in one hand and the hem of my dress in the other as Jackson came through the door behind me and shut it. We stood on a circular deck just below the top of the lighthouse, where a light rotated in a steady rhythm at least ten feet above our heads.

His wide grin had me questioning his sanity. "You look just like you did when I first saw you."

"Oh," I said softly. He remembered the beach that well?

"Here." He came close enough that I felt the heat of his skin as his arms reached around me, replacing my hands with his. "Now you can grab a hair tie if you want."

"What makes you think I have a hair tie?" I arched a brow, refusing to give in to how damned handsome the man looked in the moonlight.

"Don't all women keep a hair tie in their purse?" He nodded toward mine, which I'd slung diagonally over my shoulder.

"I'm not sure there's anything that *all women* do," I retorted, knowing full well that I had a tie in my bag. But common sense prevailed, and I surrendered my hair and hem to him, then reached for my handbag. My cheek brushed his bare forearm when I turned my head, and I muttered an apology as I quickly found the tie and restrained my hair in a quick bun.

Jackson won another point when he didn't mention that I had, indeed, had a tie as he'd assumed. Instead, he took hold of my shoulders and turned me slowly so I faced the ocean. "Worth the hike?"

My breath caught, and I moved forward to lean against the cool, metal railing, hoping it was enough to keep my skirt from flying up over my underwear. These were definitely a step up from my Hello Kitties, and I wasn't exactly ready to show them off.

"It's beautiful," I said, unsure if the wind made it too hard for Jackson to hear. The full moon played off the waves in the distance, streaking a path of white across the water that led straight to the beach, illuminating the coastline in a blend of light and shadows, softening the dramatic landscape.

"Hmmm?" Jackson questioned as he came up behind me, his head over my shoulder.

"I said it's beautiful." My mind drew a blank as I struggled to think about anything besides how close he was. How there were merely inches—if that—between us, torturous yet necessary. Those inches were all that kept the flutters in my stomach from turning into something far more potent and dangerous.

"Yeah. It sure is."

I tilted my head slightly, and his lips brushed my ear. Air rushed into my lungs as that tiny, accidental caress sent shimmers of unexpected pleasure down my spine.

"Do you see that?" He reached across my shoulder with a pointed finger.

"The waves?" I looked out to the ocean, following the path he'd given me.

"This is where the cold Labrador current meets the warm Gulf Stream. It makes the shoals shift in unpredictable ways that can cause ships to wreck." His voice was soft in my ear, his lips close but not touching me.

"How many do you think have been wrecked over the years?" The waves seemed almost harmless in the distance.

"The experts around here estimate about two thousand."

"The Graveyard of the Atlantic," I remembered, watching the waves. So beautiful, yet so dangerous. "You think there are still shipwrecks happening out there?"

"Right now? I hope not. But yeah, they happen around here more than we'd like, that's for sure." He dropped his arm and moved so he stood beside me, both of our hands on the railing. His clenched the metal as he took what looked to be a steadying breath.

"It seems almost foolish, doesn't it? To know how dangerous the water is and still choose to sail it? That seems like the definition of insanity to me. Once something shows you how deadly it can be, I choose to believe it and steer clear." The wind swept over the backs of my thighs, and I immediately missed the heat of him while simultaneously cursing my decision to wear a dress.

Pain flickered across his features, and my stomach lurched. I'd touched a nerve somehow.

He caught me watching him and forced a sad smile. "Sorry, my mind drifted. My parents died in a boating accident when I was seventeen."

"Oh God. Jackson, I'm so sorry." My stomach halted its lurch and just plain plummeted as my hand covered his. "I didn't mean…" I didn't even have words to cover my utter insensitivity. Seventeen. He'd been so young.

"Don't be. You didn't know." He looked back over the water as his fingers splayed on the railing. Mine fell into the gaps, and he tightened slightly, leaving our fingers laced. "Dad knew the waters really damn well, but the weather came in faster than forecasted and…" He exhaled slowly. "I lost them both off the coast of Maine. The thing about the ocean is she can lull you into thinking you're her equal. You understand her tides, her waves, her currents, and you begin to feel like you're partners, as though the love you feel for her is somehow returned."

"Love, huh?" I questioned softly, wondering if that's what had driven him to study oceanography. Where I had avoided everything that reminded me of my loss, he'd embraced and examined the very thing that killed his parents. Had that exorcised the demons of his grief? Or was I the only one who had those?

"Love," he confirmed. "Being out there on the water is as life-affirming to some people as sex is to others. The ocean is in their soul. And you're right, maybe it's a little bit of insanity that brings people out on those waters in particular." He nodded toward the divergence of the two currents in front of us. "But from what I've seen, the only emotions that overpower our own sense of self-preservation are obsession and love, and the ocean is both for a lot of people. They fuck up when they forget that she's too deep, too stubborn, and too powerful to love you back. There's never a partnership because she's always in control."

"I'm so sorry you lost them." It was all I could think to say. It was the only thing I'd ever wanted to hear, so maybe it was the same for him.

His fingers tightened around mine in a reassuring squeeze. "Thanks. They would have really liked you, and they would have been utterly wrapped around Finley's finger."

I made a mental note to call Mama tomorrow and absorbed his words quietly as a comfortable silence fell over us. The ocean looked exactly as he described. Inky black under the night sky, breathtakingly beautiful, and wickedly powerful. His thumb moved, stroking the edge of my pinky in an absentminded pattern. It was soothing—comforting, even—and I had no desire to pull away or put distance between us.

Holy shit, I liked the way he touched me. I liked way more than that about him, if I was being honest with myself. Sure, I liked the way he looked, but there wasn't much to *not* like. His profile was strong, his chin carved and nose straight—with a slight bump that made me wonder if he'd broken it once—and his lips somehow managed to look hard and deliciously soft at the same time. I'd seen enough of his body to know what was under that shirt, and the simple memory of him jogging toward me on the beach sent a flash of heat through my veins strong enough to kick up my pulse. He turned his head, looking down the beach, and I mentally sent up a prayer of thanks that he hadn't caught me staring at him or turned those eyes on me.

I swung my face the opposite direction and found a thick strip of scarred land that ran between the lighthouse and our own homes. "What's that from?" I pointed with my free hand so I wouldn't have to let go of his.

He followed my gaze, still stroking that swirling pattern on my skin. "That's the path from when they moved the lighthouse."

"They what? No way. This lighthouse?" My jaw dropped. This thing was *huge,* and they moved it?

"This lighthouse," he confirmed, a corner of his mouth lifting in clear amusement at my disbelief. "A little over twenty years ago, they moved it from there"—he gestured a little north, where the path ended at the beach—"to here. It was the only thing they could do to save it."

"Save it? From what? Men who mislead unsuspecting women expecting a little sightseeing and get a StairMaster instead?" I raised my eyebrows, and he laughed. *Flirting.* Oh my stars, I was flirting, and it felt…great. My heart stuttered a beat in the best possible way, and I outright smiled, reveling in both the emotion and my ability to feel it.

Jackson's eyes flared, darting between my lips and my eyes, before he shook his head slightly and blinked. "The ocean," he replied in a voice that sounded like it had been scraped over sandpaper. "They had to save it from the ocean."

"Because the shoreline changes so much."

"Exactly."

Those *eyes.* Even in the moonlight, when I couldn't see every shade of blue that made them so irresistible, they turned my knees to Jell-O. Or maybe that was just Jackson in general, if I was still on that honest-with-myself kick.

I looked back to the path. "How far did they move it?"

"Man, I'm glad I studied for this date." He laughed. "Twenty-nine hundred feet."

I didn't cringe at the word "date." "How on earth do you move something this big?"

"Just like you take on any huge project—one tiny step at a time. It took them twenty-three days and a hell of a lot of engineering."

"Did they take it apart and rebuild it?" I leaned over a little, taking in the distance to the ground and hoping it was the dizzying height that had my heart strumming faster. God, what was *wrong* with me? I'd been around Jackson plenty of times and never had such a schoolgirl reaction.

You've never been completely alone with him before. There had always been Finley, or Sam, or an entire barbecue's worth of people around us.

"No, they left it intact."

"Impossible."

He laughed. "Why?"

"Look at this thing! It's huge!" I gawked up at him.

"Don't forget old. Almost a hundred and fifty years," he added, turning his body toward mine. "Told you I studied." Like we were a pair of magnets, I moved to face him, our hands falling from the railing but staying twined. With his free hand, he stroked the back of his fingers down my cheek slowly. "But she's also too important, too unique, and too beautiful to stand by and do nothing while she drowns. While she might look delicate, she's actually incredibly strong and capable of taking a storm or two."

I stilled, knowing that he'd stopped talking about the lighthouse.

"Jackson," I begged, but I wasn't sure what for.

"Morgan." His fingers slid to the back of my neck while his thumb repeated the stroke across my cheek.

God, that felt good. A rush of longing filled my entire body, stirring parts of me I was sure had long since died—the parts that remembered need, want, and desire. The parts that remembered how it felt to be the object of someone else's desire, too. And those neglected pieces of me hungered as they roused, demanding to be acknowledged and appeased.

I fought to find a shred of my common sense amid the onslaught of pure, selfish craving that had me staring at his mouth.

"You don't want this," I told him softly, my Jackson-less hand clutching the railing as if it would keep me grounded.

"I don't want what?" he questioned, lowering his head until our foreheads touched. "Because you can't tell me that I don't want you."

Oh God. Joy, disbelief, yearning—emotions flew at me so fast I could barely process them, but one stood out the loudest. Fear. Was it fear *for* him or fear *of* him? *Yes.*

"You don't. You can't. I am a mess, and not just a little mess. I'm the kind that has a pile of wreckage for a heart, anxiety attacks I can't control, and a therapist I see every week in the hopes that I can eventually talk to my best friend again or just open the door of a truck I never wanted." My eyes squeezed shut. "Trust me, you don't want this. You don't want *me*."

"Morgan—"

"No." I retreated from his arms, and my skin ached at the loss of contact. Was I so desperate for human touch? *Just Jackson's.* "I'm not being coy or playing games, which is ironic since I used to be really good at all that. I'm genuinely telling you to run for your life."

"From you?" The skin between his eyebrows wrinkled, and I was struck with a ridiculous urge to smooth it with my fingers.

"Yes!"

His jaw ticked, and his eyes turned fierce, pinning me to the lighthouse deck with the force of his stare. "Morgan, you don't get to tell me what I want any more than I get to dictate your feelings."

I blinked, admitting the undeniable logic of his statement. "That's fair."

"If you don't want to start something with me, then that's your choice, and I'll respect it, no matter how badly I want to convince you otherwise."

"Thank you." Crap, was that a twinge of disappointment that lowered my shoulders?

His head tilted back as his chest rose and fell with a deep breath, as if he was the one struggling for control—not me. When he met my gaze again, I held my breath.

What the hell did I really want? *To press pause on this moment, call Sam and get her take on it, and then press play again so I know what I'm supposed to be feeling.* Like that was going to happen.

"I know about the anxiety attacks. Remember, I was there for one," he stated simply, like we were talking about what we'd had for lunch. "I'm glad you have a therapist because I'm well aware that you're working through something that you're not ready to let me in on, and that's okay. You don't exactly know everything about me, either, and chances are the more you know, the more you'll think you're the one who should run." He didn't move a muscle, but the way he looked at me felt like a caress all the same. "In fact, I know you'll be the one running."

"From you?" I scoffed. "You're the most together person I know." Even if he was still pining for his ex, but who was I to judge?

"Then you should meet more people." He cocked an eyebrow at me. "Morgan, I like you, and I don't just mean as my neighbor. I want you in a way that keeps me up at night, mentally calculating the steps between my door and yours. I want you so badly that I barely stop myself from taking those steps every single night. I have no problem owning my feelings about you. And while I'm not going to push you for something when you obviously don't feel the same—"

My jaw dropped. "I never said I don't want you—"

"I damn well think you deserve to know that you might preach you're a mess, but I think you're pretty fucking perfect, wreckage and all."

Every protest died on my tongue at the tangible sincerity in his voice.

"Are you struggling?" he started again. "Yeah. That's obvious. But, God, you're a fighter, even if you don't see it. You had the courage to pick up your whole life and move because you knew you needed a fresh start. You might not be able to open that truck door, but you didn't just dump it in some storage lot and run. That shit is in your front yard where you choose to confront it every day. You push your boundaries, whether it's on a surfboard or letting me drag you to a barbecue. You have loyal friends, which means you're pretty damn loyal yourself, and when death came flying at you in the form of the weathervane that time forgot, your first instinct was to protect my daughter, which is enough to make me fall at your feet without the fact that you're the most exquisite woman I've ever laid eyes on—which you are." He lifted that eyebrow in challenge again.

My lips parted, and the butterflies in my stomach fluttered so fast the friction warmed me from the inside out, even as they threatened to turn to flame and catch my body on fire. He actually wanted *me*. He saw the mess and wanted me anyway, somehow finding beauty in everything I called wreckage. Damn it, I didn't want it to be wreckage anymore. I wanted to be whole again. I wanted to have something to offer this man who took me hiking in the moonlight and pulled me away from my own shadows with his light.

My breath abandoned me as the realization hit—he made me want to *live*, not just survive and hope for the best. He'd reignited that spark within me from the moment I'd felt that flare of attraction on the beach and the care he'd taken when rescuing me from my own staircase. That spark grew every time he made me laugh, or smile, or roll my eyes. It thrived when I made plans with him, finally willing to look forward in my life. I might have been doing the work in therapy, but there was no denying that Sam was right—Jackson had become my reward for learning to live again.

"Don't look at me like that." He raked his hand over his hair. "You're gorgeous, and that's not even close to being the best part about you. Every time you let me in to that head of yours, I feel like the luckiest asshole on the planet, and there's *nothing* I've found that would make me want you any less. God, everything about you pulls me in closer without even trying. Like I said—I can own that. And sure, the way I feel about you scares the shit out of me, but that's what tells me it's real. So yeah, I'll respect your lack of feelings because I feel *way* too much, but please don't tell me that I can't want you, because I do. And I'm sure of this enough to wait until you're in a place to see just how amazing you—"

I stopped his words with my lips.

Chapter Eleven

Jackson

One second I was laying into the woman about how incredible she was, and the next, she was pressed against me with her mouth on mine.

I lost a heartbeat or two in shock, but I got with the program in the next breath, wrapping an arm around her waist and cradling the nape of her neck with the other.

"Morgan?" I whispered against her lips in question.

"Kiss me, Jackson," she demanded, looping her arms around my neck.

The words struck me like a match to a pile of kindling—the flame instant and consuming. I locked down the need pounding through my veins and kissed her gently, savoring her quick intake of breath and the way she rose against me for more. I was not going to fuck this up by moving too fast. I'd keep up these light, sipping kisses all night if that kept her in my arms. *Sound plan. Take it slow.*

She swept her tongue over my lower lip, then gently

tugged it between her teeth.

Fuck the plan.

I kissed her deep, sinking my tongue between her parted lips with a groan I couldn't contain. She tasted sweeter than I could have imagined, citrus with a hint of vanilla on her lips. Her arms tightened around me, and I tilted her head slightly so I could sink into her mouth over and over, learning every curve and line as her tongue rubbed and swirled around mine. More. I wanted more.

I wanted to kiss her until neither of us could remember any kiss that came before this one. My fingers flexed at her waist, holding her tight as our mouths moved together like we'd been kissing for years, not minutes. She fit perfectly against me, soft and curved everywhere I wasn't. My hand slid into her hair as the back of her dress whipped at my arm in the wind. *Do not think about what's under it.*

She gasped as another gust lifted the fabric, but she dove back into the kiss, her tongue darting into my mouth with little flicks that drove my need for her higher and wound me tighter. I lowered my arm over the curve of her ass and lifted, keeping my fingers splayed on her hip as I pivoted and took three steps, putting her back against the lighthouse so I could use my body to shelter her from the wind.

Her eyes flared at the contact, and I rested my forehead against hers as our breaths became choppy and harsh. Fuck me, how was I ever going to stop kissing her? She was one of those drugs you were never supposed to experiment with—one hit and I was addicted.

"Too much?" I asked, my voice rough as I lowered her feet to the deck.

She shook her head slowly, then ran her tongue over her lower lip. "Not enough." Her knee rose against the outside of my thigh.

I muttered a curse, then filled my hands with her ass

and picked her up the way I'd wanted to since the moment I'd found those curves dangling in my face. Her long legs wrapped around my waist, her ankles locking at the small of my back as I brought my mouth to hers.

She whimpered, one of her hands in my hair and the other holding the nape of my neck like I was a prisoner instead of a more-than-willing participant. The sound didn't help the current situation in my shorts, and I didn't honestly care. I kissed her deeper just so I could hear it again.

She ripped her mouth from mine and tilted her head back as she gasped for a breath. I moved to her neck, kissing a path down the slender, soft column and pausing to suck gently at the spots that made her grip tighten.

"Jackson," she moaned when I reached the sensitive spot beneath her ear.

I rocked against her instinctively, then stilled, letting my breath release slowly as I counted to five. The woman had me dancing on the edge of my self-control. I could have blamed it on my months of celibacy, but it was simply Morgan. Everything about her turned me on, and getting her in my hands and under my mouth robbed me of every logical thought, which wasn't good for either of us. I had to slow this down before we went too far.

She brushed her lips over my cheek and tightened her thighs at my waist as she made her way back to my mouth.

I groaned in surrender as I kissed her breathless, living for the caress of her tongue against mine. Fuck, I could feel the heat of her skin through the fabric of her dress. If I shifted my grip, I could slide my hand up her bare thigh—

Stop. You can't take this any further.

I mentally swatted my conscience when she rocked her hips over mine with a little moan. We were going to be so damned good together. I'd give her as many orgasms as her body could take and then start all over again, only stopping when she was just as addicted to me as I already was to her. I'd be whatever she needed—

You're the opposite of what she needs, and you know it.

I stilled against her mouth.

She didn't know. I had dumped my feelings all over her without offering her the one truth that would give her the information she really needed.

I sent up a prayer that this wouldn't be the only time I kissed Morgan. Then I fought my own instincts and slowed the tempo, gentling my mouth even as she whimpered in protest.

"We should go," I said against her lips, then gave her one last soft, lingering kiss before easing her legs from my waist. My body was never going to forgive me, but I'd never forgive myself if I let this happen under false pretense.

"Okay." She blinked at me slowly, her eyes hazy with the same desire that pumped through my veins and had me harder than the stone at her back. Once her feet reached the ground, I took her hand in mine and led her back into the lighthouse, shutting the door after us.

"Ready to head down?" I asked, trying to breathe steadily and failing miserably.

She nodded, her chest rising and falling just as erratically as mine.

I walked down ahead of her just in case she stumbled, her fingers laced with mine as I held her hand awkwardly behind my back. Unless my shoulder dislocated, I wasn't letting go.

I used every single one of those 257 steps to formulate a plan—to come up with a way to phrase the truth of what I did for a living so she wouldn't run. By the time we reached the ground, my breathing had evened out, but my mind was blank.

We thanked John for letting us into the lighthouse after hours and walked back along the sidewalk to the parking lot.

"Thank you," she said with a little sigh, smiling up at me. "That really was worth the hike."

"My pleasure." I tried to smile, but it came out weirdly enough that Morgan's brows knit.

"What's wrong?" she asked as we approached the car.

I tried to answer, but the words just weren't there. She'd been brave enough to lay her shit out—well, everything but the cause of her anxiety attacks—and here I was fumbling for an explanation.

She raised her eyebrows at me when I opened her door, but she got in without protest.

I slid behind the wheel and fired up the ignition, then slowly pulled out of the lot.

"Did I do something wrong?" Her voice trembled on the last word in a way that broke my fucking heart.

"No. God, no. You're perfect. That was perfect. Kissing you is…" I shook my head as we drove out of the park.

"Perfect?" she guessed, but her smile was shaky.

"More than. But I didn't plan on that happening." My left hand gripped the wheel as my right reached for hers.

"Right," she replied with a touch of ice, retracting her hand and placing it in her lap.

The move was a direct gut-punch, and I more than deserved it. "What do you mean, right?"

She shrugged, staring out the windshield. "I mean I'm sure you didn't plan on me basically jumping on you and kissing you like that. I'm sorry."

"You're sorry?" I snapped in surprise, my gaze jerking toward hers as much as possible while still keeping my eyes on the road. "Why the hell would you be sorry?"

"Because it's obviously not something you wanted!" she exclaimed with a sharp note of self-loathing.

"Trust me, it's definitely something I wanted. Something I still want." I was tempted to put her hand on my dick to prove just how much want there actually was. "There's just something you need to know about me first, and I was going to tell you tonight—"

"I already know you're still in love with your ex."

What?

"Hell no!" I pulled off the pavement, turning onto one of the many dirt roads that led to the beach and putting the car in park so I could turn to face her. This wouldn't wait the five minutes it would take to drive us home. "I'm not in love with Claire. No fucking way." Just the thought spiked my blood pressure.

Her face puckered with confusion. "You're not?"

"No!"

"Then what could I possibly need to know before a kiss?" she fired back. "Are you a murderer?"

"No." I scoffed.

"A kidnapper? Rapist? Do you have three other wives spread around the United States?" She shrugged in obvious frustration.

"I don't have a single wife, let alone three—"

"Then what—"

"I'm a pilot!" *Shit. Shit. SHIT.* It fell out of my mouth so carelessly that I wanted to suck it back in, hit rewind on this moment, and do it all again.

She stilled completely. No blinks, no cursing me out, no glares, nothing. I wasn't even sure she was breathing.

I sure wasn't.

"You said you were in the coast guard," she accused softly, still staring at me in what I assumed had to be shock.

"I am," I assured her, leaning on the console between us. "I'm a search and rescue pilot for the coast guard."

Her eyes flared, not in fear but with stark, palpable terror. "Helicopters," she finally whispered.

"Helicopters," I confirmed, swallowing the rising knot in

my throat. "This wasn't how I wanted to tell you. I was going to explain why I chose my career and—"

"Take me home." The demand was icy and flat as she turned away from me.

"Morgan, please. Let me explain." My mind scrambled with panic. If I could just get her to listen, then she'd understand, right?

She opened the door.

"Where are you going?" I reached for her elbow.

She turned just enough to glare at my fingers on her sweater.

I removed them immediately. Fuck, this wasn't going well.

"If you won't take me home, I'll walk. I can see the lighthouse from my deck, which means if I take this trail, the beach will lead me home." She paused, her hand lingering on the handle.

"I'll take you home."

She shut the door, then stared out the windshield as I put the car in reverse—something I wished I could do with the last five minutes of my life. We pulled onto the pavement, and I headed toward our houses. The silence between us wasn't just tense; it was sharp enough to draw blood—or break hearts.

I had to fix this. She wasn't just a friend or the woman who lived next door. I cared about her, and I wasn't willing to let whatever this was between us go without a fight. Fuck that. A battle. I put my mental armor on and prepared to go to war against her past in the hopes that she'd give me a chance for a future.

"When my parents died," I began.

"No." She shook her head. "You don't get to speak. You lied to me."

"I never told you I wasn't a pilot." I turned onto our street.

"Semantics don't make you honest, Jackson," she snapped.

When faced with which driveway to pull into, I chose mine, hoping it would give me more time. "I get that. And you're right. I should have told you sooner, but I knew you'd react just like this." I put the car in park. "And I wanted you to know *me*—not just what I did—before we had this conversa—Morgan!"

She was already out of the car.

I killed the ignition and took off after her, catching up midway between our yards. "Please, just give me a chance to explain."

She spun around and stuck her finger in my face. "You've had all the time in the world to do that, and you chose not to!"

I barely managed to stop my momentum quickly enough to keep from running her over, and then she was off again, striding toward her house.

"Kitty, come on!" How the hell was I supposed to get her to understand if she wouldn't even listen? I chased after her like the desperate fool I was.

"Oh no," she threw over her shoulder as she reached her steps. "You don't get to call me that. Never again." She marched up two of the steps and then paused, going still as a statue.

My feet froze to the very sand beneath them. I knew an approaching storm when I saw one, and she was a cat five hurricane spinning just off my coast.

Her shoulders rose slightly, and then she turned on her steps and advanced toward me. She was a storm all right, and I wasn't sure I'd be standing after she released all the wrath in those eyes.

"You knew." She flung the accusation from a few feet away, planting her feet and crossing her arms.

I swallowed.

"You knew I would shut you out the moment you told me you were a damned flyboy."

"Yes." This had just gotten *so* much worse for me.

"You know what happened, don't you?" She seethed, her jaw clenching.

Fuck. My eyes closed momentarily with the realization that I'd lost this battle long before I'd come clean in the car. I took a deep, fortifying breath and found her staring at me with the kind of loathing that only broken trust could evoke.

"I know what happened to Will," I admitted.

She blanched, her eyes flying wide, then narrowing. "Don't ever say his name!" she cried, that finger coming at me again. "You don't have the right!"

"Okay." This was so far beyond bad that my stomach took up permanent residence in my feet.

"How dare you bring him into this!" Her finger trembled.

"Morgan, he's *already* in this."

She flinched and lowered her arm. "Who told you what happened? I know it wasn't Sam. She wouldn't do that to me."

"No one told me." I shifted my weight, hoping the motion would appease my need to cross the distance between us and hold her. It didn't. "I saw the wings that day you had me get the registration out of the truck, and the name on those dog tags hanging from the mirror is the same one on the registration."

"And you what? Googled him?" she fired back.

"Pretty much." My lips pressed in a thin line as I nodded, knowing the gathering fire in her eyes was about to come right for me.

"How dare you!" Her hands dropped to form fists at her sides.

"I'm sorry. I know I shouldn't have, but you'd just had that anxiety attack and—"

"And you decided that my past was up for investigation? You wanted to see what had turned me into a neurotic shell of who I used to be?" she cried.

"I wanted to solve a mystery that I knew you wouldn't explain. And I don't think you're neurotic. I think you went through something that you're still recovering from." I tucked my hands into my pockets.

"If a woman doesn't want to tell you about the fucked-up past that she's barely survived, then you don't go searching for it, you asshole!"

My eyebrows rose. That was the first time I'd ever heard the woman curse. "You're right, and I'm so sorry."

She offered me a look that clearly told me I was an idiot. "I'm sorry doesn't remotely begin to cover this! You went looking for something you have zero right to know. If I wanted you to know, I would have told you! You. Had. No. Right!"

"I'm sorry, Morgan," I said again. "I will make it up to you, I swear."

"You can make it up to me by staying the hell away from me."

I felt the blood rush from my face. "Please don't ask that from me."

"I'm not exactly giving you a choice," she spat. "What did you think was going to happen? That I'd say it's perfectly fine that you fly those death traps, and we'd…" She tilted her head. "What exactly do you want from me, Jackson?"

"You," I replied, taking a step toward her. "I just want you."

Her chin rose. "I'm not something you can have. Not now, and apparently not ever."

She was pissed and hurt, and I knew there was a chance those words were simply a reflection of those feelings, but damn did they sting.

"I know that what you've been through has to make you scared of being with another pilot–"

"Don't presume to know my feelings just because you threw Will's name into a search engine," she interrupted. "You might know all about how he died, but that doesn't qualify you to even begin knowing the first thing about him, or the way I feel about him, or you, or anything!" Color flooded her cheeks, and her shoulders rose and fell fast enough that I started to worry about her having another attack.

"Fine, then how do you feel?" I questioned, my voice rising slightly. "Because you never talk about it. You've told me that you don't talk to your best friend and that you can't open that truck door, but you *never* go into the why of it. You know everything about me with the exception of how I make my money, and you never give me the same access. You never let me in!"

"Let you in? Like I actually want you to see inside this?" She gestured to her torso. "What do you want to know, Jackson? That I dream about him every night? That I watch the video he left for me before bed or I can't sleep? That my nightmares are full of the sound of crunching metal and gunshots, but I wasn't there with him, so my mind gives me a thousand different scenarios?"

"Morgan," I whispered, reaching for her.

She moved away from my touch. "You think I'm *scared* to be with another pilot? I wasn't even *with* Will! We never got the damned chance, and look how that turned out! I'm not scared of what you do—I'm terrified. I'm paralyzed by anxiety attacks I can't control, and they're so bad that one of my best friends has to live with me until I get through a therapy program for it! The same friend who Skypes with her husband every day because he's flying helicopters in the same fucking country that took the man I loved, and every breath I take is heavy with dread that those fucking uniforms are going to show up at the door for Sam! Is that what you want to hear?" Her voice pitched to a near-scream.

"Yes. I want to know how you feel, and I don't care if it's ugly." I would take whatever she wanted to give me—whatever she was.

Her eyes narrowed. "How I feel about you isn't ugly, and that's the problem. I moved here so I could lick my wounds in peace, and you appeared, all gorgeous and smart and funny and so damned concerned about *me*. And you tell me you're in the coast guard, and I figure oceanographers can't get hurt in the coast guard, right?"

I opened my mouth, then shut it again, because anything I said would only dig me deeper into this hole I created, and right now it was the size of the Grand Canyon.

"And then you let me get close to you! And Finley! And suddenly, I'm waking up again, and I start looking forward to things like seeing you. And I feel happy when I'm around you! And I start to realize that when I'm with you, *he* isn't with me, and as much as that fucks with my head, I accept it. You push me to start living again, and so I do, and then you take me up a lighthouse, and I kiss you and it's just..." Her eyes closed as she shook her head, and when she opened them again, she was even angrier. "It's the most incredible kiss I've ever had!"

"That's not a bad thing. It was incredible for me, too. The best I've ever felt." Hope brought my stomach back into place.

"You don't get it. Will was the last person to kiss me! That was supposed to be the best, and then there you are, blowing my mind, and you have the nerve to make me want you!" Her outstretched hands moved with every word.

"Morgan, I want you, too. I've wanted you since I saw you on that beach, and I knew we'd end up here the moment you mocked my barbecue skills and ate that burger anyway. I. Want. You."

"Damn you!" she screamed, her eyes filling with tears that caught in the moonlight. "Damn you for making me want you! For making me think I have a shot at being happy again and then snatching it away because you do the same fucking thing he did!" She pointed at the truck parked fifteen feet away, just outside the boathouse. "You do the same thing that got him killed, and I swore I would never put myself in that position again! Never! Not for you. Not for anyone!" The first tear spilled over and raced down her cheek.

"Don't cry. God, Kitty, don't cry." I moved toward her, but she walked straight past me, headed for the truck.

"Don't touch me! Stay away from me! How could you do it?" she shouted, not even bothering to look back. "How could you make me want you, make me think we have a chance, and then break me into a million pieces? It's not fair, and I hate you for it!"

My heart lurched, but there was nothing I could say or do to alleviate her pain. There was an overwhelming chance that the possibility of what we could be might not be enough to outweigh what loving him had cost her.

She grabbed the door handle to the truck and flung it open only a few inches before slamming it shut again.

Holy shit, she did it. She opened the door.

"Why? Why me? Why that fucking helicopter? Why?" she screamed, punctuating each question with another slam of the door.

Watching her breakthrough felt a lot like watching her fall apart, and it was so fucking painful that my hand grabbed at my chest.

Headlights caught my attention as a car drove down Morgan's driveway, but she didn't stop yelling at me as she abused the door. The car drove past Morgan and parked next to the Mini. It was Sam.

She got out and shut the door, then stared, drop-jawed, at Morgan before looking at me. Her gaze darted between us, her head swiveling back and forth like we were a tennis match before she approached me.

"You made me want you!" Morgan screamed, slamming the door again.

"What the hell did you do?" Sam asked, arching an eyebrow in clear warning as she folded her arms across her chest.

"I told her I'm a search and rescue pilot for the coast guard. I fly helicopters," I told her without taking my eyes from Morgan's rage.

"You have got to be shitting me," Sam seethed.

"I wish I was." At that moment, I wanted to be anything else. "I don't know what to do. Should I go over there?"

She snorted. "Unless you'd like Morgan to put your head in that doorframe between slams, I'd stay right where you are. Fucking flyboys." She muttered that last part.

"God damn it!" Morgan shouted, throwing her weight into the slams of the heavy door. "Stupid. Fucking. Helicopters!"

"She doesn't usually swear," Sam noted.

"Picked up on that. Think she's picturing me?" I questioned, my voice lowering. Every time she slammed the door, my heart felt the impact.

"Probably." She shrugged, then sighed, watching her friend.

"I never meant to hurt her."

"Guys like you never do."

"Know a lot of guys like me?" I challenged, still staring at the woman I couldn't get out of my head.

"A few." She huffed.

"Is she going to be all right? Have you seen her do this before?" God, I wanted to wrap my arms around Morgan, but I somehow doubted she'd let me comfort her when I was the one who'd hurt her in the first place.

"Open the door or rage out her feelings?" Sam questioned.

"The feelings. I know all about the door."

From the corner of my eye, I saw her look at me like I might not be as stupid as she first thought. "Huh. I'm glad. And no, I've never seen her lose her shit like this. She usually shoves it all inside for fear of hurting someone else with her own feelings. She's an expert emotional masochist."

I watched Morgan rage, seeing it differently with that knowledge. "So, while she obviously hates me, at least it's good that she's letting it out."

Morgan screamed out her hatred with another slam, proving my point.

"Did she have an anxiety attack when you told her that you're a pilot?"

"No. She yelled. A lot. But no anxiety attack that I could tell."

Sam sighed in obvious relief. "Then I'd call that tantrum over there progress, and we're just going to wait over here and let that fire burn itself out."

"God, she's so pissed at me." I shoved my hands into my pockets.

"Yeah, she is."

"How could you do this to me? You made me fall for you!" Morgan's voice was turning hoarse from screaming.

I sucked in a ragged breath. She'd fallen for me? That had to be a good thing, right? That meant I had a shot.

"You let me think we had a chance, and then you yanked the rug! You kissed me, and you told me I was beautiful! You told me we'd try! You promised we'd finally be together, and then you fucking left me! How could you do that to me? How could you die for them and not live for me? I hate you! You ruined my life! I loved you, and you ruined *me*!"

Nausea gripped me hard and fast.

"I don't think you're the one she's picturing anymore," Sam said softly, squeezing my arm to pull the sting from her words. "Why don't you head home? I'll take care of her."

"I don't want to leave her." Not like he had. Morgan needed to know that I wasn't the guy who walked away.

"That wasn't a suggestion. Go home, Jax. Give her a little space to wrap her head around what you told her. If you can't tell, the last flyboy she fell for shattered her into a million little pieces, and she's still trying to put herself back together." She squeezed my arm again. "Go. You can't help her right now, and once she calms down and realizes she's spent the better part of ten minutes screaming at a ghost and taking it out on his truck, she's going to be even more embarrassed that you witnessed it."

Logically, I knew she was right, but everything in my body rebelled at the thought of walking up my stairs. "I want her, Sam. We have something, and I'm not going to let her go without a fight."

"Fight tomorrow, Jax. She's engaged in a whole other battle right now." She patted my arm and walked toward Morgan, who was still slamming that door like it had personally broken her heart.

I ripped my eyes from Morgan and headed for my house. Halfway up my stairs, the slamming stopped, and I turned to see Morgan fall into Sam's arms. Fuck, I could hear her sobbing from here. The sound tore right through my ribs and raked giant gashes down my heart.

Sam looked at me over Morgan's shoulder and shook her head.

I got the message. Locking every muscle in my body to avoid rushing to Morgan's side, I stood silently and watched Sam lead her up the stairs and into her house. Tomorrow. Tomorrow, I would go over and plead my case.

My footsteps felt heavy as I trudged up my steps, but I made it. I gave Morgan's door a long, heavy look and then unlocked my own door, so flustered that it took me a couple tries to get the damned thing open.

I threw my keys on the kitchen counter and grabbed a bottle of water out of the fridge and twisted the top off. All the alcohol in the world wouldn't help this situation.

"It's about time you got here. I've been waiting for ages."

I crushed the bottle in my fist at the sound of her voice, and water gushed over my hand as I whipped around to see her standing at the end of the counter.

Claire. She smirked and tilted her head, her hair falling in soft auburn waves to rest below her shoulders left bare by the design of her shirt. She was beautiful, but for the first time in the seven years I'd known her, that beauty didn't stir me. It didn't so much as entice or attract me, either.

"What the hell are you doing here?" I growled.

"Me?" She blinked, all innocent, and then her expression changed into a smile that was worthy of all those movies she'd walked out on us for. "Oh, Jax, I told you I'd come home to you."

Chapter Twelve

Morgan

I don't know how to thank you for what you've brought to my life. You were there when no one else was. You pinned those wings on my uniform graduation day, and if…if the worst has happened, then I pray you use those same wings to fly.

"And those are the new windows they installed this week. Watch this!" Sam pointed the laptop toward the windows that now spanned the entire east side of the first floor. "Morgan, press the button!" she urged over her shoulder.

"What am I looking at exactly?" Grayson's voice filled the living room, and I couldn't help but smile as I reached for the remote. Sam was always happiest when she got the chance to Skype with him.

"Watch this!" I called out, then pressed the top button on the remote Steve had given me two days ago.

The line of windows split in the middle of the house,

the panels retracting and stacking on their individual tracks until the entire wall stood open to the ocean, minus the three support beams Steve swore they could do nothing about.

The breeze filled the house, ruffling the pages of my book. I sank farther into the couch and drew my knees up to shelter the hardback.

"Shit. That's impressive." High praise coming from Grayson Masters.

"Right? But all hell breaks loose if we open the front door at the same time. We learned that one the hard way," Sam told him.

My entire renovation file had turned into that letter scene from *Harry Potter.* Papers had flown *everywhere.* Just remembering the pain of picking them all up and getting them back in order was enough to make me press the middle button.

The windows reversed their previous pattern until they formed a solid wall against the wind.

"I bet it does. Hey, Morgan?" Grayson called out.

Sam pivoted the laptop so I found myself staring at the Apache pilot's face. Guy was a bodybuilder, and from the unforgiving cut of his already-carved chin, I guessed he spent most of his free time at the gym over there.

"What do you want, Grayson?" I teased, the tone coming easily. Being myself around him was easier than with the others. Then again, he'd had a front-row seat to my painfest, so it wasn't like I had to hide anything around him.

A corner of his mouth lifted to what could almost be called a smile. "It's good to see you, too, Morgan."

"It's always lovely to see your happy, shiny face." I laid on the accent thick and gave him a nose scrunch that made Sam laugh.

"Tell me you've thought about hurricanes with those giant-ass windows." His smile slipped.

I scoffed. "Turn your husband around, Sam."

"Watch this," she told him as she turned him to face the now-closed windows.

I pressed the bottom button on the remote and was immediately rewarded with a whirring sound. The room fell dark as the metal shutters descended, finally locking into place just below the deck level.

"Now that is sexy," Grayson remarked.

"European rolling shutters," I said loud enough for him to hear me, then pressed the button again and watched as the shutters rose, drenching the room with light.

Sam beamed at the laptop, and I looked away, giving my attention to my book.

"I take that back," Grayson said. "You're the sexy one. God, I miss you, baby."

"I miss you, too," she answered quietly, her voice tinged with sadness.

I looked at the words on the page but didn't read them. What if this was the last time she got to talk to him? What if his helicopter crashed just like Will's had?

"Do me one favor?" Sam asked as she settled onto the other end of the couch.

"Anything," he promised.

My heart ached, but I shook it off. Did I want a love like that? Yes. But was I jealous of what they were going through right now to make it work? Hell no.

"Tell Morgan to forgive Mr. Hottie-Coast-Guard-Rescue-Pilot next door?" she asked her husband sweetly.

My head popped up, and I gave her a good glare. She blatantly ignored me.

"Hell no. I'm not getting in the middle of that."

"I knew I loved you for a reason, Grayson," I called over to him.

Sam rolled her eyes. "Fine, at least tell her that she has to talk to him," she said, turning her head and aiming those last words right at me. "That man has left her a piece of sea glass on the doorstep every single day since she told him off. Every. Day. At least hear his side of the story."

My eyes drifted to the small pile on the side table. Six pieces in all.

"I know all the story I need to," I retorted, trying to focus on the letters that filled the page. "He flies a glorified version of the same damned helicopter as Will. End of story."

"If he's a Blackhawk guy, you tell her to run," Grayson teased. "If she's going to fall for a pilot, at least make sure he flies a real bird."

"It's a Jayhawk," I fired back before I could stop myself. Funny what you could learn on Google.

Sam sent me a knowing smile, and I glared for good measure.

"If you cared enough to look his shit up, then it's not the end of the story," Grayson remarked.

"No more love for you, Mr. Masters," I replied. "You know he looked Will up online, right?" That would get Grayson back on my side.

He swore, and I lifted a corner of my lips in a slight smirk. It felt good to be right.

"If he's that into you, I can't really blame him. If I'd thought someone stood between Sam and me? I wouldn't have stopped at a Google search."

"Traitor." My eyes narrowed.

"That's my man." Sam's smile was contagious, and I found myself shaking my head with a slight scoff of a laugh.

In truth, the only reason I hadn't googled Jackson's ex was because I didn't want to know anything about her or anyone who could walk away from their family the way she had.

The creak of a door opening sounded from the laptop,

and a muffled voice came over the speaker.

"Shit. I have to go, baby. I love you."

"I love you," she replied. "Be safe, okay?"

"Always," he answered.

Then he was gone.

Sam shut the laptop, then held it to her chest as her head fell to the back of the couch. "I miss him so damned much."

"I know you do. I'm sorry." I closed my book, then scooted so that I sat next to her. "What do you want to do today? We can do anything you want." I'd already listened to this week's recording of the Will story and rewarded myself with a trip to Christina's shop, where I'd spent an hour looking at all the gorgeous sea-glass necklaces she had, so my day was wide open.

"Anything?" Sam asked, her eyes sad as she stared up at the new, swirling ceiling fan.

"Anything," I assured her.

She sat up and put the laptop on the coffee table. "Good! Because I want you to stop wallowing and go talk to Jackson."

"Anything but *that*." I got off the couch and abandoned my copy of *To The Lighthouse* on the table.

"Come on, Morgan. You're miserable. You've been miserable for the past week! I've given you time to process, but now you're just stewing, and I'm not going to sit here silently while you push him away." She followed me as I headed toward the kitchen. It was the next major renovation.

"News flash. I've been miserable for the past *two years*," I fired back. Next week it would be exactly two years, and though I tried not to think about the approaching date, it lingered in my mind every possible minute. "And it's not like we have some relationship that I'm losing. He's just a guy who lives next door." I got out two glasses and set them on the counter. "Tea?"

"Only if it's sweet," she replied, leaning back against the

Formica.

"Honey, it's the South. It's always sweet." I poured us two glasses.

"He's not just a guy who lives next door," she argued, then thanked me for the tea as I passed her a glass. "He's the guy you want. The guy you said kissed like a god."

"Maybe I overexaggerated." I sipped my tea, knowing full well that I hadn't. Kissing Jackson was a religious experience. The man knew exactly what he was doing in that department, and he did it so well that my heart picked up the pace just thinking about it. If that man could rev me up using only his mouth, what would the rest of his body be capable of?

"Uh-huh," she challenged, lifting her eyebrow as she called out my bullshit.

"None of that matters," I grumbled. "The definition of insanity is doing the same thing over and over again expecting different results, and I'm not involving myself with another heartbreak just waiting to happen when I haven't fixed myself from the last one."

"You don't know that he's a heartbreak," Sam argued. "What if he's the love of your life and you miss out because you were too stubborn to walk across the damned yard and talk like adults?"

That wasn't possible. Will was the love of my life. Wasn't he?

But what if he…wasn't?

Damn, was I a horrible person for even thinking that?

"Morgan?" Sam asked, clearly expecting an answer.

I blinked, trying to recall what she'd said. "Even if he wasn't a pilot, it wouldn't work. The man is in love with his ex. Whether or not he denies it, I heard it in his voice when he talked about her. I'm not getting involved with someone who sees me as some kind of consolation prize. No, thank you."

Sam sighed. "And again, you don't know that. You're

assuming. We have so few chances to be happy. I almost missed out on my chance with Grayson because I was sure that he still loved Grace, and now I can't imagine what my life would have looked like without him in it."

What did my life look like without Jackson? My heart stuttered in protest, but I couldn't trust that thing, anyway. I'd been through worse. I'd survive. What I wouldn't survive was the moment he inevitably crashed into the damned ocean.

"That's different." I shook my head. "You guys are the definition of fate and happily ever after."

"We're the definition of a really good fight," Sam countered. "Look, I know the guy lied, and if what you're doing is punishing him with your silence, then I'm all for it. Make him suffer until you feel he's paid the price for being an asshole and hiding his job from you."

"Hiding his job? It's not that simple." I braced my hands against the counter as my stupid, foolish heart split in two, one side siding with logic and self-preservation and the other…siding with him.

"I know that." She set her glass down and gave me the motherlode of all sighs. "What do you like about him?"

"What?"

"Humor me." She shrugged. "What could it possibly hurt to answer? It's not like he's listening or you're giving him hope or something." Her eyebrows rose. "Unless you're scared that talking about it is going to make you rush up his stairs and jump him like you did at the top of that lighthouse, which, by the way, gives that boy an A-plus in the romantic date category, I don't care how pissed off you are."

The uninvited memory of his eyes in the moonlight and his arms around me smacked me in the heart, followed by the way his kiss had robbed me of every thought except *more* and *now*.

"Fine," I growled, ignoring Sam's little clap of happiness.

"I like that he sees me. Not just the shell that everyone does, but he actually sees *me*. It's like the man has X-ray vision for bullshit, because I can't fake anything around him, and in a way, it's so much easier because I don't even have to try."

"Okay. And?" she urged me on, hopping onto the counter and kicking her feet.

"And I like that he's a really good dad. Finley comes first, and he makes no excuses for that. His sun rises and sets on that little girl, and it might sound weird, but that's ridiculously hot."

"That's not weird. That's thousands of years of biology." Sam shrugged. "What else?"

I tucked my hair behind my ears. "I like that he pushes my boundaries, though I wish he'd let us stay in every once in a while. And I like that he's patient with me and so very careful, but he doesn't treat me like I'm breakable or weak. He just treats me like I'm something precious."

"Because you are," she assured me.

I humphed a little. "I like that he thinks so. I like that he's sure enough to tell me that he wants me and then actually throw down and fight about it. I've never had anyone willing to really fight for me before." It had always been me fighting for Will, begging him to give us a chance.

"That's definitely a plus in his column," Sam noted. "What else?"

"He knows I'm a mess. He's seen me fall to the ground during an anxiety attack, and he didn't run. He just helped me through it and came back for more. He's seen me assault Will's truck, and he's still showed up at the door every day."

"The door you refuse to open," Sam remarked with a judgy little flick of her gaze.

"I like that he keeps coming back," I admitted softly. "I don't want to, but I do."

"Hell, I like that about him, too. And I like that ever

since he's been coming around, you've begun looking at the world again. I like the hope that he gives *me* that you might just be happy one day."

I swallowed, feeling a slight burn in my throat, but the anxiety didn't kick in full throttle. Visualizing my throat opening, I slowly felt the muscles relax. "When I'm with him, Will isn't always the first thought in my mind," I admitted quietly. "I'm not saying I don't think about him when I'm with Jackson, because I do. But he kind of fades into the background. There's just not a lot of room for anyone else in my head when Jackson's around." The confession felt sinful, and I looked up at Sam, waiting for her to dole out my penance.

"I think that's a good thing, too," she said with a small, sad smile. "There's always going to be a part of you that loves Will. But that doesn't mean you don't have room in your heart for someone else, Morgan. Or that your heart won't grow to fit someone else in time."

"I feel guilty," I whispered.

"I know. And you shouldn't. Dr. Circe said that it's okay to start a new relationship, remember? In fact, she encouraged it at the same appointment she asked you to fill out that sheet about your not-so-stellar memories about Will." She nodded at the worksheet that still sat empty at the end of the counter. I had a feeling it might be my first truly failed homework assignment.

How was it fair to Will that I was supposed to trash him for homework while moving forward with Jackson?

"The homework is going to have to wait. And even if I wanted Jackson, how can I expect him to understand that my emotional speed limit rivals a sloth?"

"That's exactly what you tell him. And you want him, even if you're not ready to admit it. I know you." Her eyes softened in sympathy.

I shook my head.

"Okay. Tell me something you don't like about him," she challenged before taking a sip of her tea.

I rolled mine between my hands and brought my eyes up to meet hers. "I hate that he flies helicopters, and not just any helicopter—it's the coast guard version of Will's. What kind of messed-up fate is that? I hate this feeling that grips my belly when I think that if I fall for him—really and truly fall—that I won't survive having to bury him. I know that's really selfish of me to say considering that Grayson's in Afghanistan—"

"Stop." She fixed a determined stare on me. "You lost the man you loved, and I didn't. You get to say whatever you want to me whenever you want to say it. Now you listen. Jax isn't Grayson…or Will."

I flinched, but I held her gaze.

"Jax is a pilot, yes, but no one shoots at him. He's not going to Afghanistan or Iraq or anywhere like it. He's going out there"—she pointed toward the wall of windows—"so he can save lives. That's who that man is. He *saves* people. And you get to worry—God, I hate that it comes with the territory, but it does. Will's death traumatized you, and knowing that Jax flies is going to fuck with your head. That's understandable. That doesn't make you a mess—it makes you human. Plus, I've seen that man shirtless, and I'm shocked that didn't make your like list. Go figure, that boy is a damned pilot. You'd think we'd be better at spotting them by now."

"I guess I have a type," I drawled, rolling my eyes.

"Girl, don't we all." She grinned. "You're just going to have to decide if all those things you like about him are outweighed by the one thing you don't."

Mercy, I was an idiot for even *thinking* about it, for contemplating doing exactly what Sam suggested and talking to Jackson about my limits and our possibilities. Maybe it made me a traitor to Will's memory, but I wanted Jackson in my life.

What if he wouldn't wait for me to pull my shit together? What if I couldn't get past his job? But what would happen if I didn't even try?

"You have one more homework assignment today, right?" Sam prodded.

I sighed. "The truck."

"The truck." She nodded. "Want me to come with you?"

"No, I've got this." I forced a fake smile, and Sam rolled her eyes. "I do. I can do it."

"Okay, then get out there and open that door. Ten seconds. You hear me?" she ordered as I walked past her.

"Ten seconds," I agreed.

"And try not to beat the shit out of it this time," she called after me as I made it out the front door.

I shut it extra hard.

Embarrassed didn't even start to cover how I felt about that night—about what Jackson had seen before Sam forced him to go home. I'd been completely unhinged in my anger, and yet it had been the freest I'd been with my emotions since…forever.

I approached the truck like it was a wild animal ready to devour me if I turned my back. *Ten seconds*, I told myself. *You just open the door wide and look inside the truck for ten seconds, then close it.*

Dr. Circe had given me the assignment yesterday, calling it my next step in situational avoidance. Somehow, this seemed easier than disparaging Will on a piece of paper.

The handle was warm from the sun as my fingers wrapped around it. I took a deep breath and tugged. The door clicked open, and I swung it wide, stepping back so it didn't hit me.

One. The scent of warm leather reached me just long enough for Will to flood my mind. His voice filled my head, laughing as he put his baseball hat on over my hair.

Two. The breeze gusted, whipping past me, clearing that scent.

Three. His wings were still pinned to the visor on the driver's side.

Four. The sunlight caught on his dog tags, and I couldn't look away.

Five.

Six.

Seven. Those weren't the ones he was wearing when it happened.

Eight. His mother had that set.

Nine. She had the flag, too, when she was sober enough to remember where she put it.

Ten. I grabbed the edge of the door and slammed it home, not in anger this time but in pure desperation to shut the metaphorical door.

My chest heaved. *I did it.* There was no anxiety attack looming or anything. The memories stopped with the closing of the door. Oddly enough, I felt in control for the first time, as if I'd gained the power to open or shut the door to Will himself when I chose to.

I turned around to head back into the house and found Jackson staring at me from the middle of our yards.

My heart did a somersault.

He looked mouthwateringly good, but that was nothing different. I bet the man even looked delicious when he was hungover or sick, which was just unfair. He tucked his hands in his pockets and tilted his head to the side slightly as his mouth tightened and his eyes begged me to come closer. He was trying to give me the space I'd forced between us, and it only made me like him even more for it.

My pulse spiked, and the half of my heart that had lobbied for self-preservation turned traitor at the yearning in his expression. Oh God, how could I walk away from him?

What if I never felt this way again?

The first step was the hardest, but the others came easily as I made my way over to him.

"Morgan." His gaze raked over me hungrily, as if he was searching for some kind of answer.

"Hi, Jackson." My lips lifted in a smile, and his entire posture relaxed.

"I've been trying to talk to you. Please, you have to let me explain." He moved forward but kept his hands in his pockets.

"You don't have to explain." He was close enough that I caught the faint scent of cologne as I craned my neck to look up at him.

"No. Morgan, please." His hands flew from his pockets to gently cradle my face. "Please, don't kill this before you give me a chance to talk to you."

My hands covered his, and my thumbs gently stroked the backs of his hands. "I mean, you don't owe me an explanation. Not for any of it."

His brow knit in clear confusion.

"Your parents died in a boating accident," I said softly. "It makes sense that you would decide to become the one person who could have saved them. And as for the other thing." I swallowed but didn't look away. "I would have thrown his name into Google if I were you, too. Then I would have gone through every post on his social media and mine until I figured out exactly what our relationship had been. I can't fault you for wanting answers that I was in no place to give, though I wish you had given me the time and the chance to tell you myself."

His eyes squeezed shut, and his forehead fell against mine to rest there lightly. "I don't deserve you."

"You say that like I'm a reward, when there's every chance I'm the very trial that might drive you to drink," I teased with a hint of complete truth.

"What does this mean?" He pulled back enough to keep eye contact.

"I don't know. I'm answering as honestly as I can. It scares the living bejeezus out of me that you fly, and I'm not sure I can get past it. But I'm hoping that you might give me a little patience and grace, and maybe just wait a little bit so my head and my heart can sort themselves out."

"I'll give you whatever time you need. I'm not going anywhere," he promised. "I'll wait forever if it means I get the chance to kiss you again."

This man's mouth was going to be the death of me.

I didn't have any words to respond with, so I rose on my toes and brushed my mouth over his, then truly kissed him. It was soft and chaste, but the meaning of it hit me harder than any passionate encounter could have. "Better?"

He smiled against my mouth. "Infinitely."

I pulled back slightly when I heard his door open and close, knowing Finley would follow. "I'll tell you about Will, if you want to know more than what the articles said. You just have to be patient. I have this thing—it's called complicated grief—and it makes it really hard to talk about him. But it's getting better."

His eyes widened, and he nodded quickly. "I want to know whatever you're willing and ready to tell me."

"Morgan!" Finley called out as she thundered down the steps.

"Hey, Fin!" I pulled out of Jackson's arms and waved at her as she raced toward me.

"Shit. Morgan, there's something I need to tell you," Jackson began.

"I've missed you! Where have you been? I have so many shells to show you!" Finley's words came at me with the same speed that she did, and I barely maintained my balance as she tackled me with a hug.

"I've missed you, too!" I wrapped my arms around her and hugged her tight. "I can't wait to see the shells."

She grinned up at me, sporting two pigtail French braids.

"Wow, I love your braids!" They looked fantastic, even if a little tight.

"Thanks! Mommy did them!" She nodded enthusiastically.

Everything went wobbly as my questioning gaze flew toward Jackson. "Mommy?"

"That's what—"

"Yes, Mommy," a clipped, feminine voice asserted from a few feet away. "As in her mother. Who would be me."

Sweet mercy, the woman was breathtakingly beautiful. Her clothes were obviously couture, her body flawless, and her makeup expert. Her auburn hair was a shade darker than Finley's, and her complexion was worthy of a skincare ad. No wonder she was an actress. No wonder Jackson had fallen in love with her.

Suddenly, my shorts and tank top felt dowdy next to her silk blouse, and I regretted not wearing a stitch of makeup.

She arched a delicate eyebrow, as if she could read my mind.

"You must be Claire," I said, finding my voice and forcing a smile. This woman created Finley, and obviously the little girl was happy to have her near, so the least I could do was be happy for her. "I'm Morgan. It's lovely to meet you."

"Right. Finley mentioned you a few times." She walked forward and put her hand on Finley's shoulder, careful not to touch me in the process. "Why don't you get in the car, baby? Daddy and I don't want to be late."

Daddy and I. Good Lord, I'd found myself smack in the middle of a family. My cheeks stained with color as Finley waved good-bye and ran toward the garage.

Claire scanned me from head to toe, her eyes lingering on my feet that hadn't seen a pedicure since week one of the reward system. "Aren't you just the cutest neighbor ever when you're not losing your mind and slamming doors over and over?"

My stomach fell out of my body.

"Claire!" Jackson snapped a warning and stepped toward me.

"What?" She gave him a genuine smile. "I was just admiring Finley's friend and her exceptionally well-projected voice. Sound really does carry, you know." She motioned between our two houses.

She'd heard my entire breakdown? Wait…she'd been in Jackson's house while we were out on a date? My heart joined my stomach.

"Stop," he growled. "And you damn well know that Morgan isn't just Finley's friend. She's…she's more than a friend to me." His hand moved to the small of my back.

Well if that wasn't awkward. What the hell *were* we, anyway? And if Claire knew what we…were or were not, what did that mean *they* were? Was this just a visit? Was she staying with him? Were they sleeping together fifty feet away from my house?

It was too much. *This* was too much.

"Right." Claire offered me a sugar-sweet smile. "Well, if you're ready?"

"I'll be there in a second. Why don't you get Fin buckled?" He nodded toward the garage.

"I can wait," she replied.

I was going to die right here, right now. Had she seen me kiss Jackson? Was *she* kissing Jackson? It's not like we were exclusive since we weren't…well, anything.

"Claire." It was a clear warning.

She pouted. "Fine. I'll go. Just hurry up. You were the one who told me her pediatrician doesn't like it when we're late, and I want to make a good impression now that I'm home." Her gaze slid toward me and sharpened. "For good."

I was going to be sick.

She wiggled her fingers in a little wave and sauntered off for the car, swinging her hips expertly.

"Morgan—"

"Is *that* what you wanted to tell me?" I backed away from him.

"Yes. I just didn't have time—" His eyes were wide and panicked.

"Because I was busy kissing you. Again." I shook my head. "How stupid can I possibly be?"

"You're not!" He reached for me, but I retreated again. "Look, she's home, but that doesn't change anything between us."

"Doesn't change anything?" I challenged. "Jackson, that's the mother of your child. All you've ever wanted was for her to come home, and now she's here!"

"Claire isn't living with me. She's living with her mom. We're not together. She's just here because Fin has an appointment for her kindergarten shots. *Nothing* changes between you and me, Morgan. Nothing." The plea in his eyes nearly undid me.

"Jax! We have to get going!" Claire shouted from the driveway.

Everything this man wanted was wrapped up in that gorgeous little package, from her perfect fucking hair to her designer clothes. She was Finley's mama. She was his chance at the happily ever after he'd waited for since the day she left.

It was just too much. Too complicated. Too...*oh, screw this.*

"Morgan, we'll talk later, I promise." Jackson raked his hand over his hair.

I pushed past the pain and forced a smile. "Your family is waiting for you, Jackson."

Then I walked away, keeping my composure as I made my way up my steps.

"Morgan, please!"

"Jax!" Mercy, that woman's voice was loud, but I guess mine was, too.

"I'm at my emotional capacity for the day. Now go," I told him, because he was still standing there, staring up at me with so much angst in those eyes that I couldn't stand it. I dropped the pretense of dignity and flat-out ran the rest of the way, slamming my front door once I was through it.

"Everything okay?" Sam asked, her eyes widening as she took in my expression.

"I found another thing about Jackson that I don't like." It was the biggest understatement of my life. I was so sick of this shit. What was so wrong with me that I couldn't have just a glimmer of happiness? Was that too much to ask? Or at least a little less pain? Less pain—God, that sounded good. Numb sounded even better. Yep, that was the goal for the night.

"Oh no." She sighed.

"Call Mia. We're going out."

Chapter Thirteen

Jackson

"Two Finley-less weekends in a row?" Sawyer questioned as the bartender handed him a draft.

"She's with Claire." I sipped on ice water and stared up at the ball game playing on the flat screen above the bar.

Garrett's eyebrows shot up on the other side of me, and I didn't miss the look that passed between my friends.

"And how is that going?" Sawyer asked, trying not to make it awkward but managing the opposite.

"Well, she's made it two hours without calling me to ask a question that Finley can answer herself, so I guess that's improvement. At least she's with Vivian, so I don't have to worry about the fact that my daughter's mother knows jack and shit about her kid." I rubbed the condensation from my glass and wondered for the fiftieth time where Morgan had hidden herself away.

She wasn't at home. The minute I'd dropped Fin off for her first "weekend with Mom," I'd headed straight to

Morgan's. I hadn't even parked in my own driveway. Not that it mattered. Morgan and Sam weren't there.

Sawyer sent Garrett a beseeching look, and Garrett sighed in response. Guess he drew the short straw. "So…is she here to stay? Claire?" he asked, peeling the label off a bottle he hadn't taken a sip from.

"She says she is, but hell if I know. That woman's mind changes with the weather, and usually I don't care, but she's told Finley she's staying, and that means I'll have a broken-hearted five-year-old when something bigger and better comes along." Hence why I wasn't drinking. For all I knew, Claire would call in an hour and say she changed her mind and Finley needed to come home.

"And…are you two together?" Sawyer asked, taking a cue from Garrett.

"Hell no. Never again." Did seeing her fuck with my head a little? Sure. Was I remotely interested in rekindling something that had died so thoroughly it would need life support and a miracle? Not in the least.

"Okay…" Garrett narrowed his eyes at Sawyer and then huffed. "So that means you and Morgan?"

"What is it with the questions?" I shot both my best friends a glare.

"We're trying to be supportive," Sawyer said with a shrug, then winked at a girl across the bar.

"Well, stop. You're just making it really fucking weird." My cell phone vibrated, and I lifted my ass off the barstool just enough to slide it out of my back pocket. *Morgan*. I fumbled for the answer button, which earned me a WTF look from Garrett, but I managed to swipe it across without making too much of an ass out of myself. "Morgan?"

"No, it's Sam!" she shouted over the background noise.

"Sam? Is Morgan okay?" My brow puckered.

"Define okay," she answered.

"Is she hurt?"

"No, nothing like that, but I think I might need your help." There was a muffled scrape, like she had put her hand over the mic. "Mia! Don't encourage her!" The background noise swamped the call again. "Sorry. Look, I swore I would *never* call a guy to help me pull a friend off a bar—"

"What?" I snapped. Both Garrett and Sawyer's heads twisted my way, then Garrett asked for the tab. Morgan was *on* a bar?

"Do you think you can get to Avon? I think you might be the only one she'll listen to, or the only one who can muscle her down at this point, anyway."

"Tell me where you are. I'll be there in fifteen minutes."

Fourteen minutes later, I parked my car, killed the engine, and took the front stairs two at a time, flanked by Garrett and Sawyer.

"Jesus, who trucked in the frat guys?" Garrett asked. The college crowd had filled the bar, consuming the long, wooden counter that ran the length of the space and overflowing to the pool table area.

"Jax!" Sam called out from the right side of the bar.

I nodded, then pushed my way through the crowd. "Where is she?"

"With Mia." Sam glared up at me and jabbed her finger in my chest. "One thing first. I really need you to stop fucking with her, Jax. She hasn't had a drink since I can't even remember when, and after one conversation with you, the girl is three martinis down and sitting on the damn bar like she's holding court."

Shit. How bad was she?

"I had no clue Claire was going to show up like that, and when she did, Morgan wasn't speaking to me. What did you want me to do? Write it in a note and slip it under the door?" I shot back.

"You could have hired a skywriter for all I care. I don't give a shit how you relay the information, just that you do, because honestly, you're not my priority—she is. You let her walk straight into another shitstorm you created, after I'd spent all damned week trying to clean up your last one."

Sawyer slid to my side and grinned at Sam. "I think I'm in love. Did you hear the way she just ripped into Montgomery?" he asked Garrett.

"Yes, because we're both standing right here, you moron." Garrett shook his head.

Sam arched an eyebrow at Sawyer. "Let me guess. Cocky, good-looking, and hanging out with this guy…you're another pilot, too, right?"

"Yep." Sawyer's grin got even bigger.

"And you?" She turned her gaze on Garrett.

"Rescue swimmer. Flying is for the boys too scared to get wet."

"And you are?" Sawyer asked.

"Married," she replied, flashing her ring. "Now if you're done?"

"My bad." Sawyer's hands went up as the jukebox changed to "Sweet Home Alabama."

A flash of red caught my eye, and I leaned around the corner enough to see Morgan swaying with Mia, sitting on the bar in the middle of a horde of guys.

I sucked in a breath. It was no wonder she was surrounded. Damn, she was gorgeous. Her sleeveless, red top was cut low and tied just above the waist of an impossibly short jean skirt. I wasn't even sure I'd call the thing a skirt, honestly, since it revealed so much of those long legs. Her cowboy boots swung slightly as she sang along to Lynyrd Skynyrd, her arms loose in the air as she and Mia belted out the chorus.

She wasn't drinking—she was drunk.

"She's had three martinis?" I asked Sam as I planned my

best route for attack.

"Yeah..." She cringed.

That was a good amount of alcohol, but it wouldn't explain her sloppy motions as she brushed her hair out of her face.

I glanced from Sam to Morgan and back again before it hit me. "Oh fuck, is she on anti-anxiety meds?"

Sam nodded. "Daily. She's not supposed to drink, but I figured she deserved a glass of wine after the shit you put her through today. I guess Morgan thought she deserved something a little stronger."

"Damn, who's that girl next to Morgan?" Sawyer asked.

Sam snapped her finger in his face. "No." She moved it toward Garrett. "Not you, either. Last thing I need is my husband getting home from deployment and going straight to jail for murder."

"Noted," Sawyer replied, already scanning the crowd for his next conquest.

"I wasn't even looking," Garrett swore.

When the guys around Morgan urged her to dance on the bar top, I decided it was time to move.

I waded through a sea of Axe body spray with Garrett and Sawyer at my back. Living here for the last five years had taught me that the only thing lacking more than inhibitions with celebrating tourists was their common sense.

"Get out of my way," I growled at the polo-wearing pretty boy who was inching his hand toward Morgan's thigh.

The guy shot me a glare but took one look at my face, hopefully seeing the promised murder in my eyes, then glanced back at Sawyer and Garrett, and moved. "All yours," he mumbled, staggering away. Was I ever that young and stupid?

"Mr. Carolina!" Mia waved as I put myself between the women.

"Well, if it isn't the reason I'm drinking!" Morgan greeted me with a sweet tone and an equally sweet, fake-ass smile. "Did you come all the way over here to help me pick out a guy to go home with? There have been quite a few propositions for being so early in the evening."

"I've counted four so far," Mia added.

"The only guy taking you home is me." My gut twisted at the thought of any other possibility.

"Really? Claire didn't seem like the kind of woman who'd be up for sharing. You should probably ask her first." Her smirk lit a fire in my belly.

What had she said about the "old" version of her having a sharp tongue?

I smothered my temper, counted to three, then gripped her hips and hauled her from the bar to the stool polo-shirt boy had vacated.

"Oomph!" she grunted, bouncing slightly as she landed. "Who made you the resident party pooper?" She tilted her head back and looked up at me with glazed eyes.

"Sam was worried. And apparently for good reason. You're hammered." The harsh tone was at odds with the gentle touch as I tucked her hair behind her ears.

"Sam?" Morgan's eyes widened, and her head swiveled to see her friend on the other side of the stool.

"Girl, you need to go home, *alone*, and you weren't listening, so I called in reinforcements." She shrugged unapologetically.

Morgan's finger rose slowly, pointing at Sam. "You, of all people, called a boy to get me off a bar?"

"Man," I corrected.

Sam rolled her eyes. "This is *not* the same."

"Traitor. At least you had Will to blame for calling Jagger and Grayson on you."

Holy shit, she'd dropped his name in a casual conversation.

Was that progress or alcohol talking?

Morgan reached for the rest of her martini, but I beat her to it.

"And that's enough of that." I gave the glass back to the bartender.

"For the love of God, could y'all untwist your panties? I can have a drink. I'm legal and everything. Wanna see my ID?"

"You're also mixing alcohol with your meds," I said quietly, leaning down so only she could hear me. "One amplifies the other. It's why you feel so drunk."

"Darlin', maybe I should have done this a long time ago," she retorted, turning her face so our lips were an inch apart, if that. "It's a miraculous painkiller."

"It'll hurt plenty in the morning," I promised.

"What would you care? No doubt you'll be cuddled up with your ex." She arched a brow at me and leaned in but lost her balance.

Enough.

"Morgan, I'm not with Claire. She showed up the same night we went to the lighthouse. I had no clue she was coming, and I meant it when I said that it changes nothing between us because I. Want. You." I steadied her waist as she gripped my search and rescue tee. Fuck, her skin was so incredibly soft under my fingers.

A wicked grin spread across her face, and she skimmed my jaw with her lips. "Do you, now?"

Every muscle in my body tightened, but I found the strength to pull back. "In every way possible. When you're sober."

She huffed and nodded loosely at the crowd of college kids. "That guy didn't care if I was sober."

Ouch.

"That guy is an asshole," I ground out, reminding myself

to thank Sam for calling me. Morgan would have beaten the shit out of herself for going home with a stranger, and then I probably would have beaten the shit out of the stranger for taking advantage of her.

"I just wanted to be numb for a minute," she drawled softly.

"Yeah, I can imagine you did." I sure as hell didn't blame her. I would have been drunk every day of my life if I'd been through what she had. "Why don't you let me take you home, Kitty? Any decisions you make when you're this wasted will be the kind you regret in the morning."

She blinked away a slight sheen of tears, dropping her gaze to her hands as she smoothed them over my chest. "We're too complicated. It's just one thing after another with you. I can't get my feet under me before you knock them out."

"I'm the only complicated one in this relationship?"

Her gaze flew back to mine, but she didn't debate my choice of terminology.

"I have a dead quasi-boyfriend who I loved way more than he ever liked me. You have a helicopter that's just waiting to kill you and an inhumanly beautiful baby mama who's so desperate to mark her territory that I half expected her to pee on you this afternoon."

I stifled the laugh that tried to escape and cradled her face with one hand. "I have a helicopter that I'm damned good at flying and a heart-stoppingly gorgeous Morgan who I would really like to put to bed."

"But not take to bed. I seem to have that effect on the guys I actually like." She leaned into my palm.

What the hell had her quasi-ex put her through to make her think that?

I lowered my forehead to hers. "Don't get me wrong, Kitty. I *want* to take you to bed. I would fucking *kill* to take you to bed. I've fantasized about getting my hands on you since the moment we met, but the first time you scream my name, the only thing in your system will be *me*. I'm not about to be one of your regrets when I have the option to be your choice. Get it? I'm not trading the possibility of an entire future with you for a couple orgasms on a single night—no matter how fucking edible you look right now."

She blinked. "Okay, that was good."

"I know." I grinned.

"Are you taking anyone else to bed?" Her eyes narrowed.

"What? No. I haven't so much as looked at another woman since you moved in." Was that what this was about? Claire's timing was utter shit as usual.

"So we're exclusive? Even though we're not together?" Her hands slid up my shirt to rest around my neck.

"There's no one else. Just you," I promised.

"Okay." Her eyes softened. "Take me home." She stumbled off the barstool, and I hooked my arm around her waist, hauling her to my side.

"Well, since you asked so nicely."

Sam immediately took Morgan's stool, demanding the tab from the bartender.

Mia hopped down from the bar and grinned at Garrett. "Hi."

"I've been warned about your brother," he replied, putting his hands up.

She rolled her eyes. "The guy is half a world away and still keeps me from getting laid. Unbelievable."

When Morgan stumbled again, I lifted her into my arms, careful to make sure her skirt covered her ass as I carried her from the bar. I tucked her into my passenger seat, then clipped the belt in place as Mia got into Sam's car under Garrett's supervision a few spots down.

"Jackson?" Morgan tugged at my hand.

"Yes?" I leaned back into the car.

She locked onto the back of my neck and kissed me. Her tongue slid between my lips, and I opened on pure instinct.

Fuck, she tasted like a raspberry lemon drop, citrus and berry and the sweet burn of alcohol. I licked into her mouth, then took her deep, my fingers tunneling into her hair as she moaned. It was just as electric as the first kiss—I hadn't blown it out of proportion or romanticized it. She lit my blood on fire.

I kissed her breathless and then did it again. I fell into her so deep that I knew this thing between us would only go one of two ways—we'd end up together, or we'd destroy each other in the process of trying.

Groaning, I pulled back, breaking the kiss. "God, Morgan."

"Thank you." She let go of my neck.

"For what?"

"For coming to get me." She gave me an embarrassed smile.

"Anytime." I closed her door and turned around to see Garrett, Sam, and Sawyer leaning against her car.

"You about done over there? Because my car's at your place." Sawyer smirked.

"Yeah, yeah." I motioned him over, and we all filed into the cars.

Morgan was asleep by the time we got to her house. I parked in her driveway, then carefully lifted her into my arms after sending Sawyer and Garrett on their ways. Her head rolled against my chest, and she mumbled something about sleep and burrowed closer.

"I've got you," I said softly.

"I'll get the door," Sam said, rushing ahead to open the front door for me.

I carried Morgan up the stairs, into the house, and then up another set of stairs to the master bedroom. I'd only been here a few times when Diane and Carl had owned the place, and it looked entirely different now. Morgan had painted the room pale blue, contrasting with her white furniture. The result wasn't overly feminine but clean and minimalist.

I put her on the queen-size bed and started on her boots.

"I'll get her changed," Sam said from the doorway.

"Don't go, Jackson!" Morgan demanded, kicking her boots off the rest of the way.

This is a bad idea, Montgomery.

"I'll wait outside," I told Sam, then retreated to the relative safety of the hallway, where I counted my breaths and planned an escape that didn't include crawling into bed with the woman who'd had me hard for two months—no matter how badly I wanted to.

The door opened a few minutes later, and Sam came out, leveling me with a skeptical glare.

"She's safe with me," I promised.

"Oh, I know she is. Because my in-laws own a lot of sailboats, and the ocean is a fantastic place to hide a body." She stared at me unflinchingly.

"You are a great friend, Sam."

"I know that, too. Which is why I'm telling you that Morgan took me in when I had nowhere else to go. No questions asked. That's what she does for the people she loves. The girl is selfless to a fault, and I'll be damned if I slip on my watch and let her get hurt. You understand?" She stood in the doorway with crossed arms.

"I understand." Warning received.

She sighed, then stepped aside. "Don't do anything that will make me hide your body. You look way too heavy for me to handle solo."

"Noted." I nodded as I walked past her into Morgan's room.

The bedside table light was on, and Morgan lay curled on

her side, facing the door.

"Will you stay with me?" she asked. "Please?"

"That's not a good idea." I sat on the edge of her bed and kept my hands on top of the covers.

"I didn't say it was a good idea," she countered sleepily. "I asked if you'd stay. Just until I fall asleep? Please?"

Fuck. How the hell could I deny her when she was asking for the very thing I wanted? Easy—I couldn't.

"Just until you fall asleep."

She smiled and patted the bed behind her.

Cursing my idiocy, I took off my shoes and socks, then put my car keys and wallet on the bedside table next to her pile of sea glass, which reminded me of the present I still had in my glove box.

I killed the light and climbed onto the bed. Tomorrow was Saturday, but the flight schedule said I had to keep my word and leave once she fell asleep.

"Under the covers," she demanded, not even rolling over to look at me.

"Kitty, that's not—"

"Under the covers," she stated simply. "I trust you."

"I'm not sure I trust myself," I muttered, but I did as she asked just because I wanted to hold her. A week ago, she'd stood outside, slamming the truck door, and I thought I'd blown my shot with her. This morning, she'd come face to face with Claire and then promptly run away, so hell yes, I wanted to hold her.

I'd hold her every chance I had until she stopped running.

"I'm in. Happy now?" Fully clothed, I turned on my side toward Morgan.

She scooted until her back was against my chest. "Now I'm happy."

I curved around her, and she sighed, wiggling until her ass was firmly pressed into my hips and her legs molded around mine. My arm locked around her waist, and I gave in to temptation and breathed in the scent of her hair while telling my body to settle the hell down.

"You can't use words like relationship with me," she whispered. "You have to be patient."

"Morgan—" I stroked my thumb over her pajama-covered ribs.

"I'm a mess, and you're..."

"Complicated?" I offered.

"Right. And I like you, Jackson, I do, but you scare me."

"I'll never hurt you. Not intentionally," I promised, pulling her even tighter against me.

"I didn't used to be a coward," she muttered, her words slowing. "You would have liked me back then."

"You're not a coward, and I like you just fine now." I pressed a kiss to the top of her head.

"Just give me a second, and I'll fall asleep, I promise." Her breathing slowed as her words faded off.

"I'm not in a rush, Morgan. I can wait as long as you need me to." I meant it, and not just about her falling asleep. I could wait for her to heal, to be ready for whatever we could be. There was no deadline when it came to us.

She mumbled her assent, and I closed my eyes.

When I opened them, it was morning.

Chapter Fourteen

Morgan

The night of the graduation ball… Well, you were there. I should have known it then, but I woke up the next morning so scared that I couldn't offer you what you needed. It was never you, Morgan. It was always me.

My head threatened to secede from the rest of my body with every step I took down the stairs. What the hell had I been thinking?

Sam clattered around in the kitchen, the noise ratcheting up my pain to a seven as I came around the corner and stepped onto the linoleum. One more week and this baby would turn into hardwood. A frying pan grated against the stove burner, and I cringed.

"Sit down." Sam pointed across the counter. How the hell did she look so perky? Even her ringlet curls bounced with more energy than I had in my entire body.

I slid onto one of the stools and propped my elbows on

the Formica to cradle my aching head.

A glass of water appeared in front of me, and Sam plunked two painkillers down next to it.

"I already took the ones you left on my nightstand with the water." I lifted my head enough to catch her flash of confusion before she smiled slightly.

"I didn't leave those there. Must have been Jackson." She took the pills back with a little shake of her head. "Turns out Mr. Carolina is one of the good ones."

Jackson. Oh God, I'd made an utter fool of myself last night.

"How bad was I?" My fingers curled around the glass as Sam cracked two eggs in the pan.

"On a scale of one to me, you were probably about a seven. You definitely weren't at your best sitting up there, but you weren't dancing on the bar like it was Coyote Ugly, either." She shrugged.

Kill me now. "I didn't think about the meds."

She turned slightly, catching my eye. "I know you didn't. If you had, then we'd be having a different discussion. I shouldn't have stepped out when you were ordering your drinks."

"You were talking to Grayson. Don't blame yourself for my shitty decision making. Where's Mia, anyway?"

"She left three hours ago."

My eyes flew to the clock. "It's already noon?"

"Sure is." She slid the eggs onto a plate, then grabbed a fork and set the food in front of me. "Now eat."

I tucked in, and Sam slid a cup of coffee over as my reward once I was finished. "Thank you."

"No problem." She leaned on the counter as her lips lifted in a smirk. "Now tell me how it was sleeping next to Jackson." The woman wiggled her eyebrows.

"What? I mean..." Oh shit, I had slept next to him. I'd

begged the man to stay with me and then spooned up on him and… "I fell asleep," I whispered.

"Well, yeah. I told him if he took advantage, I'd bury him at sea, so that better have been all you did."

My eyes flew to hers. "No, Sam. I *fell asleep*. No video."

Her eyebrows rose. "No Will video?" she clarified.

"No. Just Jackson." I hadn't slept a night without watching that video in the nearly two years since I'd been given it. It had become my lullaby, my prayer, my sleeping aid, and my plea to my own brain to let him into my dreams. "What does that mean? Was it the alcohol? Jackson? God, am I using him to replace—"

"Stop." Sam's hand covered mine. "It means that you went a night without watching the video. Stop analyzing why you took the step and just be happy that you did. Be happy that you can sleep without it."

Sure, if I'm drunk and have Jackson's arms around me. The second part of that recipe was easy enough to remedy. Either way, I'd done it.

"I slept without the video." I smiled as a chunk of weight lifted from my chest, and I took a full, deep breath.

"You slept without the video." Sam squeezed my hand.

All night. In Jackson's arms— "Oh God, what time did he leave?" Had he spent the entire night with me?

"I heard the door around six a.m." She grinned as she reached for her coffee. "That man has it bad for you, Morgan Bartley."

I scoffed. "After watching me beat the tar out of Will's truck, then blasting him yesterday when his ex showed up and subsequently making him carry me home drunk and sleep next to me, I have a feeling the man is running just as fast as he can. Or he would be if he didn't live next door."

"You didn't make that man do anything. He chose to be with you during all three of those…" She struggled for words.

"Tantrums?" I suggested.

"I was going to say outbursts, but you get the point." She reached toward a small box at the end of the counter and brought it to me. "And besides, a man who's running away isn't leaving a woman gifts."

"He left this for me?" I stared at the small white box in my hand as Morgan held out a folded piece of paper.

"And a note." She waved the paper over the box. "And I've been waiting *hours* to know what's in that, so read!"

Stunned, I put the box on the counter and unfolded the note. Jackson's handwriting filled the page.

Morgan,

Fin helped me design this, so I hope you like it. This used to be a jar or a glass of some kind. All I know for certain is that it shattered at some point. It broke apart, then spent years in the waves and sand until it became something entirely new. No longer clear and sharp, but soft and opaque. When I saw this piece, it reminded me of you—beautiful, resilient, and unique. I don't mourn what it used to be in its former life, because it's precious to me exactly how it is now. I can't imagine it ever having been more beautiful—even whole—but I also know that at the center, it's still the same clear glass it always has been. The same glass, just made rare—not despite all its been through, but because of it.

—Jackson

My breath abandoned me, and a spark flared in my chest. Hope. It was hope.

"Well, what does it say?" Sam asked.

I handed her the note, then opened the little white box.

It was a teardrop-shaped piece of turquoise sea glass a little bigger than a quarter, set in gold. My fingers trembled as I lifted it from box that bore Christina's store's logo on the inside of the lid. The chain was long—a necklace. A stunningly beautiful necklace.

"Oh. My. God." Sam dragged out that last word. "I stand by my earlier comment. That man has it *bad* for you. And he could definitely teach Grayson a thing or two in the letter writing department because *damn*."

"I told him he would have liked me better before..." I swallowed, then tried again. "He would have liked me better the way I was before Will died. You know, when I was all sharp-tongued and vivacious without the alcohol."

She snorted. "If you think your tongue isn't just as sharp, then it's only because you haven't been on the receiving end of it." She set down the note as I put on the necklace. "Did losing Will change you? Absolutely. But at your core, you're the same person you always have been, with the same big, beautiful heart. The fact that he sees that heart earns him my approval, but my opinion doesn't really matter here. Yours does."

I stared down at the pendant that rested just above my breasts. "I really like him."

"I know."

"I'm really scared." My eyes found hers.

"I know that, too. Anything new is scary, and that's without you already knowing the cost of risking your heart."

"I'm not sure I have a heart to risk." But that little flare of hope in my chest argued otherwise.

"If you didn't, you wouldn't be so scared." She gave me an encouraging smile. "Now, are you ready for morning homework?"

The recording. The usual dread settled on my shoulders, but it was lighter today, easier to bear. Every day, this got a little easier. The improvement had been so small that I hadn't seen it to start with, but now that we were seven weeks into the treatment—almost halfway—the progress was obvious.

Hope, there it was again.

"It's not really morning homework since it's after noon," I quipped.

"Don't be a smart-ass," Sam shot back, already going for the tape recorder, but there was a grin on her face. "For real, are you ready?"

I really was.

"Let's do it."

• • •

I paired my new necklace with simple gold studs, put on my favorite cream dress, and walked into the school district office on Monday at ten forty-five, exactly fifteen minutes early for my intake meeting with the superintendent.

In less than four months, I would be a fifth-grade teacher.

The house renovations would be complete, and then… What then? I was supposed to deliver a list of long-term goals to Dr. Circe tomorrow, and I was drawing a big, fat blank. Did maintaining my sanity count as a goal?

Or maybe trying to ease into a relationship—I mentally stumbled over the word—with Jackson?

Jackson. A texted thank you wasn't enough, though he'd sworn it was. I wanted to see him, but he'd gone to nights this week, which meant whenever I was awake, he was asleep.

Complicated, indeed, but there was something to be said for anticipation.

I signed in at the front desk, but I was too antsy to sit, so I passed the giant stand that announced Mother's Day tea was today in honor of yesterday's holiday and perused the artwork on the bulletin board in the hallway. The district offices shared this building with the preschool, so I searched the pretty, painted rainbows until I found Finley's.

I snapped a picture with my cell phone. I'd send it to Jackson once he was awake for the night.

The door to my right opened, and an older woman with blond hair ushered a little one into the hallway.

"Why don't we try giving her a call one more time?" the teacher suggested.

A very familiar pair of Vans kicked at the linoleum floor, but I couldn't see the child's face.

"Why bother?" I knew that voice, though.

"Finley?" I walked around the teacher to confirm my guess.

Her head lifted, and I was unprepared for the flare of disappointment in those brown eyes. *Ouch.* It only lasted a second before she tried to force a shaky smile. "Hi, Morgan. Did Daddy send you?"

The teacher eyed me warily, and I checked her name tag. Mrs. Kozier.

"Hi, Mrs. Kozier, I'm Morgan Bartley. I'm Finley's next-door neighbor and the new fifth-grade teacher over at the elementary school," I said so she wouldn't call the guards on me. Then I sank down on my heels so I was eye level with Finley. "No, honey. I'm here for a meeting. What's wrong?"

"It's Mother's Day tea," she said softly, her eyes falling away.

Guess that explained the sparkly dress.

"Well, that sounds fun." I took her little hand and gave it a squeeze.

"Everyone else has their mom," she whispered, staring at the floor.

My gaze flew up to meet Mrs. Kozier's, and she shook her head. Claire hadn't come? I swallowed the ball of rage that was working its way up my throat.

"And you gave her a call?" I asked quietly.

Finley nodded, then sniffed as two fat teardrops fell from her cheeks to the checkered floor.

"Well, how late is she? Maybe she's just running a little behind, honey." *God, please let that be the case. Do not let Claire break Finley's little heart.*

Finley brought her face up, and I wiped away two more tears. "She's really late. There's only two kids left to read their poems."

My heart ached, but I managed a smile. "Let's do what your teacher suggested and call her again."

She lunged at me, and I caught her, keeping careful balance on my heels. "She's not coming. She never does."

But this time, Claire had told her she would. Otherwise, Finley never would have expected her. My dislike of the woman exploded into pure loathing. How the hell did you not show up to Mother's Day tea at your daughter's school? *The same way you walk out when she's a baby.*

"Why didn't she come?" Her little face tucked into my neck as I rubbed circles on her back.

"What can I do to help you, honey?" I didn't know how to answer her question, so I asked one of my own.

She shook her head and pulled out of the hug, but as her eyes fell, she paused. "You have the necklace!" A smile lit up her face as she snarfled up the snot her tears had brought on. "Do you like it?"

"I love it," I assured her. "I just haven't seen you to say thank you yet, so thank you, Finley. It's beautiful."

"I picked gold," she announced with a solemn nod. "Dad found the blue."

"You chose perfectly. It's the most beautiful necklace I've ever seen."

She batted away the last of her tears with the back of her hand, and I dug into my handbag for a tissue, then held it up to her nose. She blew, which solved the snot problem.

"Finley, we should really call your mom, or we need to head back in there, sweetheart," Mrs. Kozier said gently, glancing at me with an apologetic look.

"Morgan, do you want to come to tea?" Fin's eyebrows popped up as she asked.

Oh, my heart. "If you want me to, honey, I can come in. I'll just tell the desk that I'm running late for the meeting, okay?"

Finley nodded exuberantly, taking my hand, and her teacher sighed in obvious relief.

The doors swung open behind us.

"I'm here! Finley, baby, I'm here!" Claire exclaimed, her heels clicking down the hall in an obvious rush, flying right by the sign-in desk.

"Ma'am, you have to sign in!"

I stood and turned to face her, Finley's hand still firmly tucked in mine. It took every ounce of class in my body, but I channeled my manners and schooled my features to hide my disgust.

"What? But…okay." Claire stopped at the desk and signed in while I tossed Finley's tissue in the trash can.

"Look, she's here, honey. She came," I reassured Fin, whose expression flitted from joy to anger and back again.

Claire's gaze flickered between the three of us before settling on me as she reached us. "Morgan, so lovely to see you again. What exactly are you doing at my daughter's school?"

"I have a meeting with the superintendent at eleven," I answered, sweet as pie. "I make it a habit to arrive early to important events."

Claire arched a single eyebrow.

"Mrs. Montgomery, our program began forty-five minutes ago—" Mrs. Kozier chided.

I tensed.

"I know, I know," Claire answered but didn't correct her name. "But I'm here now, so can't we just get going?"

Montgomery? Nope. Not today, Satan. A wave of possessiveness I had no right to feel smacked me square in the chest and erupted out my petty little mouth.

"Lewis," I corrected Fin's teacher. "Her name is Ms. Lewis."

Claire narrowed her eyes.

"I'd hate for your mail to get mixed up," I offered with a tiny, apologetic shrug that wasn't apologetic in the least bit.

"You're late!" Finley erupted at Claire.

"I know, baby. I'm so sorry, but I had a call with my agent that just wouldn't end, and well, I'm here now!" Claire nodded and smiled, sticking out her hand for Finley's.

Finley looked from that hand to me.

"Well, let's go!" Claire insisted. "I can't wait to hear your poem!"

"I invited Morgan," Fin said so quietly it was barely a whisper.

"That's okay, Fin," I promised.

"Finley Montgomery!" Claire chastised. "Why on earth would you do such a thing? Especially when she has an *important* meeting?"

"You weren't here!" Fin shouted.

"I'm here now!"

"You can both come in. There's more than enough cookies," Mrs. Kozier assured us, no doubt seeing the same storm brewing that I did.

"Morgan?" Fin looked up at me, clearly torn.

"Are you suggesting I share my daughter with the next-door neighbor? It's our first Mother's Day tea!" Claire sniffled. "I've already missed so much because I work all the time."

I didn't mention the five Mother's Days she'd skipped out

on. Finley's eyes welled up again. Of course she was scared Claire would leave. That was all she'd ever known.

My posture softened, and I tipped Fin's chin up. "Go ahead and take your mama in for tea, you silly girl. You have a poem to read, and last time I checked, it's Mother's Day, not neighbor's day!" I tweaked her nose with a grin and let go of her hand.

Her shoulders dropped in obvious relief. "You're not mad?"

"Of course not. The understudy doesn't get mad when the star shows up! We'll go shell hunting later to make up for it, okay?"

She nodded enthusiastically. "We'll hunt glass, but Daddy already got you the prettiest one."

My fingers grazed the necklace as I smiled down at Finley. "He sure did. Off you go, honey."

"Well, let's get inside, baby!" Claire urged in a singsong voice, taking Finley's hand. Her gaze lingered on my necklace as the teacher ushered them inside.

"Ms. Lewis, right this way."

"Later, Morgan!" Finley waved as they disappeared.

I held that smile like a shield, then walked back to the reception desk and sank into one of the empty chairs along the wall.

Complicated. That's what I'd called my exclusive, non-relationship with Jackson, and that right there had been the perfect example.

What I needed right now was easy, supportive, and… easy. But Jackson? What we had was intense, emotional, and messy.

Claire was a tie for the biggest complication between us.

I'm not with Claire. I. Want. You.

I held on to Jackson's words as my fingers toyed with my necklace. I had two choices here—believe him or run as fast as I could.

Either way, the thought of losing him to Claire sent a knife straight into my stitched-together heart. She wasn't good enough for him. She'd had his love and still hadn't chosen him when it mattered.

Just like Peyton hadn't chosen Will…and yet he'd still loved her until his dying breath. He'd loved Paisley, too, even when she'd chosen Jagger. But he'd never loved me, even though I was the only one who had ever chosen him. My chest tightened. *Fucking Will.*

"Ms. Bartley?" The secretary called my name.

"Yes, ma'am?"

"Mr. Patterson will see you now. I'll take you to him." She rose and led me toward his office.

I passed by Finley's room but didn't look through the window. She wasn't mine. I didn't get to be jealous. So why did I feel that swirling green monster in my belly?

I was in deeper than I'd wanted to admit, especially after that display I'd put on about Claire's last name. Whatever, she'd taken off his ring. She didn't get to claim his name now just because she obviously wanted him back.

I wasn't giving him up without a fight.

Oh God. At what point had I decided that Jackson was mine to lose?

Chapter Fifteen

Jackson

"Because it's a school night," I said as calmly as I could possibly manage, folding my arms across my chest. Seven p.m. on a school night to be precise. I'd been on nights for the past five days, and I didn't want to spend the only night I had off this week arguing with Claire, but here we were.

I wanted to spend what time I had with Morgan, especially since I hadn't seen her since I'd crawled out of her bed Saturday morning. It had almost been impossible to make myself go.

"So let her skip tomorrow. It's preschool, for God's sake, not Harvard." She walked past me into the living room.

"Absolutely not." It wasn't the first time she'd been in my house, but it still threw me to see her taking in the pictures of Fin I had scattered around.

"But I'm making up for lost time, Jax. It's just a sleepover." Claire sank into my couch, kicked off her shoes, and tucked her legs under her, sitting like she always did. A few years ago, that familiar sight might have stirred up long-dead feelings, but not anymore.

I leaned back and shot a glance up my stairs to be sure Finley wasn't eavesdropping. "It's not just a sleepover. It's a complete disruption in her schedule."

Her lips pursed. "She's five. She doesn't need a schedule."

"She's five, which is *why* she needs a schedule. Kids like boundaries and predictability, Claire. You coming home is great, but Finley can't just bounce around like a tennis ball."

"I came back to spend time with her," she argued. "How can I do that if you won't let me?" Her face fell.

"Who says I'm not letting you?" I rubbed the skin between my eyebrows and prayed for patience. Claire had thrown everything into upheaval in the last ten days.

"You just said I can't take her tonight!" she snapped.

"First, keep your voice down. Fin doesn't need to hear any of this. Second, no, you can't just pick her up and take her when it suits you. You had her last weekend. This is my weekend, and weekends don't start on Thursday nights." I cued up a playlist on my phone, and Mumford and Sons played through the speakers. Hopefully, that would keep Fin's ears from hearing much.

A slow smile spread across Claire's face. "You still listen to this?"

"Apparently."

Her smile faded at my tone. "Why aren't you happy that I'm home, Jax? Isn't this what you wanted?"

I blew out a breath and sat in the love seat across from her. "I'm happy you're home, as long as you're actually staying."

She had the nerve to look hurt. "This time is different, Jax."

"Really? And why is that?" I leaned forward, bracing my elbows on my knees.

"Because when Brianna called and said she thought you

were really moving on, I realized that I needed to be here." Her eyes searched mine for something I couldn't give her.

My stomach twisted. "You're home for Finley, right? Because that's the only relationship you can improve."

She drew back and blinked quickly, looking away.

Shit. The hardest thing about arguing with Claire was not knowing if she was showing her real emotions or acting.

"Claire. Tell me you're here for Finley," I repeated, softening my tone.

"I don't want another woman raising my child," she admitted, not meeting my eyes.

Morgan. This was all about Morgan.

"I am in full support of you helping to raise Finley," I told her honestly. "You're her mother."

She brought her gaze to mine, and the vulnerability there caught me off guard.

"I know I'm Finley's mother. What am I to you?"

Shit.

"You're Fin's mom. That's it, Claire." I gentled the words as much as possible, but she flinched.

"You used to love me," she argued.

"Yeah, I did. But I don't anymore. I care for you deeply, and I always will. But there's no chance for us. If you're staying in Cape Hatteras, you have to accept that." Each word was clear in the hopes that my meaning was, too.

"But…" She shook her head. "This is what you wanted!" Her legs slid off the couch, and she leaned toward me. "You told me you'd wait for me! That I could come home and we'd be a family again!"

"You left five years ago!" I cringed, then got a grip on my temper and my tone. "Finley was two the last time I told you that. I held onto the hope that you'd come home for years, Claire. But eventually, I let you go."

"I never let you go!"

My eyes flew wide, and I stood. "We can't do this. Not today. Not with Fin right upstairs."

"Jax, please!" She got up and came toward me. "I gave it all up for you, for us! So we could be the family you wanted. Are you seriously telling me that you don't want Finley to have her mom and dad under the same roof? Happy? In love again?"

That's exactly what I'd wanted. What I'd prayed for. But not anymore.

"You're too late," I said simply and backed away from her. There was zero chance I was getting into any position with Claire that I'd have to defend to Morgan. None. "What Finley needs are a mom and dad who are happy and love *her*. Loving each other isn't an option anymore."

"You really mean that?" Her face crumpled, and a single tear slid down her left cheek. My jaw ticked. That was the side she cried out of for every play I'd ever seen her in.

"Yeah. I do, and I'm sorry if it hurts you, but you need to know the truth."

Her tears dried as she studied my face. "You'll change your mind."

"I won't. Now, if you'd like to discuss a schedule to see Fin so she knows when she'll see you, then let's do that. But this topic is closed."

She took a steadying breath. "Okay. Why don't we just split time? One week at my house, one week at yours?"

I blanched. "Out of the question."

"I'm her mother!"

"Claire, I can't even trust you to show up to Mother's Day tea on time, and you think I'm going to give you every other week with her?" I turned and walked into the kitchen, knowing she'd follow me, which she did.

"Of course your little girlfriend would run and tell you that."

"Actually, it was your daughter who filled me in."

"You know that I've never been good with appointments. In fact, you used to love that I was impetuous and impulsive, remember?" She leaned against my doorway.

"Yeah, and I also thought futons made great beds and ramen was a food group, because we were in *college*. I grew up because you can't be careless with a kid, Claire!"

I grabbed a bottle of water from the refrigerator, twisted the top, and chugged. Then I offered her one, because she gave me my favorite human on the planet.

"No, thanks. From what I remember, you used to like a beer right around now," she replied.

"I don't drink unless Fin is at your mom's."

"Because you're so responsible now?" She crossed her arms.

"Yes! I became a *parent*. I never put myself in a situation where I can't take care of her."

"Are you ever going to stop taking digs at me?" she fired back. "I'm here now. Isn't that what matters?"

Fuck, this was exhausting. I finished the water, hoping it would cool my temper. "You can have every other weekend and every other holiday." My heart screamed at the thought of not having Fin on Christmas morning, but wasn't this what adults did?

"Not enough. I may as well stay in L.A. and fly back twice a month for that." She brushed invisible dirt off her blouse.

"That's as good as you're going to get. If you want to schedule some dinners, we can make that happen, too, but Fin's stability is the most important factor in all of this."

Claire huffed, then stood to her full height. "Fine, then fire her nanny. I'll pick her up from school and keep her until you're off work, and I'll stay here on the nights you're flying."

"I'm not firing Sarah." I kept my hands on the counter so I didn't rip my own hair out.

"You'd rather she spend time with a stranger than her mother?" she fired at me.

"Sarah isn't a stranger, and she's proven herself way more dependable than you have! You can't have that time with Finley because I can't trust you. Don't you get that? Trust isn't something you get because you finally deigned to show up and parent. Trust is something you have to earn, and you *haven't* earned it, Claire."

She sucked in a breath. "Watch it, Jax. I might just file for full custody, and then we'll see who's begging for a little time."

Every muscle in my body locked.

"After all, I'm home full time, now, and you're still a coast guard pilot, right? Not exactly a good, dependable, predictable schedule for a little girl, is it?" She tilted her head.

"Get. Out."

She raised an eyebrow. "Just something to keep in mind, baby. There are easier ways to do this. Think about it." She walked out of the kitchen and left through the front door without saying good-bye to Finley.

I calmed myself down and got Finley bathed and put to bed while she told me all about the field trip to Roanoke she was going on tomorrow. Once she was tucked in, I kissed her forehead, then put her walkie-talkie on her nightstand and told her I'd be at Morgan's place for a bit if she needed me.

Switching my cell phone to our indoor cameras, I activated the zone right outside her room as I walked over to Morgan's in the dark.

The sound of banging came through the front door as I knocked.

Sam opened the door, but her face wasn't welcoming. "Tonight is not a good night."

I took a deep breath and reminded myself that Sam wasn't responsible for my shitty mood. There was another bang and the sound of cracking wood. "What the hell is going on?"

"She's trying to demo." Her lips flattened.

"Okay, then I can help her." Hell, breaking shit sounded great right now.

"Not tonight you can't. You look all pissy, and that's the last thing she needs."

Another bang, followed by a curse.

"Sam, I haven't seen her since Saturday morning. This is the only night I have off for two more days. Please don't stand there and tell me I can't see her because I'm in a shit mood." My jaw flexed.

Sam sighed and let her head roll back in frustration before looking at me. "Okay. Here's the deal. It's May sixteenth."

"Right."

Her eyes widened like I wasn't catching on. "It's May *sixteenth*, which is the day—"

"Will died," I guessed, then cursed when she nodded.

"So my girl is in there breaking some shit under the guise of it being demo, and you can't go in there all pissy. Got me?" She stared me down good for being such a little thing.

"I've got you." I ran a hand over my hair and tried to get my head on right.

"Okay, then come in. Just…watch your feet." She led me inside, and we walked through the foyer and turned the corner into the kitchen, where Morgan stood with a sledgehammer, wearing Will's baseball hat.

She was covered in dust and breathing heavy as she surveyed the row of upper cabinets she'd brought down.

"Hey," I said softly.

She turned quickly, clearly shocked. "Hey. I'm just, ummm—"

"Beating the shit out of your kitchen because it's the anniversary of Will's death?" I offered.

Her shoulders relaxed. "Exactly."

I took in the destruction of the room. She'd gotten the easy stuff, but there was a crapload more to do. "Look, I might be the last person you want to see tonight, and if that's the case, I get it. No judgment. I will head home the minute you say so."

She swallowed and moved her safety glasses to the top of her head.

"But I'm pretty good with a hammer, and I'd be happy to help if you want me to."

Morgan stilled.

"Or I can just sit with you while you demo," I offered.

Sam glanced between us as Morgan looked anywhere but at me, making her decision. "Stay. Sit. If you don't mind that I'm not myself."

I'd take her any way she came.

"Okay." I clipped the walkie-talkie to my belt, set the notifications so my phone would vibrate if the camera detected motion, and slipped my phone into my back pocket.

"In that case," Sam sang, "I'm going to leave her with you so I can run to the store. We're out of ice cream, and that's not good for anyone."

Morgan nodded, and Sam gave me a half smile and a mouthed *good luck* before she headed out the door.

I grabbed one of the stools from the side of the breakfast bar and sat, keeping the bar between us to give her whatever space she needed. As much as it grinded my ass to admit, she wasn't mine tonight. She was his.

She pushed the demolished cabinets to the end of the kitchen, and I locked my jaw to stop from asking her to let me help. This was the same girl who hadn't wanted me to screw down the plywood on her landing. She sure as hell didn't want me stepping in here.

Then she put her glasses back on, picked up the sledge, and swung it at the row of cabinets next to the space where the refrigerator had been. A quick glance showed that she'd moved it to the dining room.

"I bet you think I'm insane, right?" she asked, then swung the hammer again.

"Not at all."

She looked at me over her shoulder, then swung the hammer, getting it stuck through the face of the cabinet door. "Shit!"

Don't move. I folded my hands on the counter as I watched her struggle to free it, then let out a breath when she did.

"You should. I feel insane half the time. Did you know that Will and I weren't even together? Not really." She swung again, and the door fell.

"You said something about a quasi-boyfriend," I recalled.

"He never wanted me. Not really. I fell for him when I was in high school, and he only had eyes for Peyton." Another swing. Wood cracked. "And Peyton didn't want him. I never could understand that girl. Will followed her to West Point; that's how much he loved her." Another swing. The cabinet splintered at the bottom, and the sledge fell through to the counter beneath.

Fuck, I wanted her in a hardhat and some sensible boots, not shorts and sneakers.

"He was a West Pointer, huh?" I asked, just to keep her talking. I hated ring-knockers, as did every servicemember I'd ever met.

"Through and through." Her breaths were ragged as she pulled the sledge off the counter and let the business end fall to the floor. "And when Peyton died, he found the next closest person to her to love, who happened to be her little sister. My best friend, Paisley."

My eyebrows shot skyward. Holy shit.

Morgan's ponytail swished as she raised the hammer and

swung it through the cabinet next to the one she'd already massacred.

"That had to suck."

She scoffed. "It was what it was. He didn't want me. I was too loud, too brazen, too much…everything. And Paisley is the sweetest person you'll ever meet, so it's not surprising that he fell for her. Everyone does. Hell, I love her more than I love myself."

But this was the first time I was hearing her name.

She put the hammer through the door again, then struggled to get it free. "I couldn't tell her that I loved him. That would have put her through hell, and her heart couldn't take that. She had a condition back then—the same one that killed Peyton. I mean, what was the point of staying behind for college with her if I just killed her because I was too selfish to keep my mouth shut?" She yanked the hammer free with a grunt, stumbling back a few feet.

I stood but quickly sat again when she regained her balance.

She turned, leaning on the sledge as she looked at me with a mix of sadness and anger. "And then Paisley met Jagger, and *she left Will*. And he was so damned hurt, and she was so damned happy! And it slipped. I never meant for her to know, but then she did." Morgan yanked her safety glasses off. "And, of course, she wasn't mad that I'd been secretly in love with her ex-boyfriend, but then again, I'd loved him for far longer than she ever had."

I kept my eyes locked on hers and tried to appear as relaxed as possible.

"And Will. God, *Will*. I was good enough to be friends with. Good enough to help him study before he got all buddy-buddy with Josh. I was good enough to pin his wings on graduation day when his mama couldn't stand straight, and by God, I was pretty enough to kiss the night he took me to the flight school graduation ball. But I wasn't enough for him to actually *want*."

She put her glasses on, turned around, and swung three times, bringing two cabinets completely down to the counter beneath before she turned back around. Her chest heaved.

"Heaven forbid the West Point, Distinguished Honor Grad, perfect, moral, by-the-book Will Carter actually slum it with Morgan Bartley. I guess Prom Queen wasn't the resume he was looking for." Her head fell as her shoulders rose, and I stood. She gasped for a few breaths and then shot me a glare that had my ass back in the seat.

"And then he had the nerve to drive down right before he deployed and tell me that he wanted to try." She laughed, but it wasn't happy. "Finally, after *years* of loving that man, he wanted to try. But not then, of course. Heaven forbid Will act on a feeling. No, he wanted to try when he got home from that deployment. But I figured, hey, I've waited eight years for him, so what does nine months change?"

Everything, I answered myself. Even though I knew the end of the story, I kept waiting for her to give me the happy ending that she deserved.

"And he kissed me good-bye," she said softly. "And he went. Twice. I only ever kissed him twice. He died two weeks later, saving Josh and Jagger's lives, and as it happened, he told Josh that Jagger had to live for Paisley." She dropped the sledge completely. "The man I loved with my whole heart gave his life so one of the women *he* loved could have her husband."

"Holy shit, Morgan, I'm so sorry." My fucking chest ached for her.

She shrugged, like it wasn't a damned tragedy. "It was noble, right? But that was Will. I've spent the last two years wondering why I wasn't enough to make him want to live."

I stood, unable to keep still any longer.

"That's on him. Not on you," I said softly, more than aware that I was treading in dangerous territory.

"But what does it say about me that two years later I'm still so fucked-up about it that I have to be treated for a grief disorder? Why? Because I still think it's so fucking unfair that everyone else in our group of friends got their happy endings at the expense of mine? What kind of person thinks that? What kind of person can't talk to her best friend because all she wants to do is scream that it's not fair? That everyone acted like my heart didn't matter—*I* didn't matter. Paisley didn't even tell me herself, or even think about me. Ember had to tell Sam to call me. That's how I found out he was dead. And I know Paisley's husband was wounded, but a lifetime of friendship didn't afford me a moment of consideration from anyone but Sam and Grayson."

My jaw flexed as she tugged the safety glasses free and threw them on the counter.

"God, how can it still hurt *so* much after all this time? He never even loved me. I don't even have the right to grieve him like this," she cried, and I moved.

A few seconds later, I was around the bar and in front of her, gripping her arms lightly so she'd look at me.

"Morgan, grief isn't a measure of how much someone loved you. It's the measure of how much you loved *them*. You have every right to feel however the hell you want to feel. Do you understand me?"

She swallowed and looked up at me from under the brim of his cap. The man who I'd never met and would never want to. How could anyone be stupid enough to turn down Morgan's love?

"I don't want to feel like this anymore." Her eyes filled with tears, and I pulled her into my arms, resting my chin on her head as she cried into my chest.

"I know you don't."

"I want to be happy and to have a heart that's worth risking. I miss my friends. I miss *him*, but then there's you, and I want to be ready for whatever this is, and it all just jumbles in my head." Her sobs shook her shoulders.

"I'll wait for as long as you need me to," I promised her again. "You don't have to factor me in to your healing. I'm not going anywhere."

She cried herself out, then stepped back and wiped her tears away with a dusty forearm that left streaks on her face. And still, the woman was beautiful.

"I'm sorry. I probably should have asked how your day was," she muttered.

"Other than the fact that my ex threatened to sue me for custody of Fin, it's all good." I shrugged. As terrifying as the threat was, I logically knew that no judge would give her custody.

"Oh God. Are you serious?"

"Yeah. But it's okay. It won't happen."

She swallowed. "Do you want a hammer? It might help to break a few things."

I grinned. "Why don't you sit down over there and wait for your ice cream, and I'll demo the rest of this?"

She nodded slowly. "I'd really appreciate the help."

"All you ever have to do is ask."

Then I picked up the hammer and destroyed what was left of her kitchen, knowing whatever she rebuilt in the space would be even better, and I didn't think about the email I'd already fired off to my lawyer.

I didn't think about it the rest of the night.

Chapter Sixteen

Morgan

God, I wish I'd had the chance to take you up with me. I wish you knew the way it feels up there with the clouds. It's like you're an inconsequential human and a god all at the same time. You would love it.

"This is good," Dr. Circe said, looking over my list of less-than-awesome memories of Will. As much as the anniversary had taken me down a notch, it hadn't thrown me backward as much as I'd prepared for. "How did you feel filling it out?"

"Guilty," I answered honestly. "But lighter once I was done."

"Excellent. We have a tendency to put our deceased loved ones up on a pedestal, as if we can only remember the good things about them instead of who they were as a whole person." She leaned forward and put the worksheet on the coffee table. "We're past the halfway point, and I'm incredibly pleased with your progress."

"Thank you." Heat rose in my cheeks.

"How is it going with the truck?"

My pulse kicked up. "Okay. I can open the door and stand on the running board now."

She nodded, jotting something down on her notepad. "And the anxiety attacks?"

"I had one the first day that I stood on the running board," I admitted quietly. "But Sam was there, and she talked me down. I didn't have to use my rescue meds or anything."

She smiled. "Good. That's really good. And it might not feel like progress, but it is. See?" She opened my folder, flipped to a page in the back, made a mark, and then turned it around so I could see it. "These are your number of attacks a week."

The graph was decreasing.

"And this"—she flipped another page—"is your reported level of grief. Look, you started up here at ten, and now you're down here at five. It means the therapy is working. That's fantastic!"

I stared at the graph and nodded as a lump filled my throat. It was working. I was getting better.

"So for this week, I want you to put one foot on the running board and the other foot inside the truck."

I stilled, panic rising at the thought of getting in it. "For how long?"

Dr. Circe glanced at her notebook. "You don't have to hold it. Just see if you can put your foot inside. Remember, this is a marathon, not a sprint. We want you to be successful but still make progress."

"Right." Maybe I should have left that damn thing in storage instead of having the flatbed deliver it.

"Also, it's time to start talking about the interpersonal dynamics you're struggling with. You've mentioned Paisley in most of our sessions. Are you feeling up to opening that dialogue yet?" She watched me carefully, but there was no judgment in her tone or gaze, which was one of the reasons I liked her so much.

"I was actually thinking about inviting her—everyone, really—for Memorial Day weekend. I think I might finally have the words I need to say to her." Some of them had come flying out at Jackson that night in the kitchen, and others had trickled in while I filled out that worksheet. Bottom line was that I loved my best friend, and if I didn't at least try to explain my feelings, I was going to lose her.

"That's great to hear. And I know you're not quite ready for the imagined conversation with Will yet, but maybe next week?" She smiled optimistically.

Right. No.

"Maybe," I answered. "I do have one question, since I know we have to get to the story before I head home."

"How can I help?" she asked.

"Jackson..." My mouth opened and shut a few times as I struggled to find the words. "Am I using him?"

"How?"

I shifted in my seat. "I really like him, and my feelings for him get bigger every time I see him, or talk to him, or get a text. But am I just throwing my feelings for Will at him? Am I getting better because I'm rebounding?"

Her eyes softened. "Are you in love with Jackson?"

I balked. "No. At least, I don't think I am." I was wild about the guy, but I wasn't going to start throwing the L word in. "But I could see myself falling in love with him. In the future, that is."

"That's fair. Now tell me, do you still love Will?" Her voice softened.

My heart *hurt*. It wasn't the same level of pain that it once had been, but the feelings were still there. "Yes," I whispered. "It's a little softer, though, like someone turned down the stereo in the car and now I can hear other sounds, too."

"I don't think you're using Jackson. I'd be worried if you said that you were head over heels in love with him and you no longer felt anything for Will. But everything you're feeling is actually on track. You might have bigger feelings for Jackson because you're healing and becoming capable of them, Morgan. I'm really pleased at the progress you're showing in this area."

"So he's not just some kind of Band-Aid?" I fidgeted with the sea-glass necklace.

"Not that I can tell. And honestly, a Band-Aid wouldn't have touched you when you first came through those doors. You needed open-heart surgery. What you feel for Jackson appears to be genuine, but don't be surprised if a little misplaced guilt worms its way in there. Don't let it derail you or this new relationship. You're still a work in progress."

Work in progress. I needed that tattooed on my freaking forehead.

She reached for the tape recorder. "You ready?"

I nodded, and she hit the record button.

"I'm in the grocery store, and I pick up a jar of jam…"

• • •

"Okay, what am I doing here?" I asked Jackson the next day as I stood between our cars in the parking lot outside his station.

He had a devilish gleam in his eye that had me immediately suspicious. "I have an idea."

"Do you?" I folded my arms across my chest and ignored how good he looked in that flight suit.

"I want you to see what I do." He leaned back against his Land Cruiser and grinned.

"I already know what you do." Like hell was I going to

watch him fly. I already had trouble sleeping on nights I knew he was on shift.

"Right, but I want you to *see* it. I know how much it weighs on you, and maybe if you—"

"Stop." I put out my hand. "You want me to what? Stand in your control tower and watch you fly the very thing that gives me nightmares?"

His grin vanished. "Not exactly. I want you to fly with me."

Blood rushed from my face, and my stomach lurched. "You're kidding."

"Nope. I'm going to sneak you on board with my crew, and we're going to fly a quick, easy patrol. Skies are baby blue, there's not a cloud in sight, and there's zero chance of foul weather. It's the perfect day." He stared at me with an intensity that told me he was serious.

"You're not sneaking me on board anything, because there's zero chance in hell any of that is going to happen." I took a step toward him, shaking my finger.

Big mistake.

"Have you ever gone up before?" He gripped my hips and pulled me forward to stand between his thighs. Sure, it was a warm day, but that had nothing to do with the spike in temperature inside my own body. That was pure Jackson.

"No, and do not think you can charm me onto that death trap." I put my hands on his chest to hold him off, but that didn't help, either. He was firm under my touch, and I knew exactly what he looked like beneath his flight suit. I pressed my thighs together and gave him my best glare.

"Do you trust me?" He moved his sunglasses to the top of his head and hit me with those incredible eyes.

"Not fair," I whined, but I wasn't sure if it was over the question or his use of his secret weapon.

"Morgan Bartley, do you trust me?" His hands flexed on

my hips.

"With my life," I grumbled.

"I'm a damned good pilot. I graduated top of my class." His gaze bored into mine.

"Did you, now?" *Just like Will.* I pushed that thought right out of my head.

"Yep. And there is no chance I'm going to do anything that would ever put you at risk or put myself in a position that I can't get home to Finley. You know that." His hand rose and brushed my hair back just so the ocean breeze could whip it the other direction.

That was true. He'd never jeopardize Finley's future.

"Give me an hour, Morgan, and you won't be as scared of what I do out there."

I pulled my lower lip between my teeth and chewed lightly. Was I actually considering this insanity?

"Come on, Kitty. I'll give you whatever you want if you'll do this with me. I won't ask you for a single outdoor date for a month. We'll order in every night, and you can read while I rub your feet." The plea in his voice and his hopeful expression were priceless.

I sighed. An hour. Maybe it was like listening to those damned tapes of me telling the story of Will's death over and over. Maybe doing this once would suck, but it would make the future easier—the future I wanted with him.

"I know what I want." I looked him in the eye.

"Anything." That grin was back, and damn if it didn't send my heart skittering. The man was too good-looking for his own good.

"I invited my friends down for the weekend." Okay, so it had been via text, but I'd reached out.

"Okay." His brows puckered.

"I want you to meet them." I pressed my lips in a line and held my breath.

"That's it? You just want me to meet your friends?" He studied me.

"Yes. And before you agree, you should know that it has the potential to be the most awkward weekend of your life."

His eyes widened. "Those friends."

I nodded. "And they're not going to be easy on you. Sam is a cakewalk compared to Josh and Jagger." My fingertips traced the patches on his chest.

"Deal." He didn't even hesitate.

"You really should take a minute to think about it," I encouraged.

"Morgan, you just asked me for something that's within my power to give you. It's yours. I'm yours, awkward weekend and all, helicopter ride or not. I'm there." He pressed a kiss to my forehead, and I melted.

Oh God, I was really fixing to do this.

"Take me flying."

A half hour later, I was second-guessing my life choices as I stepped into the helicopter. I had on one of Sawyer's flight suits since he was shorter than Jackson, and my feet were stuffed into boots at least four sizes too big. My hair was tucked up inside a flight helmet and the visor was down, shielding my eyes. It didn't shield me from the scent, though. That metallic tang was exactly how Will had smelled after he'd spent a day in the cockpit.

"We've got choices," Jackson said through the headset as I stared at the relatively empty space. He pointed to the pair of seats at the rear. "You can have a more comfortable seat"—he swung his arm toward the front, where there were two smaller, far less stable-looking seats—"or you can be closer to me."

Garrett clipped himself into one of the rear seats and patted the one next to him. "Got room right here for you, Morgan."

The seats up front were perpendicular to Jackson's , and just behind him. I'd even be able to touch him if I needed to. "Closer to you," I answered.

"That's my girl." He gave me a grin and got me buckled into the seat. My heart pounded to the rhythm of the rotors above us as Sawyer started the preflight.

"Anyone see her?" Jackson asked Sawyer.

"Nope. Told you it would be easy. Now you just sit back and relax, Morgan. We here at Coast Guard Air would like to welcome you aboard for today's flight." Sawyer grinned at me as Jackson tightened the straps of my harness. "We have a quick flight plan for you today involving a short pleasure tour of the Outer Banks. Unfortunately, no snacks will be provided. Please keep your hands inside the aircraft at all times, and remember that vomiting is considered rude."

My stomach turned.

"I've got you," Jackson promised, cupping my cheek under my helmet.

I nodded, gritting my teeth as I prepared to kiss the earth good-bye.

In through my nose, out through my mouth. I spent the remainder of the preflight time concentrating on my breathing so I didn't let the panic win and send me running from the aircraft.

"Here we go, Kitty," Jackson said as we took off.

My stomach dropped as we rose into the air, and I squeezed my eyes shut. What the hell was I doing in this thing? I had nothing to prove and everything to lose. And the vibrations through my seat were going to numb my ass at best and rattle my spine at worst. They were even stronger at my feet.

"It's no fun when you can't see anything," Sawyer teased, looking back from the cockpit.

I opened my eyes and flipped him the bird.

He laughed. "Your girl doesn't think this is fun."

"If your ex-girlfriend went down in a bird and then died in a firefight, chances are you wouldn't think this was fun, either," Jackson snapped.

Sawyer's head whipped back, his eyes huge with apology. "Shit, Morgan, I didn't know."

"Take the controls," Jackson ordered.

"I have the controls," Sawyer responded, his focus completely devoted to the aircraft.

Jackson's hand reached back, and I took it. "You okay back there?"

"I'm okay," I lied.

"The view is gorgeous if you look out the window," he suggested, squeezing my hand.

I leaned forward and gasped. The blue of the water against the sand of the beach made for a stunning contrast as we flew down the coastline, and I had to admit that he was right. The view was spectacular, entrancing, even, and something I only could have seen from the air. We flew miles down the coast, and eventually my body adjusted to the vibration and motion of the aircraft. My brain was an entirely different matter.

"Coast Guard seven-five-three-niner, come in." The radio blared through my headset.

Jackson's hand disappeared, and my coms went dead.

Garrett nodded and his mouth moved, but I couldn't hear him. What the hell was going on? Had someone seen them sneak me on board? Was Jackson going to be in trouble? Just as I was about ready to lose my ever-loving mind, the coms came back to life.

"Morgan, we have a distress call," Jackson said, not taking my hand because he was now the one flying.

"We what?" My voice cracked.

"We have a vessel that's called in a mayday."

"Just a patrol," Sawyer muttered.

"There's no injuries, and we're the closest rescue team. I need you to just sit tight back there, okay, Kitty?"

"Yeah. Okay." My hands gripped the edges of my little seat as the aircraft changed course, pitching left. We were headed out to sea.

I closed my eyes and concentrated on the rhythmic beat of the rotors and my breathing, hyperaware of my throat. My heart pounded and my stomach dipped with the turn, but there was no looming anxiety attack…yet.

This is fine. You're fine. Jackson does this every day. He's a great pilot. Top of his class, right?

So was Will, my devil's advocate whispered in my ear. *And Josh, and Jagger for that matter.*

"Morgan, you okay up there?" Garrett asked. "Don't worry, we're the only ones who can hear you. They switched our coms to aircraft-only back here."

"I'm fine," I lied. I seemed to be doing a lot of that today, but my nerves didn't matter compared to what those people had to be going through.

"You're faking it really well," he assured me as he unbuckled.

"ETA is three minutes," Sawyer said through the headset.

Garrett rose from his seat and kneeled before me. "I need you to sit right here and not move, okay? That's all you have to do. Tell me you understand."

"I understand. Sit. Don't move." I nodded for emphasis. There was zero chance in hell I was moving from this seat or getting in the way of saving someone.

"This is totally routine, so don't stress." He stood and got ready to do whatever it was he did. He took two gray blankets from the rescue litter and set them on the seat next to me.

"Don't stress. Right," I whispered.

"Just keep breathing for me, Kitty." Jackson's voice was thick with worry.

"I'm fine." I even pitched my voice a little higher to prove it. "You just fly this thing, okay?" The last thing he needed to be thinking about was me.

"We have a visual. ETA one minute," Sawyer announced.

Garrett unstrapped a wire cage from a tower directly in front of me and took it to the floor, where he formed it into a rectangular basket. Then he hooked himself onto a belt that attached to the ceiling and opened the door of the helicopter. The noise level skyrocketed, the wind whipped through the fuselage, and there was ocean as far as I could see. Whoever waited below us was out there all alone, and though I saw the helicopter as a death trap, I realized that for them, it was salvation.

"I have a visual," Garrett said as he leaned out the freaking door. "The adult male and child are clear of the landing area."

My chest tightened. There was a kid?

"Do you need me back there, Harrison?" Sawyer asked.

"No, sir. I've got this."

The helicopter slowed to a hover.

"Prepare to drop the basket," Sawyer said.

Garrett got the thing hooked up to a wire that led outside the helicopter. "Basket ready."

"Deploy," Sawyer ordered.

"Deploying." Garrett slid the basket out the door, and it hung just outside the helicopter for a moment before he pushed a button, sending it down. Then my stomach lurched as the man leaned out again. Any farther and we'd be rescuing him, too. "Eyes on the basket."

We lost a little elevation, but that had to be on purpose, because no one panicked. Well, no one but me. This seat would probably need to be reupholstered after I dug my fingernails out of it. My heart raced, but still no throat issues.

"Hold, sir." Garrett's head swiveled back and forth at

whatever was beneath us for a minute. Maybe two. "Prepare to take the load." Another pause. "Taking the load."

I sucked in a breath as the hoist lifted the basket. We'd saved at least one of them.

"Roger," Sawyer replied.

Garrett dropped to his belly as his head hung out of the aircraft. "Load is halfway up." He rose to his knees and reached for the wire. "Basket is about ten feet below the cabin."

"Roger."

"Five feet below cabin. Bringing the basket inside the cabin."

"Roger."

Garrett scrambled to his feet and hauled the rescue basket back inside the helicopter with a terrified boy and his father as its occupants.

My breath released in an audible rush at the realization that we'd saved them both. We'd made it in time.

"Basket is inside the cabin."

"Roger."

He disengaged the wire and closed the door, then got the boy out first.

Mercy. He was soaking wet, shaking like a leaf, and his skin was pale against the bright orange of his life vest.

I grabbed one of the blankets and reached for the boy's hand. When he turned, I offered him a reassuring smile, tugged him closer, then shook the blanket once and wrapped it around him like a cape. "Is that better?" I asked, raising my voice so he could hear me over the beat of the rotors.

He nodded, his eyes wide and pupils dilated. He clutched the blanket close, and Garrett led him to the seat he'd previously occupied.

I handed the second blanket to the father, who took it with a grateful nod. The relief in his eyes was second only to shock as Garrett got them both situated in their seats.

"We're good to go," Garrett said over the coms.

"Roger," Sawyer replied again.

The helicopter pitched forward slightly, then banked left, taking us back to the coastline as Garrett took the seat next to me.

"It's a good thing we were close. That boat had another ten minutes, tops," he said through our coms.

"What sank it?" I asked.

"Not my business." He shrugged. "They're alive. That's my business. You did great, Morgan."

I scoffed. "I sat here and handed out blankets."

He grinned. "Like I said, you did great."

The father and son held hands, the son's head falling to his dad's shoulder as we flew back to the coast guard station. Ten minutes. That was all that stood between that family and the ocean. Ten minutes and Jackson's crew.

Ten minutes that Jackson's parents hadn't had.

How many lives had he saved? How many kids still had their parents because of Jackson? Or Garrett? Or Sawyer?

Had this been scary as hell? Yes.

But it was humbling.

"You okay there, Kitty?" Jackson asked.

"I'm great." I really was.

"This is going to get a little complicated, so when we land, just stick with Garrett. I have to do a post-flight. Garrett, take her to the bunk room, would you?"

"You got it," Garrett answered.

Landing was a blur, and I did as Jackson asked and waited with Garrett. First, I stayed right behind him in the hopes that no one would notice I was there as they off-loaded our evacuees. Lucky for us, we weren't the center of attention.

An hour after we landed, I sat on the farthest twin bed from the door inside the bunk room, staring up at the clock.

My borrowed flight suit, boots, and helmet lay on the bed next to me, ready to be returned to their owners. "Is it supposed to take this long?" I asked Garrett.

"Trust me, it's fine. We'd have heard about it by now if we'd gotten caught." He leaned against the door, occasionally looking through the small glass window to the hallway.

"A quick, easy patrol, Morgan." My voice dropped into a Jackson impression.

Garrett laughed. "That was his plan, trust me." A knock sounded at the door, and he looked through the glass. "About time," he said as he opened the door.

Jackson walked in, his flight suit unzipped just enough to reveal the T-shirt underneath. "Thanks, man."

"No problem." Garrett gave me a two-fingered salute and walked out, closing the door behind him.

Jackson locked the door, peered through the window, and then came toward me with an apologetic smile. "So that turned out a little more adventurous than I'd hoped." He sat down next to me, close enough that our thighs touched.

"You think?" I tilted my head.

He grimaced. "I mean, it could have been worse."

"You could have gotten caught."

"That, too." He took my hand and laced our fingers. "I'm really sorry. I never meant for you to get caught up in that."

God, those *eyes*. They made me want to swim in them—swim in him.

"I'm okay," I assured him.

"You sure? Because I'd planned on taking you for a pleasure flight so you'd see just how awesome flying can be, and instead I landed you smack in the middle of a rescue operation." He faced forward and tensed. "While I'm really proud of the rescue, I fear that I may have failed Operation Reassure Morgan." The muscle at his jaw flexed.

My heart lurched.

Letting go of Jackson's hand made him startle, but I flat-out shocked him when I turned and slid my knee over his thighs to straddle him. I settled into his lap like I'd always belonged there and cradled the back of his head with my hands.

"I'm okay," I promised, looking him in the eye so he'd know I really was. "I handed out blankets and didn't puke. You saved two people. I call that a win."

"You amaze me." He gripped my hips lightly. "But I'm guessing it didn't do much to calm your fears."

I slid my hands forward a bit so I could run my thumbs over his cheeks. "Does it terrify me that you fly? Yes. That didn't change, and I don't think it's ever going to."

"I don't blame you." His face fell slightly.

"Shh, I'm talking." I placed one thumb over his lips.

His eyes flared, and he raked his teeth over the pad of my thumb, then swiped his tongue over it.

My body flooded with warmth, and it took a second to remember what I was saying. "Yes, I'm scared, but seeing what you did out there? I understand it now, too."

His grip tightened. "You do?"

He looked so hopeful that I couldn't help but smile. "I do. There's a chance that family wouldn't be here if you hadn't been out there." I kissed his forehead. "I was so proud of you."

He sucked in a breath, then pulled back with a smirk. "Wait, you *were* proud of me?"

"I still am. Now stop fishing for compliments, Jackson Montgomery."

His eyes dropped to my lips, and I barely parted mine before he kissed me. Mercy, I loved this man's mouth. The first touch of our lips was soft, but it quickly deepened. I tilted my head as his tongue met mine, and a shock of electricity raced down my spine. He tasted sweet today, like orange soda and something uniquely Jackson, as he took my mouth in strokes that varied from hard and deep to swirling and lazy. He kept me leaning in for more, and the minute I'd get it, he'd change the pace.

When he pulled back, we were both breathing hard. I caught his lower lip between my teeth and tugged gently. I wasn't ready for this to be over.

He groaned, taking full control, and I gladly gave it to him. I rocked forward, and he grabbed my ass, bringing our hips flush. He was hard and made no apology for it as he threaded a hand through my hair and kissed me senseless.

How was it possible for a man to rob me of every single thought? I whimpered slightly when he started on my neck, his lips teasing every one of my sensitive spots like he had a freaking map. His hair was soft under my fingers, and I gripped it, seeking something—anything that might hold me to the earth while my body felt like it was gearing up for flight.

"You drive me insane. Do you know that?" he asked with his mouth at my throat. I arched to give him better access, and he took it. God, he felt good. "You're all I think about. All I dream about."

"Jackson," I moaned in answer. Every kiss, lick, and nip sent waves of need through my limbs that pooled deep in my belly. Desire rose so fast and strong it felt like a dam breaking all the way in my soul, flooding me with feelings I didn't need to keep locked up anymore.

He pressed kisses down the center of my chest, and when he reached the buttons of my sleeveless blouse, I popped them free.

Our eyes locked, and I rose slightly, tilted my hips forward, and slid down the length of him.

"Fuck, Kitty." He hissed. Then his mouth fused with mine in the kind of kiss that I had only read about. The ones that altered the universe and left you addicted. I wasn't even sure there was a universe, anymore. There was only Jackson. Jackson's hands. Jackson's mouth. Jackson's body beneath mine.

His hand slid inside my open shirt to cup my breast through my plain white bra. I suddenly wished I'd gone shopping or simply cared enough in the last couple of years to own more than two colors of lingerie.

"Please." I leaned into his touch, and he lifted my breast from the cup, rubbing his thumb over my nipple so it hardened for him.

"Perfect," he murmured against my lips, then dipped his head and lifted me slightly so he could take the peak between his lips.

I moaned at the sweet sensation, my fingers digging into his shoulders as I reveled in the pleasure his mouth gave me. His tongue was magic, and his teeth awakened every nerve ending with delicate scrapes.

My hips rolled on instinct, seeking friction and pressure—seeking Jackson.

He groaned, switching his attention to my other breast, and then he sent his free hand up the bare skin of my thigh. I rolled forward again, and he skimmed his thumb under the hem of my shorts, following the line until he dipped between my thighs.

Oh, holy hell, yes.

"Morgan, we—"

A knock at the door froze us solid.

"Shit," Jackson muttered.

My head hit his shoulder as I tried to calm my racing heart.

"One second," Jackson called, his hands already working at the buttons on my shirt.

I tugged my straps to make sure the girls were put away and slid off his lap. He steadied me and searched my eyes.

"I'm fine," I promised.

He nodded and strode for the door. "What the fuck do you want?" he snapped at whomever was on the other side of the door as he flung it open.

"You're going to be late for the briefing," Sawyer told him.

"Not sure I care." Jackson muttered a curse and shut the door in Sawyer's face. Then he closed his eyes and leaned against the door.

Certain that I had everything put back where it was supposed to be, I grabbed my handbag from the bed and slung it over my shoulder.

"Morgan, I'm—" Jackson started, apology filling his gaze.

"You owe me an entire weekend," I said before he could finish. I wasn't sorry about any of it, and I'd be damned if I let him be.

His eyes flared in surprise. "Yeah, I guess I do."

"Then I guess I'll see you at home." I kissed him gently. "Now show me how to get out of here."

He grinned, then opened the door and took me down the hallway and out to the parking lot where he kissed me again. Guess he really didn't care about being late.

When I got home, Sam sat at the dining room table, making a grocery list that included enough food to feed an army—an army I'd invited for the weekend. An army we had to feed with the grill because I didn't exactly have a kitchen.

Ember. Josh. Paisley. Jagger.

They were all headed here in three days.

Taking a helicopter ride suddenly felt like it was the easiest part of my week.

Chapter Seventeen

Jackson

By the time I got to Morgan's on Friday, there were two cars I didn't recognize in the driveway—a bright yellow Defender and a blue Jeep Wrangler.

Guess the friends were here.

There were six vehicles I knew well parked along the right side of my drive, and from the sound of music coming over the dune, the guys had everything set up on the beach.

Sam's look of relief when she opened the front door told me all I needed to know.

"That bad, huh?" I asked as she shut the door behind me.

"Not sure if bad is the word I'd use, but awkward is right up there. They're in the kitchen."

We rounded the corner and found the group standing in the unfinished area. The floors had been installed last week, and now tile that looked like hardwood covered the entire floor. The cabinets were in, and Morgan's new refrigerator had been installed, too, but there weren't any countertops yet.

There was a redhead with a small baby bump and her arm around the waist of a guy who looked to be about my height, with brown hair and eyes, and another guy with blond hair who was checking out the install job on the farmhouse sink. Next to him, a blond girl stood with an equally blond toddler on her hip, taking in the space with a smile.

They were all the same people from the flight school ball photo on Will's Facebook page.

Morgan stood on the other side of what used to be the bar but was now an island, so tense she looked like she might snap. Even her smile was brittle. I wasn't sure what her friends knew about us or if she even wanted them to know there *was* an us, but my apprehension fled the minute her eyes met mine.

Her shoulders dipped slightly, and the relief that flooded her gaze was palpable.

I crossed the floor, and when she opened her arms, I took her into mine, tucking her against my chest. Whatever we were, she wasn't hiding it from her friends.

"Jackson," she murmured, holding me tight.

"Hey, Kitty." My voice was low as I pressed a kiss to the top of her head.

"I'm so glad you're here."

"Me, too. I would have been earlier, but I needed to drop Fin off at Vivian's." I hated this new every other weekend arrangement, but if Claire was going to actually live here, then I had to get used to it.

"Man, I forgot it was her weekend." She sighed in disappointment.

"I wish I had. But she'll be home Monday afternoon."

Morgan pulled back and tilted her face up. "Well, I guess that means I have you to myself for a couple of days, huh?"

I grinned. "Well, you have to share me with Fin's pets since I'm on feeding duty, but other than that, yes."

"I find that acceptable."

The silence in the room caught my attention, and sure enough, there were four—make that five—people staring at me with blatant curiosity. The blond guy had a little skepticism in his gaze, too.

"Um. Everyone, this is Jackson. Jackson, this is everyone." Morgan introduced me, turning toward them but leaving her arm draped around my waist. "He's going to insist that you call him Jax."

"You're the only person on the planet who calls me Jackson," I told her with a laugh. "And yeah, please call me Jax."

The dark-haired guy was Josh, and his red-haired wife was Ember.

The blond guy was Jagger, and his wife was Paisley—Morgan's best friend.

"And this is Peyton." Paisley looked lovingly at her son. "Can you wave, Pey?"

The boy tucked his head into his mom's neck, but once I waved, he did, too, opening and shutting a tiny fist. Had Finley really ever been that small?

"So you're the next-door neighbor," Ember remarked with a slow smirk, glancing at Sam, who nodded.

"That would be me." I smiled.

Pretty sure this was exactly how animals felt at the zoo, because they were all staring at me. The women wore curious expressions, and the guys were flat-out skeptical.

Morgan's hand tightened at my waist as the quiet in the room became stifling. The island felt like a no-man's land, with Sam, Morgan, and I on one side and her friends on the other.

"You were right," I told Sam. "Awkward is a good word."

She scoffed and smacked my arm with the back of her hand. "So did you four want me to get the swinging lightbulb so you can sweat him out in an interrogation right here, or did you want to do it by the bonfire?"

Paisley rolled her eyes, then elbowed her husband when he looked like he was considering it.

"I'd prefer the bonfire, since my friends are down there," I said with a small shrug.

Morgan and I had set this up a few days ago, thinking it might be a little easier on everyone involved if we had a barbecue to kick off the weekend and break the tension, rather than waiting for Monday, when we'd have another one, of course.

"I second the bonfire," Sam added.

"Is that okay for Peyton?" Morgan asked, her eyes drifting to the baby. "There are still a couple of hours before sunset."

"Oh, sure!" Paisley answered. "We'll just grab his sunshade. Baby?"

"On it," Jagger answered, heading up the stairs. Guess that answered the question of where everyone was staying.

Once Jagger had the shade, we took the back deck stairs to the path that wound over the dune, and Morgan laced her fingers through mine.

"You doing okay?" I asked.

"Of course. Why wouldn't I be?" She gave me a smile that didn't reach her eyes.

I paused halfway up the dune and told Sam we'd meet them in a bit as she passed us.

"What's wrong?" Morgan asked.

Once the others were out of sight, I cupped her face in my hands and kissed her.

She melted against me, and that simple kiss transformed into something far more intense than I had planned. When I lifted my head, her eyes were slightly glazed and her posture was infinitely more relaxed.

"That's better," I said, tucking her hair behind her ear so I could see her face.

"What was that for?"

"To remind you that you don't have to put on a front for me. I know you're struggling with them here."

She looked away, and I tilted her head so she'd bring those eyes back to mine.

"What if I can't do this?"

"You can," I assured her. "And if it gets to be too much, then you can head to my house and regroup. I'll say you have to feed the guinea pig."

"Even if it takes me an hour to regroup?" she questioned, lifting an eyebrow.

"She has a fish and a turtle, too. Trust me, we can find an excuse."

She laughed, and I kissed her nose.

When we started back up the dune, I saw Paisley at the top, staring down at us with a mixture of confusion and happiness. Then her face fell slightly as she turned to walk back to the beach.

"She misses you." I took Morgan's hand as we started climbing.

"She misses who I used to be," she said softly as we crested the dune.

"I'm not going to tell you how to feel or how to handle this. You tell me what you need me to be, and I'll be that, okay?"

"I just need you." She squeezed my hand and surveyed the small gathering. "You know they're going to grill you, right?"

"They wouldn't be good friends if they didn't."

Knowing that fact didn't make the next hour any less painful. While Morgan sat with her friends, sneaking glances at me every few minutes, Josh and Jagger fired questions at me from both sides. She was close enough to hear my answers but trusted me to hold my own and didn't interfere.

I'm twenty-eight. My daughter is five. No, her mother and I aren't together. Yes, I like Morgan. We met when I pulled her out of her staircase. Yes, I know her contractor. Yes, he gave her fair estimates. On and on the questions came, until I was pretty sure they were about to ask for my social security number so they could run a credit check.

The only thing they hadn't asked—

"And what do you do for a living?" Josh asked.

Ah, there it is. "I'm a coast guard search and rescue pilot," I answered.

Morgan's eyes locked with mine.

"Are you shitting me?" Jagger leaned forward in his chair.

"Nope." I winked at Morgan, hoping she'd relax enough to breathe. Her gaze flickered between the guys. "Been stationed here five years."

"Best damn pilot in the Outer Banks," Sawyer remarked as he dragged a chair through the sand and sat on the other side of Jagger. "Other than me, of course."

"And so humble," I quipped.

Sawyer raised his beer in salute.

"You're all pilots?" Jagger glanced toward the grill, where Moreno and Garrett argued over timing.

"Nawh." Sawyer shook his head. "Javier is our best mechanic, and Garrett is a rescue swimmer. His job makes us look like chickenshits. And that's Goodwin over by the water. He's another swimmer. Hastings—the guy next to him—is a pilot, though. Those are their wives, Christina and Cassidy."

"And she knows? Morgan knows?" Josh dropped his voice.

"Morgan knows everyone. It's not like Jackson keeps her locked away or anything." Sawyer shrugged.

Josh's eyes narrowed on me.

"That's not what he's asking," I said to Sawyer before turning back to Josh. "Yeah. Morgan knows."

Appraising the level of tension, Morgan got to her feet and came around the timbers that we'd get around to lighting here in a few.

"And you know—" Josh started.

"Everything okay?" she asked, taking a seat in my lap and resting her arm over my shoulders.

"We're fine," I promised, putting my hand on her bare knee. "They were just asking if you knew that I fly."

"I know," she said softly. "I don't like it, but I know. And honestly, once he took me up and I saw him rescue—"

"You got her up?" Jagger's eyes flew wide. "As in up in a helicopter?"

"Jagger Bateman, isn't that what I just said?" Morgan fired back, arching an eyebrow. "Don't you dare go asking questions about me like I'm not sitting right here."

I pressed my lips in a firm line to keep from laughing.

Jagger sighed but looked properly chastised. "Fine. Sorry. You actually went flying?"

"I did. It was terrifying and exhilarating all at the same time." She smiled at me, and damn if that didn't make my chest constrict. "He saves lives. It's pretty incredible."

"Who saves lives?" Paisley asked, settling herself in Jagger's lap while Sam and Ember played with Peyton.

"Jackson," Morgan answered. "He's a search and rescue pilot with the coast guard."

This would have been so much more efficient if we'd just briefed everyone at once.

Paisley blanched. "I'm sorry?"

"Jax is a search and rescue pilot with the coast guard," Sawyer repeated slowly and at greater volume. "Me, too, and Hastings, over there by the water."

Paisley blinked at Sawyer, then swung her face toward

Morgan. "Honey, you're okay with that?"

"Whether or not I'm okay with it doesn't change the facts." Morgan shifted her legs.

"Well, I know that. It's just..." Paisley's worried gaze flickered between Morgan and me. "Unexpected."

"Everything about Jackson is unexpected." Her smile was slow as we locked eyes. "And besides, it's not like they deploy or anything."

My stomach sank.

"What? Hell yeah, we do. We're deploying in six weeks," Sawyer chimed in.

Morgan's face drained of color, and her body went rigid.

"I'm not going, Kitty," I said softly, cupping her cheeks. "I'm not deploying."

She swallowed, but it didn't take the terror out of her eyes.

"The guys are deploying for three months to a cushy little outfit in the Caribbean. They needed a few of us to stay behind, and because I have Finley, I'm staying." I kept my voice calm and even despite the panic trying to claw its way out of my gut. It was as if my body was responding to hers, or maybe I was just that scared of losing her.

"Finley?" she questioned.

"Right. I have a family care plan, but they took mercy on me. I don't have to go." I stroked my thumbs over her cheeks.

"You're not going." Breath by breath, she relaxed.

"He's ditching us," Sawyer complained. "But don't stress yourself, Morgan. We'll be back by the end of September."

"You okay?" Fuck, I should have talked to her about it way sooner than this, but I wasn't going, so it hadn't been at the top of my list.

She nodded.

"Paisley!" Ember laughed as Peyton grabbed fistfuls of her hair. Then her laugh turned to a grimace.

"I've got you." Sam picked Peyton up, but he didn't let go of Ember's hair.

"Peyton Carter Bateman!" Paisley chided, hopping up from Jagger's lap.

"I'll get him." Morgan chuckled and headed over to untangle Ember's hair from Peyton's enthusiastic grip.

"Peyton Carter, huh?" I asked. Damn, this guy was *everywhere.*

Paisley beamed. "Yeah. He's named after my sister and—"

"Will," I answered.

Her jaw dropped for a second before she composed herself. "She's told you about him? Sam told me she was struggling with that—talking about him."

"It's hard to ignore that giant truck in her front yard, but yeah, she's told me what she can." I tried to offer her a reassuring smile. "And every day she's capable of a little more."

Her expression shifted from shock to envy and settled on pure gratitude. "I'm glad she has you, Jax."

"I'm lucky to have her."

"Paisley, your son is freakishly strong!" Morgan called out.

Jagger moved, but Paisley touched his forearm. "I've got him." She rose from Jagger's lap and headed for the baby.

"He likes the red hair." Jagger laughed.

"Man after my own heart." Josh grinned as Paisley untangled Peyton from his wife's hair.

"So you guys done with the interrogation?" I asked as the girls walked toward the beach.

"I'm good," Josh remarked. "Sam vouched for you."

"You worried about passing muster, coastie?" Jagger challenged with a smirk.

"Nope. I honestly don't give a fuck what you think about

me. But it would sure make it easier on Morgan if you didn't think I was complete dick." I shrugged.

"You can stay." Jagger laughed. "How did you get Morgan on an aircraft, anyway? Family day?"

"I disguised her in a flight suit and walked her straight onto the bird." I watched as Morgan hefted Peyton to her hip in the dying light. She was going to make an incredible mother–if that's what she wanted. Shit, did she want kids? Was Finley an issue for her? Not every woman wanted a ready-made family.

"No shit?" Josh questioned.

"No shit," Sawyer answered. "She handled herself like a champ, too, especially when that rescue got called in."

Hell yes, she had.

"God, I can hear Carter now." Josh groaned. "Regulations state that you're not allowed on this aircraft, Morgan." His voice dropped into what was obviously an impression, but there was a soft smile on his face.

Jagger laughed. "He would have shit bricks. Can you imagine trying to get him to sneak someone on board? His little rule-loving heart would have imploded."

"Burgers in five!" Javier yelled.

"Did you char this batch?" Sawyer called back.

Javier responded with a middle finger.

"So, Will was a by-the-book kind of guy?" I didn't want to ask, but I wanted to know the answer. It was one thing to compete with a ghost, but a fucking saint? That was impossible.

"Will *wrote* the fucking book." Jagger kept his eyes on his wife and son. "He saw everything in black and white. There was no middle ground. No room for compromise."

"Even for Morgan," Josh remarked with a little headshake. "Hell, especially in the case of Morgan." His voice dropped again. "You can't wear that out in public, Morgan. What will people think?"

"Watch your tongue, Morgan," Jagger chimed in.

Her tongue? "So you're saying he wasn't perfect."

"Carter? Fuck, no. He was a ring-knocker with a chip the size of Alabama on his shoulder." Jagger scoffed. "Always had to come in first. Always had to be right." He swallowed. "Always had to do the right thing, no matter what it cost him."

Josh dropped his head briefly.

"She loved him. Hell, she still loves him." The confession was in the air before I could watch *my* tongue.

"Yeah, she sure did. But those two…" Jagger whistled. "I can't think of a time when they were in the same room where they weren't bickering."

Damn, I wished this bottle of water in my hand was something stronger.

Josh studied me carefully. "Why did you put her on that bird?"

"Because I wanted her to feel that rush at takeoff. I wanted her to experience what I do—what we do—every time we fly. My hope was that she'd see the beauty of it, and it would help conquer her fear that I'd go down like the three of you did." I kicked off my flip-flops and dug my feet into the sand.

"Will wouldn't have done it." Josh smiled to himself. "He would have told her that she was safer on the ground, and then he would have kept her there. He would have told her that her fear was unfounded because he was infallible in an aircraft."

"Will was born with this unconquerable urge to protect, and Morgan has *never* needed anyone's protection." Jagger twisted his ball cap backward. "Morgan needed someone capable of loving her and then getting the fuck out of her way."

I watched her bounce Peyton lightly and introduce him

to Christina as the girls headed back toward us.

"Bottom line, the guy was our friend. Fuck, I miss the asshole every day," Jagger continued. "But he sure as hell wasn't perfect, and the biggest thing he got wrong is something you've already gotten right."

"Enlighten me."

"You chose Morgan. He never did. He chose Peyton. He chose Paisley. When push came to shove, he even chose Josh and me. But he never chose Morgan. You did." His voice quieted as the girls reached us.

Hell yes, I chose Morgan, and I always would. The fact that someone hadn't was mind-boggling.

"You done flirting with Auntie Morgan, little man?" Jagger stood and took his son from Morgan's arms.

She smiled, but it was tinged with sadness, and a corresponding ache flared in my chest. This scene was only possible because Will had given his life for them. Hell, I only had a shot with Morgan for the same reason.

"Oh! I brought something for you!" Paisley exclaimed, dropping to her knees and digging something out of their diaper bag before standing again. "We just sent them out last week, but I wanted to give it to you in person." She handed Morgan an envelope.

"Thank you," Morgan said as she took it. She slid a card from the ivory casing, and her entire posture changed as she read it.

"Burgers!" Javier yelled.

I held up my finger in the universal symbol for *wait a fucking minute.*

"What?" Morgan whispered as her brow scrunched and her shoulders drew inward. Devastated. She looked completely and utterly devastated. What the fuck was on that card?

I rose to my feet.

"I thought you might want to come…you know. If you're feeling up to it." Paisley's smile trembled.

"Kitty?" I questioned softly, coming to her side. I wasn't going to look over her shoulder or pry into anything she wasn't ready to welcome me into.

Morgan shoved the card at my chest and stared at the sand a few feet away.

On behalf of the President of the United States, the secretary of the Army requests the pleasure of your company at the awarding of the Medal of Honor to William Carter—

I stopped reading. Holy. Shit. Will was getting the Medal of Honor.

"He would have wanted you there, Morgan," Paisley said softly.

Morgan shifted, and I forgot the card in my hand. My girl didn't have an ounce of that devastation on her face now. Oh no, it was all anger and indignation.

The storm she'd fought so long and hard to keep off her coastline was here.

"Little Bird," Jagger said softly, touching his wife's elbow as he took in the same signs I did.

"Morgan?" Paisley stepped forward, oblivious to the danger.

"I *might* want to come?" Morgan's voice was so quiet the breeze off the ocean nearly carried it away.

"Well…don't you?" Paisley took another step with obvious, honest concern.

Ember and Sam positioned themselves so the group made a square, both watching the other women with all of the caution Paisley should have shown.

"Honey," Jagger tried again, reaching for his wife's elbow.

She shook him off.

He looked my way beseechingly, but I took one look at Morgan's rigid muscles, the fire in her eyes, and remembered that this was the stage in her therapy where she was supposed to confront the people who triggered her, and Paisley was the biggest trigger she had.

I slowly shook my head at Jagger and stepped to the side, effectively getting the hell out of Morgan's way.

"I *might* want to come?" Morgan shouted. "Are you fucking kidding me?"

Chapter Eighteen

Morgan

I'm showing up empty-handed to this party, and the most amazing thing about you is that you don't care. You just want me, and I can't figure out why, but I'm done fighting it. You want this mess? It's yours. Just enjoy your last nine months of freedom—I mean, hopefully not too much or anything—because once I get home, we're doing this thing.

Paisley drew back like I'd slapped her. Her shock and hurt were obvious, and I just didn't care. I was beyond caring.

"You don't want to come?" Her brow puckered.

"You sent the invitations *last week*? You, Paisley, were given the invitations, and then you chose not to mail one to me? Not to let me know that Will—my Will—was getting the Medal of Honor?" My voice didn't even sound like mine anymore.

She blinked. "I told you, I wanted to give it to you in person. You said you were struggling—"

"I hadn't even *invited* you here when you mailed them out! What were you going to do? Wait until the week before the ceremony, just hoping that I'd be up for talking then?"

"I'd...I hoped that you'd call. And you did. Well, you texted, which isn't really the same, but—"

"Who the hell gave you the right to keep information about Will from *me*?"

Paisley's gaze darted to Ember, then Sam. Sam took a step closer. To support or restrain me? I didn't know, and I didn't give a shit.

"You said you were in therapy. That you couldn't talk about him. That you needed space! I was just trying to give you that space! I figured that when you were ready, you'd call and I'd tell you." Sweet mercy, the woman had the audacity to look hurt.

"God, I'm trying so hard!" I screamed at the sky. "I thought I was ready for this, but maybe I'm not."

"Don't walk away," she begged when I retreated a step. "Morgan, you've been my best friend all my life, and the silent treatment is killing me!"

"Killing you?" I fumbled for words as my soul scraped over a cheese grater, cut to tiny, shredded pieces by the blades of my anger and my own guilt for feeling it. "It's killing *you*?"

"Please talk to me! If it's the invitation, then you don't have to come, and I wasn't trying to keep it from you, I swear. I was just trying to protect you like you've protected me our entire lives." Her hands rose beseechingly, as if she could tug me back to emotionally stable ground.

Spoiler alert—there wasn't any emotionally stable ground. There hadn't been in years. I was more combustible than the unlit bonfire next to us.

"It's a little late to start protecting me, Paisley Lynn."

All the color drained from her face, and her hand rose to her chest, a nervous tell from when her heart hadn't been healthy. “Morgan…you have to talk to me.”

Raw, ugly emotion bubbled in that little container I kept it locked up in. I was a shaken soda, and Paisley was twisting my top.

“I can’t!” My anger would eat her alive, and that was something she didn’t deserve.

“You can!” she urged.

Those hideous feelings started to hiss as she cracked my seal.

“How long have you known he was getting the medal?” I questioned, looking for any reason to hold on to my composure. “Was it last week when the invitations came?”

Regret slackened her shoulders. “No. Daddy told me six weeks ago. Right before you told me you needed space.”

I exploded.

“Six weeks? You’ve known for *six weeks*?”

She pressed her lips in a thin line and nodded. “I’m so sorry—”

“Did you know?” I pivoted my rage at Ember.

She glanced between Paisley and me, then nodded. “Yeah, but we live right next—”

“You?” I faced Sam.

She put her hands up. “Don’t look at me. I had no clue.” She pinned a look on Josh and Jagger. “And neither does Grayson.”

“He’s got bigger things on his mind,” Josh muttered but dropped his gaze. “And mail takes longer to get there. Plus, we knew you were taking care of Morgan, and Paisley said she’s been…delicate.”

“Unbelievable,” Sam snapped.

“I should have told you.” Paisley’s voice dripped with regret.

“You should have told me he was dead!”

The whole world stilled.

In my peripheral vision, I saw Sawyer sneak away, motioning to Christina and her husband to do the same. It was just us—the Sunday dinner crew—and Jackson, who was silent and strong at my side.

"I don't understand," Paisley said softly.

"You never did," I spat, shaking my head. "How did you find out Will was dead?"

Her lips parted. "The officers came to the door. I was with Ember, and they told us Will had been killed. Then they gave us the news that Jagger and Josh were both seriously injured."

I nodded, processing the information. "I was in the jam aisle at Publix when Sam called." I tried to swallow the lump of anxiety that formed in my throat, but it wouldn't move. I arched my neck, but no matter how many times I worked my throat, it stuck there like a damned rock.

"What's wrong?" Paisley asked, moving forward.

"Give her a second." Sam stepped between us.

"Kitty," Jackson whispered, pressing an opened bottle of water into my hand.

I chugged half the bottle, then took deep breaths and visualized the muscles relaxing. I'd told this story in Dr. Circe's office for the last six weeks and listened to myself tell it every single morning. I could do this.

"Thank you." I handed Jackson the bottle and threw him a fragile smile.

He winked and squeezed my hand as he took it back.

"I was in the jam aisle at Publix, and Sam called. That jar of jam slipped from my hands and shattered all over that tacky linoleum, red like blood as it splattered my feet. And she didn't have the details. That was something only you got, since you were listed as his next of kin."

Paisley's hands fell to her sides.

"I don't remember much about leaving the store, but

slowly it's coming back to me the more I hear myself tell the story. I left the buggy in the middle of the aisle, didn't even tell the workers that I'd made a mess, and I stumbled to my car as Sam told me she was on her way to me. She was getting on a plane from Colorado. I sat in that parking lot for two hours, just staring out the windshield, and when I tried to call my very best friend, she didn't answer." I wrapped my arms around myself.

"I must have been on the plane already." Her voice was soft. "Jagger's father flew us straight to Germany."

"And you didn't pick up the phone. Not once."

"Shit," Ember muttered.

"It's okay, Ember," I assured her. "You told Sam to check on me. God knows how long I would have gone without knowing if you hadn't, so thank you."

"Oh God." Paisley's mouth opened and shut a few times as she looked at Ember, then back at Jagger. "Morgan, I wasn't thinking clearly! My husband was injured!"

"The man I loved was *dead*!" My hands flew into fists. "You don't think I made your excuses time and again? I knew you were under water. God knows I prayed for Josh and Jagger to heal quickly, and I'm honestly so grateful for their lives, but you abandoned me until the day of the funeral, and then you *invited* me to sit in the front pew like it was yours. Like *he* was yours!"

Paisley's lower lip trembled. "I didn't mean to do that."

"At what point did you remember that I loved him, Paisley? Was it when your daddy made his funeral all about Will's love for you? His sacrifice so your husband could live? Was it when I held you up at the gravesite as they buried the only man I've ever loved?" My voice cracked.

"Morgan," she whispered.

"You want to know why I can't bear to be around you? It's because every time I see your face and hear you gush about how damned happy you are, all I can think is how fucking unfair everything is!" Tears stung my eyes. "You got Jagger back. Ember got Josh. Sam has Grayson, and I have a fucking truck that I can't sit in without having an anxiety attack!"

She reached for me, and I stepped back. It wasn't in her nature to watch suffering and do nothing about it, but in this case, there was nothing she could do.

"Do you know what causes complicated grief?"

"It's a breakdown in the grieving process," Paisley answered, letting her hand fall back to her side. "Usually caused by an overwhelming guilt that you could have stopped the death from happening or the inability to accept the injustice of it. I read up when you told me why Sam was here. I would have come if you'd let me. I would have stayed with you."

I ignored her last two statements. "Your happily-ever-after came at the expense of *mine*. That's why I can't be around you. That's why I'm still crippled by a grief that you all think about from time to time. And I would never want you to feel this! Not in a million years would I ever wish this kind of debilitating pain on you. I wouldn't trade Jagger's life for Will's. How many times have I told you how grateful I am that you still have Jagger?"

"I've lost count." A tear streaked down her face.

"And how many times have you considered what life would be like if the tables had been turned? If Jagger had died for Will? If my happiness had cost yours?"

She startled. "I… We have Peyton."

"You're right. You have your gorgeous son, and he has Will's name. And I…" I shrugged. "I don't even have the right to grieve him or to be told that he's getting the Medal of Honor for choosing to die for you instead of living for me."

"That's not what I meant. Of course you do! And I know that what you had with Will was complicated, but it breaks my heart for you to think that he was your happily-ever-after when everything was so up in the air with you two, and what you have here—"

"Up in the air? We were finally on the damned ground!"

"What?"

"Paisley, why do you think he left me a secondary life insurance policy? Left me his truck? Left me his wings and his dog tags? It's because he left me with a promise, too. He drove down to see me before he deployed, and he told me we'd be together when he got home."

Paisley's breath rushed out. "I didn't know."

Ember's face twisted, and she blinked back tears.

"You didn't know a lot. I was the one who held him together after you dumped him. I was the one who had his wings engraved and then pinned them on his chest. I was the one he kissed the night of the flight school graduation ball, the one he gave a silver wings necklace to, and the one he kissed for the last time days before he died. I was the last phone call he made before that goddamned flight, Paisley, so don't you sit there and tell me that I didn't lose my chance. You were so lost in your own happiness that you didn't even know I had it to begin with."

My stomach turned at the realization that this rift had started way before Will's death. It had been growing since she'd moved up to Fort Campbell. Funny, how I'd always stayed behind for her, but she'd left at the first opportunity.

"Oh God, Morgan," she whispered.

"I was shattered and barely breathing, but I held it together during that funeral, and then I kept breathing when you shit all over my dream and pulverized my feelings between your sweet little fingers when you said he was never meant to be mine anyway."

"Wait. What?" She moved forward again, and I retreated, keeping our little dance. "Morgan, I never said he wasn't meant to be yours. I would never discourage your dream. God, we all saw the way he looked at you, the way you drove him crazy. I knew that if anyone could break through that shell he kept around his soul, it would be you. It would have been you."

I scoffed and shook my head as the horrid, disgusting feelings I tried so hard to overcome overruled my genuine love for my best friend. "So you didn't stand over Will's body and tell Josh that Will was where he was meant to be?"

Her widened eyes focused on Josh. "I..."

"What was it you said?" I tilted my head at my best friend. "*He's with Peyton*. Right? And he could have gone on to get married and have a family, but no love would ever compare to what he felt for her. I hear those words every time I see your face." They tasted like acid and ate away at what emotional defenses I had intact. I'd only ever spoken them to Dr. Circe.

"Fuck," Josh hissed, shoving his hands in the pockets of his shorts.

"Morgan, that was...you were..." Paisley shook her head and glanced around our group like they'd give her the answer.

"What? Private? Do you honestly think anything in this group is *private*?" I accused. "Ember heard you, remember? And she got understandably upset because Josh wasn't talking to her about what had happened over there, but he'd somehow managed to talk to you, right? So Ember called Sam for a little support, and Sam happened to be in my hotel suite checking on me."

"Oh, shit," Sam cursed. "I never meant for you to hear that."

"I know," I told her softly. "You were in the living room because I could barely pull myself out of bed, and you put it on speaker because Ember wanted Grayson's point of view, too. I've never blamed you. I wouldn't have made it through any of this without you."

Her lips pursed as she struggled to compose herself, but she managed a nod.

"I didn't mean that he wouldn't have been able to love you," Paisley swore.

"But not as much as Peyton," I countered. "Just because my last name isn't Donovan doesn't mean I wasn't capable of making him happy."

"I didn't think that!"

"You didn't think of me at all," I countered. "He was called home to your sister, right? Now they finally had a chance to be happy. That's what you said." My eyes stung, and my vision wobbled through the sheen of gathering tears.

Her lower lip trembled.

"How the hell can someone who calls herself my best friend stand there and say that his only chance at happiness was in *death*? You knew I loved him!" I jabbed a finger at her. "Am I that horrible, that unlovable in your eyes that you would rather see him dead with your sister than alive with me? I might not be as sweet, and kind, and perfect as you are, but that doesn't mean I wasn't worthy of him." Hot, angry tears fell from my eyes, and I didn't wipe them away. Let her see them. Let them *all* see them.

"No. Sweet mercy, Morgan, no." Paisley shook her head. "Of course you're worthy, and loveable, and it kills me that you think that—"

"Then why?" The raw cry ripped from my throat. "Why would you say he was meant to be dead instead of mine?"

She took a deep breath and glanced at Josh. "Because it was what Josh needed to hear."

"And just what the hell did you think I needed to hear?" The tears fell quickly now, their warmth stolen by the ocean breeze as they reached my jawline.

"I don't know," she admitted quietly. "But I can see now that I didn't say it to you."

"You didn't bother with me." My voice fell. "You were pregnant, and Jagger had three billion surgeries. I know that, logically. You were exhausted, and scared, and dealing with a whole host of things. I remember because when you'd call, that's all we'd talk about. And it was my fault, too. I should have told you back then, but I'd gotten so used to protecting your feelings that I didn't know how to be honest with mine. So I kept quiet and faked my way through the days, and the weddings, and the phone calls. But the nights? I can't fake those. And because no one saw fit"—I waved my hand at Josh and Jagger—"to take the time to show up and tell the woman who loved Will exactly how he actually died, I get to picture it playing out differently in every nightmare every night. But it's okay since it's just me going through it and not any of you. And hey, that's better than making you guys relive it, right? Who cares that I don't know as long as it doesn't inconvenience you? But the thing is that my therapist wants me to have this imaginary conversation with Will that's supposed to take place where he died, which is ludicrous, but I can't argue because the therapy is working. But I can't even do that because I have no idea what happened that night!"

"Shit, Morgan, I didn't realize—" Josh grimaced.

"Don't worry yourself. It's par for the course around here. And I pieced a little together between what you said at the funeral and the bits Ember relayed from the cemetery—which wasn't much. What was it you said, Josh? Paisley loved him more than all of us, right? That's why you avoided her." I leveled my stare on him, and he deflated.

"They had dated, and I knew they were still tight, and I felt so fucking guilty for living when he didn't," Josh said in explanation.

"She didn't love him most!" I screamed the words I'd held back for far too long. "I did!" I turned back to Paisley, who now had Jagger's arm around her waist. Even now, she was supported. "I loved him most. Not you. Not Peyton. She never chose him. She broke him. Then you had him and still chose Jagger, remember? I'm the one who always chose Will when I wasn't prioritizing your happiness. I. Chose. Will. You didn't. The fact that he didn't bother to choose me back until he was on his way to become a martyr doesn't change the fact that I loved him most!"

My gaze dropped to Paisley's wings, the necklace she'd been given the night of the flight school ball.

"He might have died with Peyton's name on his lips, but it was my necklace he had around his neck. The necklace that Grayson brought back with Will's body. The one he and Sam helped me put into the casket with him the night before we buried him, because if I had his wings, then he should have mine. And now it's two years later and you're all just over it! Over him! You're healed, and happy, and married, and parents, and pregnant, and even though I love you all, I hate you for it! He was supposed to come home to me, not get buried next to her!" A sob tore from my throat, and I crumpled.

Strong arms wrapped around me, and I was enveloped by the scent of the ocean and Jackson as he held me against his chest.

"It's okay," he murmured against my hairline as I sobbed into his shirt, grabbing fistfuls of the material to assure myself that he was real. He was here.

I needed to not be here.

"Morgan," Paisley pled, but Sam stepped between us. "Sam, please. I just need to talk to her. Let me make this better. I. Need. To. Talk. To. Her!"

"Paisley, you know I love you, but this is not about you or what you need right now," Sam replied in a tone that was kind but firm.

"Since when am I the third wheel around here? You

might be the one she chose to come live with her, but that's my best friend, Samantha! Move!"

"I know you are not yelling at me for your own fuck-up, Paisley Bateman. None of what's going down right now is my fault. And I get that your emotions are high, and rightfully so, but you're just going to have to let those suckers take a backseat to Morgan's for once."

I couldn't see either of their faces, but Paisley's indrawn breath said it all.

"And if you can't do that," Sam's voice softened, "if you honestly can't listen to the pain she's in without trying to fix it, then you might need to pack up that beautiful baby and your handsome husband and take them home until you can. You can't fix this, and she's not asking you to. She's just being honest for the first time in years and letting you know where she's at. And I know you want to help her. I know you love her, and you've never intentionally hurt her. We both know that this is one giant mess made by some pretty all-around shitty circumstances, but that doesn't change the fact that Morgan got lost and left behind."

My breathing regulated with Jackson's steady heartbeat as Sam gave me the time I needed to calm down. His arms felt so good around me. Safe. Secure. He held me like I was something he cherished, because he did. God, I didn't deserve this man who held me carefully as I cried out my grief for another.

"I never wanted this to happen," Paisley said softly.

My heart ached at the misery in her voice. I never wanted this, either. Never wanted my feelings to harm her. Never wanted to lose Will. Never wanted to tangle my heart up in another flyboy I'd have to bury.

"None of us did." Sam answered. "But you can't help her right now, as good as your intentions are. And as much as I value our friendship and the bond we all have, I can't stand here and let you slap a *let me make this better* Band-Aid over a festering, infected wound just because it'll help you sleep tonight."

My eye caught on the invitation to Will's ceremony as it dangled from Jackson's fingers, and I felt that same rage bubble to the surface. Maybe letting the fire out of my soul hadn't extinguished it but fed it instead.

"I need to regroup."

Jackson nodded once. "Well, as fun as this is, we're going to take a little break and feed my daughter's guinea pig." Jackson tilted his head and looked down at me. "We might need to feed the turtle, too." He took my hand, put himself between my closest friends and me, and started to walk us toward the dune.

"Are you coming back?" Paisley asked, her voice breaking. "Do you want us to go?"

I paused, gathered my composure, and then turned around to face them without letting go of Jackson's hand.

"I need a break, because when I look at that invitation, the only place I want to tell you to go to is hell, Lee. I'll be damned if I'm going to watch you accept his posthumous award while everyone cheers, because we both know his mama isn't going to sober up enough to do it."

Her eyes flared, and then her face fell.

"Right, that's what I thought." My stomach turned at the prospect of watching it all go down. "Will made you his primary next of kin, and that gives you access to all the information, and I get it, you just wanted to honor him while trying to navigate my delicate feelings that you knew nothing about. But you do now. So I'm leaving in the hopes that by the morning, this feeling will pass and I can calm myself down enough that I won't tell you to take that award ceremony and shove it up your perfect ass, because this is the last time I will ever let any of you think that your grief or your love for Will is deeper or stronger than mine. Losing that man drove me to actual insanity, and as far as I can see, you're all doing just fine."

They stared at me with varying degrees of shock, with the exception of Sam, who smirked.

"Ember, the coffeemaker is plugged into the dining room since I don't have any counters. Sam can show you where I put the extra towels, and she knows how to work the alarm and the sliding windows. And Sam, if you wouldn't mind making my apologies to our Outer Banks friends? Y'all have a good night. I sure do appreciate you coming all the way down here to see me." My eyes narrowed. "And if any of you so much as touch his truck, so help me God, there will not be enough time and space in the world to calm me down. Night!" I flashed a fake smile they all would have accepted as real before this blowup and walked over the dune with Jackson… who had just witnessed my entire tirade over another man.

"Are you okay?" he asked, handing me the invitation.

"Are you?" I challenged softly. "I never meant for you to hear all that. I can't imagine how you must feel right now."

His jaw ticked for a second, but he lifted my hand and kissed the back of it. "I feel proud of you."

"That's not what I meant." I shook my head. "I don't want you to think you're in some kind of competition with Will."

"But I am." He shrugged as we paused between our houses. "I have been since the moment we met. I'm not the guy to lay down my life—not with Fin at home. I'm the guy who figures out a way for everyone to live. But that out there"—he motioned toward the beach—"that wasn't about me."

"Jackson." My heart sank with guilt.

"It's okay." He cradled my face. "And when it comes to you, I might be a few laps behind in this race, but I've got a slight advantage on the guy."

"You're alive?" Sarcasm rolled heavily off my tongue.

"I wasn't going there." A corner of his mouth lifted. "Time, Morgan. I have time and the persistence to use it. Now, what do you want to do with the rest of our night?"

"Take me to bed."

His forehead crinkled. "I thought you wanted some space from your friends."

"Right. Take me to *your* bed."

Chapter Nineteen

Morgan

Here's the thing. If I don't make it back from this, you can't lock that big, beautiful heart away. When that guy comes along, and trust me, he will, you have to take the chance.

Substantial, scrumptious warmth surrounded me as I opened my eyes.

I blinked rapidly to bring the world into focus and tried to make sense of the heavy, masculine furniture and hunter-green comforter.

I was in Jackson's bed.

That was his arm draped over my waist, his strong body cradling mine. I waited for the panic to set in or a warning bell that I'd been reckless to crawl into his bed last night, but all I felt was calm, soothing heat.

His bedroom looked out over the ocean, and I watched the waves crash ashore with a steady rhythm that nearly lulled me back to sleep. The sky was gray and thick with heavy clouds as a storm moved in, but they didn't worry me since Jackson wasn't going to work today. Guess the weather hadn't gotten the memo that Hurricane Morgan had already made landfall last night.

I'd ripped my friends apart, and though I probably should have been nicer—gentler about it—every word I'd spoken had been true. Will would have been horrified and ashamed of me for what I'd put Paisley through.

Jackson had been proud of me for finally being honest.

Careful not to wake him, I rolled slowly in his arms and watched him sleep like the borderline obsessed woman I was. He was so beautiful that my entire body heated just looking at him. It didn't hurt that he slept shirtless, either. The man was cut in ways that had to be illegal in some states.

But even as incredibly good-looking as he was, it was his heart that held me in thrall. He was fiercely protective yet gentle when he touched me. His loyalty and persistence were unmatched by any guy I'd ever been around, and yet he never pushed me for more than I was ready to give. He let me move at my own pace without so much as hinting that it was too slow for him. He'd mastered the art of emotional seduction by patience, and that was hotter than the lines of roped muscles down his stomach or even the inked lines of latitude and longitude that ran along his side.

My heart—my stupid, foolish heart—ached with a sharp, sweet throb.

You cannot fall for this man. Not while you still love Will.

I did, right? I still loved Will. But every day that passed, every therapy assignment I conquered, softened the intensity of that emotion. The more time I spent with Dr. Circe, the more I realized that Will wasn't a sea of grief anymore. He was a mountain in my life, maybe even *the* mountain. No matter where I stood, I could still see him to the west—but I'd gained enough distance that he didn't dominate my existence anymore. He was a landmark I could guide myself by, comforting in his permanence. But somewhere in the last few months, it was Jackson who had become the ocean to my east. Deep, calming, and steady, just like those waves that pounded the shore behind me. And he was a touch reckless, too—bending the rules he found inconvenient and breaking the ones that got in his way. But for every danger he might bring, he was also gentle and tenacious enough to transform a broken bottle into a priceless piece of sea glass.

I examined the strong lines of Jackson's face, so different from Will's. And maybe it was wrong to compare, but I did it anyway. Jackson was bigger, taller, his body sharper than Will's compact, lithe frame had been, but he was also soft in the areas where Will had been unyielding. Jackson had no problem standing his ground, but he also knew when to compromise, when to concede, and when to take the risk. I would even argue that he did the latter far too often.

Will had seen the world as black and white—right or wrong.

Jackson would argue that there were ten thousand shades between the two.

My chest tightened the longer I studied him, but the butterflies in my belly were nowhere to be found. There was nothing to be nervous about anymore when I was in Jackson's arms. I couldn't do or say the wrong thing, because he wanted me just as I was, hot mess and all. He hadn't questioned my need to sleep next to him, either.

You didn't watch the video last night. That's twice.

The realization hit me at the same time that Jackson opened his eyes.

My heart skipped, and that ache increased a hundredfold as he gave me the sleepiest, sexiest smile I'd ever seen while he stretched.

You cannot fall for him. You. Cannot.

Oh God, it's too late, isn't it?

What I felt for Will was entirely separate from the emotions that overpowered me when it came to Jackson. How the hell was I capable of both?

"Good morning." His voice was scratchy with sleep as his gaze raked over me. "You look incredible in my shirt."

"Are you regretting last night's gentlemanly concern for my virtue?" I teased, hoping he couldn't see how unsettled I felt beneath my smile.

"Not even a little bit." That smile shifted to a smirk.

"You have the restraint of a saint." I rolled my eyes, knowing he could have taken me four different ways last night and I would have loved every minute of it.

A millisecond later, I was yanked against Jackson from chest to thigh, his hands like soft vises on my hips and his very large, very *hard* erection straining between us.

"Does that feel saintly?" he asked at my ear before running his tongue along the shell. "Because the things I want to do to you definitely put me in the sinner column."

"Unh." I couldn't even make an intelligent sound as he kissed his way down my neck. I was all about the sinner column.

"How the hell do you smell so good?" he muttered. "God, I love waking up to you in my bed. We need to make this a regular thing."

"I have my own house, you know." My thighs shifted against his as he found a spot that turned me on like a freaking light switch.

"Fine." He nipped at the base of my throat, and I slid my thigh over his. "We'll sleep here when Fin's home and at your place when she's not. See how good I am at compromise?"

"Uh-huh. Is she used to seeing women in your bed?"

He flipped me to my back and rose over me with a look of pure disgust. "Hell no, she's not. She's never seen me in bed with a woman who wasn't her mother, and it's been so long since that happened, I doubt she even remembers, since she was probably about eighteen months old. I don't bring women home, Morgan. Not here. Not ever. This is where I raise Fin."

"But I'm here, and I qualify as a woman."

He cocked an eyebrow. "Yeah, which should tell you that this means something to me. You mean something to me, and it's not casual."

My breath caught.

"I thought we were in an exclusive non-relationship." I raised my hand to his cheek and lightly stroked my palm over his raspy, unshaved skin. Sweet heavens, I was going to drown in his eyes if he kept looking at me like that.

"You can call it whatever you want, Kitty. Labels don't matter to me unless they matter to you. I know what we are, and like I said—it's not casual." He settled between my thighs, and I hooked my ankle around his waist. His gaze dropped to my lips as his breath hitched. "I'm all in."

That sweet ache in my heart devoured my common sense, and I pressed my lips together to keep the ill-advised words behind my teeth where they belonged.

"What's wrong?" Concern filled his eyes.

I shook my head and pressed harder.

"Morgan. You gotta talk to me." He lifted his thumb to my chin and gently pressed down so my lips parted, then touched the barest of kisses to my mouth.

"I think I'm falling for you," I admitted in a rush, then prayed that the words had slurred or come out in French, Japanese, Russian, or any other language he didn't speak.

He smiled, and it blew the previous, sexy, sleepy one right out of the freaking water. I was in trouble. So, so, *so* much trouble.

"Well, say something!"

The look he gave me was so tender, it made my eyes burn. "I don't need to think. I already know. I'm just glad you're catching up, because I am so far gone for you that I can't even see the shore anymore."

Oh. I pounced, claiming his mouth in a kiss as I grabbed onto whatever parts of him I could reach. The nape of his neck and the smooth, firm skin of his back became my only anchors as he parted my lips with his tongue and sank inside.

He kissed me so long and so hard that by the time he lifted his head, we were both panting, watching each other with lust-glazed eyes before diving in for round two. I was never going to get enough of this man. My need for him only grew each time he kissed me.

My hips arched against his, and the hard length of him stroked over the lace of my thong with enough force to push the fabric against my clit. "Jackson," I moaned as the sensation rocketed through my body, prickling my skin.

His hand clenched my hip to hold me still as he repeated the motion.

We both groaned.

Two pieces of cloth separated our skin, and it was too much. I wanted him naked so I could feel every inch of him against me. I wanted him inside me, hard and deep. The muscles of my core clenched with a need so intense that I whimpered. This wasn't just four years of pent-up sexual need talking—this was all because of Jackson. Just Jackson.

His shirt had ridden to my waist, and he tugged it up and over my breasts before lowering his head to one peak and teasing that nipple until it pebbled, and then the other, all while thrusting against me in a painfully, deliciously slow rhythm that had my nails digging little half-moons into his skin.

He moved like we had all day—like we had an eternity in this bedroom. His touches were unhurried and deliberate as he kissed every exposed inch of my skin. The man drove me insane. Every sensation pounded through my veins before it gathered low in my belly where it built a maddening tension.

"Jackson." I grabbed his hand and slid it down my stomach, between our bodies, and pressed it against my center.

He rose slightly, just enough to look in my eyes with a question.

"Please," I reiterated.

Without looking away, he pushed the lace aside and swept his fingers from my opening to my clit.

I gasped but held his gaze.

"Fuck, Morgan. You're so wet for me." His jaw clenched and his brow furrowed with the effort of restraint.

If I hadn't been wet before, the combination of those words and his sandpaper-rough voice would have gotten me there.

He repeated the stroke and swirled his fingers around my clit, bringing every nerve to life without giving me the very thing I needed.

I arched my neck, and my eyes slid shut at the exquisite pleasure his hands gave.

"Stay with me," he demanded.

My eyes flew open, and I saw it, a tiny flicker of apprehension in his depths. What would make him worry even the slightest bit when his hands were on me? *Stay with me.*

That ache in my heart sharpened with realization, and I gripped the back of his neck. "I'm right here, Jackson." I knew exactly who I was with.

He brushed his lips over mine, then plunged two fingers inside me, keeping his eyes locked on mine. The pleasure stole my very breath.

I cried out as he plunged again and rubbed his fingers

against the front of my walls before withdrawing only to repeat again and again. Every stroke pitched me higher. The pleasure sharpened, and the tension within me wound tighter.

"More," I demanded, riding his hand with greedy rocks of my hips.

"You feel so damned good." He flicked over my clit with his thumb, and I moaned. It was too much and yet not enough. "Wet and slick and so fucking perfect."

"You're killing me." His words, his touch, the very way he looked at me had me poised on a razor's edge.

"Then you know exactly how I feel." He thrust again. "Do you know how good we're going to be together? How hard it is to touch you like this and not replace my fingers with my cock?"

"Who's stopping you?" I challenged, rising to kiss him.

He groaned, consuming me with his kiss as his fingers stroked me to the edge of reason.

"Jackson." My fingers tightened at his neck as that tension rose to consume me.

"That's it, Kitty. Right there." His thumb worked my clit, and as my thighs locked, he pressed on that bundle of nerves and sent me flying.

I screamed his name as the orgasm washed over me in a tsunami of pure bliss only to ride out the next wave and the next, until my body fell limp against the sheets and my breaths came in heaving gasps. Did it last minutes? Hours? Who cared?

"I could watch you do that all day," he said against my lips as his fingers withdrew.

"I want you." I gripped his ass and brought our hips flush so he wouldn't mistake my meaning.

"Kitty," he groaned, dropping his mouth to my neck.

"Now." Now, before I could overthink my choice or give in to the guilt that was sure to follow.

He lifted his head and had the nerve to smirk, but there was a fine tremble in his arms. "Demanding little thing, aren't you?"

"Yes," I replied with a grin.

He laughed, and it was the best sound I'd ever heard. "And you're sure about this?"

"Sure enough to tell you to get a condom." I'd never wanted anyone like I wanted him. Only him. Not even—*don't go there.*

His eyes darkened.

Footsteps sounded in a steady run, sounding like they were heading up—

"She's coming up the stairs," Jackson finished my thought. "Shit!" He yanked his shirt down to cover my breasts and whipped the comforter over us.

I hadn't even noticed we'd thrown it off.

The door burst open, and Finley appeared. "Hi, Daddy!"

Kill me now. Right now, Lord. Mortification heated my already flushed cheeks. I was literally under her father.

"Hey, baby. What are you doing home?" He propped himself up on his elbows and grinned.

How the hell did he sound so calm? Why wasn't he panicked and scrambling? Why was he holding me prisoner so I couldn't panic and scramble?

"Mommy brought me! She has an audition, so I got to come home early!" She bounced with excitement and waved at me. "Hi, Morgan!"

Strike me dead this very moment. Can this possibly get any worse? "Hey, Fin," I managed with a shaky smile. I would have waved, but my hands were currently pinned between my body and her father's, not like I was telling her that.

Jackson barely disguised his confusion. "An audition, huh? Well, I'm just happy to have you home. You know, Cousteau could probably use some breakfast."

"Right! I'm on it! One fishy breakfast coming up!" She turned and ran smack into Claire. "Sorry, Mom!"

Yep, it's worse.

Claire stared at us with an open mouth, a mixture of hurt and shock twisting her features for a heartbeat. Then her eyes raked over us and narrowed in a rage so palpable the hairs on my arm stood up. "What the hell are you doing, Jax?"

He tilted his head. "What does it look like I'm doing, Claire? Better question, what are you doing in my bedroom?"

"It looks like you're confusing the shit out of our daughter, who definitely didn't need to see this. How could you?" she snapped, ignoring his question.

Jackson didn't even huff. "Funny, I could have sworn I locked the front door last night."

She snorted. "I used my mother's key. Trust me, *honey*, if I'd known you'd be up here getting your dick wet with the next-door neighbor, I would have called first."

I cringed.

Jackson tensed. "And now you've pissed me off, so you can get the fuck out, Claire."

"Why would you talk to me like that?" She pressed her hand to her heart.

"You're lucky Fin is down the hall or I would have said far worse, far louder. Now get out of my bedroom."

She blinked, as if just realizing she'd overstepped her bounds. "I need to talk to you about *our* daughter."

"Great, and we can do that downstairs. You're not welcome on the second floor. Now. Get. Out." His voice dropped to a dangerous chill that I never wanted to hear used in my direction. Ever.

She glanced between us and sighed. "Fine. I'll meet you downstairs. And just so you know, there's a line of people at the bottom of the stairs waiting to see you."

A line? My friends. Were they still my friends? Crap,

there went my buzz.

"Out!" Jackson snapped.

She fled.

His eyes were nothing but gentle when he turned them on me. "You okay?"

"You know that nightmare where you're naked in the hallway of your high school and you've forgotten your homework?"

"That bad?"

"Worse. But I'm fine. You go handle your baby mama drama, and I'll find some clothes."

He pressed a kiss to my forehead. "I'm wild about you. You know that, right?"

"I know." I stroked my fingers down his back. "Clothes, Jackson."

He sighed in sexual frustration. "I really hate her right now."

"She's five," I teased, knowing full well that he meant Claire.

"Smart-ass," he quipped but rolled out of bed. "Wear whatever you want if you don't feel like wearing yesterday's clothes," he told me after he yanked some shorts up over his boxer briefs and tugged a T-shirt over the carved lines I'd had yet to play with.

We really needed to remedy that soon.

"Get out of here," I chastised, still sitting in the middle of his bed.

He flashed a grin at me and vanished through the doorway.

I'd barely set my feet on the ground when I heard him bellow, "She's my girlfriend!"

Guess we were labeled now, huh?

I walked into his closet and marveled at the neat, organized rows he kept his clothes in. The man might be laid back in some departments, but apparently he liked his stuff tidy. I selected a soft T-shirt and settled for yesterday's shorts. I could tie the shirt, but there was no way anything of Jackson's was going to remotely fit my bottom.

Once I was appropriately dressed and had popped my head in to see Fin lost in her seashell collection, I headed downstairs and found Jackson trying his darndest to get Claire out the door while my friends pretended not to hear anything from where they sat around his dining room table.

I wasn't sure if I should kick them out or laugh at how awkward it all was.

"I'll be right in. And don't be mad at me. They looked like little lost puppies," Jackson explained from the doorway. "I couldn't leave them out in the rain."

"Uh-huh." I shook my head at him. "It's lovely to see you again, Claire."

She muttered something before Jackson closed the door, sealing them outside.

Sam was the only one to approach me as I made two cups of coffee, searched for Jackson's creamer, only to realize he didn't have any, and settled for milk, which was *not* the same.

"Give them a chance," she said quietly as I stirred in my sugar.

My stomach twisted, unwilling to face the can of worms I'd opened yesterday. But I was the one who'd lost my temper, which meant I owed them their say, too.

"Okay," I finally answered.

She let out a breath of relief and walked to the table with me.

I took the vacant seat at the foot of the table, and Sam slid into the empty one on my right. Paisley sat to my left with Jagger, who had Peyton on his lap. Josh took the head of the table, Ember to his left, next to Sam. Each one of them looked at me with resignation and a touch of fear.

I was hit with an immediate longing for Grayson, who was the most even-tempered of us all.

"I'm sorry," Paisley started, already tearing up. "I'm so sorry for abandoning you when you needed me most. I can make a thousand excuses, but the truth is I should have been the one to call you. I should have been the one to sit with you and comfort you…and, well, I should have done a lot of things. I knew how much you loved him, and I had hoped that you two would have a future. I so wanted that for you. And you're right. It isn't fair that you never got that chance, and it isn't fair that I wasn't there for you, especially when you've always been there for me."

The pure misery in her voice hurt my soul. Regardless of the last two years, she was my very best friend. Two years of neglect didn't negate a lifetime of love and support.

Jagger reached for her hand and laced their fingers on the tabletop.

"I know you had your hands full," I said softly, warming my hands with my coffee mug. "Jagger's health was your first concern, as it should have been. No one could expect you to balance a wounded husband, pregnancy, and a grieving best friend."

"You could have." She shook her head. "You should have. And I'm sorry for what I said to Josh that day in the cemetery. I tried to soothe his guilt, and instead I hurt you immeasurably with incredibly thoughtless words. You have my deepest apology, Morgan."

I swallowed the lump in my throat, but it wasn't anxiety. "Thank you."

"There are so many things that I need to apologize for, and I hope you'll give me that chance. I love you. You're the only sister I have left." She swatted away a tear.

"I'm sorry for unleashing my temper on you yesterday." I turned the cup in a nervous fidget.

"No," Ember chided. "It was a long time coming, and we deserved every word of it. I just wish you'd lost your shit on us two years ago. I'm so sorry that I didn't see how much pain you were in at the funeral. That I didn't see it at my wedding, or Sam's."

The lump in my throat grew. "That's not your fault."

"I'm mostly sorry that I didn't tell you that I talked to Will right before he came down to see you." Her face contorted as she struggled for control. "I should have told you that he said you were perfect. He told me you were funny, and gorgeous, and reminded him who he really was underneath everything else."

My chest constricted, and my nose started to burn.

"I don't think he took so long to come around because he didn't want to be with you," she continued. "It was because he thought you deserved someone who had a whole heart to give. He was trying to protect you. He wanted to be certain that he could love you the way you loved him, and when he left that night, he was hopeful about a future with you." She smiled, but it was shaky. "I'm so sorry I didn't tell you that sooner."

I tried to straighten my puckered, crumpled face and failed. "Thank you for telling me now." It was so similar to what he'd said that night. To what he'd said in the video.

"I'm sorry I'm here and he's not," Jagger admitted in a near-whisper.

"God, no. Jagger, no." I shook my head violently.

"Hey, you got to unload yesterday, and now it's our turn." A corner of his mouth lifted. "I think about him every day. I think about him in the moments I'm happiest, because he'll never get the chances I've had. He'll never get to see you wear white or watch you carry his child. I might not say it, but trust me, I think it. We all knew you two were inevitable. We just didn't know what was coming for us. I'm so fucking sorry for your loss, Morgan, and for the time it took us all to finally say it."

The warmth of the mug started to burn, but I didn't release it. "The truth is that Will had the chance to do all that. He just didn't take it. Not in time, at least. That's on him, not on you, Jagger. He wanted you to live because he made a promise to Peyton that he'd always take care of Paisley, and that's what he did. He took care of Paisley and your son. Damn if that boy didn't love a good promise."

My eyes fell to my cup and then rose to Sam when she tapped her finger on the table in distraction.

"I'm sorry I let you put the necklace in with him."

My jaw slackened.

"You wear that boy like a shield of armor around your heart, and I can't help but feel like I let you bury yourself with him that day." She forced a smile. "Oh, and I'm sorry that I left you our first day here to run for tequila that you couldn't even drink, but I guess it all turned out okay." She glanced around Jackson's house and then smiled.

"Yeah, it did." I smiled right back at her, marveling that I could discuss Will and still feel that warm glow in my chest for Jackson. "Are you guys…okay with Jackson? Not that I'm going to walk out on him if you don't like him or anything, of course. But he's so good to me, and I know it's foolish to even think of being with someone who flies the same damn helicopter–"

"Stop," Josh interrupted. "We're going to love whoever you find worthy enough to love, Morgan. Jagger and I are both flying again, too, and I'm sure Paisley and Ember feel that same fear, but they put up with us anyway. You wouldn't call that foolish, and I'm not going to let you think you're foolish, either. We can't help who we love." He shrugged. "But if you could help it, he's a damn good choice from what we've seen."

"Totally."

"Whatever makes you happy."

"I wish he flew a real helicopter, but he's cool enough."

"I put my stamp of approval on that man the minute he swam up the beach and ran by. The fact that he's just as nice as he is hot is a bonus." Sam winked.

My soul…settled. Calmed.

Josh cleared his throat. "I'm sorry that I didn't do this a hell of a lot sooner."

"Do what?" Jackson asked, coming to stand behind me with his hand on my shoulder. "Thanks for the coffee. Sorry it took so long. She's…Claire." He pressed a kiss to the top of my head.

"Pull up a stool," Josh instructed, motioning toward the bar that separated the kitchen from the dining room.

Jackson fetched the nearest stool and sat beside me, holding my hand in his lap and setting his coffee on the table.

Josh glanced at Ember, and she nodded, offering her own hand across the corner of the table. He took it and sighed so hard that his entire posture changed.

My stomach didn't just twist—it sank. What was he about to say that had him that flustered?

He looked up and met my eyes down the expanse of the table. "I was studying in my room that day in Afghanistan when Will walked in with a shit-eating grin and a bag of strawberry cheesecake cookies, asking if I was ready for his area orientation flight. That's all it was supposed to be. A quick, easy flight."

Chapter Twenty

Jackson

"You can't be serious," Morgan drawled as she settled against me on her couch. She fit under my arm like she had been made for that exact spot.

"It's a modern classic," I argued, barely hiding my grin as I hovered the cursor over the buy button on Morgan's TV. Man, I freaking loved teasing her.

"I am not watching *Sharknado* on the only night I get you alone. Nope. Not happening." She shot me a look that said she meant business as the microwave dinged.

"Come on, Kitty. It has it all. Action, suspense—"

"Sharks falling from the sky?" She got off the couch and headed for the kitchen, and I quickly followed after her, shamelessly checking out her ass in those tiny blue shorts. She wore a sweatshirt that hung off one shoulder, and with her hair twisted up into a knot, I got a sneak peek at her purple bra strap. There was nothing sexier than when Morgan was fully relaxed at home. Her home. My home. I was game for either.

I told my dick to behave, but it wasn't really interested in listening. It had one status when Morgan was in the room, and that was erect.

She reached into the new microwave and pulled out a freshly popped bag of popcorn. "Grab the M&M's."

I lifted a rather skeptical brow but did as she asked, then slid the package across the gray granite that had been installed in the kitchen almost two weeks ago. Hard to believe it was already the middle of June and even harder to think that I'd only known her for three months. She was a fixture in my world now, and every minute I spent around her only convinced me more that she was a permanent one.

I hadn't just fallen for her—I was head over heels in love with her. I'd known it in the hour it had taken Josh to tell her the story of how Will had died. She was the strongest woman I'd ever known, even if she didn't think so. I loved everything about her, from the way her face formed the expressions of the characters in whatever book she was reading to the determination with which she attacked each day. Hell, I even loved the colorful lesson plans she spent her days constructing, getting ready for the school year to start. I couldn't think of a single thing I didn't love about her.

She dumped the popcorn into a bowl, then poured the M&M's over it. I wasn't about to argue with the woman's choice of snacks, but it was definitely one of the odder things I'd seen.

"What can I do to help?"

She flashed a grin. "Just stand there and look pretty."

She'd been doing more of that since her friends had come—smiling and teasing. I wasn't going to go as far as to say that she was healed, and it wasn't for me to say, anyway, but she had definitely taken a stride in that direction.

A slim, silver tape recorder caught my eye toward the

back of the counter. "What's this for?" I asked, picking it up so I could show her what I meant.

She looked up, blanched, and the bowl slipped out of her hands, rattling on the granite for a few seconds before it came to a stop. "It's for therapy. Please don't press play."

"Okay." I set it back down carefully. "I wasn't going to, I promise."

"Thank you." She shook it off and forced a smile. "So, about *Sharknado*?"

I laughed, then picked up the bowl. "We can watch whatever you want, Kitty. After all, stay in and veg out was your idea for date night, remember?"

"Hmmm." A devilish gleam sparkled in her eye. "What about *Jane Eyre*? Or *Pride and Prejudice*?"

I grimaced but nodded. "Like I said, anything you want."

"You're only saying that because there's a storm going on and you can't drag me out to go jetpack surfing or whatever." She took a couple of pieces of popcorn from the bowl with an M&M. "Open up."

I obliged her and then groaned as the mixture of salty and sweet hit my tongue. "Okay. I take back my earlier thoughts and doubts. That's amazing. And I've never heard of jetpack surfing, but I'd be up for trying it," I teased.

She rose on her tiptoes and kissed me. It was soft and ended way too soon. There had been a crackling electricity between us since the morning we'd been interrupted in my bedroom. Between my work hours and Fin's evolving visitation schedule with Claire, Morgan and I hadn't been able to find more than an hour or two together, and the awareness between us was nearly painful.

With Sam at Grayson's parents' for the night, we were alone. Actually, truly, completely alone for the entire night.

We settled back onto the couch, and she flipped through movie options rapidly, as if she didn't care what we watched, either, because we weren't really going to be watching it anyway.

A gust of wind moved the chaise lounge on the deck, and rain fell in sheets against the glass that stretched across the back of her house.

"Do I need to worry?" she asked.

"No." I set the popcorn on the table in front of us and tucked her into my side. "This isn't bad."

"So I can stop waiting for the dune to break?" She peered over as the chaise moved again.

I kept my laugh well and smothered. "The dune isn't going to break, Kitty. That would take a hurricane or at least a healthy storm surge." My cell phone rang, and I grabbed it with my left hand so I wouldn't have to let go of Morgan, then muttered a curse when the caller ID flashed.

"Shit. It's the station," I told her with a wince. "Sorry, I'm on call."

"Well, then, answer it." She flashed me a smile and clicked on comedies while I swiped to take the call.

"Montgomery," I answered.

"Thank God." Sawyer's voice was tight, which immediately set me on edge. "Tell me you're at your house."

"I'm at Morgan's." I got up and walked to the windows. We had about an hour until sunset, so I had no problem seeing the massive white caps roiling angrily just beyond our beach.

"Close enough. A call just came in, the other crew is already engaged, and Hastings just slipped on the fucking deck. I'm pretty sure he broke his leg. Garrett's looking at him right now."

"Is it urgent?" The last thing I wanted was to leave Morgan and haul my ass out into a storm for someone who didn't actually need my help. Problem was, if they called us, they needed the fucking help.

"Life threatening. We've got a capsizing fishing vessel

with two sailors on board. How fast can you get in here?"

Shit.

"Run up the bird. I'll be there in six minutes."

"Roger."

I ended the call and slid the phone into my pocket. It would take him roughly ten minutes to get the bird through preflight.

"Don't go." The words carried the brittle sound of terror as Morgan reached my side. That same fear manifested in her wide eyes.

"Kitty, I have to." I cupped her face. "It sounds like Hastings fell and broke his leg, and Sawyer can't go out alone. I gotta go save some lives."

She ripped her face from my hands and pointed at the sea. "And who exactly is going to show up and save your life? You can't go out in this!" Her muscles locked and her pupils blew. My stomach twisted. This was bad, and I didn't have the time to reassure her like she needed. It would have been great if Sam had shown up right about now.

"I know it looks bad out there, but I've flown in far worse." I had to be out of here in the next ninety seconds. "I will be fine."

She shook her head. "No. No. No. The visibility is shit. What do you think the ceiling is? Five hundred feet?"

I glanced toward the sky. "Probably closer to four—wait, how do you know what a ceiling is?"

"Because I helped him study during primary!" Her voice pitched to a near shriek.

Fantastic. My girl was terrified and knew what she was talking about. "Morgan, honey, I'm more than comfortable with four hundred feet, and I'm just fine flying IFR." Not that I was a fan of having to fly instruments during shit weather, but it was better than letting people die.

She looked out at the ocean and back to me. "Call the

pilot in command. There's no way this can be approved. Look at it!"

If I hadn't known her past, I would have kissed her on the forehead and walked out the door, which was pretty much what I needed to do anyway.

"I already checked in with him, and the flight's approved." I grasped her shoulders lightly, hoping the physical connection would emotionally ground her. "I have to go, and I don't want to leave you like this, but people will die if I do not leave right now. Do you understand, honey?"

"Who would approve this?" she cried as the chaise slammed against the window. *Perfect fucking timing.*

"Me," I said as calmly as possible. I was down to twenty seconds, if that. "I'm the pilot in command."

Her shoulders slumped in defeat, and it crippled a part of my soul. God, I'd never wanted to be the one who caused that kind of defeat in her.

"And if I ask you not to? If I ask you to choose your own life over those people out there?" Misery emanated from her so thick I could almost taste it.

How could you die for them and not live for me? Those were the words she'd screamed at Will's truck the night I told her I was an SAR pilot.

I slid my hands to cradle the back of her head. "I'm not choosing their lives over mine. I wouldn't risk my crew like that. I wouldn't risk Finley's future or *yours*, Morgan. Do you trust me?"

She nodded slowly.

"Then trust that I won't put myself in unnecessary danger. I have to go."

"Okay." She swallowed and blinked back tears without letting them fall. "Okay. You go. I'll…wait here. But don't expect any popcorn to be left by the time you get back." Her words shook, but I'd take them. I couldn't begin to guess what saying them had cost her.

I yanked her into my arms and pressed a hard kiss to her forehead, then pulled back so I could see those gorgeous brown eyes again. “I love you, Morgan.”

Her eyes widened even further.

“I love you more than I can possibly tell you in the next three seconds, so you’ll just have to take my word for it. I will come home to you, I promise. Do you believe me?”

Her lower lip trembled, but she nodded.

I kissed her, hard and quick. “I love you,” I said against her mouth because it felt so fucking good to say the words.

Then I walked out of Morgan’s house and ran the rest of the way to my car. I was dressed and in the seat thirty seconds after Sawyer finished the preflight. We launched immediately.

Morgan was right. Ceilings were low and visibility was shit, but I hadn’t lied—I was comfortable flying in it.

I just didn’t like it.

And when that fishing boat’s mast came within inches of my tail rotor in those choppy-ass seas and gusting winds, she nearly took us down with her, but there was zero chance in hell I was ever going to tell that part of this story to Morgan.

Not ever.

Chapter Twenty-One

Morgan

I want you to be happy. Never forget that.

I glanced at my phone again and read his text message for the hundredth time.

Jackson: *Landed safe. I'll be there after debrief.*

The message had come in an hour ago, at which time I'd started breathing again.

The bowl of popcorn sat untouched on the table, and my book remained unread in my lap. I'd been staring at my wall of windows for the last three hours and twenty-seven minutes, listening to the rain pelt the glass mercilessly.

I hadn't even prayed that he'd come home like he promised for the fear that God would notice that I still existed and then take Jackson, too.

He loved me.

How could that incredible, kind, frustrating, stubborn,

phenomenon of a man love *me*? How was I supposed to be worthy of that?

This was it. If I stayed with Jackson and accepted his love, this was what my life would look like. How many hours would I stare at the windows and wait for him to come home? How many times would he kiss me and walk out the door in those kinds of conditions? How many times would he risk his life?

At what point would he be on the losing end of that risk?

At what point would I be?

But he *loved* me. Did he expect me to say it back? I was falling for him. I'd already admitted that much, but love? I wasn't sure I was even capable of that in the way he deserved. Now, if the man was interested in some hardcore infatuation, I could serve that up to him on a platter.

What was I going to say to him when he walked in that door? Was I really willing to endure this paralyzing fear every day just so I could be with him? If so, did that make me noble? Or really damned stupid?

Knock. Knock. Knock.

I jumped off the couch and raced for the door, not bothering to check the peephole before throwing it open. Jackson stood in the doorway, leaning on the outside of the frame. Humidity from the spent storm rushed at my skin, but at least the rain had stopped.

Why did he have to be so freaking gorgeous? He stared at me with a mixture of apprehension, joy, and exhaustion, still in his flight suit and boots. Our eyes locked in a wordless conversation, his tone apologetic and mine accusatory and relieved.

He didn't ask to come in or profess his love again. He simply stood and waited for my decision. Every cell in my body screamed with longing, demanding I touch him and make sure he was real.

I should have shut the door. I already walked a fine line

between sanity and...well, not, and the last thing my mental health needed was another night like this one. Logic dictated that I reexamine my commitment and then run as fast as I possibly could to the nearest guy with a desk job who would have me.

But one thing hadn't changed at my core.

I was never smart when it came to my heart, and my heart wanted Jackson.

One step and I had my mouth on his, locked in a kiss that said all I needed to. He didn't hesitate. In less than a heartbeat, his tongue twined with mine, his hands gripped my ass as he picked me up, and I locked my legs around his waist.

I heard the door slam, then found my back against the smooth surface. I gripped his hair lightly with one hand, anchored the other one around his neck, and kissed him with everything I had. It was hot, messy, and thick with a primal urgency that sent an avalanche of need barreling through my system.

He held me with one arm and tunneled his fingers through the hair at the nape of my neck, cushioning my head against the door. Even when the kiss spun out of control, he was careful with me. I unleashed all the anger and desperation that had kept me frozen these last few hours, giving my body free rein with the emotions. My teeth caught his lower lip with a scrape that I would have normally softened to a graze, but nothing about me felt soft right now.

I was a living, breathing flame, and he could either back away or choose to burn with me, because there was no putting out this fire.

He hissed softly, then kissed me harder, slanting my head and taking my mouth with deep, deft strokes that mimicked what I hoped he'd be doing with a very different body part soon. I needed more.

I needed him to torch every thought in my head until all that remained was my undeniable hunger for him.

He ripped his mouth away, leaving us both heaving with uneven breaths. "Morgan—"

"I hate you," I snapped.

"That's not true." His eyes softened, damn him.

"I hate your job," I countered. "I hate that it's not just what you do, but who you *are*."

"I know." His hand slid from my hair to cup my cheek gently.

"I hate what you do to me. Hate that I sat here tonight wondering who would call me this time when…" I swallowed hard.

"I'm here," he assured me with a soft, lingering kiss. "No one had to call because I'm here. I'm fine."

"This time," I spat.

His jaw ticked, and something I didn't want to examine flashed through his eyes.

"I hate how you make me feel." My eyes burned. "How I can't decide if the fire is hotter in the hell where I choose to live with the terror I felt when you walked out the door tonight or the one where I have to figure out how to walk away from you, because either way, how I feel about you is going to eventually incinerate me." The intensity of it was just as frightening as watching him drive off into the storm.

"All I can say is that I love you." His thumb stroked my cheek, as if his touch alone could soothe the riot of feelings warring for dominance within me.

"That doesn't make this easier!" Instead of shoving him away, I leaned my forehead against his and tightened my thighs around his waist. I felt him hard and insistent against the seam of my shorts and barely managed to keep my hips still. It didn't matter how frustrated and pissed off I was at my own feelings for the man, I still wanted him. That was the damned problem.

"I know, but it's all I have." His fingers flexed, and he gave me a little more of his weight, pinning me against the door with the pressure of his hips. "I love you."

"Stop saying that." My heart leaped and my pulse skittered as the ache between my thighs flared at the heat between our bodies.

"No." He pulled his head back far enough that I could look into his eyes. So beautiful. *Everything* about him was beautiful. "I'll stop kissing you. Stop touching you if that's what you want. I'll put you down and walk out this very second if you ask me to. I'll do anything you ask, except that."

"Quit flying," I muttered with a ridiculous pout. I may as well have asked him to carve out his very nature and set it on fire just to appease me. We both knew neither of us would like him much without it.

He snorted softly, recognizing my shit attempt at a joke, and then used those eyes of his to see into my freaking soul. "I'm going to tell you how I feel until you choose the hell that rips us apart, and even then, I'll probably still tell you. What I feel for you isn't quiet. It's loud and inconvenient and demands to be said as often as possible."

"Jackson," I whispered in a plea. *For him to stop or to say more?* I didn't know anymore. Every time I thought I had my bearings with him, I got my feet knocked out from under me again.

"I've waited my entire life to love you, Morgan. Everything that came before was just to prepare me for your arrival, to teach me how to love you."

"I don't want to fall in love with you," I whispered.

"I know that, too." The look he leveled on me was so tender I melted. Thank God for the door. "I keep my promises. I'll *always* keep them when it comes to you, and tonight made me realize that I can't promise that I'll never crash. I can't avoid every accident, mechanical failure, or act of God. That kind of promise isn't fair to you, not after all you've been through. There are some things that are beyond my control, no matter how good I am in the cockpit." He caressed my cheek, and I leaned into it, hating his words even as his honesty touched me in a way no promise ever could have.

"I know." I cradled his face. "And I know I'm irrational sometimes, but I'm so afraid that I'll lose you. I barely made it through—" I swallowed the lump in my throat and concentrated on Jackson. Just Jackson. He was the only man allowed in my headspace right now. "It will kill me if I lose you. I won't survive it."

His eyes closed as he took a deep breath, and when they opened, they shone with resolve. "I promise you that I will never put a rescue above my own life. I promise that I will never knowingly put my life at risk. I promise that while I'm the best SAR pilot at our air station, I'll work my ass off to be the best SAR pilot in the fucking country just to make sure that you don't have uniforms show up at our door, and while I can't promise they won't show up anyway, I swear to God that you'll never get that news secondhand. Never again. I'm already cautious because of Finley, but I'll double down for you. I promise that I will do everything in my power to always walk back through that door."

Oh God, the scales were tipping. My choice was fading as though it had never existed to begin with. He saw it, too. His grip shifted to my thigh as his gaze fell to my lips. Then he lowered his mouth to mine, and the sweetness of the kiss was at poignant, perfect odds with the need that had its claws in my belly. Wanting him wasn't just physical anymore. I wanted to wrap my soul around his.

"And I promise that as long as I live, you won't regret being with me. I can't even suggest that it will be easy, because that's a huge lie, but I swear that I will always make the shitty lows pale in comparison to the incredible highs. You're loved, Morgan, whether or not you want to be. But please give me the chance to show you how much."

My stupid heart picked up. I believed him. He'd mitigate what risk there was, and I'd have to pray it would be enough, because I hadn't lied—I wouldn't survive losing him.

"Okay." A smile curved the corners of my lips. "Show me how much."

His smile made my own bigger, but I only saw it for a heartbeat before his mouth consumed mine in a kiss that demanded all of my attention. It was all lips and teeth and tongue, and our touches changed from soothing strokes to needy handfuls of hair and clothes.

I broke the kiss with a gasp and yanked my sweatshirt over my head. His eyes darkened as he took in the purple lace that cupped my breasts, and the next kiss was twice as hungry.

My hands worked between us to unzip his flight suit, and I growled in frustration when my fingers found the soft cotton of his T-shirt instead of skin. "How many layers are you wearing?"

He had the nerve to chuckle, but he shifted his fingers from my thigh and cupped my core through my shorts. "Is someone impatient?"

"For someone who promised to show me how much he loved me, you're sure not showing much." I cocked an eyebrow and glanced at his torso.

His grin was pure sex, and my body responded with a wave of heat. I was fucking molten.

"God, I love you." He stole my response with a kiss, and then we were moving. I ground my hips over his, seeking any kind of relief as he carried me up the stairs. He made it to the top before bracing me against the wall and unhooking my bra. I shed it quickly.

He lifted me like I weighed nothing and sucked my nipple into his mouth.

I cried out and arched for more, gripping his shoulders for balance. His lips were soft, his teeth sharp as he raked them over the delicate flesh, then soothed the sting with a flick of his tongue. He gave the other breast the same treatment, and by the time he was finished, I was ready to shove our clothes aside and have him in the hallway.

"Your breasts are fucking incredible." He gave me one last suck and then lowered me so our mouths were level. "I'm going to devour you." Then he did. He kissed me like a starving man who had stumbled onto a feast as he took me into my bedroom. The fabric of his flight suit rasped over my sensitive skin, but I didn't care. No touch was hard enough, no kiss long enough.

The lights flicked on, he lowered me to my bed, and then he made quick work of getting out of his own clothes. Freakishly quick work of his boots, too. I reached for the button fly of my shorts, and he shook his head. "Unwrapping is half the fun."

I dropped my hands and propped myself up on my elbows so I could watch him. My mouth watered at the mind-blowing perfection of his body, and my lips parted at the sight of that deeply carved V that ran down the sides of his abs and disappeared into his black boxer briefs. I was going to trace that line with my tongue the second he got into this bed. The muscles of his arms rippled as he grabbed his wallet. He flipped it open, took out a foil packet, and held it up with a raised eyebrow. I nodded, my tongue too thick in my mouth to manage the words to affirm that's exactly where we were headed. There was a brand-new box in my nightstand, too. Something told me he wasn't a one and done kind of guy. The packet landed somewhere to my right.

His weight settled over me, and I groaned into his kiss

at the feel of his skin on mine. His mouth claimed my neck again, then lingered at my breasts before kissing a path down my stomach. My fingers threaded through his hair, desperate to hold onto whatever part of him I could.

"I've wanted to do this for so damned long." He pressed an openmouthed kiss at the inside of my hip. "From the moment I saw you on that beach." He flicked open the buttons of my shorts, and I lifted my hips so he could drag the fabric down my body.

"I thought God had taken every fantasy I'd ever had and molded you out of them. You were—you are—the most devastatingly gorgeous man I've ever seen."

His eyes locked with mine, flaring with a touch of surprise as my shorts landed somewhere on the floor. Hadn't I ever told him that before?

"I might have been broken then, but I wasn't dead." I smiled as I sat up and rose to my knees.

His eyes raked over me as he dragged his tongue across his lower lip. "The things I'm going to do to you," he murmured.

"Me first." I pressed on his chest, and he protested with his eyes but took the hint and rolled so he was on his back with his head on my pillow. My breath hitched, and my pulse kicked up another notch as I looked my fill. "I don't have words for you," I admitted, trailing my fingers from the strong line of his neck to his chest and down his abs to pause at the tattoos of latitude and longitude that ran the length of his right side. "What are these?"

"They mark places." He put one hand behind his head and ran the other down my back, but his muscles were tight with restraint. He wasn't nearly as relaxed as he tried to let on.

I lowered my lips and kissed the marks. "Where do they lead?"

He sucked in a breath, so I did it again, picking the first

line of ink. His skin was warm and firm, and he had that faint tang of metal in his scent that marked hours spent in a helicopter.

"That one is my hometown. Where I was born." His fingers drifted up my neck and into my hair.

"And this one?" I kissed the next tattoo. His abs jumped and flexed.

"Just off the coast of Maine."

Where his parents died.

I turned my attention to the last coordinates. "And this one?"

"Mobile, Alabama. Flight school. Where Fin was born."

I nodded and shifted so I could get to my original destination, selfishly glad that none of those places involved another woman.

"Kitty, you're driving me—" His fingers tightened in my hair, and he let out a groan as I licked down the V of his abs.

"These have had me distracted since day one." I got to know those two lines intimately with my mouth, inhaling his ocean and copper scent with the taste of his skin until I was drunk on him. When I reached the waistband of his boxer briefs, I found the head of his erection rising above the elastic and then swiped my tongue right over the bead of moisture that had gathered there.

"Fuck!" His cry was guttural, and I felt it like a caress.

I was going to find every single spot on him that earned me the same response and—

The world spun, and I landed on my back under Jackson. I would have asked him if he was against oral sex, but the way he looked at me was anything but angry. He reminded me of a jungle cat, a predator that had his prey exactly where he wanted her.

"That's not how this first time is going down." His voice dropped as he settled between my spread thighs.

Mercy. He was right. There. "It's not?" I asked, all breathy as he shook his head slowly.

Before I could ask him exactly how it was going to go down, suddenly he *was.* My breath came in a stuttered gasp as he slid down my body, then cupped me between my thighs.

"Damn, Kitty, you're soaked. I can feel how wet you are through the lace." His breaths came faster as he hooked the purple bands of my underwear in his fingers and looked up at me for permission.

I nodded. Hell yes, I wanted them gone. I wanted his gone, too. Naked was good.

His jaw flexed as he took them down my legs, leaving me bare. Then he sat back on his knees between my thighs, his gaze traveling my body with a heated stare. My skin flushed as if he'd actually touched me. I was going to combust if he didn't touch me soon.

He dragged his eyes to mine. "Are we still alone? I didn't see any other cars."

I nodded. "Sam doesn't come home until tomorrow. Why?" God, was he going to move? Or were we really going to lay here and discuss travel plans?

"Just checking before I make you scream." He pushed my thighs wide, held me apart with his thumbs, and set his mouth on my core.

"Jackson!" There weren't words. There were only feelings as his tongue licked long and hard through my cleft, then flicked over my clit. Holy shit, it felt *incredible.* I rocked my hips when he did it again, and he pinned them to the bed with his hands, holding me in place so I couldn't chase his mouth. I could only accept what he gave.

"I'm doing this every fucking day," he growled against my clit, and the vibration sent a jolt of pleasure so intense that I gasped. "Every." Lick. "Fucking." Lick. "Day." He sucked lightly on my clit, and I screamed. "Maybe you'll be my breakfast from now on." He plunged his tongue inside me, and my hands fisted in the covers as I moaned.

"Jackson. God, that feels so good!" Good wasn't even the right word, but my brain wasn't exactly on vocabulary.

"Or would it be better to save you for dessert?" he mused, then ran his tongue around my clit but not touching it. "My reward at the end of the day?"

We locked eyes, and he held the contact as he repeated the stroke. Erotic. That was the only way to describe it. My head fell back against the pillow as he swirled and swirled. The pleasure of it all coiled low within me, but he didn't increase the pressure to push me over.

"Jackson," I demanded with a whimper.

"You don't like it?" he asked, and I felt his smile before he licked into me again.

"Shit!" I screamed. "Yes, I… What are you doing to me?" He had me strung so tight that I was bound to break at any second.

"Making it last," he answered.

I was never going to look at his mouth the same way again.

"I've wanted you too long for this to be over quickly." He swiped again, but this time he lightly danced the tip of his tongue over my clit.

My cry was a high-pitched keen as he kept the pressure light enough to inflame but not ignite. "Both!" I shouted.

"I'm sorry?" His eyebrow rose.

My chest heaved, and every nerve in my body felt raw and exposed. "Breakfast and dessert. Have both. Just let me come."

He pressed a kiss to the line of curls just above my cleft and breathed in deep. "That's a deal." Eyes still locked on mine, he sucked my clit into his mouth and lashed at it with his tongue.

That spiral of pleasure in my belly wound so tight that my thighs locked, and when he pressed against me with the flat of his tongue and hummed, I came so hard that I wasn't sure I still inhabited my own body.

Waves of pleasure came for me as I called his name, each one a little less intense than the last as he carefully brought me down from the high. My entire body jolted when he swept his tongue through my core one last time, then rose above me.

"You are a sorcerer," I accused through my brain fog. "Pants. Off. Now."

He grinned but did as I demanded without correcting me that they weren't pants. I fumbled for the packet in the covers next to me, found it, and ripped it open as he climbed back between my thighs.

I bit my lip with anticipation at the sheer size of him. If there were perfect dicks in the world, then Jackson had one of them. He hissed, his stomach muscles tensing as I rolled the condom over him, then squeezed his length lightly. He was hard as stone and so hot that he warmed my palm.

I raised my hands to his shoulders as he hovered over me, his weight braced on one elbow as he positioned himself at my entrance with the other.

"Tell me you want this." His eyes searched mine as if there was any chance I'd changed my mind.

"It's been four years," I blurted. "And there were only two others."

His jaw popped once. Twice. The strain was evident in every line of his face as he lifted his hand to cup mine. "I'll be careful. And I don't care who came before as long as you're mine now."

"Only yours," I promised with a nod. "And don't...I don't want to know your number. Not right now, anyway." Mercy, I was babbling. The hottest, most important moment of my life and I couldn't hush up.

His eyes flared with amusement, but the rest of him was tense. "No one who came before mattered as much as you do."

I swallowed, knowing there was at least one and hating myself for letting her into this moment.

He brushed a soft kiss on my lips, as if he read my thoughts. "I've never loved *anyone* the way I love you. I don't want to just possess your body right now. I want your fucking soul, Morgan."

"Is that your way of saying you're mine, too?" The pressure of him at my core made me adjust my hips slightly, taking him inside me just the slightest inch.

There was that jaw pop again, but his eyes were still tender. "You already own my soul. I'm yours."

My heart threatened to explode; the ache was that sweet and strong.

"I want this," I assured him, hooking an ankle over his back. "I want you, Jackson."

He kissed me hard and rolled his hips, filling me with one long thrust. We both cried out. There was a slight burn as my muscles stretched to accommodate him, but it was nothing compared to the sensation of having him inside me.

His mouth tensed over mine, and his eyes squeezed shut so tight that he looked like he was in pain as he fought for control. One breath. Two. Three. Four passed before his gaze met mine. His pupils were blown, and his muscles were tight under my fingers.

"You feel so fucking good," he groaned. "Are you okay?"

"God, yes." I clenched my core instinctively.

"Good." His mouth took mine as he pulled back and pushed in again, which had us both groaning. "I'm going to live here. Right here," he promised, then set a rhythm with hard, slow thrusts.

Every stroke felt like a higher degree of heaven.

We moved together like this was our hundredth time, not our first. It was effortless and so damned good each time I met his hips with mine that I craved him in the seconds between, when he wasn't deep inside me. He never faltered, never slowed, never shortened his strokes. The man used his body like a machine to draw every ounce of pleasure possible from my flesh. My nails dug into his back as sweat beaded on our skin.

My breath caught and my eyes widened as I felt that same tight pleasure spiral deep within me. Oh God, was I really going to come again? Was it possible?

"Jackson," I whimpered.

"God, Morgan." He cradled the back of my head with one hand, pushed my knee higher with the other, and slid even deeper, changing our angle.

Tight. Everything was tight. My skin, my muscles, my very bones stiffened as my cries came in time with his thrusts.

He slid his hand down my thigh and slipped his thumb between us, then worked my clit at an alternating rhythm.

"You have to come for me, baby. I can't hold out much longer. You feel way too damned good, and I've wanted you for too long."

His words and the look in his eyes sent me to the brink, and then he pushed me right over it with his body.

I cried out his name as the orgasm barreled through me, stronger and deeper than the first had been.

"Yes," he groaned with a kiss. "I love you." His grip shifted, and his hips swung with abandon as his control snapped.

I clung to him through the aftershocks of my orgasm, and he joined me with his own, my name on his lips as his face fell to the cradle of my neck as it took him.

Moments passed while we struggled to catch our breath.

He rolled to the side so he wouldn't crush me, taking me with him so my leg still draped over his hip.

His gaze flitted over my features, taking in everything before settling on my eyes. He reached for my face and pressed a kiss to my lips.

"Mine," he said softly.

I could hardly deny it, nor did I want to. The man had just transformed my entire reality and tethered himself to my soul.

"Mine." I smiled and kissed him right back.

"True." He grinned.

We both cleaned up, and neither of us put clothes on as we slid back between the sheets.

He pulled me against him with a kiss. "I think you just changed the tides. That blew every fantasy I've ever had clean out of the water."

"Glad I could live up to the hype." I kissed his chin. How different this night had turned out, and yet this was exactly where I'd imagined we'd wind up. A thought sobered me, and I pulled away to look at Jackson. "How is Hastings's leg? I didn't think to call Christina."

He swallowed and yanked his gaze from mine, blinking rapidly. "Oh, uh. I'm not sure. I think Garrett mentioned that he might need a screw or two so they can set it."

My face puckered. "That stinks. I'll bake some cookies and take them over tomorrow."

"You are entirely too sweet." He pulled me into another kiss, and this one deepened. "Shit."

"What?"

"I only had the one condom. The rest are at my house, and I don't want to leave you here, all warm and naked, but I also know we're about three minutes away from starting up again." His brow puckered.

"Three minutes, huh? You're certain about that?" I

teased.

He lifted a brow, took my hand to his groin, and my entire body liquefied at how hard he already was again.

"Hmm. Good thing I'm a big girl and bought a box myself, because that feels more like two minutes than three." I stroked him with a pump of my hand.

He groaned, then rolled me to my back with a heart-stopping grin. "Thank God. I knew I fell in love with you for a reason."

He didn't make me wait three minutes or even two.

That box was short more than just one condom by the morning.

Chapter Twenty-Two

Jackson

I hated working nights. It meant less time with Morgan and Fin because I was always asleep when they were awake and vice versa. But tonight was my last night shift for another month, so I'd just have to suck it up.

After zipping up my flight suit, I checked Fin's room, but it was empty. The laughter coming from downstairs explained it. I found my girls in the dining room, Finley in a chair with her new cat perched on her lap and Morgan behind her, weaving her hair into another crown of braids that happened to match the very one she was wearing in her hair, but Finley's had red, white, and blue ribbons threaded through it.

"What's so funny?" I asked, leaning against the bar. God, I could get used to this. Having Morgan here with Fin made everything seem complete—whole.

"Morgan had a cat, too! He spilled glasses of water on her mama every day!" Fin exclaimed, stroking Juno's fur.

"Batted them right off the end table," Morgan added with a smile and threw a wink at me.

Fuck, I loved this woman, and it was okay that she hadn't said it back yet. Eventually my charms would wear her down.

"Oh? So just as people-friendly as Juno over here." I eyed the tabby and kept my distance. Finley had dragged the thing out of the rain a little over two weeks ago and worked her magic on her…and me. A trip to the vet later, we now had a cat that despised me and hissed at every opportunity.

"Hey, Juno likes people!" Finley argued.

"Sure, people who aren't your father," I countered as the cat stared me down.

Morgan pressed her lips together to keep from laughing and finished Fin's braid. "You're all set, my dear!"

"Thank you!" Finley sang, already headed to the nearest mirror.

"Make sure you're packed for your mom's. We're leaving in ten minutes!" I called after her.

Morgan walked straight into my arms, laying her cheek flat just below the patches on my chest.

"I hate that I have to work tonight," I said into her hair, breathing in her scent as I held her close.

"Me, too."

"You sure you'll be okay?" I tipped her chin up to look in her eyes and got knocked on my emotional ass just like I did every time.

"I'm fine," she insisted, dropping her voice to a whisper. "Don't get me wrong, I'd rather sneak over and spend the night in your bed, but Sam and I are good. Mia and Joey are coming down. Figure between us, we can get the battery changed in the truck, too. Turns out all that opening and closing of doors wears that sucker down if you don't crank the engine."

"I can do it if you want," I offered, already knowing the answer.

"I've got it. Once we get that done, we're headed to the fireworks, and we're meeting up with Christina, too."

"Out on the town with Mia, huh?" My eyebrows rose. "Does that mean I can expect a call from Sam to come use my stellar rescue moves?"

She crinkled her nose. "That was one time."

"Hmm." Her lips looked so damn kissable. They always did, but it had been a good hour since I'd kissed her, and I was already going into withdrawals. I'd had her in my bed for the last three weeks—whenever we managed alone time—and I could never get enough. I always wanted one more touch, one more kiss, one more…everything.

"Jackson Montgomery, I know you're not looking at me like that with your daughter in the next room," she whispered with a little grin.

"Looking at you how?" I teased, sliding my hand down the small of her back. This sundress was going to be the death of me. It was the same one she'd been wearing the day I met her, and I was dying to know what underwear she had on under it.

"Like you're not thinking wholesome thoughts." She arched an eyebrow but lifted her hands to twine behind my neck.

I lowered my head so I could whisper in her ear. "Wholesome? I'm thinking of a whole lot of ways to get you out of that dress, if that counts." I ran my teeth along the shell of her ear, and she shivered.

"Jackson," she warned in that breathless way that wasn't a warning at all.

"Morgan." I pulled her hips against me and kissed the spot just beneath her ear.

"Mmmm." She tilted her head so I took the spot just beneath that one, which happened to be ultrasensitive on her neck. Her breath hitched, and her pulse picked up beneath my lips.

"You smell incredible. What is that? Vanilla?" I took another nibble.

She gasped, then pushed out of my arms and made a fuss over her dress as her cheeks tinged pink. "Cookie dough."

"No wonder you taste extra sweet today." I smirked, knowing she wasn't as unaffected as she tried to look. "Get over here and let me kiss you."

Her eyes widened as her gaze darted to the living room. "Finley is going to be back down here any second."

"And?" I moved forward, and she danced backward, just out of my grasp.

"And she'll see!" She pulled the dining room chair between us, like that flimsy little thing would keep me away.

"And?" I restated as she backed her way around the table, toward the sliding glass door. I skirted the chair, and she made a mad dash for the other side of the table, putting her right back where I'd started.

"You cannot be serious." She folded her arms across her chest, which lifted the swells of her breasts to her neckline and made me groan.

"I happen to think it's pretty healthy for a kid to see her dad madly in love." I held her gaze so she knew I meant every word. I had no problem with Fin seeing me kiss Morgan. It wasn't like we were getting hot and heavy, but Morgan had kept a five-foot distance from me whenever Fin was in the room after the whole bursting-in-post-orgasm thing Memorial Day weekend. "And I am deeply, madly, wickedly in love with you, Morgan Bartley."

Her lips parted, and her posture softened just like it did every time I told her that.

I pounced, swinging onto the table and sliding straight across to land in front of Morgan. She gasped as I caged her, putting my hands on the bar on either side of her.

"You aren't human." The spark in her eyes was the stuff

dreams were made of.

"Kiss me." I dropped my voice and leaned my body against hers.

She melted and her head tipped up, but she didn't make her move.

"I don't care if Fin sees you kiss me. Hell, it would probably give her the only example she's ever had of what a healthy relationship looks like." I ran my lips up her jaw as Finley stomped around above us in her room.

"Is that your reason? Or your excuse?" she questioned, her hands fisting in the fabric of my flight suit.

"The only reason I ever need to kiss you is because I want to. And I always want to. You consume an inappropriate amount of my thoughts."

"My thoughts about you are usually inappropriate, so I think we're well matched." Her head fell to the side, and I pressed an openmouthed kiss against her throat, listening for footsteps. Kissing Morgan in front of Fin was one thing, but getting caught in the act of seducing her was another.

"How inappropriate?" I asked against her neck. "Are we talking R rating or NC-17?" I lifted my head slightly.

She turned her face so our lips were a breath apart. "I'll let you use your imagination."

My heart rate kicked up. "You'd be surprised at the things I can imagine."

Her gaze dropped to my lips.

Nearly there.

"You drive me to distraction," she whispered.

"Pot meet kettle. Kiss me, Kitty." I was going to lose my mind any second.

"So impatient," she teased, then closed the inches between us and kissed me.

I kept my groan in check, listened again for Fin's footsteps upstairs, and sank into Morgan's mouth.

She gasped and pushed at my chest even as she kissed me back.

"I can hear her upstairs," I explained against her lips.

Her hands stopped pushing and grabbed instead. I gladly went where she tugged, pressing us against the half wall as I kissed her breathless. The problem with kissing Morgan was that I lost myself in the process. There was no calm control or suave moves. There was just the consuming hunger between us and my insatiable need to please her.

Fin's footsteps thudded down the stairs, and I slid my tongue from Morgan's mouth with more than a little regret that we weren't alone. She whimpered quietly, and I gentled the kiss to a brush of my mouth as Fin came around the corner.

"There you are." She huffed like she'd been looking everywhere. "Morgan, can Juno spend the night at your house?"

I reluctantly lifted my lips from Morgan's and grinned.

She blushed bright red and gave me a good glare before turning a sweet smile on Finley. "What, honey? You need me to watch Juno?"

"She bit Mama last week." She scrunched her face as she hefted the cat into her arms. "And then she peed in Dad's shoe."

Morgan stifled a laugh.

"It's true. That cat hates me."

"Sure, Fin. Just grab her carrier and her bowls and stuff, and I'll take her home with me."

Just when I thought I couldn't love her more.

"Thank you!" Fin put Juno down and ran for the cat supplies, her unicorn backpack bobbing right along with her.

"You must really love me if you're willing to babysit Satan's personal feline." I grabbed her hips and twisted her to face me.

"I must really love your daughter," she countered with a smirk, pressing up against me. Her eyes dropped to the current situation in my boxer briefs.

"Can't help it," I said with a shrug. "If Finley wasn't here, I'd have you on your back on the dining room table and your ankles on my shoulders right now." Fuck, just the thought of it spurred my unruly dick on.

She shook her head and stepped backward, retreating. "Serves you right for kissing me in front of your daughter."

"You kissed me, actually."

"Semantics," she teased with mock shock. "You'd better do something about that. Wouldn't want the boys at the station to think you've got a going-away present for them."

"Cruel, cruel woman."

She leaned over the bar, hauled back two giant Ziploc bags, and dangled one. "Take it back."

"Oh shit, if those are half as good as you smell, then I'll take back anything you want me to."

The gold in her sea-glass necklace sparkled in the light as she laughed. "Remember to share."

I let my gaze drop to her breasts. "Never."

"The cookies, you insufferable man."

"Right. Cookies."

Once Finley reappeared with the cat carrier, Morgan cajoled Satan's mistress into the contraption and packed up the food Fin forgot into a spare bag.

She walked us out, and once Fin was in the car, I kissed Morgan good-bye long and hard outside the garage. "I love you."

"You're just saying that because I'm taking Juno so she doesn't pee in your shoes." She grinned against my mouth.

"I'm saying it because it's true." I cupped the back of her neck and lamented my work schedule for the hundredth time.

"Be safe tonight, okay?" Some of the light died in her eyes. She did her best to lock down the fear, but it was always there, a nail scratch from the surface.

I kissed her hard. "I will. I'll text you if I end up flying." She did better if I sent a before and after message, which we'd learned the week after my storm call.

"Okay."

"I love you, Morgan." I kissed her one last time, effectively keeping her from muttering something like *I adore you.*

Then I headed toward Buxton, where Vivian's house was just a couple blocks off Pamlico Sound.

Brie answered the door with a smile. "Finley!"

"Hi, Aunt Brie!" The two hugged, and I shut the door behind me so the cool air didn't escape.

The Beach Boys blared from the speakers, and Claire danced her way in, singing about California girls. I had to laugh. She really hadn't changed that much since college.

"Fin!" Claire stopped dancing and raced over, sweeping Fin into a hug. "Are you ready for the best Fourth of July ever?"

Finley nodded. "Yes! I brought cookies!" She lifted the Ziploc bag that Morgan had given her. "Morgan made them!"

Claire's smile didn't falter, but the happiness dimmed in her eyes. "Well, I bet they're just sweet as can be!"

"Come on, Fin, let's go find Grandma!" Brie took her hand and off they went.

"Her hair looks great," Claire said softly.

"It really does," I agreed, not wanting to draw any more blood than the cookies had.

"Morgan?" she questioned with a wince.

"Yeah, but if it makes you feel any better, she has Juno."

Claire's eyes widened. "That cat is the devil."

"Incarnate, and yet our daughter doesn't agree."

Finley appeared through the window, dancing across the deck with Brie, and we both smiled. It was the least antagonistic moment I'd had with Claire since she came home nearly two months ago. Two months. It was the longest she'd ever stayed.

She hadn't followed through on her threat to file for custody, but my lawyer had all my paperwork lined up just in case she changed her mind. I wasn't losing Finley.

"How did that audition go?" I asked. "The one you had for that sci-fi show?"

Claire blinked up at me in surprise, looking so much like Fin did when I caught her sneaking candy that I almost laughed. "How did you know?"

"Redhead. Eleven o'clock." I gestured to the windows.

"Oh. Right. I was going to tell you if I got it. I even asked the director about a commute-friendly schedule between here and L.A. for filming so I wouldn't have to mess with our arrangements for Fin." She tucked her thumbs in her back pockets—the same nervous tell she'd had in college.

"I think that would be great." I meant it. If there was a way for Claire to have her career and Finley to have her mom, then I was all for it. "And we could always adjust some stuff to make it work."

Her eyes lit up. "Like maybe she could come to L.A. with me?"

I stilled.

Claire pressed her lips in a line and dropped her gaze. "Figured that would be your answer. Okay, I'll make sure I can commute for the next one. I didn't get that one."

"I'm sorry."

She shrugged. "Happens. Besides, it gives me more time to house hunt. I need to find something local because my mother is killing me."

Relief socked me in the gut. "I can give you the number for the Realtor I used." House hunting meant she was serious about sticking around for Fin. This wasn't just a whim that would pass now that she realized how serious I was about Morgan.

"That would be awesome. Now I'd better go save Finley before she picks up any of Brie's dance moves. Have a happy

Fourth, Jax."

"You too, Claire."

We did the awkward nod thing, and I took off. It took all of ten minutes to get to the station, and I hummed my way through the door.

Did it suck that I had to work instead of taking my girls to the fireworks? Absolutely. But Claire had quit the vindictive witch routine around Morgan and was settling in, which made Finley happier than I'd ever seen her, and I was madly in love with an incredible woman who I had every intention of keeping for the rest of my life. Not that I was saying that to her. Maybe once she admitted that she loved me, but until then, I'd keep my name-changing plans to myself. And work on making her so blissfully happy that she'd be just as addicted to me as I was to her.

I put my stuff in my locker and glanced at the calendar. The guys left in ten days. Fuck, I hated that they were going without me, but staying with Finley was more important than feeling like I'd contributed to the mission, right? Finley was my first mission, period. Being kept back—while shitty in some ways—was the biggest blessing I could have asked for, especially considering Morgan triggered every time someone said the D word around her.

Hopefully she'd relax about it once the guys were home, and as much as she rolled her eyes at Sawyer and Garrett, I knew she'd miss them, too.

"Montgomery, Captain wants to see you," Javier announced from the doorway.

"Okay." No doubt I was about to get a rash of shit for that little maneuver I'd pulled with the ski boat last week, but hey, everyone had come out alive.

I passed Garrett in the hallway and thrust the bag of cookies his direction. "Morgan made them, and she wants you to share."

"Do I have to?" he questioned, already reaching inside for one.

"Unless you want me to tell her that you didn't." I raised my eyebrows.

He paused midbite. "I'll share," he promised with his mouth full.

"Good boy." I gave his shoulder a healthy slap, then walked the rest of the way to Captain Patterson's office. The door was closed, so I gave it a healthy knock.

"Come in."

I opened the heavy door and walked in. "You wanted to see me, sir?"

Captain Patterson looked up from his paperwork and nodded, then removed his glasses to rub the skin between his eyes. For a man who never seemed to tire, he suddenly looked exhausted. "Good to see you, Lieutenant Montgomery. Why don't you have a seat?" He motioned to the chairs.

I closed the door, which revealed Hastings in the furthermost one, his casted leg propped up on an upside-down trash can.

"Hey! How is it feeling?" I asked, sinking into the chair next to him.

He didn't answer or look at me, just stared straight ahead at Captain Patterson with a tick in his jaw. Guy must have gotten some news he didn't want, because I'd never seen him quietly pissed like this before.

Captain Patterson slid his glasses back over his dark brown eyes and leveled a pitying look on me that turned my stomach.

Oh, fuck.

"Jax, we need to talk."

Chapter Twenty-Three

Morgan

And I know I'm going to make it, because who the hell is good enough to shoot me out of the sky, right? Like I said yesterday, flying is flying no matter where you do it.

I cranked the ignition, and the engine turned over with a throaty purr I recognized all too well. Homework assignment complete for the third day in a row!

"You sure about this?" Sam asked from the passenger seat.

I slid my hands down the steering wheel and inhaled the scent of leather into my lungs.

"I don't know if I can be what you want or what you need. There are parts of me that are permanently broken, and I don't know if they'll ever work quite right. The only thing I do know is that I'm never going to stop wondering about the what-ifs if we don't give this a shot, because it's been six months, and I swear I can still taste that kiss, Morgan."

"Morgan. Are you sure you want to do this?" Sam asked again.

I blinked my way out of the memory and glanced up at the wings he'd left pinned to the visor. "Nope. I'm not sure," I answered Sam as honestly as I could.

"Okay, well, let's be certain before you put this monster in drive, because I might love you, but I'm not willing to die because you think you're ready to skip ahead in your homework and joyride." She sent me an eyebrow raise that told me she was serious. "I have four months until I see my husband, and I intend on being there when he gets off that plane."

Her voice caught with those last words, and my hand reached for hers. Last night had been rough. There had been reports of an Apache crash in Afghanistan, and while the media had reported all the facts but the names, the soldiers had been on blackout—all internet and phone services shut down—so those names wouldn't be leaked until the next of kin could be notified. That meant hours of waiting, staring at our phones. Staring at our door.

The crash hit the news around noon.

Grayson didn't get a chance to call until two a.m.

"You're so much stronger than I am." I squeezed her hand.

She scoffed and blew off the compliment. "I haven't been through what you have. Not in the same way. I don't know how Ember and Paisley ever let those boys fly after what happened."

"I have no clue." They were stronger than I was, too. All of them. But I was getting stronger. Every day. "You're really okay after last night?"

"Yeah. I'm just heartbroken for those aviators and their families."

"Me, too." We may not have gotten the knock at our

door, but someone had.

She forced a smile, but there was zero joy. "But I don't want to think about it, so I'm not going to. Besides, we're sitting in here for you."

"So I can constantly lay out my emotional baggage, but you don't have to?" I lifted my eyebrows as I teased her.

"I'm not here for my emotional baggage. I'm here for yours. Now why don't you tell me how it feels having started this truck?" She gestured to the dash, and I smiled faintly as sunlight kissed her diamond and threw tiny dots of rainbows all through the cab.

"I still hear him," I admitted quietly. "It's less and less these days, but whenever I'm in here, I swear I can hear him sitting right next to me. Do you think that will ever go away?"

"Do you want it to?"

"I don't know." I ran my fingers over the soft, supple leather of the console that separated my seat from Sam's. Will's seat from mine. "In some ways, yes, because maybe that means I'm healing. Plus, I'd really like to not have an anxiety attack every time I get in this thing, and I know I'll never sell it." That would be like selling Will's memory. "But I'm terrified that one day I'll stop hearing him, and then I'll forget the sound of his voice, his laugh, then I'll start forgetting him. And I don't want that, either."

How did I make more room for Jackson in my heart without losing Will?

"That's understandable," Sam said, pivoting in her seat so she could look straight at me. "Do you want to drive?"

I felt my throat tighten, but it wasn't as severe as it had been. "Not today."

She sagged in obvious relief. I wouldn't want to take a ride in a vehicle that gave the driver anxiety attacks, either. "You're doing great, you know. The therapy, the homework, all of it. The tapes are sounding better and better, and you even made it through that hotspot thing with the funeral memory tape, though I don't know any other woman in her twenties who would reward herself with Virginia Woolf."

"Hey now, don't mock the classics." I looked over my shoulder to the cab, half expecting to see Will's helmet bag and flight gear, but it was empty, of course. "I couldn't have done it without you, Sam. And I know you're headed home in a couple weeks, but I'm immeasurably grateful that you've stayed with me."

She smiled. "I wouldn't have had it any other way."

I looked over to Jackson's house, then checked the clock on the dash. He usually napped the day he transitioned back to dayshift, which meant he should be waking up soon. My pulse jumped with anticipation.

"It's okay to love him," Sam said gently. "It doesn't mean you loved Will any less. Or that you're replacing him. He would want you to be happy."

"That's the thing. I'm usually happy around Jackson… when he's not scaring the shit out of me and racing off to fly in a storm." My hand closed around the sea-glass pendant, as if I could hold him by proxy, and my forehead puckered. There were very few times I'd been happy around Will. Sure, there had been nights like the ball and when he'd shown up at my house, but the angst definitely ruled the bulk of our relationship. "They're so different from each other."

"Night and day," she agreed. "And that's okay. You don't have to compare them. It's not like you have to make a choice."

A choice? Between Will and Jackson? No, thank you.

She scoffed. "Girl, I said you *don't* have to make a choice."

I rolled my eyes and took another deep breath, searching my body for the usual signs that I was at my limit. "No anxiety attack."

"No anxiety attack," she agreed. "Look at you, getting all

healthy and stuff."

"Let's get out of here. Maybe I'll drive tomorrow."

"How much of that anxiety medication do you have?" she questioned.

"What? For acute attacks?" I asked. "I haven't taken rescue meds in..." I tried to think. "God, it's been over a month now."

"Right. I didn't say they were for you. They're for me riding along with you in this thing." She lifted her eyebrows.

Our eyes locked, and we laughed. I still had a smile on my face as we climbed the steps to my house. I loved my little mushroom-shaped home. The teal paint, the white trim, the new, stronger decking. It felt like a stranger who had slowly become my best friend. My very expensive best friend.

The remodel was just about finished. The two other bedrooms upstairs needed to be gutted and redone, but I'd do that after Sam left so she wasn't inconvenienced.

The whole-house generator had been ordered, and Steve was due to start the demo on the master bathroom next week.

I was finally going to have a bench in my shower so I could shave my legs without twisting myself into knots like the newest cast member of Cirque du Soliel. A bench where Jackson could sit while I straddled his lap—

Speak of the devil, why was Jackson's Land Cruiser pulling in his driveway?

We stood on the deck as he parked in the garage.

"Hey, stranger," I called out as he appeared, swinging a little paper bag.

He startled. "What are you doing up there?"

Sam leaned on the railing. "We've just been sitting here *all* day in the hopes that you'd pull up—and look! Here you are!"

My shoulders shook with laughter as he crossed our yard, but it died when he looked up at me and climbed the stairs.

He looked drained and tense. His cheeks were rough with a shift's worth of stubble, and his eyes were bloodshot. Something was off.

"Are you okay?" I asked as he made it to the top.

"Yeah. No. I'm not sure. Can I have a second with you?" He held out his hand for mine.

I laced our fingers and nodded, then took him inside.

"I'll give you guys some time," Sam said, picking up on the vibe. She disappeared upstairs, and I led Jackson to the kitchen, where I sat him down on one of the new barstools that matched my white and gray theme.

He put the bag on the counter, where it promptly fell over, but he didn't right it. He was too busy watching me like I was the one acting odd around here.

I grabbed him a bottle of water from my refrigerator, then unscrewed the top and put it in front of him.

"Thank you."

"You look…"

"Like shit?" he suggested with a smirk.

"It's impossible for you to look like shit. But you do need a nap. Why didn't you go to sleep when you got off this morning?" Where the hell had he been all this time?

"I needed to grab something I'd ordered last week, and then I just kind of drove." He picked up the bottle and downed half of it.

"Did something happen? Could you not sleep?" Oh God, was Claire threatening a custody suit again? I stepped between his outstretched thighs and braced my hands on his shoulders. "Tell me what has you worried."

He studied me like he'd never seen me before. "You're beautiful." He threaded his hand through my hair and palmed my waist with the other, then pulled me closer. "Kiss me, Kitty."

Now that was something I could do.

I fit my mouth to his like so many times before and kissed him slow and deep, winding my arms around his neck. The world and its problems faded into the hazy background, leaving only Jackson and the way he made me feel. He changed the tempo with deft flicks of his tongue, and the kiss turned hungry and urgent…desperate, even. By the time we broke apart, our breaths were ragged. My pulse raced, and my lips felt swollen.

Never in my life had I been with a man who could erase the world in a single kiss the way he could. The power Jackson held over me was terrifying, but I knew he'd never use it against me. He loved me.

And I…I adored him. I was addicted to him. My heart leaped for him, and my soul felt whole when I was in his arms. Need, infatuation, connection…those were all things I felt for him, but loving him? That was an emotion—a power—I wasn't sure I was capable of giving anyone else again. Love was a gift. I knew that. I felt it every time Jackson gave me those words. But loving someone also gave them the power to obliterate you.

"I brought you a present," he said against my neck, pressing his lips to that sensitive spot beneath my ear. The scruff on his face was a delicious contrast to his soft lips.

"Does this present involve getting me naked? Because although I could be absolutely in favor of it, Sam's upstairs." I tilted my head to give him better access.

"It's in the bag." He lifted his head, and I nearly groaned at the loss. The thing about finally having Jackson was that I never felt entirely satiated. I wanted more and more of him. "Don't look at me like that, or we'll be at my place in thirty seconds, and there's something we have to talk about first."

I pouted. It was childish, and I didn't care. "Fine. We talk, then we go to your place."

"Open your present." He flashed me a grin that nearly

took my panties clean off and pushed the little brown bag my way.

I slid the box from its bag, lifted the lid, and unwrapped the delicate layers of tissue paper. *Mercy.* This book was incredible. In simple block text, the words *Night and Day* stood out where they'd been embossed in rich, dark leather. It was cracked and worn in places, and though it had been protected in a clear library jacket, it was easy to see that it had passed through many hands over the course of many years to find its way here.

"Jackson, is this…" I didn't want to open the cover. Didn't want to even think it might be.

"A first edition? Yeah. But don't worry, it wasn't as expensive as you'd think. I didn't dip into Finley's college fund or anything." His eyes were bright with the simple joy of making me happy.

But this…this was anything but simple. It was a gift chosen with such thought and care that tears prickled my eyes and my chest expanded with a glow I was sure had to be visible.

Oh, my heart. Do not fall in love with this man.

Don't fall? Or don't admit it?

My stomach twisted and did its own falling.

His eyes dimmed. "Kitty, if you don't like it, I can return it."

"What?" I blinked myself free of my thoughts. "Oh no, Jackson, this is exquisite. Not just that you found a copy, but it's the only one I haven't read yet!" I flipped the cover and, sure enough, there was the publication date: 1919.

He flashed a smile. "I knew you were on a Virginia Woolf kick and checked your shelves. I figured it was a fitting present since you finish therapy in what…three more sessions?"

"Two," I said softly. My grief had been at a nine—mostly because I refused to use my ten—when we'd begun, and last week's session it had rated a three.

Three. It hadn't even seemed possible when we'd started. And sure, I still had my triggers, but Dr. Circe said there was a chance those might never go away. There were some things that simply couldn't be fixed, but they sure could be avoided.

"Well, now you have the last Virginia Woolf book to read as your reward."

I carefully wrapped the book and put it back in the box to protect it. "You are incredible, Jackson. Thank you." I kissed him.

"You might not think so in a few minutes, so I'll take it."

My brow furrowed. "Why?"

He shifted his attention to the box. "How are you going to read it in the box?"

I blinked. "I'm not. I'm going to buy one of those airtight display cases and protect it like the piece of art it is."

His gaze whipped back to mine. "What's the point of having it if you don't read it?"

"What's the point of having a first edition, priceless book if you don't protect it?" I countered with a grin.

"You are an astounding woman, and I love you." He shook his head, and the atmosphere in the room shifted as he took a deep breath. When his eyes met mine, there was a plea in them that I didn't understand, and I wasn't sure I wanted to. "There's no easy way to say this. I have to take a trip."

"Okay?" I sat on the nearest stool and faced him so our knees touched. "Are we talking a few days or a week?"

"A few months."

The world tilted on its axis. "I don't understand."

He leaned toward me and took my hand. "Hastings's leg isn't going to heal in time. He isn't cleared to go. He's livid, but there's nothing he can do."

"Go where?" My pulse skittered, and nausea threatened to bring my lunch back up.

"It's basically a three-month vacation, when you think about it. Just a rotation." His voice was level and calm, but his eyes weren't.

"Jackson," I warned. "Half answers are bullshit."

He flinched. "You're right. Okay. I have to deploy with the unit."

The edges of my vision blurred, and his words all jumbled together.

"I wish we had better timing, but I have to deploy."

My heart beat like a bass drum.

"It's just three months, Kitty. That's all. Three months and I'm back. Three months and then we have forever."

"I mean, how hard could it be for us to wait nine months, considering how long we've been dancing around this?"

It was impossible to blink free of his voice. Couldn't shove the memory back in the cassette tape and store it like I'd been taught by Dr. Circe. I ripped my hand from Jackson's and pressed my fingers to my temples. *Breathe. Breathe. Breathe.*

"Shit. Babe, I can't imagine how this sounds to you, but it's nothing like what you're thinking." Jackson reached for me, but I leaned away from his touch. "I'm just going somewhere else to do the same job I do here. That's all. Just flying."

"It won't be that bad, so I don't want you to worry, which I know you will anyway, but flying is flying no matter where you do it."

I slammed my eyes shut and tried to steady my breathing. This wasn't happening. It wasn't possible.

"Morgan, honey—"

"You said you couldn't go!" I shouted, the sound echoing off the tile floors. "You told me that because of Finley, you couldn't go!"

When he reached for me again, I slid off my stool and stumbled backward until my back hit the island.

"No, Kitty." There was so much pain in his eyes. "I said

that I had a family care plan, but the captain decided to leave me behind because of Finley. It was a decision made for both the needs of the unit and compassion. Being a single parent doesn't get you out of deployments."

That fucking word was the bane of my existence. I gripped the edge of the counter to stay upright.

"And Captain Patterson knows Claire is back, so I'm not parenting by myself. The entire reason I was being left behind no longer exists." His jaw ticked, and I knew there were parts of that conversation he was leaving out.

"But if Hastings can't fly?" God, there had to be a way out of this, right? I couldn't do this again. It wasn't even in the realm of possibility.

Jackson rose from the stool but stayed a couple feet away. "The guys from Elizabethtown will cover it. We're just an offshoot of them, anyway."

Something soft twined between my ankles. Juno.

"Have you told Finley?"

Jackson shook his head and smashed his lips in a flat line. "I told you first." He took the bottle of water from the counter and slammed the rest of it back, then crushed it in his fist. "I can't imagine what you're thinking right now."

"I can't." My breaths came faster, like a steaming locomotive gained speed as it left the station.

"It has to feel just like—"

"No!" I shouted, pointing my finger at him. "No." I couldn't stay here. Couldn't think. Couldn't catch my breath. Couldn't slow my heart. I couldn't do this. Not any of it.

"Okay." He laced his fingers on the top of his head and took a calming breath. "Let's look at this logically."

"Fuck your logic." A lump grew in my throat. *No, no, no.*

"It's just search and rescue, baby. It simply happens to be a rotation at an air station in the Caribbean so we're on hand for hurricane season. It's more like a three-month TDY than it is a deployment."

Fuck that word. Fuck all of this.

The stitches I'd sewn meticulously into my heart began to pop one by one.

"This isn't like him," Jackson said so softly that I almost didn't hear it.

"I'm sorry?" I snapped, arching my neck slightly to dislodge the damn lump.

"My deployment is nothing like Will's."

"We are not talking about Will!" He was already in my damned head as it was.

"Kitty, we have to be able to talk about him, especially with this."

"He's not..." I sucked in a breath and rolled my head, but the lump wasn't going anywhere. It was growing. "He's not in this conversation." Because if he was, I couldn't be. Deployment...I couldn't do another one. Couldn't get that news again. God, I could still feel the gum-like texture of the strawberry jam on my shoes.

Jackson took a step toward me, and I moved again, heading straight into my kitchen. He couldn't touch me. He took every ounce of logic the minute his hands were on me, and I had to be able to think. I had to survive.

"Baby, he's in every conversation when it comes to my job."

My gaze snapped to his, and my hand stilled on the handle to the refrigerator.

"He may as well be standing in this room." He gestured between our bodies. "Right here in between us." There was such care, such compassion in his gaze, otherwise I might have started throwing things at him. Didn't he know how hard I was trying to keep that from happening?

My throat constricted, and I ripped open the refrigerator door, grabbed the pitcher of sweet tea, and drank straight from the glass. I gulped and swallowed, but nothing would shake that lump, the tightness that I refused to believe was the harbinger of what I'd been working myself to the emotional bone to get rid of.

I slammed the refrigerator door and put the pitcher on the counter.

"I can't do this." I shook my head to emphasize my point.

He winced. "We can do this. It's three months."

"No." There. How was that for setting my emotional boundaries?

"Morgan, you're reacting out of fear, and I get it. I can't fathom how you must be feeling right now, and the fact that I'm even asking you to go through this again is..." His face crumpled, and he looked away.

"I. Can't. Do. This." It wasn't possible. I wouldn't just regress. I'd be on the fucking floor.

"Baby." He came for me, and I slid right around him, making it to the entrance of the kitchen before he could stop me. "Morgan, nothing is going to happen to me!"

"You don't know that!" I screamed at the top of my lungs as I reached the foyer. "You have no fucking clue what can happen. You just *think* you do."

"I promised you that I'd never put a rescue above my own life, and I meant it. I'm the best SAR pilot on—"

"Oh, shut up!" I shouted. "You're the best? Funny, Will thought he was the best! Jagger and Josh? Yep, I've heard those words out of their mouths, too. You all think you're the best until you fall out of the sky, because when push comes to shove, you're not the gods you think you are, so don't you dare stand there and tell me that *nothing* is going to happen to you!"

That drew him up short, and we faced off in the entrance hall.

Throwing my head back, I stared at the lofted ceiling,

praying for my throat to open, but it wouldn't. I was a little girl caught in the middle of a hungry boa constrictor. Tighter and tighter it drew, taking my air supply.

"Maybe we should sit down? I'm getting worried about you over here."

"You're worried?" I spat back. "You're deploying. I'm the one you expect to sit here and wait and worry, and I'm not going to do it! Not again. No!"

"Kitty, please listen to me. I'm not going to a war zone. I'm going to the beach."

My heartbeat wasn't a bass drum anymore. It was a staccato snare, and my breaths came so fast that the room around me felt distant, but I forced my mind to work. "Twenty twelve, four dead. Twenty ten, three dead. Two thousand eight, four dead. Two thousand four, six dead—"

"Fuck," he swore, low and soft. "I know what happened with every single one of those crashes."

"Coast Guard. Search and rescue crashes," I added between gasping breaths as my back hit the wall. "You can't. Make. Me do. This again. I won't. Not for you. Not for. Anyone." My head buzzed.

"Kitty," he begged, and the agony in his eyes was more than I could stand. "Okay, talking about this is putting you at risk, and I don't want—"

"Ha! Exactly!" I shouted at him as my throat closed even tighter.

"I won't be at risk. Not any more than usual. No one's going to be shooting at me, Morgan. It's not the same, baby. Please."

Shooting. Will. First the RPG that crashed Jagger. Then the next one that took down the medevac with Josh and Will on board. Then the small arms fire that hit Will in the sweet spot that wasn't covered by Kevlar. Even the best pilots weren't immune to bullets, right? We had no control in fate. No control. None. People died. And he bled out right there, in some dusty, rocky valley in Afghanistan, all because he'd been ordered to deploy. He was dead. And Jackson was deploying. Jackson, who had become my whole world. Jackson and that same helicopter. Jackson. Jackson. Jackson was talking. What was he saying? Jackson was deploying. Deploying. Deploying. Why had I let this happen again? My past was repeating because I was too stupid to stop it. The jam was sticky. The shoes went into the trash. The necklace. The necklace. The blues—

The air ceased. Pain erupted, so sharp it stopped my hurricane of a brain. I concentrated on my neck muscles and visualized them opening. Air rushed through again, and I gasped.

"Can you hear me?" His hands were on my shoulders. "You're having an anxiety attack. Let me get Sam and your rescue meds—"

"No!" Using them was defeat. It was a step backward, and I was supposed to be moving forward. I was at a three. A three!

Unless I was triggered. Deployment? Trigger. Jackson flying? Trigger. Jackson himself…

"Sam!"

I ripped out of his arms and slid down the wall. Once my butt hit the tile, I drew my knees to my chest. *Breathe. Open your throat. It's in your mind, not your body.*

"What is going— Holy shit."

Thudding footsteps.

"She's having an anxiety attack." Jackson dropped to his knees before me. God, those eyes were so blue. Just like my sea glass. Blue. Blue. Blue. So beautiful. Of course I fell for him, and because I did, now he would go.

"Okay. Give me a second."

"Just breathe, Kitty." His voice was calm. Why was he

so calm? Why was he still *here*? Didn't he understand that I couldn't do this?

My fingernails dug into my kneecaps.

"It's okay." He reached for me but thought better of it. "God, I wish you'd let me hold you."

Can I hold you? Just this once before I go. The next time I kiss you will be after this deployment.

The vise around my throat squeezed.

"Move," Sam ordered.

Jackson slid to the side.

"Here we go." Sam held out a white, oval pill and a bottle of water.

"No," I denied. "Over. A month."

Her eyes softened for a heartbeat, and then she was steel again. "Yep, so this time we'll push for two months between. We set the goals we can attain, remember?"

She thrust the offering my way and waited for me to decide. She gave me power in a moment I had none.

I swallowed the pill. It took half the bottle of water to get it down my throat, but it was in. A small brown paper bag appeared next. I grasped it with two hands, brought it to my face, and began breathing.

"There we go," Sam said softly. "You just breathe and wait for the meds to kick in. What the hell did you do?" That last part wasn't aimed at me.

"I'm deploying."

Sam drew back and her wide eyes flew to mine, interrupted by my paper bag every few seconds as it expanded. "Oh, Morgan."

"It's not the same, Sam."

"To her, it is."

They both fell silent as I breathed like it was my full-time job. For the last four months, it had been. How had I only lived here for four months? Is that really how long I'd known Jackson? God, and I was already so far gone that I was breathing through a paper bag. This wouldn't be the only time he deployed. This was who he was.

Slowly, my breathing returned to normal and the buzzing faded in my head. My throat was still constricted, but that would pass once the meds kicked in. Not that it mattered because I'd be asleep soon after that.

I dropped the bag to the floor and sat with my head against the wall, arching my neck. "You should go."

"It's okay. I've got her, Sam," Jackson said softly.

"No." I lowered my head and found him watching me. Beautiful, kind, magnetic, head over heels in love with me—and a loaded freaking gun when it came to my mental health. "You should go, Jackson."

"Morgan?" His eyes flared.

"Go. This isn't going to get any better the more we talk about it." My heart screamed in protest. "I need you to go."

He warred with himself, with my words. It was all over his face. "Okay. I need to talk to Fin. And Claire. Shit. Okay. I'll come by for breakfast tomorrow?"

Quick cuts were better. I shook my head. "No. I need you to go for good."

"This is not over. This is...I don't know what this is because it's not a fight. This is a blip on the radar, Kitty." Agony. That was the only way to describe the look in his eyes and the rending of those stitches in my heart.

Sam stood and backed away, staying by the edge of the foyer. She never went far after I'd had an attack.

"This is over," I said softly. "I won't do another deployment. I won't take another phone call. I won't bury another man I—" I snapped my mouth shut. God, when were the meds going to kick in?

"Love," he accused. "You love me."

I locked my jaw and dropped my gaze.

"Fine. Well, I love *you*, even if you won't say it, and I'm not giving you up. It's only three months, Morgan. Nothing will change in three months."

"Try three days," I whispered. "I'm not ready for this. I'm not strong enough for this. I will not do this. Do you know what happens when no one chooses you?"

"Kitty, that's not what this is," he whispered.

"You learn to choose yourself. And that's what I'm doing. I'm choosing me. I'm choosing no anxiety attacks. No deployment. No…" My face crumpled, and I fought the tears that stung my eyes.

"No me." His mouth tightened as he fought for emotional control.

"If you love me, you'll go."

He flinched.

"You won't ask me to do this. You won't ask me to stay with you, knowing the cost is this happening to me every. Single. Day. You won't ask me to undo everything I've fought so hard for." Air flew freely through my throat, and the ache lessened.

"Morgan, no. God, please." He clenched his hands but didn't reach for me.

One touch was all it would take to break my resolve, and I couldn't let that happen. Not unless I wanted to dive right back into daily attacks, and if I had to go through another deployment…that's exactly where I'd be.

"Jackson, if you love me as much as you say you do, you will walk out that door and you won't come back. You'll let me heal. You'll let me go."

Despair. Conflict. Anger. Frustration. Defeat. They all visited his face in the span of thirty seconds—some twice. I gripped my knees to keep from grabbing him as he stood. I locked my jaw to keep from begging him to stay.

He walked to the door and then through it but turned

around once he was on the deck. "I love you more than any torture you could ever ask of me. So, if I love you enough to walk away, can't you love me enough to stay?"

The last stitches in my heart ripped free, and my damage bled out all over me. "I never said I loved you." It was barely a whisper, but he heard it.

"Right. I guess you didn't." His expression would haunt my dreams for as long as I lived.

"Sam, close the door," I begged. The meds were kicking in, and while I could move, I was sluggish as hell, but at least the ache in my throat was fading.

His face tightened, daring me to do it myself, but I couldn't.

"Morgan…this is… Maybe take some time?" she asked softly.

I leveled her with a stare. "Remember when you showed up at my house with a truckload of furniture and begged me not to tell Grayson where you were?"

"Shit." Her mouth tensed, and her gaze flew between Jackson and me.

"Please shut the door." My voice broke, and my shoulders rose as the first sob racked through me.

Jackson moved, heading my direction, but Sam was faster and shut the door before he got there. And because Sam never did anything half measure, the deadbolt followed.

What was left of my pulverized heart shattered into so many pieces it may as well have been sand.

Sam sat and pulled me into her arms while I cried.

"It's going to be okay," she whispered, even though we both knew it wasn't.

So I did what I always did. Wiped my tears, lifted my chin, and waited for the pain to pass.

Chapter Twenty-Four

Jackson

I finished packing my second duffel and placed it next to the first in my entryway. All I had left to do was pack my carry-on.

Our flight left tomorrow afternoon.

The last week had both flown immeasurably fast and dragged like hell. The time I spent with Fin disappeared in a heartbeat, and the moments I stood at my window and blatantly stared at Morgan's house…those seemed to last forever and hurt like hell.

If you love me as much as you say you do, you will walk out that door and you won't come back. You'll let me heal. You'll let me go. Her words had played on repeat inside my head for the last eight days. The sound of her sobs came in a close second. Her telling me that she'd never said she loved me? I blocked that out as much as possible.

Every day I climbed her steps and left a single piece of sea glass next to the one I'd left the day before. She was amassing quite the little pile, and I was paying quite the bill to Christina, since I didn't have much sea-glass hunting time left. But unlike the last time I'd left daily reminders that I wasn't giving up, this time she hadn't accepted them.

The situation wasn't hopeless, since she still lived next door, but it wasn't exactly hopeful, either.

"You should take Phillip," Finley said.

I turned away from the window to see the world's saddest little girl staring at me. I hoisted her up and sat her on my forearm so that we were eye level. "You think I should take a blind turtle on deployment?"

She nodded solemnly.

"Maybe I should have asked *why* you think I should take him?" I tried to match her serious expression and failed.

"Cousteau is a fish. He can't go. Barnaby would escape, so he can't go. And Juno pees in your shoes." She wrinkled her nose. "But Phillip would fit in your pocket." She tapped the breast pocket of my button-down shirt. "Not that one, of course. It's too small."

"So I should take Phillip because he can breathe without water, he's too slow to escape, and he won't pee in my shoes?" I raised my eyebrows at her.

"Yep. Plus, he fits in your pocket." Her big brown eyes were almost impossible to deny, but in this case, I was going to have to hold out.

"I won't have a lot of time for pets, Fin. It's mostly flying and paperwork. Is there some other reason Phillip needs to come?"

Her little lips pursed, and she stared long and hard at the floor.

"Finley?" I asked gently.

"So you don't forget me." There were no tears, thank God, but the misery in her eyes broke my heart, then trampled it.

My chest constricted, but I managed not to lose my shit in

front of her. “Fin, sweetheart, there’s no chance I could forget you. Zero. I don’t need to carry Phillip around when I have you right here.” I took her hand and put it on top of my heart. “Will it make you feel better if you hear the plan again?”

She nodded.

“You have a brand-new phone!” I made a jazz hand with the one that wasn’t holding her and was rewarded by a tiny smile. “Now, what are the rules of this brand-new phone, Finley Montgomery?”

Her eyebrows furrowed with concentration. “Only use it at home or at Grandma’s.”

“Correct.”

“Keep it charged.”

“You got it.”

“Answer when you call for video chat.”

“Bingo. Every day at seven before school and every night before bed as promised. You’ll be so sick of my face you won’t want me to come home.”

She giggled. Oh, sweet victory.

“And what happens if I have to go rescue people and can’t make it to a call?”

“You’ll send a text or call earlier…or later!” There was a grin, too.

“And what happens to that phone when I get home?”

She twisted her puckered lips from side to side. “I have to give it back.”

“Yep. This phone is for deployment only, so consider it a perk.” I tweaked her nose. “But what is the number one rule of the deployment phone?” I set my features as sternly as possible.

She huffed out a sigh. “No calling boys.”

“That’s right. No boys. None. Everyone you love besides Daddy is a girl, anyway.”

“What about Uncle Sawyer?” She raised her brows.

Well, she had me there. "I might make an exception."

"Will you put Morgan's number in, too? Just in case?"

"I can do that." Leave it to my brilliant little daughter to twist the knife. I didn't have the heart to tell her no, and I knew Morgan wouldn't want me to when it came to this. Fin had caught on that Morgan hadn't been around, but since I'd never outright told her we were together, I didn't think I needed to announce what might be the opposite now.

"Thank you!" She threw her arms around my neck, and I held her tight, breathing in the scent of her strawberry shampoo. This deployment was going to suck on every fucking level possible.

"I love you, Finley." God, how was I going to leave her for three months? I hadn't been apart from her for more than three days since she was born.

"Love you, Daddy." She smacked a kiss on my cheek.

Knock. Knock. Knock.

"Maybe it's Morgan!" she exclaimed, wiggling down from my arms. She shot off like a bolt of lightning before I could tell her there was zero chance in hell Morgan was here. She'd even sent Juno back with Sam the day after she'd thrown me out. "Mommy!"

Shit, I'd forgotten what time it was.

I walked into the entry to see Claire hauling in a massive suitcase.

"You still sure about this?" she asked as Fin took her purse.

"Sure that it's better for Fin if her routine is as close to normal as possible? Yes. You still promise to move out when I get back?"

She arched an eyebrow. "How about I promise to move out when you get back if you still want me to?"

I tilted my head and blinked.

"Okay, fine." She rolled her eyes with a smile. "I promise.

This is just the first one. I'll bring the others over tomorrow before you go."

"Thank you. I've got all the feeding schedules up in the kitchen."

"For Finley or the menagerie?" she joked.

"Yes," I answered.

We both laughed, and it was awkward but easier than it had been.

Knock. Knock. Sam stood behind the glass storm doors with a beach bag slung over her shoulder.

"New girlfriend?" Claire asked.

"Don't start," I warned, keeping my voice level since Finley was here as I opened the door. "Sam?"

Her gaze darted to Claire, then her suitcase, then me. "Bad time?"

"Not at all. Come on in." I stepped back, and Sam walked straight through the entry to high-five Finley.

"How's it going, Fin?"

"Hey, Sam!" She leaned around Sam and stared at the door, which served as another slice to my soul. Not that it mattered. It was pretty much death by a thousand tiny cuts around here right now.

"Just me today," Sam said with enough perk that Finley's face fell only slightly. "But she did bake you some cookies this morning!" She dug into her bag and produced a Ziploc full of chocolate chip cookies.

"Really? Yay!" Fin took the cookies and disappeared toward the kitchen, still wearing Claire's purse.

Cue the most awkward moment of my life.

"How about I take Fin down to the water for..." Claire glanced between Sam and me. "A while. Text me when you're ready?"

I nodded my thanks, and Claire ushered Fin and her cookies out the door.

"Can we sit?" Sam asked.

"Sure."

Once we were at the dining room table, Sam pulled out her phone, a laptop, and the small, silver tape recorder that usually lived on Morgan's counter.

"Does she know you're here?" Even asking was painful.

"Hell no. She'd slaughter me for what I'm about to do, which means I'm trusting you to keep this between us. But, before we start, do you want to explain why your ex has her suitcase in your entry? Or should I just jump to conclusions?" Her eyes narrowed slightly.

"Claire is moving in so Finley can stay in our home while I'm gone," I answered easily. "We're not together. We're never going to be together again. I'm just trying to make it as easy as possible on my daughter."

Sam studied me for a second and then nodded, as if accepting my answer. "Okay then. Because I'm not about to risk one of my closest friendships if you're already moving on. Get me?"

"I'm not moving on. I'm not exactly hopeful, but not moving on." I rested my elbows on the table. "It's only three months, Sam. She threw me out and slaughtered me for three damned months."

Sam sighed. "You're not wearing her glasses."

"She doesn't wear glasses," I countered.

"Not the kind of glasses I'm referring to." She rolled her eyes. "When you think about this deployment, what's your first concern?"

"Easy. Who is taking care of Finley? Where is she staying? How do I keep connected to her? How do I make her feel secure and safe? Not that Morgan isn't a giant clusterfuck—"

"Nope, you're good. I get it. You see this deployment with your daddy glasses on, as you should. Being Finley's dad colors everything in this world, even Morgan. And you might flip your boyfriend lens onto a situation, like you did when you came to tell her about the deployment, but no matter what, your daddy lens comes first. It's permanent."

"Right. I can see that." It was true. Morgan's love for Fin only elevated my attraction to her.

"You aren't using Morgan's glasses," she said again, then set up the laptop. "Before you two got together, Morgan would watch this video every night before bed. Some nights she'd watch it a hundred times." She took a deep breath and muttered a prayer for forgiveness at my ceiling before she pressed play.

The background was a white wall with a picture of a Blackhawk helicopter and the tops of chairs. A dining room table. Then he slid into the picture, and I was faced with Will Carter.

He looked exactly like his pictures online, of course. Serious, clean-cut face, brown, wavy hair, brown eyes…and a delicate pair of aviation wings around his neck. Morgan's.

A pang of jealousy hit me harder than I'd felt myself capable. Jesus, the guy was dead, and I was growly. He still owned the heart of the woman I loved, and I couldn't even fight him for it.

He sighed, then looked straight into the camera. "Morgan. Elyse. Bartley." He flashed a smile that transformed his features, but it faded quickly. "God, I hope you never see this. I hope that I get home from this deployment and delete this file so I can tell all of this to you in person. And yeah, I just got back from your place last night…" He smiled and looked away. "But there's a lot I didn't say, because it wouldn't have been fair seeing that I asked you to wait around until I get home."

Shit. Just like I had.

"So yeah, I'm praying you never see this. But…" He swallowed. "But if something happens, and you do, then I want to make sure you know that you are the most infuriating, stubborn, button-pushing pain in the ass I've ever known." He nodded.

My eyes flew wide. What the actual fuck?

"They were always at each other's throats," Sam commented with a sad smile.

"But you're also ridiculously smart, and compassionate, and loyal, and so gorgeous that you make my teeth hurt when I look at you. There is nothing about me that deserves everything you bring to the table." He scoffed. "I'm showing up empty-handed to this party, and the most amazing thing about you is that you don't care. You just want me, and I can't figure out why, but I'm done fighting it. You want this mess? It's yours. Just enjoy your last nine months of freedom—I mean, hopefully not too much or anything—because once I get home, we're doing this thing. And I know I'm going to make it, because who the hell is good enough to shoot me out of the sky, right? Like I said yesterday, flying is flying no matter where you do it." His grin turned cocky, and my stomach twisted. Fuck, he sounded just like I had.

"Shit, that's pretty much what I said to her." I cursed.

"I figured." Sam's face scrunched in pity.

"But in the interest of being prepared, let's do this. I took out a secondary life insurance policy this morning, and you're the beneficiary. And I know you're going to want to fight it, but please, take the money. Use it. Don't just give it to charity or stick it in a bank account, Morgan. Spend it on something that brings you happiness. Use it to leave like you always planned. I just wish I was going with you."

The video continued for about fifteen minutes while he said good-bye to her. While he confessed the things he hadn't felt strong enough to say in person. Those fifteen minutes transformed him from a two-dimensional ghost to a flesh and blood man who I might not hang with in real life but I could respect. We were alike in miniscule ways and complete opposites in the ones that really mattered.

"So, I guess, I'll see you later. And I'm hoping you come to the redeployment ceremony, because that's when it's all going to start for us." A slow smile spread over his face. "And I'm going to kiss you so hard that the last few years will have all been worth it." His eyebrows popped up. "We should go to the Outer Banks for a whole week when I get back. Remember how much fun we had there? Maybe this time I'll actually get you off the beach and onto one of those surfboards. Yeah. I'll plan it all. And I guess now I have to delete this file when I get back or it will ruin the surprise." He sighed, long and hard. "See ya later, Morgan. Nine months."

He reached forward and killed the recording.

"So that's Will," Sam said with a sigh, shutting the laptop and bringing over the tape recorder.

"I already knew that she loved him, but thank you for making him real." My voice was gruffer than I intended. If that night in Afghanistan had gone differently, maybe I still would have met Morgan, but she would have been a tourist wrapped around her boyfriend. I never would have had the chance to fall in love with her.

"You're welcome. Now, you know that every week Morgan has to record the story of his death and listen to it, right?"

"So that's the tape recorder."

"You got it. This is from this week." She pressed play, and Morgan's sweet, clear drawl came through. She told the story from start to finish, then the funeral, without so much as a hiccup. There was pain, grief in her voice, but she was concise and in control.

"That therapy sounds a lot like torture," I remarked as Sam hit stop.

"It has been." She slid her phone in front of her, swiped

it open, and thumbed through her media. "Now listen. I only have this because I was an idiot and thought I was supposed to record it. But when you stand there all frustrated, preaching at her that you'll be fine and it's only three months of a beach vacation? This is what goes through *her* head." She tapped her phone, and Morgan's voice came through again.

"I'm…in the grocery store—" Holy shit, she sounded broken. Every word was a struggle. "—picking out a jar of jam, and my phone rings." She gasped, sucking in air. "It's Sam," she cried with a sob.

I braced my head in my hands as my eyes fluttered shut. Like I could somehow block out her pain if I didn't see the fucking phone.

"She…she…" Her breath was ragged. "I can't do this. I just can't."

"You can, Morgan. You just have to get through it once today. Go as far as you can," a soothing voice sounded. That had to be her therapist.

"Sam said that there was a crash." Another pause. "And our friends are hurt."

"Have some water," the therapist suggested.

"Thank you." Another pause. "And Will…he didn't make it." Her sobs crush my soul, my ego, my very foundation. "He's dead. He's only been there three days, and he's *gone*." She cried so hard my eyes burned, and when I glanced at Sam, she was swiping away her tears.

"I can't listen to this," I snapped.

"If she could get through it, so can you," she retorted.

I locked my jaw as my legs began to fidget, looking for any action I could take to lessen Morgan's pain.

"And…and…" She sucked in a harsh breath. "I drop the jar and it shatters, but who cares? Will is dead. Will! *My* Will! And I can't breathe! How am I supposed to breathe?" She screamed that last word, and I felt it reverberate in every cell of my body. The gasp she took was familiar, and I tensed every muscle in my body as I heard it. "I can't. I can't. I can't." The chant went on another ten seconds before the therapist jumped in to help with the anxiety attack, and the tape stopped.

Sam pocketed the phone and wiped her cheeks again.

Defeated. Drained. Heartbroken. I couldn't put a finger on which emotion trumped the rest. "I love her," I whispered.

"Yeah, I know you do. And beneath all this that's swimming in her head? I think she loves you, too. And you can be as mad as you want to be that she's shut you out, as long as you understand that it has nothing to do with what she feels for you and everything to do with self-preservation so she doesn't become her"—she lifted her phone—"again."

"So I'm just supposed to do what? Walk away from the woman I love?" I lifted my head. "Because that's not in my nature. What we have is something worth fighting for, and I'm climbing into the ring, ready to take the punches, but she's already left the arena."

Sam sighed and rubbed her forehead, then glanced at her wedding ring. "The truth is I'm torn. I honestly think she needs you just as much as you need her. I…" She shook her head and muttered something to Will. "I think you're her match. But I also know that you are jumping up and down on the biggest trigger she has."

"I can't help it. If I could do anything about this, trust me, I would."

"I know that, too." She stood and put everything back in her bag. "Which is why I'm telling you that it's not going to be enough for you to fight for her. You're going to have to fight *her*, too. And that might be more than you can take."

I got up to walk her to the door, then stared through the storm glass at Morgan's house. She was in there, right now, and I couldn't do a damn thing about it. Or could I? "I can take it," I told Sam. "Whatever she dishes out, I can take. Now, during the deployment, and after. I'm all in."

She studied me, then nodded. "Okay."

"But how am I supposed to love her without triggering her right now? Because I don't want her on the ground for the next three months." I never wanted to hear the voice on that tape again.

"Just keep doing what you're doing. Show up, but don't force her hand. Morgan's the long game."

"No, Morgan's the endgame."

Sam chuckled, dug through her bag, and pulled out a clear package with…

"Are those knee pads?" What the hell?

She pushed them into my chest. "I was told by the guys that if you were willing to fight, you'd need these. It's basically your invitation to the boys' club. We'll back you up as much as we can." She winced as I took the pads. "And sorry about the door last week. I owe Morgan, and she called it in. Honestly, I'm only here because I remember those months without Grayson, and it would have been a lot easier if we'd just communicated."

I raised my eyebrows.

"I thought he was in love with his ex-comatose ex-girlfriend. Long story."

"Apparently."

"Be safe, Jax. She might have thrown you out, but all of that girl's happiness is wrapped up in you making it home. No matter how safe you think you're being—be safer. You understand?"

"I understand."

She hugged me and walked out the front door. "Oh, and Morgan has an appointment tomorrow to have some sea glass set in a bracelet."

I blinked. "Okay?"

"It's at Christina's at eleven thirty a.m., which to my understanding is five hours before you're due to show at the hangar for deployment."

I grinned. "Thank you, Sam."

"Don't fuck this up, Jax."

I wasn't going to.

Chapter Twenty-Five

Morgan

These months are going to fly by. I promise. And then it's you and me.

"It would look good in platinum," Christina mused, laying out the small pieces of sea glass on her lightboard as we stood in the workroom at the back of her shop.

"Or gold?" I suggested, fingering the pendant around my neck. Jax and I might be done, but it felt wrong to take it off.

"It would definitely match your necklace," she said with a nod. "You know, I just wanted to say that I'm really sorry Jax has to go."

I stilled.

"Peter is so angry that they won't let him wait for an upslip there. He knows…what this is costing you two, and we're both very sorry." She squeezed my hand.

Trying—and failing—to neatly box the pain of losing Jax, I brought my eyes to hers. "It's not your fault."

"You two would still be together if Peter hadn't slipped on that deck." She bit her lower lip.

"Christina, don't. Whether it was this…trip or the next, it was bound to happen. Getting out now just makes it hurt less than later." My smile was shaky and fake as hell, but she didn't call me on it.

"Well, I still feel like shit about it. You two have something very real, and I love you both. So I'm hoping you'll forgive me." She patted my hand and headed for the door that led to the showroom of her shop. "You know, I have just the clasp that will hold this together for you. Give me a second and I'll grab it from the display."

"Clasp? But we didn't even decide what metal—"

She closed the door, and I heard the audible click of a lock. *What in the actual hell?*

The back door that led to the parking lot opened, and Jackson walked in.

My heart jumped, like someone had used the paddles to get a rhythm back. I'd missed this man so much that I wasn't sure I was still a complete person.

He closed the door behind him but didn't throw the lock. Instead, he faced me and leaned back against it, which pretty much felt like the same thing. His face was clean-shaven, his baseball hat was on backward, and his MIT T-shirt stretched across muscles I knew all too well. Every single part of him looked good enough to eat, but his eyes…those brought me to my knees. They were red-rimmed and swollen. He looked haunted.

"I thought you left today," I said, breaking the silence but not the tension.

"Five hours," he answered, tucking his hands in his pockets.

"Finley?"

"Claire and Brie took her up to the water park. Figured

keeping her busy would be best. We…" He swallowed. "We said our see-you-laters this morning to make it easier on her."

"I'm so sorry." That explained the swollen eyes. My heart ached for him.

"Thanks. I put your number in her cell phone. She asked for it. The phone's only for deployment, so we can FaceTime, and I doubt she'll bother you—"

"It's fine. I'll pick up whenever she needs me." I missed Finley just as much as I missed Jackson, and I hadn't been prepared for that. Hadn't been prepared for any of this.

He pushed off the door and came toward me but stayed on the opposite side of the line of worktables that divided the small room in half.

My gaze flew to the door.

"You can leave at any time. I'm not trying to trap you. Just talk to you," he said softly, bracing his palms on the table between us.

"Nothing's changed." It couldn't. It didn't matter how I felt about the incredible man standing in front of me. Survival had to be my first priority.

"I know." He nodded, a slight smile curving his kissable lips as his eyes dropped to the necklace he'd given me. "I didn't really get a chance to talk last time. And while you're free to walk out that door any second you see fit, I'm really hoping you'll give me five minutes."

"Five minutes?" My pulse jumped. Five minutes with this man was dangerous to my heart, but didn't I owe him that? Hell, I owed him far more. "And you stay on that side of the table?"

If he touched me, I'd be a goner.

"Five minutes, and I stay on this side of the table," he agreed.

"Deal." I tucked my hair behind my ear, wishing I'd worn it up today.

"I love you, Morgan." He nailed me with those eyes, and

his words shattered what little defenses I had against him.

"Jackson, don't," I whispered as my heart thudded to life.

"Five minutes." He lifted the corner of his mouth into a sinfully sexy smirk.

Ugh. I nodded.

"First, I have a really bad habit of not telling you things first, so I'm telling you that Claire is living at my house with Finley while I'm gone."

I sucked in a breath, and that heartbeat that had started slugging its way to a dependable rhythm stuttered. Ten days. It had only taken ten damned *days*.

"Kitty, it's not what you think, and damn, that face is making me want to jump this table and hold you, but I made a promise, so I won't. Claire and I aren't together. We'll never *be* together. She's living at my place so Fin can keep her life as normal as possible. Plus, Juno raked her claws down Vivian's couch, so that option is off the table."

I smiled, then pressed my lips between my teeth so he wouldn't get encouraged.

"She's moving out when I get back. It's just for Finley, and it's probably the most maternal decision she's ever made... after moving back. But now you know, so you won't be shocked when she's coming down the stairs or asking to borrow sugar... not that she bakes. You'll probably see a ton of takeout."

I glanced toward the clock and raised my eyebrows. *You're using your five minutes, Jackson.*

"You're right. Morgan, I love you. Taking a three-month trip isn't going to change that. I'm not sure a lifetime would change that, honestly."

My eyes widened and my stomach tightened, but there was no anxiety...at least not yet. If it came to that, I was going to have to leave for my own good. *He didn't use the D word.*

"And I understand why you had to end this, and I don't blame you for choosing your own health. You've earned every inch of ground you've gained, and it would kill me to take that from you. I never want to be the cause of your pain."

"Thank you," I whispered, knowing I was now the cause of his.

Weren't we just a pair?

"You told me that if I loved you, I would walk out the door and wouldn't come back. But the truth is that I love you enough to walk out the door *and* come back."

My breath hitched.

"You can give me up. That's okay. My love is strong enough to carry us both through this." He leveled a look on me that said he was completely serious, and despite every plea my brain sent my heart, my posture softened. Defenses gone. His eyes flared, and he took a quick breath. "I'm not giving you up."

"I'm sorry?" My eyebrows reached for the sky. "That's not your choice to make."

"Five minutes." He pointed to the clock.

I folded my arms under my breasts and felt no small satisfaction when his eyes followed and heated. Ten days hadn't squashed the chemistry between us. If anything, it apparently had the same effect as a starvation diet—I was ravenous. Hungry but not stupid enough to take the cheese from a time-delayed trap.

He looked at the ceiling, and I could almost see him count to five before he locked eyes with me again. "Right. Back to the point. I'm not giving you up, Morgan. Not today. Not tomorrow. Not ever, if I have my way."

I scoffed and narrowed my eyes. Didn't he realize kidnapping was illegal?

"I'm leaving on a trip in five hours, and as far as I'm concerned, I still have a girlfriend. And in case you're missing the point, that girlfriend is you." He grinned, and my body temp rose. Damn it. "You think I'm leaving on this trip and

I'm not going to come back."

I swallowed and shoved the panic as far away as I could.

"So you think that if you don't love me—if we're not together while I'm on this trip—you'll save yourself the heartache of that possible future."

Bull's-eye.

"And I understand that, too. If you want to shove that love you *don't* feel for me into a little box and file it away in your emotional basement so you can survive these next three months, then be my guest. It's not like I get a say anyway, right?" His words were at odds with the smirk he wore. "So fine, file me away, Kitty. Live your life. Start your new job. Finish up your therapy and heal. But just like I can't make you stay with me, you can't stop me from loving you."

The man was insane. Maybe he was the one who needed therapy if he couldn't see that I was rejecting him. *Are you, though? Nice necklace.*

"So that's exactly what I'm going to do. I'm going to love you so hard that three months will be a pencil dot on our timeline."

Mercy.

"I'm going to love you so well that you'll never doubt that I choose you. Every day. Every situation. I choose *you*."

I melted. I'd waited a lifetime for those very words.

"I'm choosing you today by telling you that your well-being is more important than my ego or my need for reassurance. I'll choose you every single day that I'm gone, every mission that I fly, every second that I breathe. You don't have to be with me. I'll be with *you*."

I swallowed. "And what if I start seeing someone else?" Not that I was going to. Jackson was it for me. That's what made this whole thing so fucking impossible.

"Five. Minutes." He pointed to the minute remaining on the clock, and the pulse leaped in his neck. His knuckles whitened, and his jaw ticked twice. "If you want to see someone else, then I guess that's your prerogative, seeing as you're single."

Well, that hadn't been the response I'd expected. Did that mean he—

"As for me, I have a girlfriend I love more than life, so the only action I'll be getting is this hand"—he raised his right—"fueled by your picture and enough memories of making love to you to last way longer than three months. You don't have to be mine. I'm yours."

My lips parted and my thighs buzzed. Stupid sex drive.

"And you'd better tell whatever guy you date to be prepared for a fight, because the minute I get off that plane, I'm coming straight for you. When I tell you that I'm coming home, I mean it. And, Morgan, you. Are. My. Home." His eyes churned with longing and resolve.

Fuck my life, he was breaking down my own resolve.

He glanced at the clock. Ten seconds. His eyes raked over me like he was memorizing every detail of my face and body. I couldn't help but do the same to him. This was it. He was leaving.

"I choose you. And if I have to let you lose me so you can save yourself, then I'll hold on enough for the both of us. That's how much I love you."

Time was up.

He gave me one last, longing look and walked toward the door. My heartbeat matched the rhythm of his steps. What if this was really it? The last time I saw him? What if I never had the chance to hold him again? To see the light in his eyes when he smiled or the way his lips formed the words *I love you*? What if this was the last…everything?

My soul screamed in protest and ripped her claws into whatever was left of my defenses.

"Jackson!" I cried out as his hand reached the doorknob.

He turned, and everything I felt was so clearly etched on his own face that I whimpered.

"Kiss me."

He jolted forward but froze when I lifted a finger.

"This doesn't change anything. We *are not* together. And I know that makes this a really selfish, really screwed-up request. But…this trip…" I blocked out the D word and lifted my chin. "I want one last kiss." My hand fell to my side.

"This isn't our last kiss." In four strides, his hands were in my hair and his mouth was on mine.

Home. Everything in my body sang at his touch. He felt so right under my fingertips as they laced behind his neck.

I opened under him, then moaned as his tongue curled around mine with swirling, deft strokes. He kissed me so thoroughly, so deeply, that I couldn't remember why I'd ever stopped. Every time he moved to soften the kiss, to pull back or pause, I kissed him harder, pulled him closer. This couldn't end. Not yet. Not while I felt alive and whole.

"Morgan," he growled when I reached for the hem of his shirt and slid my hands under it. I was met with smooth, soft, warm skin over tight, hard muscles. I gripped his waist and tugged, bringing him hard against me—oh, and *he was.* His arousal pressed into my stomach, and my hand wrapped around it through the fabric of his shorts.

Fire. I was on *fire.* My skin flushed, my breasts swelled, and my thighs dampened. He was a triple raspberry lemon drop, sweet on my tongue and going straight to my head, and I wanted more. I would always want more when it came to Jackson. Touching him had been a bad idea, but it felt so damn *good.*

"Fuck," he groaned against my mouth as I stroked him. "Morgan, baby, you have to stop. You're killing me."

"I don't want to stop." I never wanted to stop. I wanted this moment to last forever—for there to be nothing beyond these walls that would rip us apart. I wanted an eternity in this little room with the man I couldn't have outside it.

Jackson lifted me to the worktable, stepped between my thighs, and stole my thoughts with a deep, carnal kiss. He took control, slanting his head over mine and erasing the world with the stroke of his tongue and the rasp of his teeth. In this moment, I was his—we both knew it.

His hand slid under my sundress and bra to cup my breast. I moaned my approval and then gasped when he abandoned our kiss only to tease my neck, my throat, my collarbone.

I unsnapped, then unzipped his shorts so I could feel him—hard, hot, and smooth against my palm.

"Kitty," he groaned, in part warning, part plea.

I pumped him in answer. I was done with the warnings. We were in the eye of the hurricane that had become our lives, and if this was the only moment we had, I was taking it.

His hands slid up my thighs and under my dress, lifting the hem to pool at my waist. Then he gripped my ass and yanked me forward, bringing us within one scrap of satin of what we both wanted. We locked eyes, and I nodded before his fingers slid under my panties and through the proof of my need.

"Fuck, you're drenched." His dick leaped in my hand.

I whimpered and rolled my hips, gripping the back of his neck, worried he'd think about what we were doing and stop. I led the head of his arousal to my cleft, and he hissed.

"You have no idea how badly I want you, but I don't have a condom. I wasn't exactly planning on this." His forehead rested against mine, his breaths ragged.

"I'm on the pill. Please, Jackson." I rolled my hips against his fingers, and he gave my clit a quick, hard flick of his thumb that made me clench him even tighter.

"Are you sure?" he asked, looking me straight in the eyes so I couldn't pretend I didn't know what I was doing.

"Fuck me." I couldn't be any clearer than that.

He raised an eyebrow. "If that's what you want to call it, I'll let you believe that." He dragged my panties down my legs and off, then tugged the waistband of his boxer briefs to just below his ass. Then he was at my entrance, throbbing and insistent, and his eyes were on mine, giving me one last out.

"This doesn't change anything between us." I hooked my ankles around the small of his back and took his face in my hands as I rocked my hips forward, taking him inside me slowly.

"Kitty, that's exactly what I've been trying to tell you." He gripped my hips and thrust forward, filling me completely.

He swallowed my moan with his mouth, kissing me deep as he moved within me with hard, powerful strokes that sent pleasure radiating through my limbs and wound it tight at my core. "You feel so fucking good," he said against my lips, kissing me again when my whimpers became keening cries.

Our bodies strained as we moved together, both giving and taking, clinging and saying good-bye. My muscles tightened as the pleasure built to a peak, and I tried to fight it—to make this last as long as possible—but Jackson reached between us and stroked me exactly like I needed. He knew my body, my cues, my needs the same way I knew his.

I swirled my hips in time with his thrusts, and he groaned, our kiss breaking so we could breathe but our lips staying close enough to brush as we fought for air—for time. Everything within me tightened, drew back like an arrow, and as I felt him swell within me and his thrusts lost that steady rhythm that meant he was close, I kissed him again, pouring into it everything I felt but couldn't say.

And then we were there, falling over the edge together in an orgasm that blew apart my body and my heart. He caught me, just like he always did, pulling me against his chest before my body fell limp, then stroked me through the aftershocks of the bliss until the last waves drifted away.

I buried my face in his neck as he stroked my back in long, soothing sweeps. Slowly, like the trickle of winter air through a drafty door, the cold truth of the reality that waited for us sank in.

He kissed me softly, then slid free.

I'd never felt so empty in my life.

He tucked himself away, then cleaned me up and helped me back into my underwear, and what could have been awkward was just incredibly sad.

"I love you." He cradled my face and took another chunk of my soul with the look in his eyes. "Do me a favor and check in on Fin once or twice while I'm gone?"

I nodded. How could I not? I loved her.

"Thank you," he whispered.

"This doesn't change—"

"Shh." He kissed me quiet, then smiled. "I know. And I love you, anyway. Three months, Morgan." He kissed me hard and deep, then ripped his mouth from mine and strode for the door without looking back.

I sank to the floor as the first tears fell. *Please, God. Don't take him. I'll do whatever you want, just don't take Jackson, too.* I wasn't capable of living in a world where he didn't. It wasn't possible.

With careful breaths, I waited for the anxiety to come, but only fear and misery rose with my tears, and those grew to outright sobs. When Sam found me, I didn't question how she knew. I simply sank into her hug and cried until I was empty.

"I know," she whispered, rocking me back and forth like a baby. "I know. It'll be over before you know it, I promise. You'll get stronger every day. Just hold on and breathe."

Did she realize her words applied to us both?

"You'll get stronger. It'll get easier."

It became my mantra.

Chapter Twenty-Six

Morgan

Just promise me that you won't let this break you. The idea of being your tragedy kills me.

Sam left two weeks after Jackson did. She'd protested the entire time, swearing she could stay longer if I needed her, but she'd taken all the time away from her life that she could, and I wasn't going to make her miss a single day of graduate school.

Besides, Dr. Circe had cleared me from complicated grief treatment, and though I still saw her for anxiety, she assured me that the loss I still felt regarding Will was on a healthy, normal track.

The loss I felt from Jackson? Well, that was of my own making.

He'd been gone three weeks now, and breathing… it wasn't easier, and when the anxiety gripped my throat and threatened to close it, I took my mind elsewhere and reminded myself that I didn't have a boyfriend, so there was no need to be such a wimp about it.

I climbed into the truck and cranked the ignition. It roared to life, and I grinned. Today was the day, and since I had three weeks before school started, a brand-new master bathroom, and newly gutted spare bedrooms to make over, it was time to head to the hardware store.

Seat belt fastened and driver's seat adjusted from Will's last ride to my shorter frame, I put the truck in drive and… drove. "What were you listening to?" I asked him as I flipped on the stereo.

Johnny Cash filled the speakers, and I laughed. "Of course you were." The scent of leather and Will still permeated the cab, so I rolled the windows down and let the humid ocean air fill the space as I drove the streets of the little town I'd decided to call home.

I bought supplies, put them in the bed, and climbed back into the driver's seat. It was all so…normal, and yet Will was still everywhere. It wasn't my truck—it was his. I brushed my thumb over his wings. Not those. They deserved to stay. My eyes drifted to his dog tags.

Carefully, I unwound them from the rearview mirror, clasped them tightly within my hand for a moment, then put them in the glove box and clicked it shut. A little less him… but it needed more *me*. I slipped my sea-glass pendant from my neck, then secured the chain carefully around the mirror. The glass swayed like a pendulum.

That was better. Now I was in here, too.

And so was Jackson.

I parked the truck in my driveway, gathered what supplies I could carry, and trudged up my steps.

"Oh, thank God," Paisley drawled from the deck chair. "I took a cab from the airport, and when you weren't here, I thought I was going to end up sleeping on your porch for the weekend!"

I dropped the bags and enveloped my best friend in a tight hug. "I'm so glad you're here."

And I meant it.

• • •

"You want to explain that giant basket of bath bombs that arrived this morning?" Paisley asked as she sipped her tea.

I glanced toward the obnoxious gift basket that took up at least three feet of counter space. "Nope."

Her eyes narrowed. "Jackson."

"I said I didn't want to explain." I gave her a sweet smile.

"Uh-huh. And that giant teddy bear taking up the corner of your living room?" She motioned her head sideways.

"Not talking about that behemoth, either."

"What about the three boxes of classroom supplies on your dining room table?" She arched a blond brow.

"Maybe I bought those myself." I shrugged.

"Maybe, but you didn't." Her mug clicked on my granite as she set it down. "That man is in love with you."

"Well, then that's his fault, now isn't it?" And speak of the devil, my phone buzzed.

Jackson: *Taking a bath yet?*

I snorted.

Morgan: *I wouldn't tell you if I was.*

Jackson: *That's okay, I have a great imagination.*

Morgan: *You know in some states, they'd consider this stalking.*

I tapped my fingers on the granite, waiting for his response and blatantly ignoring the way Paisley watched me with a that's-what-I-thought grin on her face.

Jackson: *The minute you feel harassed, call the station and tell Captain Patterson.*

Jackson: *I'll get the message. Trust me.*

I frowned. Was he being ridiculous and a little obsessive? Yes. Did I want him to get in trouble for it? Of course not.

Did I want him to stop? That was another question entirely.

Jackson: *Until then, I'll just be over here, picturing you in that new bathtub.*

Morgan: *You are incorrigible.*

Jackson: *I think you might be catching on.*

Morgan: *Go save someone.*

Jackson: *I love you, Kitty.*

I didn't answer, but I knew he never expected me to. That familiar ache consumed my soul and began to throb. It was more than longing. More than saying that I missed him. That ache beat against my ribs with the force of my heartbeats, demanding that I acknowledge my emptiness. I felt…incomplete without him. He had a piece of me, and the rest noticed.

I put away my phone with a sigh and found Paisley staring at me with a little smirk.

"You ready to talk about that yet?" she asked.

"Nope."

"Fine." She sighed. "So, what would you like to do today? I'm not even sure what to do with myself without Peyton underfoot. A movie? A pedicure?"

I grinned. "Grab your swimsuit. We can make the paddleboard yoga class that starts in forty-five minutes!"

Her jaw dropped.

• • •

I knew she craved quiet since her life now had none, so we spent the next day curled up in the living room reading as a summer storm made the tourist-heavy beaches quiet.

The best thing about having a librarian for a best friend was that she didn't talk when there were books to be read.

Page after page flew by as I devoured *Night and Day*, despite my better judgment. The book belonged in a display case, protected and preserved, but it felt like a betrayal to put it up without reading it, so I did.

The only sounds were turning pages as we soaked in the quiet, and from time to time, I would stop and pause over the beauty of a well-written line as I savored the last book in my binge of Virginia Woolf novels.

I see you everywhere, in the stars, in the river; to me you're everything that exists; the reality of everything.

Though the confession belonged to a man who had never lived, published in a book that had been written over a hundred years ago, my chest tightened and my breath caught because I knew that feeling with an intimacy that shook my very being.

I saw *him* everywhere. He was in the ocean and on the beach. He was in my bedroom and my kitchen and in the clouds that blew by overhead. He was in the rain that pelted my glass and the sun that warmed the deck in the morning.

Somewhere in the last five months, my existence had shifted. My center of gravity had moved. *He* was my reality of everything.

Jackson.

I closed the book and held it to my chest as an ache of longing consumed me.

"What's wrong?" Paisley asked from the other end of the couch, looking over her e-reader.

"How did you let Jagger fly again?"

Her eyes widened, and she sat up, placing her tablet on the coffee table. "What do you mean?"

"He almost died. *Will* died saving him, so I'm asking you how you *let* him fly again." I held the book like a shield.

"Well, I'm not sure you really *let* Jagger do anything," she muttered with a sigh.

"You do. If you asked him never to fly again, he would. That's how much he loves you."

She pressed her lips in a line and looked around my house, her eyes never focusing as she thought about my question. "I fell in love with Jagger just the way he was, and asking him not to fly would change him into someone I don't know. It's a part of him. I could no more ask him to stop flying than he could ask me to stop reading."

"But reading won't get you killed," I challenged.

"My heart almost did." She shrugged. "You don't have to go to war to put your life in danger. You can just get in the car, or walk down the street, or step into the ocean."

"But after...what happened...aren't you scared?" I whispered the question, afraid of the answer. Afraid that I might be the coward in the pair of us.

"Terrified," she admitted. "Every time I see his scars, I'm reminded. Every time he flies, I hold my breath. I'm amazed I don't pass out some days."

"But you put yourself through it, anyway."

She sighed and adjusted the blanket over her lap. "I do. How long does he have left on his flight school obligation?"

I didn't feign ignorance. "Six years."

"So he can't stop flying even if you asked him to." Her

voice softened.

I shook my head. "It doesn't matter, anyway. We broke up. We're not together."

Her eye roll involved her entire head. "Right."

"I can't go through it again. If something ever happened to Jackson..." I swallowed past the lump in my throat and slowed my breathing. *Not today, Satan.* "When Will died, he took my heart."

"I know." She nodded with a sad smile.

"But Jackson..." I pulled the book from my chest and laid it across my lap. "He would take my soul. There wouldn't be anything left to keep me breathing."

She moved to my side, and I turned so we sat shoulder to shoulder.

"You have to decide what's bigger—your love for him or your fear of losing him. And you'd think they go hand in hand, but they don't. My love for Jagger wins out by a hair. And it's the smallest darn hair, but it's there. I'd rather risk losing him than spend my lifetime not loving him." Her green eyes locked on mine.

"But I don't love Jackson," I whispered.

She took my hand. "Call it what you want. Whatever you feel, if it's bigger than your fear, then you grab onto it with both hands and you don't let go."

"But what's the point? What if I do, and I'm not enough for him? What if I can't let go of the past? What if..." I sighed.

She pinned me down with her gaze. "What if you don't learn from that past?"

I startled. "I don't know what you mean."

"Oh, Morgan." She squeezed my hand gently. "There is someone who *loves* you. And he tells you every day, and you can't accept him because you're scared. Scared that you don't have a whole heart to give him. Scared that you won't be able to love him in the way he deserves. And he challenges you, and he pulls you out of your comfort zone, and the chemistry between you is obvious to anyone with eyes, and when your chance for happiness is staring you in the face, you push it away and blame the timing. You push him away because if you let yourself love him, and he dies, you won't survive burying him. You know because you've done it before. You've buried the love of your life, and you'll be damned if you'll risk that kind of pain again." She stared at me, daring me not to connect the dots.

"Oh God," I cried, crumpling in on myself as the pain of my own ignorance cut me to the core.

I'd worked so hard to protect myself from feeling another loss like Will's that I'd become just like him, but instead of my heart being on the line—it was Jackson's.

• • •

My first day of school, there were two dozen roses on my desk from Jackson. The note was simple:

> *Today it begins. And yes, I'm singing "Hot for Teacher" all day long. X Jackson*

I scoffed, then laughed. The man never outright called, but he made his presence known in every way. He was tenacious. I'd give him that.

Next to those glorious roses sat a small vase containing a single gerbera daisy. He didn't have to tell me what to do with it.

While my students had to wait outside for the bell to signal the beginning of the day, the kindergarten kids were allowed in fifteen minutes earlier, and we were in that window. I took the flower down the hall, smiling at the other teachers and adjusting my lanyard so they could see I was one of them.

I still wasn't sure who the hell decided I was mature

enough to be a teacher, but I'd fake it until I made it.

The kindergarten rooms were at the opposite end of the wing, and the noise was astonishing. I opened the door on the left and was met with a barrage of nervous parents and excited children, all scrambling to put away their supplies and find their backpack hooks.

The redhead I was looking for spotted me over the heads of her classmates.

"Morgan!" She parted the seas like the social butterfly she was and flew into my arms. I dropped down to her eye level, careful to keep my skirt from riding up.

"You look amazing!" I held my finger out, and she obligingly twirled in her fluffy skirt and sequin-covered shirt. Her hair lay in perfectly formed ringlets that I knew wouldn't last past the first recess.

"Mommy did my hair." She grinned.

"You did a great job." I smiled up at Claire, who looked as uncomfortable as humanly possible, but she was here. She might be living in Jackson's house and sleeping in his bed, but she was doing it for the good of Finley. They weren't together...at least that's what I reminded myself to keep my claws sheathed.

Besides, Jackson and I weren't together, so she had every right to sleep in his bed.

Right.

"Thanks." She offered me a tight smile. Things weren't exactly easy between us, but I appreciated that she'd at least turned off her seek-and-destroy glare when it came to me.

"Finley, your daddy sent this for you." I handed Fin the daisy, and her entire face lit up.

"It's beautiful." She drew out the word with reverence. "He FaceTimed this morning. He told Mommy I could wear my skirt!"

"Against my better judgment," Claire muttered, sending

an obvious glance around the much less ostentatious outfits in the room.

"I'm putting it on my desk!" Finley carried the flower like it was a nuclear bomb, dodging her classmates every step of the way.

"Did you know you're supposed to volunteer?" Claire asked in a hushed whisper as I rose to my feet. "And not just every once in a while. They want classroom aides, and story-time readers, field-trip chaperones, and I *work*. There are a thousand sign-up sheets over there!"

"It can be a lot, but school resources aren't always what we'd wish, so having parents step in can really help stretch our budget," I explained with a small smile. "But you don't *have* to. That's the whole point of being a volunteer, and I know you're taking on a lot right now."

"Right, and all these other parents are just going to think I'm the loser mom who can't show up for story time Thursday, and they all know that I haven't been here as much as I would have liked. Gossip in a small town never dies." She pursed her lips.

"How well I know it." That was pretty much the story of my life. "But the more you're here, the more they get to know you, the less they'll talk."

She shook her head. "How does Jax do all this and still get to keep his precious career?" There was an edge of panic in her eyes.

Ugh, and there went my stupid heart with the aching again.

"Well, first, be a little easier on yourself. Jackson hasn't been a kindergarten dad yet, so he hasn't done all this. It's brand-new territory. Is something else stressing you out, Claire?" The level of agitation seemed a bit unjustified.

She warred with herself for a second, then sighed. "I have an audition today, and they agreed to do it through video chat, which is pretty much unheard of. But the only time the director has is exactly when Fin gets out, and Mom has a doctor's appointment, and Brie has some meeting, so I'm going to have to cancel it. I'm trying so hard to do both—to figure out how to be Finley's mom and not lose my career, but…" She shook her head and looked away.

I bit my tongue and reminded myself that I couldn't judge her for the way she'd abandoned Fin for the last five years since she was here now and obviously trying her best. "Why don't I bring her home with me?"

Her gaze snapped to mine.

"Really. Just leave her booster at the front office, and I'll carry her home. No big deal. It's not like you live across the island, remember? Just come grab her when your audition is over." I could get Fin's opinion on the paint colors for the guest room and maybe even sneak in some shell hunting.

"I can't ask that of you," she protested, but there was a spark in her eye.

"Yes, you can. I love Finley. I love spending time with her, and honestly you'd be doing me a favor." I lifted my badge. "And I'm background checked and everything."

"But you and Jax…" She hesitated.

I suddenly wished I had his pendant around my neck instead of in the truck. "This isn't about Jackson. It's about Fin."

She glanced nervously as parents snapped pictures of every conceivable "first" of the morning. "Okay. Thank you. I guess I didn't realize it would be this hard. Or maybe I did, and that's why I stayed away so long."

"It's not a problem," I assured her. "I'm always available to help, if you'll let me."

She flashed a Hollywood smile, but it was tinged with a note of desperation.

I started taking Finley home every day.

Chapter Twenty-Seven

Jackson

There was no such thing as a three-day weekend here, so the fact that it was Labor Day weekend made no difference to me. I sat in the operations center with my laptop, scouring the internet for the world's most obnoxious blow-up apple for Morgan's classroom.

Hastings rolled his eyes every time I sent him on random missions, but he never complained. The guy's cast had been cut off last week, but he'd been denied his request to replace me down here. Honestly, I couldn't be pissed. This was my job, and like it or not, deployments were a part of it.

A fact Morgan knew all too well, which didn't exactly work in my favor. Once I got home and had her back in my arms, it would only be a matter of time before we went through this again. Hell, I'd be up for Lieutenant Commander in two years, so a PCS wasn't going to be far behind.

I missed both my girls like hell, and we weren't even halfway through this deployment. Seeing Fin's face every morning and night was its own special form of torture. I could see her, but I couldn't hug her, and each time the screen went black hurt my heart more than the last. I'd missed her first day of kindergarten, which was something I'd never thought I'd say.

But she'd had Claire, right?

And Morgan.

Fuck, I missed Morgan. I missed her smile and her laugh. I missed walks on the beach and the moments she'd open up. I missed waking up in the middle of the night with her body wrapped around mine and her head on my chest. Did I miss the sex? I was a guy, and it was the best of my life, so yeah, of course, but I missed the connection more. I would have given up sex for the rest of my life if it meant I could just hold her every day. I'd probably negotiate a few kisses, though. I missed her kisses so much I nearly groaned just thinking about them. She'd never been able to hide her feelings when her mouth was on mine.

The fact that Finley spent her afternoons with Morgan gave me hope. Not that I was using my kid to keep my girlfriend or anything. I wasn't sure there was anything I could do to actually keep Morgan, but that didn't mean I wasn't fighting like hell. I'd meant every word I'd said to her the day I left. I loved her enough to carry us through this. Hell, I loved her enough to carry her through a thousand of these, but I still hated myself for putting her through it. There weren't enough gifts in the world to make up for the spike in her anxiety attacks.

But a giant blow-up apple still might help.

"You know girls like chocolate and flowers, right?" Sawyer asked, smacking my shoulder as he took the seat next to me. "I mean, if you're ordering blow-ups, there are way better models that serve way better purposes."

I scoffed.

"Leave the man alone. He's long-distance wooing," Garrett remarked from the corner of the room where he was playing a video game.

"Just saying." Sawyer waggled his eyebrows. "And who the fuck says wooing, anyway? What is this, the eighteen hundreds?"

"Wooing is the only word I can describe for what's going on over there," Garrett threw back. "What else would you call constant effort with zero dates and zero encouragement?"

"Harassment," Sawyer quipped, then cringed. "Shit, that was a step too far."

I leveled a look at him over my laptop screen.

"I said I was sorry!" He put his hands up. "We all like Morgan. We're all pulling for you. We all understand why she…did what she did, and we all think she's worth it."

"Don't say *we all*, like we sit around gossiping about Montgomery's love life," Garrett chided.

I honestly didn't give a fuck if they approved of my actions or my relationship—or lack thereof. The only two opinions I cared about in the world were Morgan's and Fin's. "Right. Thanks."

He spun his chair to face the monitor behind me. "You keeping an eye on Ingrid? She's starting to look nasty."

I looked over my shoulder at the named storms heading our way. "Nah. Looks like she might skirt by the Bahamas, and she's only a two. The boys at Clearwater will handle her. Jerry's got my eye, though."

When the fuck had I become callous enough to think of hurricanes as rescues and aftermaths instead of destruction and lives lost? We were called in for storms every year up and down the coast, and it never failed to affect me, but I'd stopped panicking at model projections years ago.

Sawyer whistled low. "He's a big son of a bitch."

"And headed this way, if those models are right." The last

thing Puerto Rico needed was another fucking hurricane, but we were here and ready to help if he hit.

"What do you think he'll end up at?" Sawyer rocked back on his chair.

"That guy?" Garrett slid his chair out from the console and peered at the monitor. "He's going five."

"Fuck that. Three," Sawyer countered. "He'll lose steam as he passes over the islands there." He pointed to the model that took the storm south.

"Let's pray he doesn't hit them at a three." I looked at the models closer. "And if he follows that middle projection, then I'm with Garrett. He's going big."

Moreno skidded into the room, grabbing the doorframe. "We've got a call."

I shut my laptop. "Time to save some lives."

• • •

I cracked a yawn and reached for my phone when the notification went off. I'd already talked to Fin this morning, but the coffee hadn't quite kicked in yet. It was still weird as hell to see Claire in my home, moving around in the background.

My screen flashed with Morgan's name, and I immediately smiled.

Morgan: *Why is there a giant apple in my classroom?*

I grinned.

Jackson: *Because you're a teacher, duh.*

Morgan: *This thing takes up my entire whiteboard space.*

I had half a mind to FaceTime her, but I knew she wouldn't accept. She never picked up my calls, either. That was the demarcation line of our relationship. Text was fine. Voice was not.

Jackson: *I don't believe you.*

A minute later, a picture came through of a giant red apple consuming her instruction space.

Jackson: *I fail to see the problem.*

Morgan: *You. Are. Impossible.*

Jackson: *I. Am. In. Love. With. You.*

Just like it always did after I dropped the L word, the conversation fell quiet. At least she wasn't hot and cold. The woman made her choice and was sticking to her guns.

Jackson: *Are you leaving for Washington tomorrow?*

Morgan: *Right now. I just stopped by to grab something.*

My chest tightened. I couldn't imagine how hard the next two days would be on her, and I wasn't even there to hold her hand.

Jackson: *I'm sorry I'm not there.*

Morgan: *Me, too.*

It was the closest she'd come to admitting that she missed me.

Jackson: *Eight more weeks.*

We'd already been here seven.

She didn't reply.

I grabbed chow, then headed to the op center for another fun day of briefings, workouts, and waiting to be needed.

"We saved you a seat, honey," Sawyer said as he patted the office chair next to him at the long conference table.

"Thanks." I slid in between him and Moreno, with Garrett just across the table. Every one of the twenty-two guys in this room was from our unit at Hatteras, and it was standing room only by the time the captain walked in.

"Good morning, ladies and gentlemen," Patterson said as he stood at the head of the conference table. "Daily brief is as follows."

He launched into the mundane and saved the important stuff for last, probably so we didn't sneak out or fall asleep.

"Jerry continues to be our primary concern. Warren, you want to talk weather?"

The meteorologist stood and nodded, heading to the monitor. "Jerry is absolutely a concern. We're predicting a category four landfall, but if he follows this model, he could pick up speed in the warm waters here and elevate to a five."

Damn, if that thing came anywhere near us, it was going to level the place.

"I told you," Garrett mouthed.

"Shut up," Sawyer retorted.

"Either way, we're looking at widespread destruction from here"—he pointed to a string of islands—"to here, which means we'll need all hands on deck. We're hoping this model is correct, and he'll miss us, but you know how finicky storms can be." He pushed his glasses up his nose. "Sir, would you like to—"

"Go ahead," Patterson said, his voice tight.

"Though this storm"—he changed the monitor, and my stomach turned—"won't affect us directly, it is cause for concern, as you can see why."

"Holy shit," Sawyer muttered.

"How the hell did that happen?" Garrett snapped, like Warren controlled the weather.

"To be honest, the projections were off," Warren answered. "She went right around the Bahamas, picking up speed to a three, and we thought she might spin off into the Atlantic, but…well, early this morning her winds measured 113 knots." His jaw ticked.

Captain Patterson took pity on the guy and grabbed the remote for the monitor. "These are only projections, and you all know how quickly the models can change. That being said…" He clicked the remote, and the monitor changed to show the projected path.

The entire room erupted with questions.

I had my phone to my ear before I'd even cleared the room, leaving the briefing before I'd been dismissed.

"Pick up. Pick up," I muttered. Morgan was already on her way to Will's ceremony.

"Jax?" Claire's voice came through.

"You've got less than forty-eight hours. Get Finley and evacuate. Don't wait."

Chapter Twenty-Eight

Jackson

There was nothing quite as ironic as an SAR pilot watching helplessly as a hurricane headed straight for his home while he was a thousand miles away.

Evacuations had been ordered yesterday.

Finley and Claire had left earlier this evening. It was later than I'd wanted, but at least she'd gone. Vivian, however, was a die-hard. She'd weathered every hurricane—including Irma—from her home, and since Brie took a volunteer position at one of the shelters on the mainland, that left Vivian alone.

Alone, with a category four headed straight at her.

"I know this is killing you, especially those of you with families on Hatteras, but we just have to sit tight and see," Patterson told those of us who sat in the conference room bleary-eyed, glued to the news coverage.

I wasn't sure exactly what he thought would change. There weren't a lot of models forecasting anything but a direct hit on Hatteras in the next twelve hours.

There was about an hour before my morning Finley call, and then I'd try to talk Vivian into getting the hell out of there, not that she'd listen. The woman was probably planning a hurricane party.

The reporter stood at the end of one of the smaller piers, getting pelted by rain as waves crashed at his feet. "As you can see, the winds have increased here to eighty miles an hour, and it's very hard to stand!" He leaned into the wind. "We're seeing enormous whitecaps, and the surge is already approaching the tide line."

"Moron," Sawyer mumbled.

"Right. And Ryan, could you tell us what makes this particular hurricane so dangerous to the Outer Banks?" the anchor asked through the earpiece.

"Sure, Sarah. No matter what, we're looking at a massive impact here on Cape Hatteras. Even if Irene veers into the Atlantic over the next twelve hours, the storm surge is projected to be devastating because it will coincide not only with the high tide, but tomorrow is a full moon."

"So, in effect, would you say that this is a perfect storm, of sorts?" the anchor questioned as the reporter was hit with another wave.

"He's going to get knocked on his ass," Garrett noted.

"Exactly. Hatteras has ordered all residents to evacuate, but we've been told that as many as fifty percent of the residents have not. All hospitals have been evacuated to the mainland, the ferries have shut down, and the bridges are only open to outgoing traffic. The residents here are being told that emergency services will *not* be available, and the governor has warned them that they are putting their lives at risk."

"Shit," someone cursed behind me.

"And yet this dumbass is standing out there," Sawyer

added.

My foot tapped impatiently in my boot, and I'd decided the pressure in my chest wasn't going to ease up until we knew that Vivian had made it out.

"And we've heard that some streets are already flooding?" the anchor prodded.

"Yes! The low-lying areas are already taking on water, and as you can see, the sea is rapidly advancing!" He leaned back into the wind.

"Ryan, we've just gotten news that Ingrid has been downgraded to a three," the anchor announced.

There was a small sigh around the table, but it wasn't big. The difference of a couple of miles an hour in wind speed wouldn't mean as much as that storm surge.

"That's great—"

A wave slammed into both the reporter and the cameraman, sending them sloshing down the pier.

"We told you," Sawyer said at the television, like they could hear us.

I followed Patterson out of the conference room. "Sir, you cannot expect those of us with families to sit here."

"I don't. I expect you to do your jobs. Jerry is still—"

"Jerry has been downgraded to a one, sir. Are you telling me that you think we'll be effective at rescuing people here, knowing our families are in danger at home?"

His jaw flexed. "I'm telling you that until Jerry's path is certain, I can't do anything. Now, your daughter evacuated, right?"

"Yes, but not her grandmother."

"I can't do anything about that, Lieutenant."

"This is complete and utter bullshit. I don't care if you think Elizabethtown has this covered. It's bullshit," I snapped.

His eyes narrowed, and I knew I'd overstepped but couldn't find it within me to give a shit. "There's nothing I can do. Replacements are on their way, but until they get here or Jerry dissipates, no one is leaving this island. Do I make myself clear?"

"Crystal."

I left him standing in the hallway and headed for my room, trying to calm down before I called Fin. The last thing she needed was me to worry her. Maybe she didn't even know Vivian had stayed.

Once my pulse settled, I propped my phone up at the back of my desk and reached to dial Finley.

Claire rang through instead.

"Hey," I answered, putting the phone to my ear. "I was just getting ready to call Fin."

"I just checked on her—they're fine," she said, sounding out of breath.

"What do you mean you checked on her?" I snapped.

"Relax. I mean I called and checked in. That one's mine!" she called out.

My stomach hit the floor. "Claire, what the fuck is going on?"

"I got a call for that sci-fi show! They want me!"

I sucked in a deep breath and counted to three.

"Please tell me that you're not in L.A."

"Just landed and got my bag. They said I could only have the role if I was here and ready to film this morning, so I caught the red-eye out of Raleigh."

Holy fucking shit.

"Tell me you have my daughter!" I shouted.

"Jesus, Jax. Stop yelling. Of course I don't. You told me I couldn't bring her to L.A., remember?"

I pulled the phone from my ear and stared at it like this might be an error. "Where. Is. Finley?"

"I left her with Mom. Hi, yes, I'm Claire Lewis."

I froze. Me, the guy with the lightning reflexes and the

great judgment. The one who never got into a situation I couldn't get out of. I fucking froze.

"Jax, are you there?"

"That hurricane is headed straight for them." My voice shook with the effort to not scream at her.

"Pssh. Don't worry so much. Mom has lived through every major hurricane, and she said there is nothing to worry about. Besides, it's already been downgraded from what I can tell. They'll stay inside. It'll be fine. Stop overreacting."

"I'm not fucking overreacting! You left our daughter with your mother on an island in the middle of a hurricane and you want me to what? Calm down?" I paced the small confines of my room.

"God, have you always been this angry? I had your windows boarded up and secured your house, Jax. Everything is fine."

Rage filled every cell in my body. "I don't give a fuck about the house! I want my daughter safe!"

"I don't have to sit here and listen to you yell. We're not married, remember? Finley's safe, Jax. You didn't grow up there. I did. Everyone freaks out, buys all the bottled water, and then the storm passes, we clean up, and move on. Your job has made you paranoid, baby. Now, I have to go. My car just got here."

"Go to hell, Claire."

I hung up.

Chapter Twenty-Nine

Morgan

Bury me at West Point, would you? My mom is going to say I should be in Alabama, but I belong at West Point. I'm asking you because I know that out of everyone I trust, you're the strongest, the most capable of picking that fight, and I need you to.

I slipped into my dress and tugged the zipper up my side. It was a navy-blue sheath with a boatneck collar and three-quarter sleeves. Classic. Demure. And exactly what Will would have wanted me to wear to his Medal of Honor ceremony.

I clasped my pearls around my neck and applied minimal lip gloss.

The ride from our hotel—just south of D.C.—to the White House would take over an hour, so it wasn't like I couldn't reapply in the car if my lips got dry. I'd foregone mascara for the good of everyone.

My FaceTime rang, and Finley's picture popped up. Now

there was a reason to smile.

"Good morning, Fin," I said as I rested the phone against the bathroom mirror.

"Hey, Morgan!" She waved, her hair a riot of curls against her pajamas. Guess I was ready pretty early.

"What's up, buttercup?"

"Not much. You said call when I want, right?" Her eyebrows rose in question.

I glanced at the clock—plenty of time. "I sure did. How does Juno like the road?" I asked as the tabby settled herself in Finley's lap.

"She hates it here." She shrugged.

"Travel is hard on kitties." I took the phone into the room and sat on my bed.

"He peed on Grandma's shoes this morning, but she doesn't know yet. She's already mad about her leg," she whispered. "That's why I'm upstairs."

I blinked. "I thought your grandma didn't want to evacuate?"

"She didn't! She says we're safe."

"What do you mean *we're* safe?" Nausea hit me hard. From what I'd seen on the news reports, Vivian's place was anything but safe. They'd pulled out all emergency workers, shut down the hospital, and were preparing for landfall in the next twelve hours.

"I'm at Grandma's, silly!" She grinned. "She said we'll get to watch the water rush under the house and everything."

Oh God. Oh God. Oh God.

"You're on Cape Hatteras?" I tried to keep my face as relaxed as possible.

"Yep! Mommy had an audition, so she went to L.A."

My jaw dropped before I managed to close it. "So it's just you and Grandma?"

"Yeah, but she's downstairs." Her voice dropped to a

whisper again. "She fell off the ladder a little bit ago. It's so windy."

Mercy, God. Please, mercy.

"Is she okay?"

Finley pursed her lips, then sighed. "It took forever to scoot to the couch." Her face fell. "She told me to go upstairs and play because it hurt so bad."

My thoughts raced. "Okay, I want you to take me to her. Go downstairs and take the phone."

"I'll get in trouble!"

"No, you won't. I promise. Go."

She sighed but did it. The phone bounced at different angles as she plodded down the steps.

"Grandma? Morgan wants to talk to you." The phone moved forward, and Vivian came into view. She was on the couch, just like Finley had said.

"Morgan?" She was pale as hell, and the lines of her face were etched with pain. "How are you, dear?"

"How hurt are you?" I asked, throwing manners out the window.

"Oh, it's nothing." She tried to force a smile.

"Vivian. Please. You have Finley. So let's not beat around the bush." My hand gripped my phone so tight I was surprised it didn't crack.

"I think I broke something," she said quietly. "I can't move anything from my hip down."

Shit. "Did you call 911?"

"They pulled all the emergency responders, dear. It's okay. We'll just wait it out." Her eyes closed as she breathed heavily. "Sorry. It's a bit uncomfortable."

"What were you doing on a ladder?" I asked, unable to stay quiet.

"There's more that goes into hurricane prep than boarding up windows, young lady." Her lips pursed.

"It's going to be days until someone can get to you if you guys don't get out now. Can you drive? Or call someone who can?"

She shook her head. "I can't move, and I'm not calling people to leave the safety of their homes. The winds are already up around eighty miles per hour. Now don't you worry that pretty little head of yours. I've weathered far worse hurricanes than this one."

The phone beeped on their end.

"Oh, that's Daddy. I'll talk to you later, Morgan!" Fin exclaimed.

She didn't wait for me to say good-bye. My screen went black.

My chest heaved and my mind raced. I'd seen Vivian's house. It was only a block or two from the sound, and the reporters had just said the surge would be unprecedented. She was immobile, and she had Fin.

Go. The urge punched me in the gut.

And do what? They'd closed the bridges to incoming traffic. Was there anyone I could call? Christina had already evacuated, and I would never ask her to put herself in danger.

Go. The urge filled me with unreasonable urgency. Instinct? Worry? Overreaction? Maybe all three.

How the hell had Claire left Finley on an island facing a hurricane?

Oh God, what if something happened? There were no emergency responders. No Jackson. He had to be sick with worry. And what the hell was I doing? Sitting here in my hotel room while that storm barreled toward them?

She's not your daughter. There's nothing you can do.

It didn't matter that I loved her. I had no control over the fact that Claire had left her there like an inconvenient carry-on in an over-full plane.

Fin might not be mine, but she was Jackson's.

And while I might not be Jackson's…well, he was *mine.*

Go.

I scrambled off the bed and threw things into my suitcase. The dress had to go.

Knock. Knock.

I was mid-unzip as I reached the door and found Paisley and Sam on the other side. "Come in." The zipper was down by the time I was back to the bed.

"Hey, are you ready to… What are you doing?" Paisley asked.

"Finley's on Hatteras. Claire left her there." I stepped out of my dress and let it fall to the floor. "Vivian fell and broke something. I think it's her leg."

Sam's eyes widened, and she quickly shut the door. "Oh my God, did they call someone?"

"Emergency services were pulled two hours ago. There's no one."

"You're not thinking of going down there are you?" Paisley questioned.

I stepped into the only jeans I'd brought and yanked them up my legs. A shirt came next.

"Morgan!" Paisley yelled.

"I can't stay here and do nothing, Paisley! Hatteras is six hours away, probably less since I'll be the only one going that direction. At least there's no traffic, right? I can make it before the storm hits." Socks.

"You…you can't be serious." Paisley's eyes flew huge. "Morgan, tell me you're not serious! You can't just drive into a hurricane!"

"Sure I can." I grabbed my shoes, thankful I'd packed some sensible sneakers, and put them on. "I have the truck. Not the Mini. The storm surge will start about two to two and a half hours from landfall, which means I have…" I looked up at the clock. "Eight and a half hours to get to Vivian's and get them back to my house. That's a two-and-a-half-hour window for error. Plenty of time."

I hopped up and raced to the bathroom, throwing my toiletries into a bag and pausing long enough to pull my hair up so it wouldn't get in the way.

"I can't let you do this." Paisley stood there shaking her head.

"What would you do if it were Peyton?"

Paisley sucked in a breath.

"I can't leave her. I won't sit here and do nothing." I tossed everything else I saw into the suitcase and swung my purse over my shoulder.

"You'll blow away! The winds are already throwing reporters left and right!" There was enough panic in Paisley's eyes to make me pause.

"Darlin', I have a seven-thousand-pound truck, and we're not talking a tornado like that one—" I pointed at Sam.

"Hey, now."

"Now as much as I love you, you're just taking time." I zipped my suitcase closed and hoisted it to the floor.

"I'll come with you," Sam said.

"You cannot!" Paisley shouted.

"I'm sorry? If Morgan's driving into a hurricane, she at least needs someone riding shotgun!"

I took in her beautiful black dress and perfectly done hair. "No, she's right, Sam. You are needed here."

Sam narrowed her eyes at me.

"Tell her," Paisley huffed.

"Grayson was given leave for the ceremony. His plane lands in about an hour. He'll be waiting for you at the White House."

Sam's jaw dropped. "What?" she asked softly.

I nodded. "Go. You only have two days with him, and you're not wasting them driving to North Carolina, so go."

She was torn. It was all over her face.

"I'll be fine, Sam. Go be with Grayson." I hauled my suitcase through the door.

"But what about the ceremony?" Paisley followed me down the hall.

I hit the elevator button and turned around. "I think this is exactly what Will would want me to do today. In fact…I think this is why he left the truck to me."

The doors opened, and I got into the elevator, then punched the button for the bottom floor. "I love you, Paisley."

"I love you, Morgan!" she cried as the doors shut.

Chapter Thirty

Jackson

My bag was packed. There was nothing else I could do but wait and think myself to death.

I sat on my bed with my back against the headboard, uncaring that my boots were leaving footprints all over my bedding.

Finley was at Vivian's.

Vivian had most likely broken her leg, if not her entire hip.

No one could get to them.

Hastings had flown the birds to safety, and Christina was already in Tennessee with family. Everyone else I knew was here.

The hurricane was due to hit in four hours.

Replacements were on their way. It wasn't like we could leave the people here without aid. Logically, I knew that. Emotionally, I was clawing at the sides of my cage, cursing my own inability to protect my daughter.

My phone rang, and I startled. The power had gone out in Buxton an hour ago, and I'd told Fin to conserve her battery.

Wait. Morgan?

"Morgan?" I swiped the phone to answer. Shit, today was the ceremony, wasn't it? Was it still the same day?

"They shut the Virginia Dare Bridge!" she shouted. "How do I get over the sound?"

My heart beat just a little softer with the sound of her voice. God, I missed her.

"What? Kitty, it's really fucking loud. Are you in a car wash?" Why was she asking about the bridge?

"No, I'm not in a car wash! Why the hell would I be in a car wash? They shut the Virginia Dare Bridge, Jackson. I drove an hour out of my way because I knew the others were already closed, but now this one is, too. How do I get over the sound?" she shouted.

I sat up straight. "I know you didn't ask what I think you just did."

"Cut the shit!" she yelled.

"Kitty, please tell me that you're in D.C. with your friends." My chest constricted.

"I can tell you that, but I'd be lying. Jackson, I need to get across the sound. Please, it's already so bad out here."

My eyes slid shut, and I pulled the phone from my face as I fought for control. *No, God. Not Morgan, too. No.*

"Jackson!"

"You turn around and go inland. Those bridges are going to be hell, and the storm surge is already at the high tide line. Fuck, I don't even know if you can get across the Oregon inlet bridge if you *do* make it across the sound, so *please*, Morgan. Please do not do this." She couldn't know, could she? How would she?

"I'm not leaving without Finley, and Vivian can't move."

"Fuck! How do you know?"

"Finley called me!"

My door opened, and Sawyer leaned in, no doubt because I was screaming like a madman. "Morgan, you can't do this. The Mini will get swept away. Please, baby. Don't do this."

"I have the truck, and I know the rule. If you can't see the bottom of the water, don't drive through it."

My eyes flew wide, and Sawyer must have heard her because he nodded. "It's a heavy-ass truck."

"That doesn't apply to ocean waves." I wasn't scared. This was three billion levels beyond scared. I was fucking terrified.

"They're expecting a twelve-foot storm surge. I've seen Vivian's house, Jackson. It can't take it. We both know it. And we both know there's only one house that can."

Hers. There wasn't enough oxygen in this fucking room.

"I'm the best shot Finley has!"

Sawyer leaned against the wall and nodded slowly.

"Are you seriously going to sit there and let this happen? I'm right here, Jackson. I'm an hour away at most. That's three hours before landfall. I can make it!"

"I can't lose you, too!" My voice shook as hard as my hand.

"Driving is driving, no matter where you do it."

She did *not* fucking go there.

Sawyer walked across the room, took the phone, and hit speaker. "Where are you, Morgan?"

"Sawyer?"

"Yep."

"Don't you fucking dare put her in danger," I hissed at my best friend.

"She already put herself in danger. *For Finley*, Jax. All I'm doing is helping her out. Where are you, Morgan?"

"I'm just outside the Virginia Dare Bridge. It's closed to incoming traffic."

"They're evacuating as many people as they can. Okay, I want you to go north to the William Umstead. Find it on the GPS."

"I fucking hate you," I seethed.

"Hate me tomorrow, brother." His mouth flattened.

"Got it. I'm on my way."

"Stay on the line, would you, Morgan? I think it might make Jax feel a little better."

"Okay. God, it's hard to see. The rain is coming in hard."

"And it's just going to get even sportier out there," Sawyer responded.

"I see the bridge. It's closer than I thought. Shit, there's a guy and a concrete barrier."

Shit. Wait. I was supposed to feel relieved. I didn't want Morgan on the island…but if Morgan didn't get to Finley, there was a high chance she wouldn't make it. Morgan was right—Vivian's house wasn't made to sustain that high a surge. Was I seriously about to risk Morgan's life for Finley's? How the hell could I ask her that?

"There's always a guy and a barrier," Sawyer noted.

"Go to the left. There will be space to the left. I know how they set those up," I said, hating myself the whole time.

"Okay, I see it. I can make it." The rain filled the gaps in conversation hard enough that it sounded like she was in a storm of golf balls. "Sorry!"

I snorted a laugh. Only Morgan would apologize to the guard when she blew right by him.

"Tell me you have gas."

"Three quarters of a tank," she confirmed. "It's raining, but I'm okay. The bridge is good."

"Well, yeah, she's not out there yet," Sawyer whispered, his face tense.

"She shouldn't be out there," I snapped. But she was Finley and Vivian's only chance.

"Okay, I'm in Manteo. How's the weather down there, anyway?" she shouted over the barrage of rain.

My eyes just about popped out of my head. "Could you just concentrate on driving?"

"Bet you're glad I'm not in your ear during a rescue, huh?"

"Don't even start with me, Kitty." Fuck, I was going to throttle her the next time I saw her. Then I was going to kiss the shit out of her. *Just let them live.*

"Here we go, there's sixty-four. Sorry! I know, I know! Sorry! I think I just pissed off whatever's left of the State Patrol out here, Jackson."

"Trust me, they have bigger fish to fry than to chase you down. Now listen to me. You're getting out to shore, and the wind is going to start throwing things around, so keep your eyes open." I leaned forward, as if it would help.

"Okay."

A minute, maybe two, passed with only the sound of the rain against the truck.

"I'm on twelve!"

"Good job, baby. Now just take it steady."

"Whoa, whoa!"

"Morgan?"

"Sorry, there, um... I think that was plywood, but it missed me!"

My heart jumped into my fucking throat.

"Oh look, there's another person out here! Nice to know I'm not alone. It's really windy, though."

"It's just going to get windier." And harder. And rainier, and then the surge would hit.

Sawyer flipped his phone around so I could see the screen. The station clocked the wind at ninety-six miles per hour five minutes ago. Fuck.

"Morgan, what's in the back of the truck?" Why the hell

didn't I think sooner?

"About four hundred pounds of sand! Grayson called before I got too far and told me to stop and buy some."

"Good. Good." Grayson was my new favorite person in the entire fucking world. "Can you see the water yet?"

"I'm just now clearing the residential— Holy shit."

My head fell to my hands. "How bad is it?"

"It's…everything is white. And huge. Holy shit, Jackson. It's coming up the beach. It's past the high tide line."

The storm surge was coming.

Sawyer leaned his head back against the wall and shut his eyes.

"Okay, let's, uh…let's look at the road, Kitty. Can you still see it?"

"The rain is coming at me sideways, but there's no standing water on it."

I nodded, like she could see me or some shit. "I need you to listen to me. Can you hear me?"

"I've got you."

"Morgan, this is the easiest part of the drive. Soon, you're going to have to go over the new Bonner Bridge. Do you remember it?"

"God, I hate that thing!"

"Yeah, well, just be careful. It should drain the water, but you want to make sure you go a little slower on it so—"

"So I don't hydroplane. I know how to fucking drive, Jackson!"

I threw my hands up, and Sawyer snorted.

"Okay, I'm coming up to the bridge," she said after what felt like forever. "And I'm on it."

She'd be up in the air for two-point-eight miles.

"This thing is moving," she sang.

I could almost see her biting her lip and gripping the wheel. Why the hell weren't we there? What good were we all the way down here when our families needed us?

"How's the bridge?" Sawyer asked.

"I'll tell you when I'm off it."

He lifted his eyebrows.

Tense moments passed where all I could do was stare at the phone and pray.

Sawyer flashed his phone. The winds were up to ninety-nine.

"I'm off! Thank you, sweet baby Jesus!"

My shoulders sagged in relief.

"It really pushed me around up there, but I'm okay. It's getting hard to see, though. The windshield wipers can't keep up!"

"Okay. Now before you bite my head off, do you remember asking me about the road washing out? The day I took you to Avon?"

"Yeah. That's where the road's close to the beach, right?"

"You got it. Listen to me, baby. If that road is washed out, turn around and go back. You have no idea how deep and fast that water will be. It would be like driving the truck straight into the ocean. Do you understand me?"

Silence.

"Morgan?"

"I understand. I'm not leaving Finley to get washed away, Jackson."

"I can't lose either of you." My head dropped.

Sawyer put his hand on my shoulder.

"You won't. I'm going to make it in time. I promise. The surge isn't up that far. It can't be. Now hush and let me drive."

But it wouldn't be the surge. That section of road would go down to the waves.

"Holy Lord, that water is creeping up. I'm at Rodanthe," she called out the update.

"Okay." I didn't want her to think she was alone. My nails

dug into my arms.

“Shit!” she shouted.

“Morgan?” Pretty sure I drew blood.

“The wind.” Another minute passed. “I’m okay. The wind just pushed me clean onto the shoulder. I’m okay.”

If I never heard the sound of rain again, I’d be just fine with it.

“Avon! Oh my God, I think that’s a porta-potty! There’s stuff flying everywhere! Shit, there’s water on the road, but it’s not up to the curb yet.”

I was going to vomit any second now.

“Leaving Avon.”

She was getting close. “Do you know if the road is still there?” I whispered to Sawyer.

He lifted his shoulders and shook his head.

She could be driving straight into the water.

“The waves. I can see the waves and— Shit!” Skidding tires. “Okay, well, the water’s coming up over the road here with every wave.”

I jolted. “Turn around.”

“No.”

“Morgan! I love you. Please, turn around! Go back to Avon!”

“What did you say to me that night? People will die if I don’t leave right now?”

Every muscle in my body locked. *Don’t do it. Don’t do it.*

“I’m okay, Jackson. It doesn’t look that deep. I’m going to get your little girl.”

The rain cut out.

The sound stopped.

“Morgan? Kitty, are you there? MORGAN!”

Morgan was gone.

The call had ended. I grabbed the phone and dialed her number.

Ring. Ring. Ring. Ring.

"All circuits are busy—"

"Fuck!" I screamed and slammed my phone on the bed. *She's okay. It's the cell tower. Not her. She's okay.*

"What can I do?" Sawyer asked quietly.

"Put me on a fucking plane!"

Chapter Thirty-One

Morgan

Morgan, when it's time to let go, you have to let go. Fall in love. Get married. Have all those babies you want. Just be happy. I hope the guy knows just how lucky he is, because I took way too long to recognize it. Go. Love. Live. I'll be watching, cheering you on.

My hands cramped around the steering wheel. I wasn't holding on so much as I was clutching the damned thing.

NC 12 was washed over but not washed out. Not yet. I made it through and onto Hatteras Island. Visibility was shit, and I'd skirted two pontoon boats before curving with the road into Buxton.

The roads were under water. How much? It couldn't be *that* much, right? I kept an eye on anything that could clue me in to the depth and made my way slowly through the streets.

Go away, Ingrid!

You're not welcome, Ingrid!

There were countless variations painted on the boards of houses I passed. Some had previous hurricane names lined through and Ingrid painted over. Rain pelted the back window now that I'd turned, increasing the visibility slightly, but I knew it would only be twice as bad once we were headed back.

There it was. Vivian's house.

I pulled into the driveway, then said a prayer that she'd forgive me for assaulting her grass and pulled up so the doors opened right in front of the staircase. I put the truck in park but left it running. I still had a half tank, and I wasn't taking any chances that something would happen and it wouldn't start again.

I zipped up the raincoat I'd bought at the Virginia border and scoffed at the umbrella from the same store. Like that was actually going to help. Then I pocketed my cell phone in the water-resistant pocket of the jacket. It was a gamble, but I wasn't going to chance missing his call if Jackson could get through.

God knew it had only been his voice and steady, calming presence that had gotten me through Avon. I hadn't felt alone in those terrifying miles.

The truck doors were sheltered from the worst of the wind because of the garage, and I got the driver's door open easily. The steps up to the front door were slick, and though the house was now blocking the wind, there was no quieting the sound of rending metal as the gutters ripped from the house.

Keep going. She's right here.

I made it to the deck and then pounded on the door. "Finley! It's Morgan! Open the door!" I waited what seemed like an eternity before starting again.

Finley opened the door and looked up at me with wide eyes.

I scooped her into my arms and slammed the door shut. The house was dim.

"Morgan?" She clung to my neck. "You're all wet!"

I've got her, Jackson. I made it. She was here, and safe, and alive. Now I just had to keep her that way.

"Hey, Fin." Taking a selfish, extra moment to hold her tight, I pressed a kiss to her hair, then put her down. "I'm so glad to see you!"

"I thought you were gone!"

"I was, but I heard you needed some help, so now I'm here!" I smoothed back her hair from her face. "Take me to Grandma, would you?"

She nodded and led me through the entry, past the dining room, and into the living room, which was only lit by three small, exposed windows that topped ones that had already been boarded up.

"Hi, Vivian. How are you feeling?" I asked, sitting on the edge of the coffee table.

"Morgan?" Vivian was in the same position as when I'd called last, but she struggled to sit.

"No, don't move. I came to take you guys to my house." My eyes darted around the room, looking for something that would keep her leg stable. "Fin, honey? Why don't you get dressed"—Juno wound herself through my feet—"and pack up the menagerie. We're getting out of here."

"Okay!" Fin took off upstairs.

"I'm not leaving." Vivian stared me down with a look of authority that might have gotten me about five years ago. "I stayed during Irene, and I'm staying now."

"Can I see your leg?"

She pulled back the blanket and lifted the hem of her shorts.

That sucker was broken, and if I had to guess, it was in multiple places.

"Right. That's broken. What's the highest storm surge this house has ever seen?" I raised my eyebrows at her.

"Nine feet." She nodded.

"They're now expecting fourteen. It's hitting at high tide on a full moon." Maybe I could break apart a chair or find some kind of bench to strap her to.

"They always overestimate." She waved me off. "Lunar tide…now that's a pickle, but I'd be willing to gamble that we don't see over ten."

Ten would put water in her first floor.

"Are you willing to gamble Fin's life?" I asked, keeping my voice quiet so Fin couldn't hear.

Vivian startled. "You really think it's going to be that bad?"

"Do you think I would have driven down from D.C. if I thought you'd be okay? Your leg is broken. Fin is five years old. What would you do when water gushes in your door? I can't leave Fin here. She is coming with me. But I won't leave you here, either."

Her mouth pursed as fear skated over her face. "But where would we go?"

"My house can take a fourteen-foot storm surge. It can probably take eighteen. I remodeled to hurricane proof it this year. It's supposed to stand through a cat four, and this is just a strong three. But we have to go now. The water is rising, and if we don't make it to the shore in time, we'll be stuck here." I scratched Juno's head and mentally started counting. If she wouldn't come with us in the next five minutes, I was going to have to knock her out and drag her.

"Imagine heading toward the shore and not inland." She humphed. "Let's go, then."

My shoulders sagged with relief, but I couldn't afford the time to savor it. We had to move quickly.

I found a shorter length of two-by-four by the door and

used belts to splint the area under her leg the best I could. I apologized the whole time she screamed.

Finley's eyes were wide as she watched.

"Are the animals all packed up?" I asked, watching the clock. The house *moved* with a groan.

Fin nodded. "Except Cousteau."

Right. The fish.

"Okay. Get everybody by the door and put on your raincoat." I patted her on the back, and she ran off.

Five minutes later, I had Cousteau in a water-filled Tupperware container. Phillip and Barnaby were in separate carriers at the bottom of a large beach bag. I slid Cousteau in on top and met Finley in the entry, where she had Juno in her carrier.

I got down to her eye level. "Okay, Fin. It's windy and rainy and *really* scary out there, okay?"

She nodded, but her mouth trembled.

"We have to go because Grandma's house isn't high enough to keep you dry. So we have to get to my house. Understand?" I zipped up her raincoat.

She nodded.

"I need you to listen really carefully and do exactly as I say, and sometimes it might be scary, but we're going to be okay. I'm going to take Grandma to the truck, and I want you to wait right here until I come get you." I needed Finley in the safest place, and right now, that was the house. In an hour, it wouldn't be.

"My mommy left," she whispered, tightening her grip on Juno's carrier.

I bit back the anger that saturated my tongue when I thought about Claire heading to an audition. That was the last thing Finley needed.

I cupped her cheeks in my hands. "I. Will. Not. Leave. You. Not now. Not today. Not ever. I promise."

"Because you love Daddy?" Her eyes filled with tears.

"Because I love *you*. I came all the way back—that's how much I love you. I even made a policeman very mad to get to you. I won't leave you, Fin. You're the only reason I'm here." I wiped her tears with my thumbs. "Are you ready?"

She nodded, and I pressed a kiss to her forehead.

"You wait right here with Juno. Promise."

"I promise."

The winds blew impossibly harder, and the rain fell in driving sheets as I took Vivian out of the house, dragging her by her armpits. "Hold onto the bag," I ordered her, and she pulled Fin's pets closer. Then I walked backward down the steps, dragging her along at an angle so that the two-by-four slid instead of thumped.

"Hold on!" I shouted once we made it to the bottom.

A trampoline flew by, flipping end-over-end down the road.

Don't even think about it. Just keep moving.

I got the back door open, and with Vivian hopping, we managed to get her across the backseat. "Buckle up! I'm grabbing Fin!" I shut the door, which was no easy feat, even given the shelter from the garage.

I raced up the stairs and looked out over the neighborhood from the top of the deck. The surge was here. Water pushed in with each wave, and it had already overtaken the houses up the block.

The dune will protect your house. You can get there.

I threw open the door and held my arms out for Fin, silently thanking Jackson for buying her backpack carrier.

Fin rushed at me with obvious relief, and I lifted her into my arms. "Do you have your phone?"

She nodded. "But not my clothes. They're upstairs."

"We don't need them. Okay, hold on tight, Fin. No matter what. Understand?" I locked one arm under her butt and clamped the other one around her back. Then I took the little girl I loved more than the world out into the storm.

She plastered her face against my neck as I made my way down the steps, careful not to slip. Everything was slick. I opened the driver's door and lifted her inside. "Crawl over the console."

She did it.

I climbed in and grunted as I hauled the door shut. It closed, thank God.

"I'm not allowed to ride in the front seat." Fin looked at me with raised eyebrows.

"And without a booster, too." I shrugged. "I'm hoping your dad will forgive me." Wasn't I just mother of the year? Or stepmother. Or quasi-not-quite-girlfriend-current-custody-haver. Whatever.

"Buckle up," I ordered as I did the same. She put Juno's carrier on the ground and buckled. Then I drove through the grass of Vivian's front yard. "I'm sorry!"

"Don't mention it," she said from the backseat. Her voice was weak, and I knew that both bracing her broken leg and moving her down to the truck had taken what little strength she had left.

It was impossible to see. The rain drove straight at us. I memorized as much as I could between the squalls and crept carefully onto NC 12.

"Oh my word," Vivian exclaimed from the backseat.

"What's that?" Finley asked.

"Hold on," I ordered, watching the huge shape fly toward us. The wind took it left, and I swerved right.

"I think that was a roof," Vivian said softly.

I was too busy gulping for breaths to say anything.

We passed the bakery I loved, and the auto parts store as the wind and rain tore at us, pushing us the way it wanted us to go as I fought to keep us on the road. There was a lot more water now. But it looked like rainwater. There was no foam.

We turned onto Old Lighthouse Road, and I cringed. Here was the foam blowing in from the ocean in giant streaks of white between the huge beach houses. Sand had blown all over the road, making it hard to see the edges.

"Think of it as off-roading," I told Finley as a powerful gust of wind pushed us close to the curb.

"Have you been off-roading a lot?" she questioned, looking out the side because she was too short to see over the dash.

"Actually, yes. In this very truck, as a matter of fact." I gripped the wheel and forced our way through the sludge of water and sand. The houses drew closer to the shore, but I refused to look and see if the dunes held.

We were committed now. We'd either make it to my house or be swept away trying.

The houses ended, and we entered the tiny stretch of road that belonged to just Jackson and me. Without the other houses to shield us from the wind, we were exposed, and it took twice as much effort to keep us on the road.

Almost there, Jackson. We're almost there.

I would have given anything to hear his voice through the speakers. To hear him tell me that I'd made the right choice in bringing them here.

We pulled into my driveway, and I nearly wept with relief. Until I saw the water cresting the dune, then breaching it. The waves came in time with my slamming heartbeats as the water carved a rivulet that quickly became a creek.

It would be an inlet in a matter of minutes.

I hit the gas, careful not to spin out, and took us toward my stairs. The wind was impossibly strong, and the water oozed forward, reaching my pilings. I parked with my side closest to the stairs.

"Okay, same thing, just in reverse, got it, Fin? You're

going in first, and then I'm bringing Grandma."

She nodded solemnly, and I'd never been so glad that she was short. If she could see what we were walking out into, she would have sobbed like I wanted to.

The door wouldn't budge.

The wind was too strong.

"You have got to be kidding me!" The water was coming in faster. There was no telling how long we had. We needed the height of the steps to get us all out safely.

Think, Morgan. Think.

Got it.

I drove forward, then turned us around in the middle of our yards, taking out a section of Jackson's fence in the process. This time, I angled the truck close to forty-five degrees and threw it into park when Fin's side was closest, pocketing the keys.

"Come here, Fin." I lifted her through the backseat to stand in front of Vivian, then climbed into Fin's seat. Bracing my back on the console, I placed my feet on either side of the handle, opened the door, and pushed with everything I had.

The wind did the rest.

The door whipped open unnaturally, slamming into the steel on the other side and destroying the hinges. *Forgive me, Will.*

Even with the relative shelter of the dune, the wind did its best to keep me inside the cab.

"Time to go, Fin!" I lifted her over the console, then stepped onto my stairs and held out my arms. "Close your eyes, baby!" Through the slats of the staircase, I saw water gush beneath us. The dune was going quickly.

Finley reached, and I gathered her tight. Her little legs wrapped around my waist as I took the steps one at a time, fighting for each and every one. I kept one hand on the railing and the other locked around Fin as we climbed.

My legs strained and burned with the effort it took to make it. Category three meant these winds were probably up over a hundred miles an hour by now, but I didn't want to think about it.

We made it to the deck, and I struggled across the few feet that lacked a railing to make it to the alcove that sheltered my front door.

The scant amount of windbreak made all the difference, and with a twist of my key, we were inside. I lowered Finley to the ground. "Go wait in the armchair right there in the living room, okay? I'm getting Grandma Vivian."

Her eyes seemed frozen in the widest position, and I thanked God that I'd closed the steel shutters. Otherwise she would have had double the reason to be terrified. We were about to be surrounded by water.

"I will come right back. I promise. You are not alone."

Fin nodded, and I raced for the door.

The wind knocked me on my ass as I ran for the deck, sweeping my feet clean out from underneath me.

"Damn it!" I shouted, already fighting to get to the staircase. I bumped down on my butt to give myself the smallest profile possible. The water was up to the rims on the truck, and Vivian's back filled the front passenger doorway. "How did you get up here?" I shouted over the roar of the wind.

"I'm not helpless!" she yelled back over her shoulder, the beach bag safe in her lap.

I gripped under her arms and hoisted her from the truck, then began the long trek back into the house. By the time I reached the foyer, I was exhausted. My muscles shook with the effort it took to get Vivian to the couch, but I got her there.

Now to close the door.

"Juno!" Fin cried.

I turned, expecting to see the cat involved in something awful as usual, but Fin stared at *me*.

"She's in the truck!" She sobbed. "I forgot her!"

"Okay," I said, mostly to myself. "Okay." I was not going to let her cat drown in a damned backpack.

I was more cautious this time crossing the rain-slick deck and made it to the truck as water crept up the rims. A quick glance behind me showed a canyon forming in the dune... and not just one. The ocean was coming.

I stepped into the truck and grabbed Juno, slinging her onto my back. Then I looked up. Will's wings were still tacked to the visor, and my sea-glass pendant from Jackson dangled from the rearview mirror. I had time. I could get them.

The dune gave way behind me.

Wings or sea glass? There was only time for one. The water was coming.

Wings.

Sea glass.

Will.

Jackson.

I gripped the sea-glass pendant in my fist and yanked with all the strength I had in me, breaking the clasp on the chain. Then I lunged for the staircase.

Water soaked my shoes as it flowed through my stairs all the way to the third step, and I stumbled up a few steps higher to relative safety before I turned around.

The sea rushed into the cab through the open door, and I watched in horror as the truck rocked slowly toward the driver's side. The next wave came—they were only seconds apart now—and swept the truck away with the torrent of water that now flew freely from the ocean.

"Good-bye, Will," I whispered into the howling wind. Then I made my way up the stairs and into the house, shutting and locking the door behind me as the storm raged hungrily against the frame of the house.

"Juno!" Fin came rushing at me, and I slid the backpack down my arms and handed it to her.

She undid the top, and Juno scurried out and away with Finley trailing after her.

I took my cell phone from my pocket.

No bars. No service. The towers had to be down.

We made it, Jackson.

Then I collapsed against the wall of the foyer, just like I had the day Jackson told me he was deploying. How scared I'd been that I would bury him, when I'd just spent the better part of three hours taking every chance that he'd bury *me.*

I could have died and left it all unspoken—left him wondering how I really felt when I'd known along. Known and been too stubborn and scared to voice it. And for what? To protect my heart from the very pain I nearly caused him?

The house groaned as the ocean rushed beneath us. I'd rebuilt this house as I'd rebuilt my soul—strong enough to withstand the storm—but where I'd hurricane-proofed the frame so I could survive, I'd failed to rebuild my heart to *live*, and I desperately wanted to.

I wanted a life and a future.

I wanted kids and laughter and sleepless nights.

I wanted those things with Jackson.

I wanted Finley.

I wanted everything that came with loving both of them.

And the minute the cell service turned back on, I would tell him. I wouldn't waste another day avoiding the things beyond my control, and instead I would grasp every chance at happiness that came along. I made my vow, held the sea-glass pendant to my forehead, then tucked Finley into my side and prayed we'd survive till morning.

Chapter Thirty-Two

Morgan

Was this how Noah felt the first time he cracked the door open on the ark? By noon the next day, the winds had died, the rain had ceased pummeling the windows, and I finally felt brave enough to raise the steel shutters.

I held my breath as the ocean came into view, still angry and white-capped.

"How bad is it?" Vivian asked as I opened the sliding glass door. The wind blustered, but it wasn't a full-on assault.

"I'm about to find out." I glanced from my cell phone, noting the lack of bars, to Finley, who sat at my dining room table, playing with my iPad.

The deck felt solid beneath my feet as I walked toward the railing, where my knees nearly gave out.

The dune was demolished.

So was Jackson's house.

My hand flew to my mouth when I saw the devastation. The pilings had completely collapsed, taking Jackson's house down to the sand. That must have been the thunderous crack in the middle of the storm. Half of his home had washed away, leaving the rest like an open-faced dollhouse that had seen a war.

My heart ached for what he'd lost.

"Can I come out?" Finley asked from the dining room.

I whipped around and forced a smile to my face. "Not yet, Fin. It's still pretty windy." She wasn't able to see the damage from where she stood, and I wasn't about to break her heart.

I closed the door behind me and kissed the top of her head. "What do you say we put on a movie?"

She nodded, her eyelids already drooping with exhaustion as I set her up in the armchair so she wouldn't bump Vivian, who took up the couch. There hadn't been much sleep last night.

"Give me a couple minutes to check things out," I said softly to Vivian.

"I'm fine. Don't worry about me."

Of course I was worried—she was in some serious trouble. I opened my front door and sagged with relief. This portion of the deck had made it, too, and the stairs were still there. Seaweed covered most of the steps, and there was a scent I couldn't quite place that would probably have overpowered my senses had the wind not still been whipping.

My stomach sank. I didn't need to trudge through the mud around the base of my house to check on my Mini Cooper.

It was lodged in the wall of the boathouse.

My garage door? Who knew?

There was no sign of Will's truck.

We were good and stranded, and we weren't the only ones. According to the emergency radio, Hatteras Island had been cut off when a stretch of NC 12 washed out south of Avon. It could take weeks to repair. Vivian didn't have weeks…or even days. She needed medical attention now.

I looked up to the skies and assessed the ceiling. It was still overcast but safe for flight. We just needed a big enough signal.

In hushed tones, so I wouldn't wake Fin from her well-deserved nap, I explained my plan to Vivian.

"You're sure you want to do this?" Her face was tight with pain that Tylenol wasn't touching.

"I think it's our only shot. Cell service is still out. Your leg needs to be set, and we didn't grab your insulin while making our escape. If you have another idea, then I'm all ears, but right now, this is all I've got."

She sighed, the skin puckering between her eyebrows. "Okay. But only if you let me help repaint once the weather is nice enough."

"Deal," I offered, though I had zero intention of taking her up on it. "I'll be right back." I pulled the five-gallon bucket of red paint from the storage closet, stuck a paintbrush and screwdriver into my back pocket, then carried it all onto the deck.

Then I started painting.

It took the better part of an hour, but I was now the proud owner of a giant red X on my deck and enormous letters that read H-E-L-P.

Then I checked on Vivian and Fin and settled in for the long haul. I evaluated our supplies, then gauged the fuel level in the generator.

Just as I'd come inside and made peace with becoming a somewhat more eccentric version of Tom Hanks in *Castaway*, the sound of rotor blades beat the air.

"Daddy!" Finley raced for the sliding glass door.

"Hold up!" I barely beat her there. Sure enough, hovering above us was a rescue swimmer descending from the rope of a Coast Guard SAR helicopter.

I knew it was impossible, but my heart skipped, anyway. I hadn't seen Jackson in almost two months, and while these weren't the best circumstances for a heart-to-heart, I was ready to keep the vow I'd made last night.

"Are you Montgomery's girl?" he shouted as his feet hit my deck.

I nodded. "Is that him?"

The guy looked at me like I was crazy. "No. He's deployed, right?"

"Right." Guess this was not my movie moment.

"Hastings is flying. He saw the X. The entire island is cut off. They'll probably start evacuating who they can tomorrow, but we have room for two more." He had to yell the words to be heard over the noise.

Two. Not three. This wasn't even a made-for-television moment.

So I did what any woman in my situation would do—I sent Vivian and Finley to safety, even though they both protested, one loudly and with many tears because I couldn't hide what had happened to her house.

Then I was alone…unless I counted the four animals I was now responsible for. Juno wound herself through my legs, confirming that she counted. I was one of the only humans she found acceptable, but I still made a mental note to hide all my shoes.

Finley and Vivian were safe, and my house still stood. I sent up a prayer of thanks.

Exhausted beyond all belief, I curled up on the couch and propped my cell phone on the coffee table, watching those service bars like a hawk in hope they'd return.

I had a vow to keep.

Chapter Thirty-Three

Jackson

"You fucking *what*?" I charged at Hastings in the middle of the Elizabethtown air station.

"I only had room for two more, Montgomery!"

"So you just left her there?" I came around the table at him. "She's been out there all alone since yesterday?"

"There are hundreds of people out there! What did you want me to do?" He put his hands up, which caught me off guard long enough to stop myself from beating him to death.

"I wanted you to rescue my girlfriend!" I shouted. That term didn't even remotely come close to what Morgan meant to me, and she'd probably deny it was even true.

Sawyer flanked my right, and Garrett took my left.

"We're running round-the-clock evacs on serious cases, Jax, and I rescued your daughter and her grandmother because Morgan chose to save *them*. Now calm the hell down." Three other pilots stared at us like we were the evening entertainment.

"Calm down? Where's Christina right now?" I spat.

"In Tennessee with her family."

"Morgan is on a hurricane-ravaged island! I have no idea how much food she has, or gas for her generator! So do *not* tell me to calm down!"

"Why don't we back this up a little," Garrett suggested, laying one hand on my shoulder.

Recognizing that I was only six inches away from Hastings's face, I retreated a few steps and rubbed a hand over my eyes. My eyelids felt like sandpaper.

"Finley's at the hospital?" I confirmed, making sure I'd heard him right.

"Yes. They admitted Vivian for observation, and they're all safe and sound," Hastings assured me.

Finley was safe. Morgan wasn't.

"Give me your helicopter."

"I'm sorry?" Hastings's eyebrows shot up.

"You heard me. I want your fucking helicopter." Did I stutter?

Startled, Sawyer's gaze swung between Hastings and me. "Yeah, what he said. We want your helicopter."

"Exactly how much crew rest have you had, Jax?" Hastings folded his arms over his chest.

"Eight hours," I answered with a shrug.

"Over the last three days," Garrett muttered.

I turned a slow glare on him.

"Just trying to keep you alive, my friend. Love you like a brother, and you know I'm down for going after Morgan, but you're not safe to fly."

"I didn't say I had to fly it."

Hastings tilted his head. "I'm listening."

Chapter Thirty-Four

Morgan

I had a fish in a vase on my kitchen counter, a turtle in my bathtub, a guinea pig in what was supposed to be a shabby chic, decorative birdcage, and a cat curled up on my lap as I rested on the couch.

Fin had been a ridiculously responsible pet owner and packed food for all her charges in a pocket of the cat carrier, but since Juno had gone through her two allotted cans of cat food, she was now licking tuna from my pantry off her paws.

My hands ached from setting my garage to rights, which had consumed my morning, but I still managed to hold my book.

I checked my cell phone for the hundredth time in the last hour, but there was still no service. Logically, I knew Fin and Vivian were fine—they'd probably been airlifted straight to the hospital—but I wanted a little reassurance, and I would have killed to hear Jackson's voice. Hopefully, he knew they were safe. I had a billion things I wanted to tell him, none of which included the state of his house.

Rotors beat the air, but I didn't jump off the couch. The coast guard had been up and down the island, evacuating emergency medical cases, so the sound had become more than commonplace.

The police officer who stopped by this morning told me they were hoping to have cell service up by tomorrow, and they were evacuating people by ferry based on levels of need. With Finley and Vivian safe, I figured my need wasn't as pressing as the others around me, and I definitely wasn't about to ask to evac Fin's zoo.

The steady thump of rotor blades didn't retreat.

Bang. Bang. Bang.

I jumped, looking up from my book to see a coastie at my sliding glass door. Guess Hastings had come back. I climbed off the couch and tried not to trip over Juno as I made my way to the door. Then I flipped the lock and slid the glass open to look up at my own reflection in a visor.

"Hi! Can I help you?" I shouted over the noise of the hovering helicopter.

He said something into his helmet, and the bird flew away.

He'd unhooked his tether. What the hell?

The guy unsnapped his helmet, yanked it off, and tucked it under his—

"Jackson!" This had to be a dream, right? But the air still smelled like post-hurricane funk, and surely, I wouldn't imagine *that.*

I threw myself at him.

He caught me, tugging me close as the air fell quiet around us. *Thank you, God.* We stumbled backward, and he set his helmet on the table, then wrapped both his arms around me and held tight.

It was the first time I'd felt safe since he'd deployed.

"Tell me you're okay," he said against my temple.

I lifted my head and smiled. "I love you."

His eyes flared wide.

"I love you, Jackson," I said again, just so he knew I meant it. "I promised myself that the minute the cell service came back up, I'd tell you, but doing it in person is so much better."

Our mouths met in a kiss, and the world righted itself as his lips moved with mine. It was sweet and desperate all in the same breath.

He yanked back with narrowed eyes. "But you're okay, right? You're not hurt?"

"Well, Finley and Vivian were evacuated. Fin was fine, but Vivian's leg was a disaster, and we didn't pack her insulin when we fled her house, but I'm assuming they're okay since Hastings flew them out. How are they?"

"He told me, and we'll get to that in a second. I'm asking about you." His eyes raked down my frame.

"Wait...you haven't seen them yet?"

"I told you that the minute I got off that plane, I was coming for you, remember?"

Mercy, I did, and he'd come for me. My heart didn't just fly—it soared.

"And I knew they were safe, but you weren't, so I'm here. Now put me out of my misery and tell me if you're hurt." His eyebrows furrowed.

"I'm fine. A little scraped up in places, but nothing to worry about." My stomach dropped. "Oh, Jackson, your house..."

His mouth set in a firm line. "I know. It was kind of hard to miss as we flew up, but there wasn't anything in it that can't be replaced. Except the house itself. That might be a little tricky with the location, but I'm not worried. I was scared shitless about *you*." His hands rose to cradle my face. "You came back for Fin."

"Of course I did. But I also put her in so much danger. We almost didn't make it in time." Had I made the right judgment call?

"You saved her life. And Vivian's. That house, and three more on that block, collapsed. I'll never be able to thank you enough." His voice broke.

"You don't have to thank me." The thought of what could have happened was enough to weaken my knees. "I only did what you would have."

"I don't deserve you," he whispered, setting his forehead on mine.

"I could say the same exact thing. So why don't we agree that we deserve each other and go from there?" His neck was warm and strong under my fingers. "I love you, Jackson. And I'm sorry it took me so long to say it."

"I don't know if I can stay," he blurted, stroking his thumbs over my cheeks. "They granted us all emergency leave, but it's still up in the air if we'll need to return."

My belly churned, but I nodded. "Okay. Then we'll deal with it no matter what they decide."

He startled. "What changed? Two months ago, that would have put you on the floor."

"And it still might," I confessed. "But my love for you is bigger than the fear, and I'll handle the months you're gone if it means I get a lifetime of loving you."

He kissed me hard and quick. "I get it now, and I don't blame you for telling me to get out months ago. That half hour on the phone with you was fucking terrifying. You were in so much danger, and I couldn't do shit but sit there and pray."

I cringed slightly. "I put the rescue above my life, and I'm sorry, but I'm not. I also recognize the irony that I couldn't keep the very promise you made for me."

He huffed a laugh. "I knew you were doing it for Finley. You risked your life to save my daughter. I was so furious with you, and yet I'd never loved you more."

I smiled. "So you do still love me."

"I love you more than my own life, Morgan. You're all I want. You, and me, and Finley. For the rest of my life, you're it. I will spend every day making you impossibly happy, and incredibly aggravated, but I hope the first more than the last, if you'll have me."

My heart leaped. "That sounds like a proposal."

"If I thought I had the barest shot of getting you to agree to marry me, it would be, but I know you're cautious—"

"Yes," I blurted.

His eyebrows rose, and his eyes lit up.

"Yes," I repeated. "I'm done waiting to be happy or looking for the other shoe to drop. I'm done being careful and keeping my heart in a box when it already belongs to you. If anything, the last few days have shown me how quickly it can all vanish, so I'm grabbing onto this." I slid my hands down to his chest and gripped his flight suit. "Grabbing onto you with both hands and a full heart."

"Kitty," he whispered.

"And if you were just joking, that's okay, too. But if you really meant it, then feel free to ask whenever you want, because my answer is yes."

He laughed. "I should plan it all out, but I'm not going to."

"Wait. Do you want kids? More kids, I mean. That's probably something I should know." Because I did. Lots of them.

He blinked, then smiled with his whole face. "I do. Do you want the one I already have?"

"More than anything," I answered. "It would be a shame to toss her out after all the work I just went through to save her."

"God, I love you." He kissed me, soft and slow, and when our lips parted, he swept in deep. My fingers curled in his flight suit, and I returned his kiss with all the love I felt for him. "Marry me, Morgan Bartley."

Two years later

The peach cobbler looked perfect. Everything about this weekend was pretty perfect, actually. The weather was gorgeous, I'd scored six uninterrupted hours of sleep last night, and Jackson even managed to have all of Labor Day weekend off.

"Whoa, that smells good. Need any help?" Sam asked as she walked into the kitchen, tying her curls into a ponytail.

"Thanks! I could definitely use a hand. I think that's the last of it." I pointed to the gallon of ice cream I'd just pulled out of the freezer.

"Got it!" She grabbed the gallon by the handle and nodded toward the door. "Let's get out there."

I stacked the peach cobbler pans so they didn't get smooshed, then followed her out of the beach house. She shut the door behind us, and we started down the steps. It was still in the low eighties, but the late-afternoon breeze kept it tolerable.

"Boathouse looks good," she said as we reached the bottom. "Last time I was here, it still had a giant hole in the side."

I scoffed. "That was almost two years ago, which tells

you how long it's been." I eyed the spot my Mini Cooper had gone through. We'd long since rebuilt, but I still missed that little car…and the truck. It had been found a few days after the hurricane, thank goodness, and though we'd had to salvage it, I'd gotten back the only two things I'd cared about. Both Will's wings and his dog tags now resided in the bottom drawer of my jewelry chest.

Jackson had offered to frame them for me, but it felt right to tuck them away, safe and sound.

"It's been too long," Sam agreed. It really had.

"You'd think you were still stationed in Colorado instead of Fort Bragg," I teased, hip bumping her as we turned and walked toward the dune steps.

She laughed. "We've been there a month. Cut us some slack. I'm sure we'll harass you guys plenty in the next six months."

Six months from now, we'd be at our new duty station in Cape Cod.

"We're keeping the house, so just let me know whenever you guys want to come and use it," I told her as we climbed.

"You guys thinking you'll retire here?"

"That's the idea. We both love it, and Vivian and Brie are both here." The breeze whipped the strands of my hair that had come loose from my braid as we crested the dune.

The sight brought an immediate smile to my face. The bonfire was set up, ready to be lit at sunset, and our friends had already staked out their seats.

Garrett and Sawyer manned the grill while Javier lectured and Christina laughed at something her husband had said.

"I said I would help!" Paisley chided as we carried the food past the giant, empty sunshade and put it on the table.

"You're not supposed to be carrying things," Sam lectured.

"I'm pregnant, not useless," she grumbled.

"And how is little Ms. Bateman?" Sam asked, hunching to put her hands on Paisley's growing belly.

"I'm still voting he's a Mr. Bateman," Ember stated with a smile.

Sam scoffed. "No way. I'm telling you this little one is going to skew the scale to the girl side in the Bateman household. Aren't you?"

Paisley rolled her eyes. "Whatever this baby is, it's the last in the Bateman household, that's for sure. Three kids under five will be more than enough."

"But you make such pretty babies," I pouted, throwing my arm over her shoulder as Sam stood.

"Speak for yourself, Morgan Montgomery."

I glanced down at my wedding ring, smiling as it twinkled in the sunlight. It had been over a year, and I still got giddy whenever I heard my new name.

"However many we have, you have to admit, they're freaking cute," Ember said with a laugh, pointing toward the beach. "And I don't just mean the babies."

My heart melted, and we all headed in their direction.

The guys stood in a line, just far enough that waves came over their feet, all decked out with various sizes of baby carriers.

Josh stood on the left, wearing his and Ember's two-year-old, Quinn, in a rugged, framed backpack. Next to him stood Jagger, with Annabelle, his and Paisley's thirteen-month-old, in a front carrier. Then came Grayson, who somehow managed to look even bigger with Delaney, his and Sam's fifteen-month-old, strapped to his chest. Finley walked Peyton through the smaller waves just in front of them.

And then there was Jackson.

My Jackson.

I slipped my hand into his and peeked at our sleeping son, who was tucked away in the sling Jackson wore. Grant was three months old, and he was…everything. His little breaths were even through his tiny, perfect lips, and Jackson had him completely shielded from the sun as he napped peacefully. We'd named him after Jackson's father, and all three of us had fallen in love with those big, blue eyes at first sight.

Jackson pressed a kiss on my forehead and slid his arm around my waist, pulling me close. He was an amazing father—no news there—and Finley had jumped headfirst into the role of adoring older sister. We were now a family of four…with six pets.

"If you wake him, you wear him, Kitty," he joked in a whisper.

I laughed. If the roaring of the ocean and the booming voices of the men beside us didn't wake Grant, nothing would. The kid slept like a champ.

"You're fixin' to have some pretty awkward lines with that thing," I noted, devouring the bare skin of his chest and stomach with my eyes.

"You can always lay out naked with me and help them fade." His lips brushed my ear.

A shiver slid down my spine.

"Jackson Montgomery, we have company!" I dropped my jaw and raised my eyebrows in mock indignation.

He laughed.

Leaning my head away from Grant, I cupped my hands around my mouth. "Fin, there's cobbler!" It had become her favorite dessert this year. Last year it was apple pie, and who knew what she'd pick next summer?

Her eyes lit up, and she raced out of the waves, her hand still gripping Peyton's.

"Can we get some?" Fin asked, looking up at me with an excited smile.

"Fine with me, but he'd better ask his mama." I smoothed back an errant curl.

"Aunt Paisley, can Peyton have some cobbler?" Fin asked down the line, where Paisley stood with Jagger. "You want cobbler, right?" she asked Peyton like an afterthought.

"Mama, please?" he asked, jumping. That boy might have looked like Paisley, but he was all Jagger, constantly moving.

"It's okay with me," she answered.

"Yes!" the two exclaimed at the same time.

They took off at a run, kicking up sand.

A few years ago, I never would have thought I'd be raising my kids with Paisley's, and sometimes the sheer reality of it, the happiness that flooded my heart when we were all together like this, was too much for words.

We wouldn't all be together like this again for a while. Jagger had just gotten home, but Josh was headed out one last time in a couple of months—his last deployment before his six years was up and he'd be eligible to get out of the army. Grayson would be gone before Easter.

This was a rare, complete moment, and I knew none of us would take it for granted. We'd all learned that we couldn't control the storms in our lives, but we weathered them better when we were together. Phone calls, Skype, texts, and visits—we always made time, and I had the feeling that we always would. Friendships like ours, forged in fire, were the kind that lasted.

Ember lifted Quinn from the carrier, then took off after the spitfire toddler when she made a dash for the waves, scooping her up and blowing kisses on her neck. Slowly, everyone but Jackson and I headed back to the barbecue, leaving us alone on our beach.

"What are you thinking about?" he asked, stroking my side.

"How long it will be until we're together like this again." I hooked my arm around his waist and leaned into him.

"Bittersweet?"

"A little, but I'm just happy for the time we have." I looked up at him, and my heart filled to bursting. "I'm happy for every day I have with you."

"And I'm happy for every night, so we're even." His smile made me glad I'd passed the six-week postpartum mark a while ago.

"I love you, too." I rose on my toes and kissed him long and slow.

Rotor blades beat through the air, and we broke apart, watching as the Jayhawk flew overhead, heading out to sea. My stomach clenched, but it wasn't in fear. Even though I knew Jackson wasn't on call, there was always the chance he'd get called in, and I didn't want to miss him for a single second this weekend.

"Do you think they'll need you?" I asked as the bird grew smaller and smaller. When I tilted my head to look up at him, I found his eyes already on me.

"No." He cupped my face and pressed a soft kiss to my lips. "I'm right where I need to be."

God, I loved this man.

"Daddy!" Finley yelled. "I saved our seats!" She pointed to the beach chairs she'd claimed.

"We'll…" Jackson started to yell, then glanced down at Grant and thought better of it.

"Go ahead, I'll be right over," I assured him, letting my hand trail down his side, where two more coordinates had been inked. The first led to the very spot we were standing now—where we'd first met. The second, the hospital where Grant had been born.

"Don't be too long," he said softly.

"You going to miss me?"

"Nawh." He smirked, and I felt it between my thighs. The man was lethal. "I'm just not sure I can keep our daughter from eating your share of the cobbler."

I shook my head as he threw me a wink and walked away, cradling our son carefully.

The water was cool as it washed over my sun-warmed feet, and I let the peace of the moment sink in and fill my soul. My toes brushed against something hard, and I bent down, scooping the object free and letting the water rinse the sand away.

It was a piece of green sea glass the size of my thumb. Its edges were soft and worn, much like the pendant I wore around my neck. I smiled softly at my find, then tossed it underhand back into the sea.

"Why did you do that?" Fin asked, appearing at my side.

"So someone else can find it." I glanced from my daughter to the water where the glass had disappeared. Maybe one day it would turn up at the feet of another brokenhearted girl and speak to her the way countless pieces had spoken to me as I'd carefully rebuilt myself.

Her brows puckered. "You don't want it?"

"I think someone might need it more than I do. I have enough." I took her hand and smiled.

As we walked back to the barbecue, I looked out over our little crowd.

Jagger, Paisley, and their kids were camped out in a set of chairs, with Ember, Josh, and Quinn taking the next set over. On the other side, Grayson held both Sam and Delaney in his lap as he pretended to eat his daughter's cheeks, much to her delight.

Jackson glanced tenderly at our son, then smiled at us as we made our way to him.

I had more than enough.

I had everything I'd ever wanted.

Acknowledgments

First and foremost, thank you to my Heavenly Father for blessing me beyond my wildest dreams.

Thank you to my husband, Jason, for being my rock. For loving me more than your wings and pushing me to fly. For being the real-life Jagger, while giving pieces of yourself to Josh, Grayson, and Jackson. Thank you to my children, who never cease to amaze me with their ability to adapt to every new situation—including quarantine—with grace and love. To my sister, Kate, for always listening. To my parents who always understand what "I'm on deadline" means. To my best friend, Emily Byer, for Sonic shakes and Cake.

Thank you to Karen Grove, not just for editing this last Flight & Glory book, but for picking up the first one out of the slush pile. You've never let me settle or allowed my writing to slip into complacency. I've grown not only because of your faith and encouragement but also your friendship. Thanks for always picking up the phone.

Thank you to my team at Entangled. To Liz Pelletier for agreeing to give the Flight & Glory fans the book they've been asking for. To Heather and Jessica for answering endless streams of emails. To my phenomenal agent, Louise Fury, who makes my life easier simply by standing at my back.

Thank you to my wifeys, our unholy trinity, Gina Maxwell and Cindi Madsen, who hold my sanity in their capable hands and keep me at the keys. To Jay Crownover for being my safe place and the wolf to my rabbit. To Shelby and Mel for putting up with my unicorn brain. Thank you to Linda Russell for chasing the squirrels, bringing the bobby pins, and holding me together on days I'm ready to fall apart. To Cassie Schlenk for reading this as I wrote it and always being the number one hype-girl. To every blogger and reader who has taken a chance on me over the years. To my reader group, The Flygirls, for bringing me joy every day—this one is for you.

To the amazing servicemembers in the United States Coast Guard and their families, thank you not only for your service but for giving me a little creative license since Jackson's station on Cape Hatteras is entirely fictional.

Lastly, because you're my beginning and end, thank you again to my Jason. None of this would be possible without you.

About the Author

Rebecca Yarros is the *USA Today* bestselling author of more than fifteen novels, with multiple starred *Publishers Weekly* reviews and a *Kirkus* Best Book of the Year. A second-generation army brat, Rebecca loves military heroes and has been blissfully married to hers for more than twenty years. She's the mother of six children, and she and her family live in Colorado with their stubborn English bulldogs, two feisty chinchillas, and a cat named Artemis, who rules them all.

Having fostered, then adopted their youngest daughter, Rebecca is passionate about helping children in the foster system through her nonprofit, One October, which she cofounded with her husband in 2019. To learn more about their mission, visit oneoctober.org.

To catch up on Rebecca's latest releases and upcoming novels, visit RebeccaYarros.com.

About the Author

Don't miss the rest of the Flight & Glory series...

FULL MEASURES

EYES TURNED SKYWARD

BEYOND WHAT IS GIVEN

HALLOWED GROUND

Also by Rebecca Yarros...

WILDER

NOVA

REBEL

THE LAST LETTER

GREAT AND PRECIOUS THINGS

THE THINGS WE LEAVE UNFINISHED

FOURTH WING

Discover more New Adult titles from Entangled Embrace...

TALK FLIRTY TO ME

a novel by Livy Hart

When it comes to my brother's best friend, smart-mouthed firefighter Sam O'Shea, avoidance is key. But when my dream audition falls in my lap, I'll do anything to kickstart my career—including making a deal with the devil himself to read with me. The problem? We land the job. Together. Oh, and the book is an erotic romance. Nothing like narrating steamy lines in a tiny studio with a man who lights a fire under your skin...

AN UNEXPECTED KIND OF LOVE

a novel by Hayden Stone

Bookstore owner Aubrey Barnes likes his quiet London life exactly how it is, thank you very much. His orderly world is thrown into chaos when a film company leases his shop and he crashes into distractingly hot American actor Blake Sinclair. And keeps crashing into him. Aubrey isn't cut out for the high-profile life of dating a celebrity, especially one who's not out yet. Good thing their tryst is absolutely not going anywhere...

Under a Storm-Swept Sky

a novel by Beth Anne Miller

An eighty-mile trek across the stunning beauty of Scotland's Isle of Skye isn't something I imagined myself doing. Ever. This isn't a trail for beginners. Rory Sutherland, my guide on this adventure, is not happy. We clash with every mile, but we recognize a shared pain. The tension between us is taut with unsaid words. And hope. He's broken. I'm damaged. Together, we're about to make the perfect storm.

Chaos and Control

a novel by Season Vining

Wren Hart never thought she'd stay in her sleepy Midwest town, until she met Preston. Gorgeous, mysterious, Preston's life is ruled by routine and order. But while their relationship grows in a delicate dance of chaos and control, the danger lurking in Wren's past is inching ever closer...and could destroy them both.

Made in the USA
Monee, IL
18 February 2024

53706711R00277